"One of the best works of gothic suspense that this reviewer has read this year ... The questions left dangling add to the thrills that this book delivers. *The Murder Stone* is an unforgettable reading experience."
—*Midwest Book Review*

A FEARSOME DOUBT

"Brilliant ... who would have thought that Charles Todd's brilliant concept for a mystery ... would not only continue but grow stronger from book to book."
—*Chicago Tribune*

"This atmosphere-dripping series set in post–World War I England is always on my must-read list."
—*Miami Herald*

"Todd raises the stakes in this series to new and nearly unbearable levels."
—*New York Times Book Review*

"An atmosphere thick with melancholy and longing, one that showcases sympathetic characters brilliantly."
—*Washington Post Book World, Book World Raves*

"If everyone would just read one book, any book by Todd, and pay close attention to what he's saying, there would never be another war."
—*Kirkus Reviews*

"A tragic conspiracy of greed and betrayal. A compelling unique story."
—*Chicago Tribune*

"Todd is a mystery writer who can make you feel the fog and suffer the despair of a troubled police officer. Characterization and description are outstanding. A warning though: Once you've read one of his novels, you'll have to go to the bookstore, the library or the Internet to find the others."
—*Oklahoman*

"Todd continues to provide a superior look at a people and a country trying to recover from the devastation of war. *Watchers of Time* so thoroughly immerses the reader in 1919 England that it's startling to realize that the authors are American. What's even more astounding is that this seamless story has been written by two people."
—Oline Codghill's Best Mysteries of 2001,
Florida Sun Sentinel

"Storytelling at its finest." —*Mystery News*

"A spot-on re-creation of the 1919 period...and the most persistent plaguing by a ghost since *Macbeth*. Todd fans will queue up for this one."
—*Kirkus Reviews*

"Atmospheric...unsettling...psychologically astute."
—*Publishers Weekly*

"A unique and timely psychological thriller that explores the different ways that people cope with traumatic loss and personal tragedy...The rich detail of rural life and characters, and polite British dialog and manners, makes for a satisfying historical read."
—*Drood Review of Mystery*

"This is the best series of mysteries being published today—bar none. If you love mysteries, don't miss these."
—*Somerset, (PA) Daily American*

LEGACY OF THE DEAD

A *New York Times* Notable Book of the Year

"A searing story." —*Booknews* from The Poisoned Pen

"A great mystery as well as a haunting human drama."
—*Midwest Book Review*

"Todd is a skilful and sensitive writer able to limn
characters quickly and convincingly and Ian Rutledge
is a unique and uniquely compelling sleuth."
—*Booked and Printed*

"Magnificent entertainment." —*Mystery News*

"Charles Todd is a talented storyteller.... The setting,
the cast of characters—notably, in this volume,
an outspoken elderly woman who survived
the Indian massacres—and the dovetailing plots
all make this the kind of book that is hard to forget."
—*Contra Costa Times*

"The word 'superb' hardly conveys the outstanding
quality of the brilliantly conceived and elegantly
executed Inspector Ian Rutledge mystery series."
—*Strand Magazine*

WATCHERS OF TIME

"One of the best historical series being written today...
In the grand tradition of English murder mysteries...
Todd's great gift is an ability to weave an atmosphere
thick with melancholy and longing, one that
showcases sympathetic characters brilliantly.
These emotional connections make *Watchers of Time*
a compelling mystery rich with depth and shading."
—*Washington Post Book World*

"If anyone can turn a simple village mystery into a brooding Greek tragedy, it's Charles Todd. Todd handles . . . grave issues with great compassion for his morally bewildered characters, who have had enough of guilt and retribution and long only for peace."
—*New York Times Book Review*

"This is a series that just keeps getting stronger with each book." —*Tales from a Red Herring*

"A most impressive effort." —*Chicago Tribune*

"Truly captivating." —*Drood Review of Mystery*

"Todd writes a gripping and atmospheric novel of war, guilt, and belonging. . . . A very absorbing read."
—*Murder Past Tense*

SEARCH THE DARK

"I won't soon forget author Charles Todd's Ian Rutledge in *Search the Dark*." —*Cleveland Plain Dealer*

"The third compelling Ian Rutledge mystery takes the sensitive and appealing Scotland Yard inspector, a former WWI officer, to the countryside of Dorset. . . . [A] fine period mystery." —*Publishers Weekly*

"A well-crafted historical." —*Library Journal*

"Nightmares abound. . . . Todd's finely crafted post-war atmosphere, his superb exploration of human motives, his deftly sketched supporting cast, and a challenging plot are rewardingly combined here as he compassionately probes the dark scars left by nearly unbearable psychological wounds. But the best thing about *Search the Dark* is Ian Rutledge. Gentle when he can be, relentless when he must be, tormented he cannot help but be, Todd's Ian Rutledge is as fine a piece of literary work as appears today."
—*Strand Magazine*

WINGS OF FIRE

A *New York Times* Notable Book of the Year

"A remarkable village mystery ... driven by characters
of great psychological complexity ... [Todd wraps]
his challenging plot, complex characters and
subtle psychological insights in thick layers
of atmosphere."
—*New York Times Book Review*

"Fine writing. A spectacular conclusion that rejuvenates
the cliché 'It was a dark and stormy night.'"
—*Washington Post Book World*

"A strong mystery, filled with fine characterizations,
a superb eye for Cornwall and for post–World War I
attitudes, and a wise and wily explanation of
how some of us deal with guilt."
—*Boston Globe*

"Todd writes exceptionally about a time when people
found not just meaning but healing in poetry,
when intuition was viewed as a kind of 'second sight,'
and when everyone was stamped by war—not just
the legless men, but also the women who lost
their loves and so their futures."
—*San Jose Mercury News*

"A brilliant return ... Memorable characters,
subtle plot twists, the evocative seaside setting
and descriptions of architecture, the moors and the sea
fully reward the attention this novel commands."
—*Publishers Weekly* (starred review)

A TEST OF WILLS

A *New York Times* Notable Book of the Year

"Todd gives us a superb characterization of
a man whose wounds have made him into a stranger
in his own land, and a disturbing portrait of
a country intolerant of all strangers."
—*New York Times Book Review*

"Todd depicts the outer and inner worlds of
his characters with authority and sympathy as he closes
in on his surprising—and convincing—conclusion."
—*Publishers Weekly* (starred review)

"The emotional and physical carnage in World War I
is used to remarkable effect." —*Chicago Tribune*

"With his tortured detective Ian Rutledge and
the ghost who inhabits his mind ... Charles Todd has
swiftly become one of the most respected writers in the
mystery genre.... The pair is unique among sleuths."
—*Denver Post*

"A first novel that speaks out, urgently and
compassionately, for a long-dead generation...
A meticulously wrought puzzle and a harrowing
psychological drama."
—*New York Times Book Review*

"More than an ordinary whodunit, this literate thriller
raises disturbing issues of war and peace."
—*San Diego Union-Tribune*

"A standout debut." —*Minneapolis Star Tribune*

"Strong, elegant prose, detailed surroundings and
sound plotting characterize this debut
historical.... Highly recommended."
—*Library Journal*

Also by Charles Todd

THE MURDER STONE

Charles Todd

BANTAM BOOKS

THE MURDER STONE
A Bantam Book

PUBLISHING HISTORY
Bantam hardcover edition published November 2003
Bantam mass market edition / September 2004

Published by Bantam Dell
A Division of Random House, Inc.
New York, New York

Library of Congress Catalog Card Number: 2003056299

ISBN 0-553-58660-2

For Kate Miciak,
whose book this is...

THE HATTONS OF RIVER'S END HOUSE:

Francesca Hatton—central character, a young woman who has spent the early war years in London as a Red Cross worker meeting trains from the coast; burned out, she comes home to the Valley when her grandfather has a stroke.

Francis Hatton—who has lived secluded in the isolated Exe Valley. After his death, Francesca discovers that he may have been a very different person from the loving grandfather she remembers.

Francesca's Dead Parents—**Edward** had a gambling problem and was exiled to Canada, where he and his wife were killed in a car crash, leaving an infant daughter. Or did they?

Francesca's Uncle and Aunt—**Tristan and Margaret Hatton**, who seldom came to the Valley, but had a family of sons. They died in Hampshire—or were they murdered?

Francesca's Cousins:

Simon, the warrior, who played war games and then went off to real war, only to die. He it was who gave the white stone at the bottom of the garden the name Murder Stone.

Robin, the practical one, who always sought explanations for everything. Did he, in the war, before he died, see the wretched business for what it was?

Peter, the engineer, who made the props for all their games, and then became a sapper in the war, only to die a horrible death when one of his tunnels collapsed around him.

Freddy, the musician, whose talent was silenced in the terrors of destruction.

And Harry, the charmer, the youngest who was everyone's favorite and who was the last to die, in the first weeks of the Somme offensive.

Mr. Gregory—the children's tutor.

Mrs. Lane—for years the housekeeper for the household at **River's End,** and who lives in the village now, coming to clean and cook every day.

Wiggins—long-dead gatekeeper and gardener.

Bill Trelawny, the coachman, who has served the family all his life and is devoted to Francis Hatton.

Bill's sister Beth Trelawny—who died in Francis Hatton's youth.

Tyler—the old dog that had belonged to Francis Hatton.

RESIDENTS OF HURLEY—the tiny hamlet where a bridge crosses the Exe River, a stone's throw from the gates of River's End.

William Stevens—the young war-wounded rector of St. Mary Magdalene Church and the village choice to marry Miss Francesca.

Mrs. Horner—the housekeeper at the Rectory, and neighbor of Mrs. Lane's.

"Tardy" Horner—her husband, the sexton, and always late.

Mr. Chatham—the former rector, now retired and living by the sea below Exemouth.

Mr. and Mrs. Ranson—who own the village inn/pub, The Spotted Calf.

Miss Trotter—the old woman who lives alone in a cottage beyond the church, offering medicines and advice with equal vigor, as many eccentric people did in the past.

Daisy Barton—a dead serving girl whom Mr. Hatton took pity on.

Mrs. Markley—another resident of the Valley.

Betsy Henley—a Valley child.

Mrs. Tallon, husband George, daughter Mary—a prosperous Valley family beyond the hill.

Mrs. Danner—the verger's wife.

Tommy Higby—who had a cow in his care shot before his eyes, on **Mrs. Stoner**'s farm.

BEYOND THE VALLEY—

Dr. Nealy—who lives in Tiverton and serves Hurley when called.

Miss Honneycutt—the nurse he provided during Francis Hatton's last illness.

Mr. Branscombe, of Exeter—the Hatton family solicitor, his family having served the Hattons for generations.

THE LEIGHTON FAMILY—from **Sussex**

Richard Leighton—war-wounded, and searching for the grave of his vanished mother.

Thomas Leighton—his father, who has remarried and has a young daughter.

Victoria Alice Woodward MacPherson Leighton—the missing wife and mother, who is thought to be dead.

Alasdair MacPherson—Victoria Leighton's fiercely determined father, still living as the book opens, and unwell.

Carter—the MacPherson butler.

AND FINALLY—the bit players from other parts of England, who knew Francis Hatton in one way or another.

Elizabeth Andrews—a young woman who claims Francis Hatton saved her life.

Walsham—the man who claims that Francis Hatton cheated his father out of an estate.

Mrs. Perkins—the housekeeper of that house, and her

husband, **Ben,** the groundskeeper, clubfooted, and unable to serve in the Army.

Lydia—her twin sister who lives in Cambridge.

Mrs. Kenneth—who keeps an inn in the village of **Mercer, Essex,** and sister to Mrs. Perkins and Lydia. A gossip . . .

Mrs. Gibbon—the woman who runs the orphanage established by Francis Hatton in **Falworthy, Somerset.**

Mrs. Passmore—a woman whose child was left at the orphanage for placement years ago. Widowed, she's now searching for him.

Miss Weaver—Francesca's governess for the first year or so in the Valley.

Sergeant Nelson—an Army man sent to the Valley.

The Scotsman—who had lost something to Francis Hatton and wants it returned.

And finally, **the shooter** in the hills whose real identity is obscured by doubt and silence . . .

CHAPTER 1

Devon, Autumn, 1916

It always stood in the back garden—what my cousins called the Murder Stone.

They teased me about it often enough.

"Put your head here, and your brains will be bashed out."

"Lie down here, and the headsman will come and chop your neck!"

Nasty little beasts, I thought them then. But they're all dead now. Lost at Mons and Ypres, Passchendaele and the Somme. Their laughter stilled, their teasing no more than a childhood memory. Their voices a distant echo I hear sometimes in my dreams.

"Do be quiet, Cesca! We're hiding from the Doers—you'll give us away!"

But the Murder Stone is still there, at the bottom of my grandfather's garden, where it has always been.

And the house above the garden is mine, now. I've inherited it by default, because all the fair-haired boys are dead, gone to be real soldiers at last and mown down with their dreams of glory.

CHAPTER 2

It seemed quite strange to be sitting here—alone—in the solicitor's office, without her grandfather beside her.

Francis Hatton had always had a powerful presence. An impressive man physically as well: tall, strongly built, with broad shoulders and that air of good breeding Englishmen wear so confidently. Someone to be reckoned with. Women had found him attractive, even in age.

He had carried his years well, in fact, his face lean and handsome, his voice deep and resonant, his hair a distinguished silver gray.

Until 1915.

In 1915 the first of the cousins died in France. They had hardly had time to grieve for Simon when Robin was killed at the Front. Freddy and Peter soon followed, and Francesca watched each blow take its toll. The man she had always adored had become someone she barely recognized. Silent— dark. And then Harry died ...

She stirred in her chair. Mr. Branscombe had always toadied to Francis Hatton. The solicitor fussed with the papers before him now, setting the box marked *HATTON* aside and uncapping his inkwell, as if hoping to delay matters until his true client arrived. Reluctant somehow to begin this final duty.

And had she failed in her own duty to her grandfather? She had hated the change in him, that gradual withdrawal into himself, leaving her behind. Instead of mourning together, for the first time in her life she had felt shut out of his love. When Harry died on the Somme in the late summer of 1916 —scarcely two months ago—she had witnessed Francis Hatton's descent into despair.

In the weeks following his stroke she had prayed for her grandfather's death, and at night, walking the passages in restless repudiation of approaching death, she had wished with increasing fervor that she could hasten it, and be done with it at last. For his sake. For release...

A surge of guilt pressed in on her.

Mr. Branscombe cleared his throat, an announcement that he was ready to begin the Reading of the Will. Ceremony duly noted...

The servants—the older ones, the younger ones having gone off one by one either to fight or to work in the factories— were in an anteroom, waiting to be invited into the inner sanctum at the proper moment.

" 'I, Charles Francis Stewart Hatton, being of Sound Mind and Body, do hereby set my Hand to this, my Last Will and Testament...' "

The Devon voice was sonorously launched on its charge.

Francesca found it difficult to concentrate.

My grandfather is only just dead, she wanted to cry. *This smacks of sacrilege, to be dividing up his goods and chattels before he's quite cold... I haven't earned the right to sit here. Oh, God.*

But who else was there to sit in this room and mark a great man's passing? She was the last of the Hattons. A long and distinguished line had trickled down to one girl.

Mr. Branscombe paused, glancing over the rims of his spectacles at her, as if sensing her distraction.

"Are you with me thus far, Miss Hatton—?"

"Yes," she answered, untruthfully.

He seemed far from satisfied, regarding her intently before returning to the document.

Francesca felt pinned to the hard, uncomfortable chair provided for the solicitor's clients—chosen, she was certain, to prevent them from overstaying their welcome—and wished she had the courage to stop him altogether. But listening was her duty, even if she cared little about provisions for her future, and she had absolutely no idea what she ought to do about the house at River's End. Close it? Live there? Sell it?

Ask me next month—next year! I'm so weary—

It was haunted, River's End. Not by ghosts who clanked and howled, but by the lost souls who were never coming back to it. She could almost feel them, standing at the bottom of the stairs each night as she climbed to her room. Shadows that grieved for substance, so that they, too, could come home again.

It was a stupid obsession on her part, and she hadn't told anyone of it. But the old black dog also seemed to sense their presence, and ran up the stairs ahead of her, as if afraid to be left behind among them.

Just that morning the rector had said, worried about her, "This is such a large, rambling house for a woman alone. Won't you come to us at the Rectory and stay a few days? It will do you good, and my housekeeper will take pleasure in your company…"

But Francesca had explained to him that the house was all that was left of home and family. An anchor in grief, where she could still feel loved. She knew its long dark passages so well, and its many rooms with their drapes pulled tight, the black wreath over the door knocker. River's End was peaceful, after the tumult of her grandfather's dying. And the ghosts were, after all, of her blood.

Mrs. Lane came in to cook and to clean. It was enough.

There was the old dog Tyler for company, and the library when she tired of her own thoughts. Her grandfather's tastes had run to war and politics, history and philosophy. Hardly the reading for a woman suffering from insomnia. Although twice Plato had put her soundly to sleep—

She became aware of the silence in the room. Mr. Branscombe had finished and was waiting for her to acknowledge that fact.

"Quite straightforward, is it not?" she said, dragging her attention back to the present.

"In essence," he agreed weightily, "it is indeed. Everything comes to you. Save for the usual bequests to the remaining servants and to the church, and of course to several charitable societies which have benefited from your grandfather's generosity in the past."

"Indeed," she responded, trying to infuse appreciation into her voice.

"It's an enormous responsibility," Mr. Branscombe reminded her.

"I understand that." What might once have been shared equally with the cousins would be hers. She would rather have had the cousins—

It was clear that Mr. Branscombe was uncomfortable with a woman dealing with such a heavy obligation. He fiddled with the edges of the blotter, and when no questions were forthcoming, he asked, "Do you wish to keep the properties in Somerset and Essex? I must warn you that this is not a propitious time to sell—in the middle of a war—"

He had her full attention now, as she stifled her surprise.

"Properties—?"

His thin lips pinched together in a tight line, as if he'd finally caught her out, as he had known he would.

Trying to recoup his good opinion of her and conceal her ignorance, she asked, thinking it through, "Were these estates destined for my cousins? You see, my grandfather told me very little about them."

He told me nothing—

"The properties have been in his possession for many years. Quite sizable estates, in fact. Whether he intended to settle either of them on one of his male heirs in due course, I don't know. He didn't confide in me." It was grudgingly admitted. "I can tell you that the property in Hampshire that belonged to your uncle, Tristan Hatton, was sold at the time of his death. It would have been prudent for your grandfather to provide in some other fashion for his eldest grandson. Sadly, Mr. Simon Hatton is also deceased."

Simon. The first of the cousins to go to war . . . the first to die.

Francesca was still trying to absorb the fact that her grandfather had owned other estates. But if it was true, why had he always chosen to live in the isolated Exe Valley? It was the only home she had ever known. And as far as she was aware, that was true of her cousins as well. Even Simon had had only the haziest memory of his parents.

Why had he never taken us to visit houses in Somerset or Essex, if they were his? There hadn't been so much as a casual "Shall we spend Christmas in Somerset this year?" Or "Since the weather is so fine, we might travel to Essex for a week. I ought to have a look at the tenant roofs. . . ." If he had gone there at all, it had been in secret.

The thought was disturbing. Why should secrecy have been necessary? Hadn't he trusted her? Or had he never got around to telling her, after Simon was killed? Or at Harry's death? The last of the five grandsons to die. Francis Hatton had abandoned interest in everything then, including the will to live . . .

"Before I summon the servants to hear their bequests, there is one other matter that your grandfather wished you to deal with. A recent Codicil, in fact."

"Indeed?" she said again, still wrestling with the puzzle of the properties.

"It involves the Murder Stone, whatever that may be."

Caught completely unawares, Francesca stared at him. "But—that's nothing more than a jest—a largish white stone in the back garden that my cousins were always making a part of their games!"

"Nevertheless, your grandfather has included in his will a provision for its removal from Devon to Scotland."

"Scotland? My grandfather has never been to Scotland in his life!"

"That may very well be true, Miss Hatton. But I shall read you the provision: 'I place upon my heir the solemn duty of taking the object known to her as the Murder Stone from its present location and carrying it by whatever means necessary to Scotland, to be buried in the furthermost corner of that country as far away from Devon as can be reached safely.'" He returned the Codicil to the will, and cleared his throat again. "I was summoned to River's End after his stroke especially to add this clause."

Mystified, Francesca said, "The deaths of my cousins must surely have turned his mind—"

"Perhaps this stone reminded him too forcibly of their lost youth," Branscombe suggested gravely, with an insight she had not thought he possessed. "When men are old and ill, small things tend to loom large."

Francesca shook her head. "It's such an insignificant matter..."

"Perhaps to you, my dear. But I assure you, to your grandfather it was quite important. I was under the impression that Mr. Hatton was—um—extraordinarily superstitious—about this matter. Speaking to me about this stone seemed to agitate him. The nurse had cautioned me not to allow him to exert himself unnecessarily. And thus I neither questioned nor inquired but wrote his words down directly as he spoke them."

"My grandfather was never superstitious! And he allowed my cousins to use the stone as they pleased. It was always a part of our games—we were never warned away."

"I have no answer to that. But I can assure you that this responsibility is yours and must be regarded as a binding charge. He was absolutely adamant on that score."

"But surely not right away—not while the war is going

on?" She couldn't begin to imagine how she would manage to dig up the stone—it most certainly weighed more than the elderly gardener and the coachman put together! There was no one else who could be spared for such work—help was short as it was. And how could she arrange for it to travel to Scotland, when petrol and tires were so dear? It was an enormous undertaking, and one she couldn't face just now.

"At your earliest convenience, of course." Branscombe's tone indicated disapproval of using war as an excuse.

Francesca was about to protest, but the solicitor sat waiting for her to agree to the terms of the Codicil, as if her grandfather's unfathomable anxiety had invaded him as well. She nodded and was relieved when he finally seemed to be satisfied.

He set aside the thick sheets of the will. "I have already taken it upon myself to send a Death Notice to the *Times*. And I've ordered the grave to be opened, and instructed the rector that the services are to be held on Friday of this week. If that's agreeable..."

Whether it was or not, she couldn't do much about it. Men arranged such matters, as a rule. And all the cousins were dead....

There were other papers in the box labeled *HATTON* in a fine antique copperplate. Most likely Branscombe the Elder's hand. "What else is in there? Besides the will?" More surprises? Other secrets?

"Our family has always handled the legal affairs of your family," Branscombe reminded her with satisfaction, glancing at the contents. He plucked out several folded documents. "Here we have your great-grandfather Thomas's will, and *this* is Francis Hatton's grandfather George's. *He* fought at Waterloo with the great Duke of Wellington. *His* grandfather Frederick was with Cumberland at Culloden. Amazing history, is it not?" A reminder that she would be expected to leave her own affairs with the firm that had mounted guard over it for generations.

On the papers she could see the faded handwriting. A family's continuity preserved in old ink…It was a heritage she had been taught to revere. The Hattons had always served their country well. She, the only girl in a family of six cousins, had been expected to do the same. It was why she had volunteered to serve with the Red Cross in London.

"All quite regular and in order." Branscombe returned the documents to the box with affection, as if he counted them old friends. "Ah. There's also a letter here that your grandfather deposited with the firm—"

"May I see it?"

"I know of no reason why you mayn't. As heir…" He lifted it out of the box and passed it across the desk to her.

Curious, she examined it. It was wrapped in a piece of parchment on which was inscribed over the seal in her grandfather's beautiful hand, "To be held and not acted upon."

Before Branscombe could stop her, she broke the brittle wax under the writing and drew out a letter. There was no envelope, only the single fragile page.

It read, "May you and yours rot in hell then. It is no more than you deserve!"

There was no signature.

What in God's name, she thought, shocked, had her grandfather done to be cursed like this?

And on the heels of it—

If he hadn't given credence to such a savage indictment, why had Francis Hatton sent this letter to his solicitor for safekeeping?

CHAPTER 3

After the letter had been returned to the box, Branscombe rose and went to summon the servants to hear their bequests. Francesca watched their tired, drawn faces as they filed into the room.

They had loved and admired her grandfather. His death had been difficult for them, and before he had breathed his last, each of them had come to the darkened room to file past his bed, their eyes wet with tears.

Francis Hatton, she knew, would have preferred to meet Death standing, head high, those dark green eyes undaunted by Fate. She had done her best to restore a little of his self-respect. She had bathed his hands and face with lavender-scented toilet water and sprinkled a little over the bed to disguise the sour smell of age and sickness, the last indignity for a man whose pride had been as fierce as his will.

She had longed to believe, as she spoke each name aloud, that he'd known his servants were there and how they were grieving. She knew too well they had believed that he would go on forever, a stalwart man who had always been their bulwark as well as hers. . . .

That night, as the nurse slept soundly, he had drifted into the final darkness, his hand clasped in his granddaughter's. She had held back her tears, talking softly to him until his breathing ceased, and then for another half an hour, until the hand in hers grew cold.

Leaving Exeter, they drove home up the Valley, Francesca Hatton at the wheel of the family car with Mrs. Lane, the housekeeper, while the rest of the staff—the coachman, the man who kept up the outbuildings and the park, the woman who helped Mrs. Lane with heavier chores such as ironing and turning the beds—traveled in the family carriage behind.

The Valley narrowed as it drew toward its source, a river winding its way between the rolling hills and the road following as best it could. Sometimes a ford carried them to the other bank of the Exe, and sometimes a bridge carried them back.

You would think, traveling along this road, Francesca told herself, that no one lived here. The rounded, ridgelike hills rose from the water, sometimes blotting out the autumn sun, and the only creatures for miles were sheep or cattle where the grass was greenest, and a fox sunning itself on an outcrop of rock. The horses had gone to war, like the men who had once worked this land and cared for the animals and the houses that sometimes stood over the crests out of sight from the road. Women and elderly men did the heavy work on farms now, or it wasn't done at all.

From time to time where the hills dipped, late afternoon sun threw long golden beams across the water and through the trees on her right, spears of light. Prehistoric, she thought. Before Time began and Man had come trudging up this Valley. Somehow deserted—

And now that her grandfather was dead, it was. Deserted by the remarkable spirit that had made this emptiness her home and seemingly held the life of the Valley in the palm of a powerful and graceful hand.

She hadn't realized just how much she had loved Francis Hatton. Not even in his last illness. Or rather the final heartbreak—for no mere illness could have struck him down so ruthlessly as the deaths of the cousins.

Beside her, Mrs. Lane said in a voice still thick with tears, "I don't know how we shall get along without him!"

"We shall have to try," Francesca answered the housekeeper, in an effort to offer comfort. *I'm the head of the household now. Such as it is. It's my duty....*

"Yes, Miss Francesca. But it won't be the same. First the five lads, and now Himself."

"Well. We must go on. He'd want that. We aren't the only family in England to suffer—"

"No..."

But one could tell, Francesca thought, that Mrs. Lane believed that the Hattons had carried the heaviest burden.

"Did you know," she asked, suddenly reminded, "that my grandfather owned land in other parts of the country?"

"No, Miss." The finality of the word indicated that Mrs. Lane didn't care. Like so many of the Valley's inhabitants, her universe was here. The rest of England might as well be across the Channel.

Silence fell between them.

Behind them the carriage rumbled over the rough, winding road like a ship wallowing in the sea. Mr. Branscombe had pressed Francesca to stay the night in Exeter, but she had chosen to travel home with her grandfather's servants. Hers... Hers, now. She must remember that.

Below the road the Exe ran like a tangled ribbon, meandering of its own will, sometimes dark in the heavy shadow of trees, sometimes bright with slanting sunlight. A pretty, secretive river that cleft the hills, dividing neighbor from neighbor. Most of them preferred it that way.

When the funeral was over, Francesca told herself, she

must return to London and her duties there, interrupted by her grandfather's illness and death. He would expect it.

But she had little heart left for meeting troop trains on their way to the ports, offering men hardly older than boys tea and buns, pretending to be cheerful, happy for them as they went off to glory fighting the Hun. She had also stood on the same drafty station platforms in the depths of the night when the wounded came through, carriage after carriage of them. No flags or tea or pretty smiling faces greeted those unheralded trains. The Red Cross came to them to see to bandages and offer water, to press cold, frightened hands, and to light cigarettes for those able to smoke. It was a bloody, barbarous business, walking through the carriages where so many lay in torment. And to think that these were the survivors. There were no trains for the dead. They were buried where they fell.

It had exhausted her, the suffering she had witnessed. She could face anything but that stoic *suffering*.

And the war that was to be finished by Christmas, 1914— the war that had swept away her five cousins in the madness of enlistments—was dragging on into its third year of stalemate and death, with no end in sight.

Her grandfather's illness had come at a time when she would have given anything, done anything, to escape her duties. But the summons home had been bittersweet, and all she could do yet again was to sit and watch another man's silent suffering.

I must be careful what I wish for. . . .

At first Francis Hatton could speak, although with some difficulty. She had looked forward to those brief conversations, and they had sustained her. Too soon, he had slipped into rambling monologues, leaving her behind. And finally that dreadful dark silence had engulfed him. Trapping his indomitable spirit in a slowly dying body. She had found it unbearable—

The horses clattered past the bridge and turned from the main road into the gates of River's End.

Francesca sat forward, looking out at the small stone gate-house where Wiggins used to live with his wife. Empty now and locked. Both had died when she was fourteen and never been replaced. Their daughter, Ellen, had cooked for the household until last year, when she had gone to live with her own daughter, war-widowed in Cornwall. Continuity...

Ahead the house was hidden by trees, but the road looped up the hill toward it as if confident of finding it in the end. And the old horses pulling the carriage just behind the motorcar knew their way, sensing home and oats and a blanket for the night.

The coachman, Bill Trelawny, had been with her grandfather for as long as she could remember, his back stooped now with age, but his hands on the reins still sure. He had taken Francis Hatton's death the hardest. A man of few words, Bill had come sometimes in the evening to stand dumbly by the bed, such anguish in his eyes that Francesca had realized he would have happily died in her grandfather's place if God had asked it.

At the breast of the hill the drive widened into a loop, and the uncompromising shape of her grandfather's house rose with authority, like the man, gray stone pointed with white, chimney pots lined like soldiers across the roofs. Hers...

When the servants had been settled over their late tea, Francesca took the motorcar and drove herself (much to the horror of Bill—the coachman still tended to treat her as Mr. Hatton's little granddaughter) to the church in what passed as a village but was in fact no more than a hamlet. Hurley had come into being to serve the needs of medieval drovers and carters who had passed up the Valley, and it owed its church to a benevolent Hatton in the sixteenth century whose eldest son had served with Drake and come home safely from savaging the Great Armada. Francesca had always wondered why the church had been consecrated to St. Mary Magdalene, the repentant sinner. An odd choice if it had truly been built to celebrate a valiant captain's survival.

Small, stone, with a belfry barely worthy of the name, the building boasted nothing of special importance—no rood screen, no marble knights and ladies in the ambulatory, and only a single brass, which it had actually inherited from an earlier church in Somerset.

Francesca had stepped over the long memorial brass set in the flagstones on her way to the Hatton pew every Sunday she had attended church services here. The only time she could remember looking at it closely was when the cousins had attempted to duplicate the spectacular armor the figure wore. Otherwise she'd passed by what everyone in Hurley simply referred to as the Somerset Brass, without giving it a second thought.

But now this name had taken on a new meaning.

Do you wish to keep the properties in Somerset and Essex?

She walked down the aisle, her heels echoing in the autumn silence, and stopped to look down at the figure.

Early armor. The time of the Edwards, Simon and the cousins had decided, eagerly examining each detail. That wonderful chain mail. The sword in its elegant belt. The spurred, steel-clad feet. A man of some standing, to merit a memorial nearly as long as he must have been tall in life.

She knelt on the chill stone floor, and tried to read the Latin that bordered the figure. Tracing the incised letters with her fingers, she could make out part of the inscription. Something about peace...

The door of the church scraped open, and Francesca looked over her shoulder to see the rector just stepping into the shaft of sunlight that pointed, like an accusing finger, in her direction.

"Miss Hatton!" William Stevens exclaimed, shocked to find her on her knees in the middle of the church. "Is there anything I can do for you?"

"Good afternoon— No, I've just come to look at the brass.

I don't think I've ever really examined it before. Can you read the words here?"

He came toward her, limping. He had been wounded at Mons, his face raked and part of a foot cut away by shrapnel as he ministered to the wounded and the dying. A man of perhaps thirty-two, old for the shredding flail of war. And sent here to a secure and undemanding living while he healed in spirit as well as flesh. There were whispers that he walked the churchyard late at night, talking to the dead. Francesca thought perhaps he simply found it hard to sleep without dreaming.

"It's Medieval Latin," he was saying. "I'm no scholar. I've often wondered myself how it should best be translated. See, there's an abbreviation. I know that much. And that word is *peace*—and there is the word for *sin* . . ."

"I expect he lived a rather brutal life," she observed. "And needed whatever forgiveness he could find."

"Most likely. At a guess, it reads, '*For the sins of my youth, I have paid. God accept my soul and grant it peace.*'" He grinned. "It depends on where you start deciphering it. But it's a prayer we could all make."

"It's always been called the Somerset Brass. Do you know why?"

"Not really. But I've heard that this church was scraped together from bits and pieces languishing elsewhere. Your grandfather could have told us, I'm sure. The flagstones in the choir are said to be from a convent in London. The brass here is from Somerset—and that baptismal font from Essex."

"Essex—" she echoed.

"Yes. A good many villages vanished in the plague years, you know. People died, houses and churches fell to rack and ruin. And of course not much later there was Henry the Eighth letting Cromwell loose on the monasteries. I shouldn't be surprised if these things were rescued and brought here by the founding family to give the sanctuary some air of age. A baptismal font was not a common thing, you see—in the old days, it gave a church status to have the right to baptize. A mark of religious significance."

"I didn't know that." She rose, dusting her hands and the front of her skirt. "But why Somerset—and Essex? Did the Valley have ties with such places?"

"Lord, no, not to my knowledge. Although, as I said, whoever gave us the church may have done."

He paused, as if not wanting to change the subject until she was ready. "About Friday—"

"The funeral." Francesca sighed. "I understand Mr. Branscombe has made all the arrangements."

"But you may change whatever you like," Stevens assured her. "I don't expect—given the war—that we shall see a great throng here for the service. What's important is that it should please you."

"That's kind." Her eyes filled unexpectedly with tears. "I should like to be sure the music includes his favorite hymns—"

"I'd thought of that, and believe I've managed to do rather well." Stevens's scarred face smiled, giving the sinister set of its lines in repose a warmer appearance.

"Thank you." Looking around her, Francesca said, "We have no memorials to my cousins, do we? I'd thought my grandfather would have seen to that."

"Your grandfather had a difficult time coming to terms with their loss. Especially young Harry. I don't think he needed reminders in brass or stone. Would you care to see to it?"

"Yes. By all means. Would black marble be out of place here, do you think? Black for mourning..."

"The church is gloomy, too dark perhaps for black. White is also the color of mourning. And of youth dying before its time."

"Yes," she said again, thinking about it. "I like that choice. I'll see to it—afterward." Looking into the troubled brown eyes, she added impulsively, "You were in the war. Was it very terrible? I've seen the wounded in London, and that's grim enough. I can't imagine being on a battlefield, and knowing that death was coming—watching the men beside me drop and not move again—" She faltered, and then confessed, "I wonder about my cousins, you see. No one told us *how* they died—the letters only said that they'd been brave and didn't suffer. Which is a lie if I ever heard one!"

"Some of the men suffered terribly." Stevens answered her with bitter honesty. "Screaming in pain, or lying there in silence, which is somehow worse, trying to be—brave about it. But sometimes it's quick enough. With no time for thought or grief or pain. They may be the lucky ones."

Francesca nodded. "I pray my cousins were among them."

As she drove from the church back to River's End, Francesca could feel exhaustion sweeping over her. She'd slept poorly during her grandfather's last weeks of life. And the reading of the will had been unexpectedly unsettling. Now she craved only a cup of tea and her bed, not necessarily in that order. Comfort, to dispel the encroaching shadows.

There was a man standing beside the steps to the main door; his horse stood waiting to one side. It stirred uneasily as the motorcar swept past. He was silhouetted against the setting sun, tall, broad-shouldered, and for an instant she caught her breath.

How many times had she seen her grandfather waiting for her just there, when she had gone riding or was traveling home from London? Coming toward her, smiling, taking the reins of her horse or handing her down from the motorcar—

But this man didn't move until she had stepped out of the vehicle, and then, reluctantly, he took off his hat.

He looked nothing at all like Francis Hatton.

How silly of me—she thought, blinking back hot tears.

Strangers weren't commonplace here in the Valley. She regarded him, still unable to trust her voice. This man was too young to have been an acquaintance of her grandfather's. And she was nearly sure he hadn't attended any of the brief memorial services at St. Mary Magdalene for her five cousins. But perhaps he had been at the Front and couldn't get leave. . . . He had the bearing of an officer.

"Miss Hatton?" he asked, his voice neutral, as if he wished to be certain who she was before proceeding.

"Yes, that's right." Fifteen steps separated her from the door and the solitude of the house—and yet it felt like a mile to go.

"My name is Leighton. Richard Leighton. Does it mean anything to you?"

"Should it?" she countered, wondering if perhaps Simon had spoken of him, or Peter. Had Leighton written to her grandfather when Harry died? So many people had, people she had never met. Harry's charm had touched so many. She waited for the usual words of condolence and explanation: "*I was a friend of Robin's. Didn't he tell you? I heard that he was wounded, I'd hoped he would make it. . .*"

Instead, her response seemed to anger him. She could see that in the flush that rose in his face, although he went on to answer civilly enough. "I had expected that it would be familiar to you."

Nothing to do with the cousins, surely! What, then? There was now an intensity about him, as if he wanted something from her, and she had no idea what it was. Francesca said, in an effort to hurry matters, "As you can see, I've just returned from a rather long journey—"

"As have I. I would be grateful for a few minutes of your time, Miss Hatton."

"Mrs. Lane will have gone home for the day. I don't care to receive visitors when my housekeeper isn't here."

"Mrs. Lane was—persuaded—to wait for your return. Give me five minutes. If it isn't too much trouble—" The last words were thrown down like a challenge.

Francesca examined him more closely. Hard, dark blue eyes stared back at her. The high-bridged nose, the firm mouth, the chin that belonged to a man certain of himself, determined on his own course.

Like her grandfather, she thought unexpectedly.

And like her grandfather, a shadow of illness was there as well. . . . She knew the signs: the brackets of pain on either side of the mouth, the strain across the cheekbones, the tightness of the jawline.

It didn't matter. Her determination could be as firm as his. "You may tell me here whatever it is you wish to say. I don't intend to admit you or anyone else today."

Leighton glanced across at the coachman, who had come around the corner of the house to drive the motorcar back to the stables. Bill, silent, stood his ground, eyes on Francesca's face. The stranger's horse stamped, jangling its reins, as if it sensed the tense atmosphere.

Finally Leighton said, as if he would have preferred no witnesses, "Very well, then. I've come to ask if, in your grandfather's papers, you've run across my family's name. Or to be absolutely clear, the name of my mother, Victoria. It's important to me if you have." The deep voice was curt, cold.

Francesca felt a stab of uncertainty. Was this something else she was expected to know—and hadn't been told? She wasn't prepared for more secrets! And then annoyance took over. "My grandfather's been dead only a matter of days. I certainly haven't spent that time going through his papers or anything else!" Heaven knew, it had been hard enough listening to the reading of the will—

The man gestured impatiently, as if he felt she was being intentionally intractable.

"I'm staying at the inn that stands on the fork of the road. The Spotted Calf. I shall return to call in five days. Will that be sufficient time?"

The Spotted Calf was the small inn set on the green down the road from the Rectory. It had been named over a century ago for the ghost of a small calf seen wandering across the Exe bridge when drovers passed through. The inn was mainly used by sheepmen, anglers, and travelers caught in storms, and was neither a comfortable nor a picturesque accommodation. Only the sign—a calf standing on the little stone bridge and bawling—showed any originality or imagination.

"I'm in *mourning*," Francesca rejoined acerbically. "Can't you understand that? I bid you good day, Mr. Leighton!"

With a nod at Bill, releasing him from duty, Francesca went up the three steps that led to the door and lifted the knocker. If Mrs. Lane, she thought, had been foolish enough to stay at the bidding of a stranger, she could answer the door a second time.

When the elderly housekeeper opened to her, Francesca stepped inside and was about to shut the door in Leighton's face.

Bill was already starting the motorcar, and the roar of the engine almost drowned out Leighton's voice as he said swiftly, urgently, "It's likely your grandfather killed my mother. If he did, I—the family—would like to know where she's buried. *My* grandfather is still alive, you see. And he hasn't much time left!"

Stunned, speechless, Francesca stared at the stranger standing on the lowest step.

Unbidden, the words of the unsigned letter in the legal box came back to her.

May you and yours rot in hell then. It is no more than you deserve!

"It's not *true*—dear God, I refuse to believe a word of this!" she exclaimed, offended. But the stark pain in his face told her he was convinced he was right.

"Look, I'm not trying to hold you to blame for what your grandfather did. But we've waited a very long time. And now that he's dead, Francis Hatton can't be brought to justice. He can't be questioned or hanged. We can't even prove our suspicions. It will do him no *harm*—"

Unwilling to hear more, she nodded to Mrs. Lane, who shut the door on Leighton's last words.

And then as the door latch clicked, Francesca had second

thoughts. If she refused to listen, what would he do? Spread these lies through half the village? Driven by such anger, he might make all manner of trouble! Who could say? Francis Hatton's funeral was at the end of the week—she couldn't bear to see it disrupted—

She opened the door again herself, and said to the tight-lipped man still standing there, "I've changed my mind. Call tomorrow. At eleven o'clock."

To her surprise he didn't answer. He simply turned on his heel and walked back to his horse.

As he swung into the saddle, Richard Leighton grimaced. Touching his heel to his mount's flank, he told her harshly, "I'll be here."

With that he rode off.

Mrs. Lane said, watching him go, "He knocked at the door no more than a quarter of an hour ago, Miss. I told him you weren't receiving visitors. But he wouldn't take no as an answer. I stayed on, for fear he was trouble brewing."

"Yes, that was kind of you," Francesca replied absently, closing the door again. Her heart was thundering in her chest. "You've lived here in the Valley all your life. Did you ever hear of a Leighton family? Or of a missing wife? Or of someone of that name whom my grandfather might have known?"

The housekeeper was shaking her head. "I never did. It isn't a Devon name, or I'd have recognized it on the instant. What did he mean, saying your grandfather may've killed his mother?"

"It's all nonsense, I'm sure," Francesca answered wearily. "I don't even want to think about it! I hope you've left something nice for my tea. I didn't feel much like eating in Exeter."

"I saw how you picked at your food." Mrs. Lane took her mistress's coat and gloves. "There's a bit of the roast beef still, and I've made potatoes the way you like them. And a little tart. Miss Hatton . . ." It was a measure of the woman's anxiety that she had used formal address. "Why should your grandfather have murdered *anyone*? I don't understand!"

CHAPTER 4

That night, as Francesca lay listening to the sounds of the old house stirring around her in the cool night air, she put her hand on the old dog's head for comfort and remembered her grandfather's final weeks.

She had been sent down from London on the seventeenth of August, when the heat of summer stilled the air and dust lay heavy on the roads.

Francis Hatton had been ill for a week by that time, one side of his body frozen forever by the seizure that had nearly killed him.

He had recognized her, but had turned his face away, as if ashamed to be helpless. The doctor, standing across the bed, watching his patient, said with false heartiness, "Mr. Hatton. It's Francesca! Come for a visit..."

And the dark green eyes had swung to fix themselves on his granddaughter without warmth or welcome, as if she had disappointed him by being there.

"Folly to bring you away from London with a war still on,"

he murmured. And then his voice grew stronger. "Was it this old fool's idea?"

Dr. Nealy smiled. "Yes, indeed it was. Leaving the city will do Francesca a world of good. She's pale, and too thin. Spending all her days in railway stations is not healthy for a young woman. If you behave yourself, so that she can take an hour now and again to sit in the sun or walk over the hills, so much the better."

"Hmmpf."

"Well, then, that's settled. She's off now to rest after her journey. And I've to look in on another patient."

Francesca leaned down to the bed to kiss her grandfather's dry, whiskery cheek.

And the old man said, quite clearly, "Cesca? Where are the boys? Did you bring them with you?"

He had slipped quietly into the half-world of memory and illness. Francesca, her heart aching, went quickly from the room.

Each day Francis Hatton had strayed for longer periods into the past. Sometimes reliving his own youth, calling to his wife, his two dead sons, sometimes remembering the end of July, when he had been whole and the fifth black-edged telegram had come.

This time it had reported Harry's death on the Somme.

Hatton had written to Francesca in London, telling her the news, and ending sadly with *I've given everything I have to England. Simon and Freddy, Peter and Robin, and now Harry. All gone. It will be a long winter for me...*

That night the seizure had struck him down. He had been sitting at his desk, reading a book of poetry, translating line after line of elegant Latin into elegant English. It had been a way of passing time that had settled into a hobby years before—a hobby which had even produced an anonymous volume or two of annotated works. The pen had suddenly

The Murder Stone   25

scratched across the page, splattering ink over the print and trailing off into an indecipherable scrawl.

Francesca had found the book just where he had left it and looked with tears in her eyes at the open page and the ink stains and the abrupt, infirm strokes of the pen. She had closed it gently, as if she had trespassed. And somehow she knew he would never come back to find it waiting there.

After that she had sat for hours listening to Francis Hatton ramble through the long span of his life.

Sometimes she recognized names. Her grandmother Sarah. Edward, her dead father. Tristan, her uncle. And of course Tristan's sons, the orphaned cousins she'd grown up with. Sometimes she heard her own name spoken with love and affection, and once or twice in admonishment. For the most part she'd been a good child, but even she hadn't been immune to the high spirits of five lively boys in the house. From Simon, the eldest, to Harry, the youngest, they had been mildly riotous and often in trouble, but never unrepentant.

Or as Peter, the middle brother, had told her before marching off to war, "It was a glorious childhood. I couldn't ask for any better. I hope I can bring up my own family by the same standards...."

They had never lived long enough, any of them, to hold their own sons.

Francesca, slowly pulling together the tangled narrative until she believed she could picture the whole history of this man, had been grateful for an intimate glimpse into Francis Hatton's past. Loving husband, good father, unstinting surrogate parent to his grandchildren, his life had been clearly above reproach. But she had thought, once, after the rector had come and gone, that it was just as well her grandfather had lived a blameless existence, since he was doomed to repeat it now for anyone to hear.

She hadn't known—then—that Francis Hatton had kept secrets from her. Nor that he would be accused of murder. Such was his discipline that even in the vague ramblings of delirium her grandfather had managed to hold tight to a private core she had never even dreamed existed. . . .

Throwing off the bedclothes, she found her slippers and robe, unable to close her eyes although her very bones ached with weariness. Lighting the lamp by her bed, she left the dog asleep and went down the dark passage to her grandfather's room.

She opened the door to the faint smell of sickness that lingered there. A nurse had come in to look after him in his final days, to bathe him and change the sheets and see that he was continent and comfortable. A severe woman, with hair drawn back in an unforgiving knot at the back of her head, and a face that was closed as if she kept her feelings buried well inside. But Miss Honneycutt was competent and unexpectedly kind, a Devon woman with deep roots in the land, and Francis Hatton had accepted her tactful ministrations without complaint.

Francesca set the lamp down on the table that stood by her grandfather's favorite chair, and looked around the room. It was large and cheerful enough, with cream brocade covering the walls above the dark wainscoting, and deep blue hangings on the bed and at the windows. The floorboards were bare, the wood polished to a high sheen. The furnishings were Regency, which her grandfather had preferred to heavier Victorian designs. A man's room more than a woman's. She couldn't remember it any other way, and now she wondered for the first time whether her grandmother had slept there, or in the adjoining bedroom. Her grandmother had been dead before she, Francesca, had been born. . . .

It was too bad that her grandfather had never been fond of family photographs. He had claimed it was a Victorian fancy—that frames cluttered up tabletops and mantels, the solemn, outgrown faces an embarrassment as one grew older. But she would have enjoyed seeing her grandmother's likeness or recalling the cousins when they were young. As far as she knew only one frame, holding a photograph of her parents, had ever stood by Francis Hatton's bed. And that had been more for her sake, she thought, than his own. He had sat her on his knee, pointing to it, when she was small and bereft and had wept at night for her mother.

"Look, there she is. Smiling. Pretty. Happy. You mustn't miss her, Cesca, and want her back again. It would be selfish, don't you see?"

And Francesca had stopped crying....

Trailing her fingers over the glossy surface of the desk that stood between the windows, she looked across at the bed as if asking forgiveness for prying. And then she let down the top.

There wasn't much to find. Francis Hatton had kept the ledgers for his estate in an office at the back of the house, where his tenants reported each day on the running of the farms and the upkeep of the property. Here were family matters, from a copy of his will to the reckoning for his last pair of boots. Francesca looked at each item, and folded it again to put it carefully back where her grandfather had kept it.

The book of poems he'd been working with as his stroke brought him down was where she had left it, on the desktop. She lifted it to touch the leather binding with tenderness, riffling the pages as if through them she would reach out to his last coherent thoughts. And then put it away again.

From time to time the boys had written to their grandfather in London on his occasional visits there, dutiful letters after a gift of money or some other treat. Her own were there, too:

Dearest Grandpapa,
I am no longer spotted with the measles, and I miss you terribly. I do not enjoy needlework in spite of what my tutor says about the duty of a lady to make her stitches neat and tiny. I have learned a new piece for the piano and will play it for you when you come home...

Freddy, the fourth cousin, three years older, had taught it to her, and she smiled now as she remembered his longer fingers showing her small ones where they should strike the keys next until she had the positions by heart.

> *Dearest Grandpapa,*
> *Thank you for the new book. I have read it, although it is quite long. I fell from a tree in the garden and hurt my knee. I was very glad to spend the afternoon in bed. Peter feared I had broken my leg, and Simon told me that I would have to be shot, like a horse. But Bill laughed at him and carried me into the house. I cried only a little...*

And another, slipped under the study door in an effort to return to her stern grandfather's good graces.

> *Dearest Grandpapa,*
> *I am sorry that I hit Simon so hard. I hope he is feeling better. But he was very mean to Arabella, and I wanted him to stop teasing me. I shall beg his pardon at dinner, for I truly didn't intend to hurt him. But I will not forgive him until he begs mine as well...*

Simon had buried her favorite doll, telling her that it had died on the Murder Stone, a victim of whatever war he was currently waging in the gardens.

Peter was right. It had been a glorious childhood in many respects. Francesca and the cousins had been orphaned too young to mourn long for what they had lost. Instead, under Francis Hatton's watchful, caring eye, the six children had made their own family, and basked in laughter and affection.

Francesca turned to the handful of letters from her cousins, each boy's personality shining through the words.

Simon, the warrior. Robin, the pragmatist. Peter, the engineer. Freddy, the musician. Harry, the charmer.

Harry had written—when all five were in trouble for painting the dog red to stand in for a Highland deer—

Dear Grandpapa,
We did not mean to make Napoleum so unhappy. But
we were in desperate need of a deer to hunt, and Robin
refused to play the part. Cesca was already angry at us
for dunking her for a witch into the pond. Simon had
made the best bows I have ever seen, and Peter found
raven feathers to fletch the arrows, and it would have
been such a waste not to have a deer. We would never
have hurt him! Freddy was Walter Scott and could say
his lines by heart, and you would have been very proud
of him. I beg your pardon on behalf of all of us, and
hope we shall be allowed to come to tea after all. We
shall each save a treat for Napoleum, so that he will
know that we are very very sorry . . .

She had loved them so dearly—

Putting aside the letters, she searched through the remaining drawers with some care, hoping to find—what?

Certainly not proof of murder, but something that would explain to her why the man Leighton had accused her grandfather of such a thing. But she couldn't think what there might be. Hardly a confession! Correspondence, perhaps—

But there was nothing to enlighten her. Not even a passing reference to the Leightons. No letters marked *"To be opened after my death."* No cuttings from a London newspaper about a long-ago disappearance. Not even a scrap of paper about the property in Somerset—or Essex. *Nothing . . .*

Had Francis Hatton had some vague warning of his death—and culled the contents of his desk before he was felled by the stroke? It looked that way.

Had he simply overlooked the bitter letter in Branscombe's document box? Or trusted that she would open it and take its warning to heart? But how could she, not knowing what or who it referred to?

She closed the desk, lifted the volume of Latin poetry, and sat in the chair where her grandfather had often sat. "Why did you tell me nothing of this business?" she asked into the silence.

"Who is this man Leighton? Who wrote that letter cursing you? And why am I to travel all the way to *Scotland* to bury that silly stone from the garden? Why did you own other houses and never say a word to me about either of them? I don't *understand*—"

But it was too late for her grandfather to answer....

CHAPTER 5

Precisely as the tall clock in the hall struck eleven the next morning, the door knocker sounded through the house like a death knell.

Mrs. Lane hurried from the kitchen, where she had been preparing Francesca's luncheon, and opened it to Richard Leighton, who stepped into the hall in a swirl of rain.

His hat and his coat were drenched, and his leather gloves, wet from handling the reins, must have felt like eelskin under her fingers. Francesca saw Mrs. Lane hold them with distaste, like a bit of meat gone off.

"Miss Hatton will receive you in the sitting room, sir. If you'll follow me."

She led the way, her head held stiffly as if she was anxious that he should say nothing to upset Miss Francesca. That morning she had already given Francesca her opinion that murder was not something decent people had anything to do with. Indeed, she knew better than most that Mr. Hatton had been a good and God-fearing man all his life.

Watching from the first landing, where it turned and no one would think to look up and find her, Francesca could read indignation in the set of Mrs. Lane's shoulders.

The housekeeper settled the visitor in the small sitting room, and then came to the foot of the stairs, where Francesca could see her.

Francesca walked down the steps and went into the sitting room herself. Leighton was standing there as if he owned it and she were the visitor with unpleasant business to discuss.

His glance swept the paintings and the marble of the hearth, and then met the eyes of his hostess as she crossed to one of the rose chintz-covered chairs. There was hostility in his face.

And a tiredness. She thought, considering him, that he had slept no better than she had. Possibly for a very long time.

Francesca asked him to be seated, but offered no other hospitality.

"Before we begin," she said, with coolness, "I want to make it clear that I have allowed this visit solely out of courtesy, and not because I have any reason to believe I can help you in your search. Do you understand me?"

"I understand." He listened to the fire for a moment and then went on in measured tones, as if detaching himself from what he had to say. But Francesca, watching his eyes, could glimpse a little of what seethed just below the surface. "My mother has been missing since I was a child. My grandfather managed somehow to live with that grief without the satisfaction of knowing how she died—or why—or where she may lie buried. My father eventually moved on, married again, and has been reasonably happy. But the anxiety is always there. For all of us. My family has a right, I think, to want these questions finally answered. When I saw the obituary in the *Times*, I believed that there was no reason now why the past can't be set straight. Privately, to my family's satisfaction. I've come to ask you to tell me what you know."

"First of all, I've never heard the name Leighton spoken in this house," she answered truthfully. "And I can't think why you believe my grandfather had a hand in your mother's disappearance, much less her death! That was—by your own admission—years ago. I'm not sure I had even been born! How would I know what may have happened? How could *you* know?"

"My grandfather is Alasdair Murchadch MacPherson. *Her* name was Victoria Alice Woodward MacPherson. Do you recognize either of those?"

"I've never heard the name MacPherson in any connection," Francesca responded firmly. "Is your grandfather Scottish?"

"His forebears came from Scotland. What has that to say to anything?"

She couldn't tell him that she had become acutely aware of certain places in the last twenty-four hours: Somerset, Essex—even Scotland. Instead she asked, "It might help if you told me exactly what became of your mother. Why should you believe she was murdered? It's hardly a common thing, is it, to have a murder in the family!"

"She walked out of the house one spring day, intending to call on a friend on another street. And she was never seen again."

"Where was this house? Here in Devon?"

"My parents lived in Sussex at the time, along the South Downs near the Dykes. When she failed to come back, my father couldn't live there any longer. He sold the property and moved away. Away from the memories. I never forgot that house. I can describe it still—in every detail. I spent the next ten years waiting for her to return—I was more faithful than my father, you see. I didn't believe she would willingly leave me."

The image of a small boy waiting by the window for the mother who had never come back slipped into Francesca's mind. She, too, had waited for her own parents to come back...but they were dead. Far away in Canada.

"What brought my grandfather to *Sussex*? And why should he abduct a woman he didn't even know!"

"But he did know her. He was a close friend of my father's. He was the best man when my parents were married. The two men had met abroad, in Italy, I think. My father was some years older than my mother—"

Her grandfather had always been interested in Greece and Rome—his collection of books on the ancient world was exceptional. But why hadn't he said anything about his travels there? Her thoughts leapt to the next question: Had her grandfather been intent on hiding any association with the Leightons? Certainly she would have sworn he'd never been abroad.

Another secret—? Or was this man lying?

Leighton reached into his breast pocket and took out a wallet. "I have their marriage lines, with your grandfather's signature as a witness." He passed a folded paper to Francesca.

She unfolded it with a sense of unease and scanned the sheet. And, in truth, her grandfather's fist was there—she recognized it at once. Next to it was the name Thomas Gerald Estes Leighton.

The date indicated that Leighton's parents had been married three years before Tristan and Margaret Hatton, her uncle and aunt. Therefore Leighton himself must be of an age with Simon, her eldest cousin. Perhaps a year or two older.

Barely glancing at the rest of the document, she handed it back to Leighton, her mind still on her grandfather. "When was your father in Italy?"

"He went abroad a number of times before he met my mother."

Which meant that Francis Hatton must have traveled after her grandmother's death, during the years her own father was at Oxford.

"I'm not here to talk about my father's travels," Leighton reminded her impatiently.

"You were saying—my grandfather was a witness at your parents' wedding. Surely there were dozens of other guests! You're asking me to believe that alone of all those people,

Francis Hatton came back some eight—nine—years later and carried off the bride? Why? Even if he'd wanted to marry Victoria, your father stood in the way! And to be frank, I don't think he ever looked at another woman, after my grandmother's death."

Yet how could she be so positive—given the other secrets she'd uncovered? It was like a quagmire, where the most dangerous places appeared to be the most solid.

"I've never suggested he wished to marry her! We're speaking of abduction and murder, not a grand passion—"

He stopped abruptly, his face suddenly white, one hand gripping the arm of the chair with such force the knuckles were rigid. With her experience in the care of the wounded, Francesca could tell that he was in great pain, nearly gritting his teeth as he waited for it to subside.

"What is it?" she asked quickly.

Leighton cleared his throat. "Nothing. I was wounded not long ago. I'm sorry—where was I?" But his voice was tight with the agony.

"Is there anything you need? Would standing help?"

With an effort of will, he brought himself back to the matter at hand, ignoring her unwilling sympathy. "What sort of monster breaks up a family for his own amusement?"

Francesca countered hotly, "Precisely my point! It's a monster you ought to be searching for. Did no one consider a vagrant wandering on the Downs that day? And what about someone in the village with a history of instability? Or it could have been sheer jealousy, someone who secretly disliked your mother! Look there before you accuse my grandfather!"

"The police were quite thorough. They even questioned my father—asking him what might have caused his friendship with Francis Hatton to turn malevolent. Who knows what lay between them? Francis Hatton had seen my mother no more than a handful of times. He'd put up no objection to the marriage. It's true he seldom came to our house, but he continued to meet my father in London from time to time. What happened? Why, years later, did he come back into our lives and destroy them! It was as if he couldn't get her out of his mind, and in the end, was willing to do anything—hurt anyone—to have her."

"But when did suspicion turn my grandfather's way?"

"Not until the next morning. At midnight—when Victoria still hadn't come home—my grandfather telegraphed everyone he could think of to come and help in the search. Alasdair was desperate. Victoria was his only child. The village police were getting nowhere. In fact, they were waiting for someone to come down from London. Time was slipping away. My father was afraid for her—afraid she was hurt—lying helpless out there waiting for someone to find her."

"Where was your father that day? At home?"

"He was at the British Museum giving a lecture on the Elgin Marbles—there was an American society of antiquities in London that week. He blamed himself for not being home to initiate an immediate search. She'd been gone nearly five hours when he learned what had happened. And nothing had been done. Of all the people Alasdair contacted, Francis Hatton alone refused to come."

"Where was the search centered? Why did it require so many people?"

"The village at first. But it was my father's opinion that when the friend didn't answer her knock, Victoria had walked on toward the Downs. She often did that—she enjoyed being alone and sometimes she poked about among the Stone Age rings and barrows that clutter that part of Sussex. She'd come home in time for tea, content and somehow restored. And so there was no way of knowing how far she'd gone or in which direction—and it would take more than a handful of men to scour the countryside."

"Did my grandfather give any reason for not coming to help?"

"When my grandfather pressed him, Hatton told Alasdair in no uncertain terms that he was a fool to think that Victoria was lost or had been spirited away. He was completely unsympathetic. My grandfather was shocked—angry."

"Hardly proof of guilt, if my grandfather knew anything about your mother! He must have believed she was able to take care of herself. You just told me she'd walked in the Downs any number of times."

"Or was he covering his own tracks? It appeared that he must have been watching her that day. Your grandfather's carriage had been seen in Chichester that very morning, heading toward the Downs. He must have known she would go walking."

"Why should anyone in Chichester notice my grandfather's carriage? Much less remember which day it was?" she retorted scornfully.

"And," he went on, this time ignoring the interruption, "late that afternoon a smith on the road near Upper Beeding had examined a mare's hoof for a stone, and found none. The carriage's driver refused to pay the man for his trouble, and the smith remembered that. There was a woman in the carriage, but she was heavily veiled. Still the smith's description of the driver was quite good. Tall, dark-haired. Light eyes, blue or even green."

"It would be very unlike my grandfather not to pay the man for his time—he was always generous."

"Nevertheless—"

"All you've done is vent your wretchedness on my family! My grandfather is dead, he can't defend himself! And you haven't bothered to see his point of view! For instance, how do you know your father hadn't offered rewards for any information? And this blacksmith—and the witness who saw the carriage—simply lied to claim the money."

Something in his face changed.

"He did, in fact, didn't he? Offer rewards?" she pressed. "Then your proof is no proof at all!"

"There was the blood—"

Blood. Her heart flipped and then settled back into a more or less normal rhythm.

"What do you mean? Where?"

"On the Downs. The searchers found Victoria's shawl in a

dip in the land, where she must have taken shelter—or attempted to hide. The fringe was black with blood. She was never seen again. No word, no body. Just silence and that stiff patch of blood on silk. My grandfather begged yours to come stay with my father, to offer what comfort he could—they'd been friends once. And he wouldn't. It was as if Francis Hatton couldn't face us. He never spoke or wrote to my father again. That hurt my father, I can tell you. If it wasn't guilt that kept the man away, what was it, for God's sake? What made him behave with such callous disregard for an old friendship?"

"For all I know," she countered, "something your father had done could have driven your mother away. Or perhaps she went of her own free will, and my grandfather wanted no part in dragging her back again. Why should *your* family stand blameless? Grandfather was no fool—"

"She left behind a small *child*. If my father had mistreated her, do you think she'd have willingly left her own son to face the frustrated brunt of his fury?"

It was a telling argument, and Francesca had no answer for it.

But he seemed to take her silence as disbelief, and his anger, never far from the surface, flared. He stood up, towering over her. There was menace in his face.

"I was old enough to *remember*. My father did nothing to Victoria—nor to me. And I've questioned my grandfather again and again about your family. He swears it was something in Francis Hatton's nature that was perverted, vicious. It's your family that has a history of instability, not ours!"

All at once she could see a different side of Richard Leighton. One she'd glimpsed on the drive—one he had striven to put aside this morning. This man was filled with a fierce and abiding anger that welled from the deep recesses of his soul. Francesca couldn't be sure whether it was his own— or whether it was a reflection of childhood in a family torn apart by tragedy. But it was there—and very real.

"You don't have to look any further than Francis Hatton's

sons to see that there was something wrong in *this* house," he went on before she could even frame an answer. "Both of them died young, in disgrace! Don't ask me to search for evil in my background. My mother was brought up with joy and happiness. Search for the darkness where it began, in your own family. If you're honest, you'll find it!"

Leighton crossed the room, and at the door said, with his back to her, as if struggling to regain his composure, "I shan't let this matter rest. If you learn anything, you can reach me through the card I presented to your housekeeper yesterday."

And then he was gone, leaving Francesca sitting there with no answer to his accusations.

A storm in the night set a shutter to banging, and Francesca got up to do something about it.

The noise led her to the sitting room, and she lifted the sash to reach out and fasten the shutter again. Afterward she walked through the dark house with the shades of her cousins, living and dead forlornly searching for comfort.

In the drawing room was the piano that had been dear Freddy's pride. She touched the case, suddenly inconsolable, wanting more than anything to hear his music again. The fourth-born, tall like all the Hattons, a superb rider, an excellent tennis player, he could coax the most beautiful sounds from any instrument. Francis Hatton had asked him once, jesting, where such a talent had come from. He'd been intensely proud of him, as he was of all his orphaned grandchildren.

"Nowhere," the grinning boy had promptly answered, "It's my very own."

It was Peter the engineer who had laid out a tennis court behind the shrubbery, and it had seen hard use. Even her grandfather had played on summer evenings, and they had all worked toward the day they could defeat him.

Weeds were overtaking the court now.

There wasn't, she realized, a single corner of River's End

that didn't echo with memories....Everywhere they whispered to her, beckoned to her, reached out for her, as if refusing to let go. They offered—comfort.

In the end she went up to her grandfather's room and sat in his chair again, looking across at the empty bed where he had spent so many of his last hours.

"Did you do these things, Grandfather? Or are they lies?" she asked the pristine coverlet and the folded sheets and pillow slips that lay at the foot, where Mrs. Lane had set them after ironing them.

Francesca could almost picture him lying there, his green eyes fixed on her....

A memory came rushing back to her, shocking her. Leaning back in the chair, she gasped, as if a hand had slapped her across the face.

The words that her grandfather had muttered in his halfsleep not a fortnight ago—

It was late afternoon and Francis Hatton lay quietly as he so often did now. Francesca couldn't quite be sure what was wakefulness and what was that limbo between sleep and unconsciousness. It didn't matter; she could feel his presence, and that alone was enough.

Sitting by the side of the bed, she began to talk to him, a habit she'd fallen into of late, almost like thinking aloud. The post the day before had brought a letter from a friend in London. It had been painful to read. Her own emotions had been raw enough, but the despondency in the letter had overwhelmed her. And as she had done as a child, Francesca found herself pouring out her anguish to the one person who always listened.

"It's the endless lists of dead and missing and wounded. There's always someone we know, someone we met at a party—a brother—a friend. It numbs the heart, until it's impossible to feel anything any longer. Everyone we meet is in mourning. The newspapers tell us almost nothing—mainly lies. The correspondents who did go over write mostly platitudes about gallantry among the allies or atrocities by the Germans. The Army won't allow observers at the Front. Even mail is heavily censored! And how can we be winning when the dead go on piling up, and nothing has changed in France? The Exeter newspapers only repeat what they're told by the War Office, that we'll soon be victorious on the Somme. But Sally writes that the wounded tell another tale, that we lose as much as we gain. And that the only end we can hope for is stalemate."

She turned to look out the window, struggling to regain her composure. But after a moment tears got the better of her. "I can't *bear* the thought of going back to London!"

There was a slight movement on the bed, as if her grandfather had heard her. As if her need had reached him.

It was unimaginable relief to unburden her soul.

"It's not cowardice," she went on earnestly, trying to explain why she should be so derelict in her duty. If the other women could stand it, why couldn't she? She answered herself aloud. "It's helplessly watching so much *suffering*—I can't close my eyes to that, try as I will." But the figure on the bed was still. "I wish it would *stop*, that's all. The fighting. I'm no longer sure we shall be able to win!"

But here at River's End, where there had always been sanctuary—here was another man slowly, painfully dying before his time. In her dreams, she was beginning to tangle them together—the cousins living and starkly dead, the long trains filled with bloody bandages and white faces, and her grandfather's helpless body, no longer moving resolutely to his iron will but locked in a silent, hopeless defeat.

Dr. Nealy had told her two days before that there was no possibility of full recovery—that Francis Hatton's torment could go on for months—a year.

Reaching out for something, some response, she cried, "Is it all in vain? Did we lose Freddy and Simon and Peter—did this happen to *you*—all for *nothing*?"

And as if her wretchedness had gotten through the fog of

his damaged mind, he seemed to rouse himself, there on the bed, to struggle to answer her ... to reassure her.

"*Victorious ... victorious ...*" he said, over and over again, his hand moving a little on the coverlet.

It nearly broke her heart with joy. For the next several days, it buoyed her spirits and let her sleep a little.

But what if he hadn't? she asked herself now.

What if he wasn't predicting the outcome of the war? What if, in the darkness that clouded his brain, it wasn't her words that had reached him? What if somehow her anguish had touched a chord of memory, and sparked an anguish of his own? What if he was saying the name of a woman he had once cared deeply for—or hated enough to kill ...

Victoria—Victoria ...

Not *victorious.*

In the name of God—she couldn't have mistaken him—

Yet his words had been dreadfully slurred, the result of his stroke.

No. *No—!* She fought the fear now, and felt the doubt drive through the certainty.

I wish I had never heard her name, she thought. I hate the very sound of it! I wish I had never set eyes on Richard Leighton!

The room seemed to grow colder, shutting her out.

As if Francis Hatton was furious with her.

She got up hastily and went back to her own bedchamber, listening to the storm climbing about the hills as if searching for something. Or someone.

How long had it taken all those men to comb the Sussex Downs for Victoria Leighton? Days? Weeks? While husband and child waited in desperate hope?

Had it been difficult to cover the terrain? Had the searchers come back tired and depressed, only to be chivvied by Alasdair MacPherson's fears into setting out again at first light? Had Richard's father searched with them, dogged and determined?

Had it rained—or had sun reddened their faces? Had it been summer hot, or windswept cold?

It didn't matter, Francesca thought, climbing back into bed and drawing the old dog nearer, for the living warmth the devoted creature offered.

Nothing she, Francesca Hatton, could do now would ever bring Victoria Leighton back again. Whatever had become of her...

Why couldn't the woman rest in peace?

Because Victoria's father and child couldn't let go.

THE COUSINS

Simon ... the warrior

I was sixteen that summer. I'd begun to think ahead
to Oxford, and I was already of two minds about
that. It's what I'd studied toward, of course, but not
what I really wanted. I told myself, if I do well in the
first term, I'll ask to go to Sandhurst. Perhaps then
Grandfather will listen to what I have to say and give
me permission to become a soldier.

Would it seem odd, when the time came, to go
away from here and live among strangers, leaving
behind all that was familiar? My brothers. The house
at River's End. Cousin Cesca. Grandfather ... The
Valley had been the center of my life for so long I'd
taken root there. I couldn't remember any other
home. And I'd had a feeling for some time that
Grandfather was hoping I'd give up my dream of
Sandhurst and take over the estate's management,
training for the day the house would be mine. I
wasn't certain I should inherit it. Peter called me

mad. I called it independence. God knows he talked incessantly about building railroads in Patagonia or across Burma. My brother ought to have understood why the Army called to me.

It was late July, I think, when we finished a hard-fought game of tennis, Robin and I, and we threw ourselves down afterward on the cool, thick grass, looking up into a cloudless summer sky.

I hadn't intended to say anything. It wasn't something I wished to talk about. But the words came out anyway, as I lifted myself to one elbow. "I'm having that nightmare again."

Robin was tossing the tennis ball to Maggie, one of the dogs, watching her race across the court and catch it, flinging up her head in glee.

"I don't remember when you didn't have it," he told me. Ever practical.

He'd heard me pacing the floor God knows how many times in the small hours of the morning. And being Robin, sometimes he'd come tap at the door, to inquire if I was all right.

"It stopped for a while," I said finally. "For nearly six months, in fact. I don't know why. Now it's back."

"Same as before? The nightmare's course, I mean?"

"Yes." I hesitated. I'd never described it before this. It was as if putting it into words gave it a reality a dream never owned. Robin didn't press. And after a time I went on. "I see a woman, smeared all over in blood, lying on the Murder Stone. I don't know who she is—or why she's there. Or how I came to see her. But I am quite certain she's dead, and I'm walking into the garden, the sun is high overhead, and there's no one else about. The dogs are inside—with Grandfather, at a guess. One of the woman's hands moves, then she's still. I'm terrified; it's as if I've never seen someone covered in blood before—and the shock is intense. And then Grandfather is striding across the grass, and he says something as he puts an arm around my shoulders and leads me away. And that's the end of it. No explanation, no sense of when or how or why it happened. All the same, it's vivid. As if I could touch the woman and feel real flesh."

Robin took the ball, smeared with saliva now, and threw it again before wiping his hands on his trousers. Maggie went dashing madly after it. "It wasn't real to start with, you know. It's those bloody games you played out there—it's no wonder you've had nightmares!" I couldn't tell whether he was joking or not.

I didn't reply.

"Ever ask Grandfather about it?" Robin turned his head to look at me. I was glad to see only concern in his face.

"Lord, no!" It was my turn to throw the ball. Maggie was waiting, her body quivering with anticipation. "I never quite screw up my courage somehow. It's rather like opening a door you know is better left closed. . . ."

Robin grinned at me. "Old man, you can't have your cake and eat it! Either you make peace with this wretched dream—or you ask Grandfather what might have triggered it. Simple as that."

I returned the grin. But inside I knew it had never been that simple.

It was not until the night before I left for Oxford that I finally spoke of it to my grandfather.

He listened intently, his face impassive. When I'd finished, I said, "It would help if I knew whether the nightmare was real or not. Is there any way to explain it?"

Grandfather said nothing. Then he clapped a

hand on my shoulder, as he'd done when I was a child and had pleased him. "I've never found a dead body on the Stone. Unless it was one of your ragtag army slain or melodramatically dying. Still, I'm glad you asked," he said. "If only to set your mind at rest."

It did. I couldn't have said why. But it was as if a great black cloud had been blown away. Perhaps because I'd never known him to lie to me.

Later, what I remembered most about that conversation was how sad Grandfather's eyes were.

I told myself at the time it was because I was leaving River's End and he knew how much he would miss me.

On the train to London, I watched my smiling reflection in the rain-streaked window, lighthearted, already pulling away from my childhood. Grandfather sat quietly beside me, as if he understood. He was looking down at his hands clasped quietly in his lap. I was the first to leave; it couldn't have been easy for him.

She hadn't been there.... It was only a childhood nightmare that had grown steadily worse because I'd been reluctant—afraid?—to tell anyone.

And yet that dream had been as vivid as any real memory I possessed. Odd what tricks the mind can play.

"I've never found a dead body on the Stone...." Grandfather had told me.

So why was I haunted by the certainty that I had?

CHAPTER 6

The next morning was cool and clear, with a fresh wind blowing down the long valley of the Exe.

Francesca was awake and dressed well before Mrs. Lane came walking up the drive.

The housekeeper was surprised to find her mistress buried in the back of the linen closet, intent on sorting sheets.

"Miss Francesca!" the older woman exclaimed in dismay. "Whatever are you thinking of!"

"The funeral is tomorrow. I was restless. I couldn't sleep— I needed something to keep my mind and hands occupied."

"But this will never do—"

With a sigh, Francesca relinquished the sheets in her arms and let the housekeeper persuade her to come down to the kitchen for a nice cup of tea. The English panacea for everything.

As if to distract an unruly child, Mrs. Lane launched into an account of her own morning.

"I was never so surprised," she prattled, rinsing the teapot with cold water, "to find Mrs. Horner, the rector's house-keeper, on my doorstep before seven!"

Mrs. Horner lived in the cottage next but one to Mrs. Lane. Childless, both of them, the two women had found service a way to fill empty lives, and each was loyal to a fault to her employer.

"That's unusual," Francesca dutifully answered. "She's usually at the Rectory by that hour to prepare breakfast for Mr. Stevens."

"Indeed she is! But she was that upset she wanted a word with me before she left for the Rectory."

Waiting for the water to boil, Mrs. Lane turned a worried face toward Francesca. "That man who was here yesterday—"

"Mr. Leighton?"

"That one." It was a measure of her condemnation that Mrs. Lane refused to use the name. "Just after tea yesterday, Mr. Stevens thought he saw someone walking in the church-yard, and went to discover who it was. And it was that man! Poking about among the graves, first this one and then that, and by the time the rector got to the churchyard wall, he was up the hill where that stump of a cross is, the old one."

It had been, once, a fine Celtic cross put up by a Devon family for a son killed in a storm. And the cross itself had been toppled in another tempest in the 1700s. The general opinion was that God had expressed his wrath twice, and no one was willing to risk it a third time by putting the head back on the shaft. Green with old moss, they'd lain side by side ever since.

"What did she say the man wanted?" Francesca asked with trepidation.

"He was looking for a grave—or so he said. And he asked the history of that broken cross."

"It has nothing to do with the Leightons—for that matter, it's a good three hundred years old!"

The teakettle began to whistle. Mrs. Lane turned back to her stove. "He was on about that mother of his being missing, and Mr. Stevens told him roundly that it was not likely he'd find her here in Devon!"

"So Mrs. Horner reported?"

"Indeed, and in the end, Mr. Stevens invited the man back to the Rectory and tea, though he'd long since had his own."

"And what did they talk about?" Mrs. Horner had long ears—and a lively imagination.

"About his mother, mostly. That's how Mrs. Horner got the whole of the story. Mr. Stevens asked how a son, age eight, could remember whether his mother was a good woman or a bad one. How he could judge in what way her own character might have contributed to her downfall or her death."

That was very blunt! Francesca thought. Aloud she asked, "And how did our Mr. Leighton reply?"

"He said that he was not interested in defining his mother's character, he only wished to know what had become of her."

"Did he make any mention of murder? Or my grandfather?"

"Mrs. Horner said nothing about that—nor did I wish to ask outright." It was Hatton business, and not for the ears of the village at large.

Francesca felt a sweep of relief. "Well, if he's only telling people that his mother is missing— But who can say what he might reveal if he stays here long enough? I wish he would be satisfied and go!"

"Not much chance of that, is there?" Mrs. Lane poured two cups, set one before Francesca with a linen serviette, and went on with her account. "Afterward Mrs. Horner asked Mr. Stevens how he could have been so patient with such a one. And Mr. Stevens, good Christian soul that he is, answered that he rather thought the man was ill and needed absolution."

"A strange way to go about it. Seeking a murdered woman."

"Well, as to that, if he's ill, it could be his mind is playing tricks with him. You know as well as I do, dwelling on the past because there's nothing much else to do, day in and day out, can warp his thinking. What angered me the most was Mrs. Horner telling me that Rector had agreed to look through the church records for his mother's name. Mr. Stevens is a good-hearted man, but in my book he's being led on!"

"What, does Leighton believe my grandfather killed her, and then out of a bad conscience gave her Christian burial in St. Mary Magdalene's churchyard!"

"It'll only encourage him," Mrs. Lane agreed. "But I thought you ought to know—"

Francesca left her tea untasted. "This is more serious. I shall have to speak to Mr. Stevens, before this goes any further."

"I'd not want to get Mrs. Horner in trouble—"

"She won't enter into it, I promise you."

"And there's tomorrow—" Mrs. Lane interjected, as if trying to keep Francesca occupied. "I've not liked to ask you what we're to be serving to the funeral guests."

Dear God, Francesca thought, appalled. "I hadn't considered—"

"I'll be baking most of the day. But if you could bring back that large box from my kitchen, after you speak to Rector—I was intending to ask Bill to fetch it this morning. After the storm last night, his joints are aching something fierce."

"Yes, I'll see to it. Perhaps Mrs. Horner can help out tomorrow—"

Times had changed—where once River's End and other such houses in the Valley had boasted large staffs inside and out, few were left to do the ordinary work of big households, much less the extra preparations required for guests, parties, or important events like weddings and funerals. Now everyone's staff had shrunk to those too old for war or for the factories, and the towns were crying out for anyone to fill the vacancies left by men called up. Village girls had always been glad to earn money by helping out when needed, but they too had vanished, some of them patriotic and eager to serve, others drawn by the better pay. All over England, able-bodied men were a rarity almost as soon as the call had come, but it wasn't long before the young women followed them to London or Manchester—to all the larger cities—where the excitement—and the work—could be found. Now the Valley was reduced to asking favors of those who remained, everyone doubling up to lend a hand where it was needed, refusing to complain, offering with a wry shrug, "There's a war on, you know." The new French expression, *"C'est la guerre,"* had become the watchword in London. As if that excused the increasing hardships. The elderly minded children, helped where they could in the fields or small shops, and cooked meals for the women doing heavy labor in their husband's or brother's place.

"I've already asked Mr. Stevens if he could spare her. He offered the Rectory instead of River's End, if you'd prefer it that way. But it's not fitting, is it, Miss? Mr. Hatton wouldn't have cared to be so shamefully neglectful of his friends."

"I daresay there won't be many friends who are able to travel this far," Francesca replied. "But all the same we must see that the meal is done properly. Whether two people or twenty or two hundred come to the service."

Francesca drove herself into the village, and found the rector in his study, considering what he was to say tomorrow about a parishioner twice his age and whose life he knew only briefly and at its very end. William Stevens welcomed Francesca with the air of a man badly in need of rescue.

"I've come about Mr. Leighton," she said. "I'm told he's asking questions about his mother, claiming she must be buried here in Devon. He's already been to see me, haranguing me for answers. I'm beginning to think the man's obsessed."

"He didn't put it quite that way. But yes, Leighton's looking for information. And there's none to give him. I've searched the parish records rather carefully, and nothing comes to light. In fact, I hadn't expected it would. He's probably dying, you know. Leighton. And people who are dying are often...single-minded."

Even Mrs. Lane had said as much.

"Dying? Did he tell you that?"

"No. But there's a sense of urgency about him, a darkness that seems to drive him. As if he knows his time is short. And there are brief spells where he almost blacks out. As though the pain had grown unbearable. I've noticed too he can't sit in one place for very long—that seems to distress him the most." Stevens smiled wryly. "I've had some little experience myself with the wounded and hospitals, as you know. I've come to recognize the symptoms of fatalism."

"Well," she retorted in exasperation, "accusing strangers of foully murdering his mother is stretching obsession beyond belief!"

"Who has been accused— *Murder?* Francesca, what are you talking about?" The rector's face was severe with concern.

Francesca bit her lip. She had let her tongue run away from her, let anger get the better of judgment. "He swears Grandfather abducted and killed his mother, then buried the body where it couldn't be found. I can't think why he's so convinced of that, but he is."

"He told me only that she had ties to the Valley—Francis Hatton? But that's *absurd*!"

"Yes, I told Mr. Leighton as much. He called on me again yesterday morning and all but accused me of hiding the Family Secret and refusing to divulge what I know."

"That's even more absurd. If your grandfather had committed *six* murders, he'd hardly have unburdened himself to *you*! It's to me he'd have turned, his priest and confessor, as he lay dying. And I can tell you he did nothing of the sort!"

"But how am I to refute it, pray? And what if Leighton badgers the funeral guests tomorrow? 'Did you know my mother? Do you think she was murdered by the man we're burying here today—'" She caught herself and sat down unsteadily, as if the air had gone out of her. It was an appalling thought.

Stevens asked, "You haven't slept well, have you?"

"Does it show so clearly? No. But that's not the point—"

"I think it is. Ordinarily you'd have the good sense not to

heed what a man you know nothing about has told you. I believe Leighton to be sincere, but even I can't be certain he's telling the truth! Two very different matters! The problem is, you see, you're vulnerable now. And alone."

And how had this stranger learned so much about the Hattons....

"My grandfather did keep secrets," Francesca confessed, forced into honesty by Stevens's open concern. "I'm only just learning some of them! It's not a matter of good sense—not any longer. The seeds of doubt have been planted, you see, and I'm starting to question everything I thought I knew about Francis Hatton! By any chance, *did* my grandfather confide in you? You visited often before I came home and in those last weeks before the end. Did he tell you things he never told me?" she pleaded. "I'm so in the dark!"

"How can I know the answer to that? I will say that what was uppermost in his mind—as you'd expect—was the loss of his grandsons. He was struggling to comprehend it—he sometimes railed against God, calling Him merciless. 'First both of my sons,' he would say, 'and now my five boys. I would have offered my sons up like Isaac, but not my boys.' I told him that that was madness. That he'd loved his sons just as much as he had loved his grandsons. His other concern, naturally, was keeping you safe when he wasn't there to cherish you. 'Who will guard my girl?' he must have asked me a dozen times. The Valley will look after her, I replied, but that didn't appear to satisfy him. In his view no one could take his place." ·

"How did he answer you? About his sons?"

"His answer was unexpected..." The rector paused, as if debating how to finish the account. Finally he added, "He said that his sons had disappointed him. For what that's worth."

In disgrace...

"What had they done to disappoint him? Besides dying before their time?"

"He didn't explain what he meant. He changed the subject after that."

Unsatisfied, Francesca considered asking Stevens if Francis Hatton had told him about the properties in Somerset or Essex. If he had spoken of the Murder Stone. But something made her hold her tongue.

"I can understand his railing," she answered after a moment. "I sometimes railed myself. It seemed so unfair, to take them all. Even Harry."

"Harry is only one of many. You have no idea how the youth of England has been squandered," Stevens said bitterly. "You can't imagine the slaughter." He shook his head in denial. "Battles used to be set pieces—a few hours—three days—and then both sides withdrew to lick their wounds. The killing might have been horrific, but it was finite. Trench warfare is different. The Battle for the Somme—we were trying to relieve the pressure on the French, you see. But somehow the Germans guessed what we were about. And here it is, October, four months later, and the butchery continues. We're dug in on one side of No Man's Land, and they're dug in on the other, and it's a war of attrition. How many of you can we kill before you've killed all of *us*? There's no respite, no space to stop and think and *survive*. And no one was prepared for that! Certainly not the Army General Staff!" He stared into space at something she couldn't see, something ugly that seemed to fill the room with his doubts. "My faith was tested in ways I'd never dreamed of—how does anyone tell a mere boy that it's his *duty* to climb out of the trenches and race across that barren hellscape until he's cut down—?"

Stevens caught himself, made a deprecating gesture that was half resignation and half apology. "But that's *my* particular obsession. We were saying about your grandfather—" He tried to smile, and failed.

But he couldn't hide the pain. Francesca wanted to comfort him—and knew that that was the last thing he could endure just now.

"My grandfather—yes. What was he like as a man?" she pleaded, trying to define her own enigma. To her he was

Grandfather, the rock of her world. She'd never before questioned—she couldn't see him through the eyes of other people.

"He was one of the most forceful men I have ever met. Whatever decisions he made, he stood by them. He was intelligent, compassionate, and sometimes unyielding—even cruel. I have to tell you that as well."

"How do you mean—unyielding?"

"He had an Old Testament view of life. Retribution, an eye for an eye. Where I would have tried to find the charity to forgive, he would say, 'They brought it on themselves. Now they must learn to live with it. That's their punishment.' And serenely walk away while I tangled myself in knots over the thorny question of duty and responsibility." Stevens made a wry face. "But it's in my nature to want to find a way out of a dilemma, to uplift and comfort."

"Give me an example," she pressed.

He shook his head. "I can't think of one that doesn't involve parish business. Of course that's where I dealt most often with Mr. Hatton. I'm sorry, I shouldn't have brought it up—"

"But do you think—*was* there something mean—vicious—in him?"

"Good Lord—!" Stevens began earnestly. "No, not that kind of cruelty! I promise you!" He was embarrassed, and added with a wry grin, "I was trying to say that your grandfather saw good and evil rather starkly. Black and white. Without the compassion I'd been taught in Seminary. I found myself wondering what kind of experiences in his own life had taught him such—bitterness."

But Francesca wasn't content.

"Do you think my grandfather was truthful? That you could trust what he told you?"

"You're letting this soul-searching eat away at you! And that's Leighton's doing, of course. The man ought to be horsewhipped for it!" He was angry. "Do you think you could be so far wrong about a man you'd loved all your life? Do you really believe you could be such a poor judge of his character?"

"You haven't answered me. Was he truthful?"

"He said to me once, 'You believe now that absolute truth is a virtue. When you're my age, you'll understand that it isn't.' But in a way I did know what he was trying to tell me— I'd written letters home to the parents and wives of dead soldiers, I'd held the hands of the dying and offered them more grace than they deserved. Sometimes truth has to be put in context. Harking back to what we talked about earlier, if Francis Hatton kept secrets from you, he must have had a very good reason for doing so. And you must give him the benefit of the doubt there. You must trust to his wisdom and his good judgment."

"All right, I'll hold on to that. Thank you!"

"Not at all—"

Mrs. Horner stuck her head around the study door. "Mr. Leighton to see you, sir. I told him Miss Hatton was with you, but he insisted his business couldn't wait."

Leighton came striding into the room on the heels of the announcement. His nod to Francesca was the briefest acknowledgment of her presence. Then he said to the rector, "I've just been speaking to an old woman who lives on the edge of the stream, in that hovel that passes as a cottage."

"That's Miss Trotter, I think—"

"Her mother worked for the Hattons. That's why I sought her out. She told me that some twenty years or more ago a body was found in the river. The dead woman was given decent burial in the churchyard. Francis Hatton paid the sexton to dig the grave and the rector of that day Chatham, I think Miss Trotter said he was called—to speak a few words, although the question was whether the woman was a suicide or the victim of a storm."

"Before my time, of course," Stevens agreed. "But I recall seeing a reference to that death last evening as I was searching the church records for you. She was a serving girl who had run away from home."

"Who decided that she was a servant girl?"

"The records don't tell us that sort of thing. Someone must have recognized her—the name given was Daisy Barton, occupation, servant."

"Odd that Miss Trotter didn't know that, as she was living here at the time. She swears no one recognized the girl. I'd like to see the grave, if you will tell me where to look."

"Mr. Leighton, I can understand your desire and your impatience. But Miss Hatton was here before you, and there's the matter of her grandfather's funeral tomorrow. If you will come again in an hour—"

You could see, Francesca thought, that Leighton didn't relish the rector's polite refusal to answer him on the instant. That urgency again . . . She felt herself enjoying his discomfiture. And at the same time felt a twinge of guilt. A grudging understanding. She had never seen her own parents' graves, and sometimes wondered what it was like in Toronto in the winter . . . if anyone brought flowers for them in the summer.

Richard Leighton was no different than she, surely, in wanting closure.

But not at the sacrifice of Francis Hatton's good name!

"I can follow directions, if you will give them," Leighton was saying.

"No." It was firm. "I am occupied at the moment with other matters. You must wait until I am free to help you."

Leighton turned on his heel and stalked out of the room, but on the threshold he staggered, clutching at the sides of the door for support.

Stevens, with a smothered oath unbecoming to a priest, was across the room and at his side, his bad foot forgotten. But Leighton brushed him off. "It's nothing!" he snarled on an indrawn breath. "I missed my step—the carpet—"

It was a naked lie, but Stevens let him save face. "Yes, of course."

The door closed behind Leighton, and Stevens limped back to the desk, smiling ruefully at Francesca. "I'm sorry—"

The peace she'd achieved moments earlier was shattered.

Anger had swallowed her again, and she fought to keep her temper.

"He'll go to any lengths, won't he, to show my grandfather killed that woman! I'll be hearing from his solicitors next!"

"I think he sincerely believes—"

"Yes," she interrupted grudgingly, "he probably does. I don't know whether it was his father or his grandfather who cultivated it, but he's utterly single-minded! That makes him dangerous."

"Dangerous?" Stevens repeated in bewilderment. "Hardly that!"

"It isn't *your* grandfather being accused of something unspeakable, like murder, when he can no longer tell his side of the story! Don't you see? It's only a matter of time before the whole story spills out, and the Valley learns why that man is here! And after he's gone, I'll have to look everyone in the face, wondering how much of this wild tale they believe. Can't you find a way to get rid of Richard Leighton before tomorrow? So he won't attend the funeral? Send him on a wild-goose chase to Exeter? Or back to London."

"I'd have to lie—"

"No, you'd only have to speak the truth—that murder hasn't been done here in the Exe Valley in half a century."

As she said the words, Francesca found herself thinking, "Even if Grandfather killed Victoria Leighton, it wasn't *here*. He'd never have done such a thing here where we were living. But there was always Somerset—or Essex—"

You believe now that absolute truth is a virtue... There were many ways of lying. What kind of man had her grandfather become, far away from River's End?

CHAPTER 7

The house, when Francesca returned, smelled of pastry and yeast and roasting pork. The funeral baked meats, she thought, remembering *Hamlet*. All I need is the ghost of my grandfather come to warn me.

Instead, had he sent Richard Leighton? She shook away the thought.

After delivering the sought-after box from Mrs. Lane's pantry, she went upstairs and took off her hat and coat, still dissatisfied with the way her interview with the rector had ended.

In spite of everything, she decided, Stevens was more than a little sympathetic toward Richard Leighton. A fellow soldier, a fellow sufferer. The comradeship of war, Peter had once called it, she remembered. Fear and courage and death made men brothers in ways that had nothing to do with birth.

She, on the other hand, didn't trust the man at all.

"Please God nothing happens tomorrow—!" she said aloud into the silence of her room. "I couldn't bear it!"

She went down the passage, looking at the shut doors that closed off her cousins' rooms, and the door at the far end which led to her grandfather's suite.

"I've hardly had time to grieve," she said to him, as if he were still there and could hear her. "Or to say good-bye."

The knocker on the door clanged loudly, and at the head of the stairs, she watched Mrs. Lane cross the hall below and open to the undertakers from Tiverton. They had brought Francis Hatton home for the last time.

The massive oak coffin stood on velvet-hung trestles in what had been the drawing room when the Hattons had felt the need to entertain. The room hadn't been used in years—not since the war began, certainly. Most people had given up entertaining on a formal scale. Francesca stood watching as the undertaker's men arranged swags of black crepe across the tops of portraits and over the closed drapes at the windows, then veiled the lovely oval French mirror. The room seemed excessively warm and suffocating, with candles burning at either end of the coffin and above the mantel, their reflection glinting in the polished surface of the wood.

A macabre setting fit for a Gothic melodrama.

Grandfather wouldn't care for it—he'd fling the windows wide and say bedamned to them all! I wish I had the courage to do the same.

She turned to see a broad man standing in the drawing room doorway, staring fixedly at the casket. She thought at first that he had come to make certain that everything was done properly. His words told her differently.

"It's true, then." A rough voice, strongly accented.

"I beg your pardon?"

"He's dead." His eyes swept the room, examining it as if he were the tax man come to assess the price and the quality of the household goods.

"I'm sorry, we aren't receiving guests—"

"I'll be back tomorrow." And with that he was gone, tramping out the door as if furious to be put off.

"Who was that?" Mrs. Lane asked, standing in the hall and staring at the slammed door.

"I have no idea." Francesca gestured to the drawing room and its grim decorations. "I thought this sort of thing went out with the Victorians—"

"It's Mr. Branscombe's taste, I expect. He's one for ceremony."

Francesca sighed. "You must be right."

The men were setting about the task of opening the coffin lid.

"No—!" Francesca cried out, before she could stop herself. "Leave it closed, if you will!"

The undertaker's men gaped at her. "You don't care to have it opened now, Miss? Will you be opening it before the service instead?"

"No—no, I don't want it opened at all!" She felt an unreasonable panic, knowing suddenly that she couldn't bear to look down at that still face, the eyes shut, the mouth an unyielding line. Or were the eyes shut? The nurse had closed Francis Hatton's eyes when she'd been summoned to pronounce him dead. A gentle hand passed over the lids. Had they opened again?

Francesca shuddered at the thought.

"No—please. Leave it as it is!"

They must have been accustomed to grieving family wanting to look a last time on the face of a loved one. The four men stood there and waited, as if expecting her to change her mind.

She could feel her heart thudding against her ribs. What was she to do? "Please—if you've finished, go now! I—I need time alone—"

That seemed to be an emotional response they recognized. With polite bows in her direction, they left the drawing room in single file, like penguins, she thought, as she went to the door, firmly closing it behind them.

She turned, trembling, to Mrs. Lane. "Does it have to be here? The coffin?"

"There, now, it's what's always done, Miss Francesca. Don't you remember? And I think your grandfather would have liked coming home a last time. After all—"

"Well, then, I shan't look at it!" She walked firmly back to the drawing room and shut the doors with as little fanfare as possible.

"There's the candles, Miss, they'll have to be seen to—"

"Then I should be grateful if you'd see to them, Mrs. Lane."

She picked up a shawl she'd left on the table by the passage to the rear of the house, and went quickly down toward the kitchens and out through the yard door.

How am I to sleep tonight with that casket in the drawing room? I shan't be able to set foot in that room ever again, without seeing it all in my head!

But what had she to fear from her grandfather?

Throwing the shawl over her shoulders against the afternoon chill, she walked briskly down the path through the kitchen plots, and let herself out the gate into the landscaped lawns. At the bottom of the garden was a small pool that had in its time played the role of baptismal font, witch's pool, Cape Trafalgar, and whatever else her cousins could conjure up in their fertile imaginations.

Halfway to the bench that was set above the pool, she stopped to look down at the Murder Stone.

It lay there, mocking her, a long white curved lump of stone that had always seemed as alive as the five boys who played upon it. Or had they made it so! Yet something there was. Perhaps that was why her grandfather had been so set on removing it now that they were gone.

But in God's name—why to Scotland? Why not simply break it into pieces and throw them into the river?

Francesca put a hand down to the cool dampness of the rock, expecting that vivid response yet again, as if the stone knew she was there.

And felt stone—only stone—under her fingers.

It's as dead as they are now. Nothing—I can't feel anything here!

Or could it be that she was the one who had changed?

Francesca ran her fingertips over the rough surface again, then began to brush aside leaves that had drifted down with the changing of the season.

How creative the cousins had been—and how often they'd inadvertently made her life a misery.

"Yes, yes, I *know* your mother and father are buried in Canada!" Simon had repeated impatiently. "But let's pretend you're *another* girl, Cesca, kneeling to mourn the murder of your father in Scotland, and I'm Rob Roy, come to avenge his barbarous death. And Harry is the Red Indian that killed him—"

"Rob Roy never met any Red Indians," Robin had scoffed. "It's not in the story!"

"Well, he might have, you can't know for certain!" Simon had retorted, and Freddy had agreed with Simon. "Besides, we cut off Harry's hair yesterday, and now he *looks* like a Red Indian."

"I'll only do it if you're sure there aren't any spiders," Cesca had told them resolutely. "Push the grass aside, and be *sure*."

The grown Francesca's fingers were busy pushing the grass back from the stone, as Freddy's graceful pianist's hands had done, and it was then that she noticed that something—mouse? vole? fox?—had been scratching around the edges of the stone in the night. As if to see what the dimensions were, and where it could best burrow under.

She hastily drew away.

Or had Leighton been here? Had that obsessive search for his dead mother led him to consider every bizarre possibility? It was a disconcerting thought.

That man kept thrusting his family nightmare into her private world at every turn! And she was helpless to stop him. What demons of guilt or uncertainty or delusion had driven his family to fix blame on Francis Hatton, of all people? What did Leighton *really* want?

Had her grandfather been capable of committing cold-blooded murder? A few days ago, she would never have believed such defamation of his character. Now—now that she knew how many other secrets he'd kept from her—she was filled with uncertainty. There was the property he'd never told her about—the visits to Italy as a younger man—his unexpected obsession with the Murder Stone. There was even a suggestion of something disgraceful in the lives of his sons. And now a charge of murder. What else lay beneath the seemingly smooth surface of his life?

Would it matter to her if he had killed someone?

What if a murderous nature ran in families?

She looked down at the silent white stone. What would the practical cousin, Robin, have to say to Richard Leighton? Would *he* have questioned their grandfather's character as she'd been doing? Or would Robin simply have knocked Leighton down for even voicing such a malicious accusation?

The Murder Stone.

How had it come by such an appellation? Even the cousins' tutor didn't know, although he'd told them that the stone was of ancient origin, possibly hand-hewn like those at Avebury and Stonehenge, and from a forgotten culture that was even older than either of the famous rings.

"It's been lying here far longer than any house built in this Valley," he'd said, making the most of their curiosity for his lessons. "Think of that! Try to picture those early people setting it here to honor a great king or a heathen god. Even Arthur, if he had come to the Valley, wouldn't have been able to tell you how it got here or by whose hand! It was shrouded in time even then."

That had launched a round of Arthurian wars, Merlin and Lancelot battling the Druids.

Francesca felt a shiver of fear. Murder had a harsher reality now. It was no longer games in the back garden.

A stark reminder to her to be about her duty and remove

•

the stone to the far north of Scotland, as her grandfather had commanded. Even if she didn't understand why it had to be done.

She slept poorly again that night, all too aware of the candlelit coffin in the room below. Even the dog had deserted her and gone to sleep across the threshold, wishing to be as near to his master in death as he had been in life.

The Tyler by the door ...

If her grandfather had walked a last time through the empty rooms of River's End, he had not come to visit hers. Consideration—or condemnation?

She wished he would confront her and say whatever had to be said, and let her mourn him properly.

Or was he being cruel—leaving her to her own conscience?

An eye for an eye—

A secret for a secret—

What did my father do that was so disgraceful? she asked the silence out in the passage. Or my uncle Tristan?

Is there a darkness in our family that you kept from us as long as you could?

Mists clung to the river in the early dawn, but it was turning fair when the pallbearers arrived to shoulder their heavy burden and carry Francis Hatton to his final resting place. Burly men, but older, they took their time, and Francesca followed them with the servants. It was not a short walk to the church, and the men were red-faced by the time they arrived. But no one would have asked Francis Hatton to make his last journey on a cart or in a hired hearse. Such were their feelings for the man who had all but ruled them for most of their lives. Old loyalties ran deep in these people. For her grandfather, they would have perjured themselves, many of them, and taken the blame for his sins, real or imagined.

Mourners were waiting inside the church. Neighbors and villagers for the most part, faces she'd grown up with, names she knew. Greengrocer, sexton, innkeeper, smith, butcher, sheepman, farmer...Most were middle-aged, with children still in school as well as sons at the Front and daughters in London.

It was as if the Pied Piper of War had lured the older boys to France, and the girls had rushed to the cities to fill their empty shoes. It hadn't happened just in Hurley; all over England the story had been the same. Would this displaced generation ever come home again? Or, like the cousins, had they left never to return?

The organ was playing one of her grandfather's favorite hymns, now. Francesca's throat closed.

Standing apart from the Valley families was a sprinkling of strangers. To be expected, of course. One of them she knew: Leighton, his eyes unreadable in the shadows cast by one of the clustered columns that separated the nave and the aisles. She also recognized the gruff man who had intruded at River's End yesterday, the one she had mistaken for an undertaker's assistant. He glared at her as if he could pierce the dark veil she wore and know what was in her mind. But who was that woman, also in a veiled hat, as if sharing her mourning? A second woman stood in the next row, her face half hidden by the handkerchief she was pressing to her mouth. Then Francesca's eyes passed on to an angry man, who stood upright as the coffin passed, and all but spat at it.

Who are these people? Have they come here to grieve with me—or, like Richard Leighton, have they brought bitter memories to be exorcised? It was a horrid thought. *Please, God...! Not today of all days. Let him be buried in peace!*

But as she found Branscombe's satisfied face in the last row but one, she recalled the obituary in the *Times*. Had that brought them, just as it had brought Leighton? It was a long way to travel on a whim, to say good-bye to someone they couldn't have known well...Or perhaps they had, and it was she who was the stranger to them.

Close as she was, she could hear the muffled sounds of the oak casket being settled firmly on the black velvet draped trestles.

As she took her place, the rector stepped into the pulpit. The wheezing box organ produced a final musical chord and stopped, as if choking on the sound.

Francesca listened to William Stevens extol her grandfather for his kindness and his charity, and wondered if Francis Hatton was laughing quietly in the darkness of his oak coffin. He had indeed been a generous man and a kind one, but he had also given short shrift to fools, carried himself with a haughty sense of his own worth, and put his family above all else. He had made a home for his orphaned grandsons and his orphaned granddaughter, giving of himself, in time and money and love, to make each of them feel safe and happy.

How much of that was a lie, how much the truth? Why had his sons died in disgrace? In spite of the rector's attempt at comfort, Francesca had lost her faith in herself. And that was making it impossible now to read the actions of a man she had once believed she knew to the very core. But she couldn't tell Stevens that, could she? Without raising other ghosts...

The rector was saying that Francis Hatton had cared for the church, seeing to its needs and recognizing its pastoral duties. But Francesca knew that for another lie. Francis Hatton had viewed the church as a social obligation, and given God only a passing nod. He had insisted that his grandchildren attend services with strict regularity, but it had always been the tutor, Mr. Gregory, who accompanied the six youngsters.

So many secrets—

The voice of the rector echoed in the church, rising to the rafters and bouncing off the cold stone as he ended the funeral eulogy.

Francesca found herself devoutly wishing that the cousins were still alive and sitting here with her, their shoulders comfortably touching, Harry's hand clasping hers, sharing her burden.

But there was no one, except the old dog who wasn't allowed in the church...and a dead man in his coffin. It was beginning to dawn on her just how alone in the world she was. A frightening thought—she must muster the courage to cope with it. As she had mustered her courage the night Francis Hatton died.

When the final prayers had been said and the coffin had been carried into the churchyard, a passing shower of rain dotted the polished oak with what seemed to be myriad tears.

And I haven't cried at all, she realized.

The committal was brief and ceremonious. Stevens pressed Francesca to let the first handful of earth fall back into the open grave, dust returning to dust. She heard it strike the wood, a hollow sound, as if the body within had already departed and there was nothing left but the shroud of his best suit of clothes.

Bill was waiting beside the motorcar while she spoke to a number of people at the graveside, and then he drove her steadily, with an air of state, back to River's End.

Mrs. Lane and her friends from the village, including the rector's own housekeeper, hurrying ahead, were putting the finishing touches to what was a feast by wartime standards— a roasted hen, an enormous ham scavenged from one of the outlying farms, platters of sandwiches, and plates of cakes and tarts. Tea was already steeping in the silver teapots by the time the motorcar arrived at the door, and the fragile porcelain cups were sitting in rows like a waiting army.

With relief, Francesca relinquished her hat and veil to Mrs. Lane. Peering through the closely woven black silk threads was beginning to give her a headache. She felt as if she were drowning in darkness.

She was waiting at the door, the assiduous Mr. Branscombe at her side, when the first of the mourners came to accept hospitality from the bereaved household.

She spoke to each villager, bidding each welcome as he or she shyly passed through the door and into the high, paneled hall with its tall medieval chairs and the great curve of the newel post ending in a carved leopard. The doors of the drawing room stood wide, and the candles struck fire from the gold trim. No amount of black bunting disguised the fineness of the French love seats, or the grace of the table covered now with a crisp white cloth and the Georgian silver tea service. Francesca had not meant it to be overwhelming—but Mrs. Lane had insisted that River's End reflect its late owner.

"They'll expect no less!" the housekeeper had warned. "Wait and see."

Many of the mourners had never set foot here except as tradesmen come to the kitchen door or tenants stepping, hat in hand, into the estate office. They looked around them with subdued interest as they made their way across the checkered tile of the hall floor.

Richard Leighton, taking her hand perfunctorily, said, "A fine send-off for a murderer, I must say."

"Do shut up," she hissed. "This isn't the time or the place."

"No, you're right. I apologize." He nodded stiffly and walked on into the room.

The gruff man she'd seen the night before with the undertakers slipped from the hall into the drawing room past a neighbor who was cajoling Francesca to consider spending a few days with them up the Valley. "We'd be delighted to keep you as long as you like," Mrs. Markley was saying. "You know you can be comfortable with us, my dear."

Francesca thanked her, keenly aware it was true. But she wasn't ready to abandon the house yet, and if she did it would be back to London that she traveled, her leave nearly up. Back to the trains of misery that came in the dark of night, and made her heart break.

The young woman in the veil was next in the line of guests. She pressed Francesca's hand as if she had known her for years, and spoke briefly. The older woman followed her, and then the angry man she'd noticed in the church, his face still blotched with fury. He merely nodded curtly, as if he couldn't force himself to say even the platitudes of polite condolence.

"I wonder who he is," Branscombe was saying, staring after him as he also passed on into the hall and from there into the drawing room.

Finally the last of the guests had straggled past, and Francesca turned to find Mrs. Lane at her elbow with a cup of sweet tea. She drank gratefully, and was looking for a place to set the cup when Richard Leighton came up to relieve her of it. "Sit down," he said. "You have done your duty."

It was an unexpected kindness, and she turned to anger to strengthen her backbone.

"I wish you'd had the decency to stay away today! You've been prowling the cemetery—talking to the rector—asking questions of half the village— That makes a mockery of coming to honor the dead."

"It's true. I've no reason to mourn the man you called your grandfather. I suppose I wanted to be sure he was dead. If there's any justice in heaven, he's already answered for his crimes."

"You're rude," she said impatiently, and walked away, only to be cornered almost at once by the angry man.

He said in a low, strained voice, "Look, my name is Walsham. I've come about the estate in Essex."

Startled, Francesca said, "Indeed?" They were standing a little distance from the other mourners, and no one could overhear them.

"Yes. My father, a rather foolish man, lost it to your grandfather at cards. I demand the right to buy it back. I ask your permission to speak with your solicitor on Monday morning."

"I know nothing about the property in Essex—" she began, but faltered. Tall and fair, his face flushed, he would surely have reminded Peter of a Viking on the attack, but Francesca wasn't amused. It was as if the man believed that sheer persistence would persuade her. Or was used to having his own way by the force of his choleric personality.

"I can afford to pay a fair enough price for it." He was clearly trying to hold his temper in check. This wasn't, she could see, a recent resentment but a long-simmering rancor. "The Essex estate has been in my family for four hundred years or more. I have the right to ask for first consultation."

"But I haven't even *seen* it—I can hardly decide—"

"That has nothing to say to anything," he told her hotly. "The property is *mine*. My father was cheated, I tell you! But I'm offering you—"

Leighton was unexpectedly at her elbow. He said, staring at Walsham, "It doesn't matter what you're offering. I suggest you say farewell to Miss Hatton. Contact her solicitor at your convenience and his."

Walsham opened his mouth to argue, but something in the younger man's face made him think better of it. Leighton escorted him out.

Her head throbbing, Francesca slipped away to the small sitting room down the passage. Stepping inside, she leaned against the door, her eyes shut and her whole body struggling to soothe away the tension of the morning. She had been so afraid something untoward would happen—and it had been a close run thing.

She nearly gasped when someone in the room cleared his throat.

It was the gruff man who had appeared with the undertakers. She hadn't seen him standing there between the windows. He made no effort to introduce himself, but said, "Where is it? I should like to be allowed to look at it."

"Where is what?" she asked, irritated. "And what are you doing in here? The rest of the company is in the drawing room!"

"I've searched the house," he replied baldly. "It isn't here as far as I can tell. My box. The tricky devil refused to hand it over, even after I'd met his exorbitant price! I'll not be cheated, I tell you. I want what is mine."

Francesca had no idea what he was talking about. "If he won this box from you at cards, I know nothing about it! Now if you'll please leave—"

"It wasn't lost in a card game, woman! Are you witless? I *paid* for it. And I want to see it. Francis Hatton knew what I was about—he knew why I wanted it. And he agreed I should have it! Now I've come for it, and I won't be denied." He spoke English with a pronounced Scottish accent in the r's. "He was a bastard, Hatton was, but I always believed he was honest. Now I know differently!"

"I suggest you see my solicitor if there's something you want from this estate," she told him coldly. "I am not discussing business on the day my grandfather is buried!"

"It's none of the solicitor's bloody business! If you had any sense, you'd see that. Nor is it yours to keep—it never *was!*"

Francesca whirled and went to find Branscombe. The man reluctantly followed.

One of the women she hadn't recognized in the church, the younger one, stopped her in the passage with a hand on Francesca's arm, a tentative touch that indicated shyness. The man on Francesca's heels brushed past contemptuously.

"I wanted to ask you," the woman began diffidently, "if Mr. Hatton had left anything to me in his will. My name is Elizabeth Andrews, and your grandfather saved my life when I was a child. I'd have been put into an orphans' home, if he hadn't found a family to take me in. I wondered if Mr. Hatton had remembered me at the end...."

Her head giving her no peace, Francesca said, "I'm afraid I've never heard your name until now."

Miss Andrews looked crestfallen. "I—I do apologize!" she stammered. "What he did loomed so large in my life—I thought perhaps it might have mattered to him as well—"

"My grandfather was a secretive man in some ways," Francesca heard herself saying. "I didn't know anything about his business affairs."

Miss Andrews stepped back, her cheeks flushed with embarrassment.

Will these people never go—

But then Francesca took pity on the girl, no more than a

few years younger than she was. Eighteen? Barely! Perhaps a small legacy would have helped her find a decent start in life—

"You must speak to my solicitor," she said, summoning kindness to her voice. "He knows more about my grandfather's dealings than I do. He's the man who was beside me as I was greeting guests."

The gray eyes were tearfully grateful. Francesca felt a stab of shame.

Why didn't you tell me all these things? When you were rambling through the events of your life, why did you leave out so much? What was Elizabeth Andrews to you—!

A Valley woman came up to her, taking Francesca's hands and holding them as she spoke of Francis Hatton with affection and warmth. A good neighbor, she was saying. "We will remember him that way, too. Now, if there's anything George and I can do, you have only to send word! Or are you returning to London?"

"I don't know, Mrs. Tallon—I haven't thought much beyond today."

"Of course you haven't!" Then Mrs. Tallon added, with some feeling, "Mary is grieving still for Freddy. I hadn't realized there was so much affection there. I can't believe they're all gone, all those wonderful boys."

Francesca said, "It would have been a happy match, I think, my cousin and your daughter." There the conversation ended. Francesca made her way through the crowd of people, finally reaching Stevens.

The rector smiled down at her as she laid a hand on his arm.

"Just talk to me. About anything—the weather—the service—I don't care—as long as no one else interrupts."

"What's wrong?" he asked, instantly concerned. "Is there something wrong?"

"People are coming up to me *wanting* things—I'm half afraid to speak to anyone anymore. It's impossible to tell what's true and what isn't."

Looking at her sharply, Stevens asked, "Did you eat any breakfast this morning?" He took her hand and tucked it through the crook of his arm. "Never mind! Come along, we'll step outside where you can breathe a little fresh air." He led her out the door and across the drive to the lawn. "Is that better?"

Francesca brushed a hand across her eyes, letting the quiet sink in. Then she thanked him with a smile.

"You haven't let yourself grieve properly, you know," he reproved gently. "Your grandfather lived a long and full life. It isn't like your cousins, cut down in their prime. We ought to rejoice that he has gone on to a better life, no longer bound to his bed and suffering."

It isn't his death that has dismayed me, it's his life, she thought. "You must have noticed them. That man who looks as if he's an undertaker—the Scot—claims my grandfather stole something from him. Mr. Leighton you know about. There's a young woman who feels he ought to have left her something in his will—another man is demanding that I return his Essex estate. He claims my grandfather cheated his family at cards. I've never heard of any of them before—"

"Funerals often bring vultures in their wake. Money is usually what they want. In one fashion or another."

Francesca wondered if that was what Leighton wanted— a sum to keep his mouth shut? How much would it cost to make them *all* go away? But even as she thought it, she was ashamed. Her cousins would have faced them down. Was she such a coward? No ... It was the anxiety of the last few months that had drained her spirits. If only she could *sleep*—

Mrs. Lane was coming across the lawn, her face distressed. "That man," she said even before she reached the rector and her mistress, "was wandering about in Mr. Hatton's *bedchamber*! I have never seen anything like it!"

"Who? Mr. Leighton?" Francesca asked, alarmed.

"No, the other one, the one with no manners—"

"I'll see to him," Stevens said. "Find another cup of tea for

Miss Hatton, if you will, Mrs. Lane. I don't think she was allowed to finish the first one."

The housekeeper said worriedly, as the rector limped back to the house, "I hope they don't come to blows—it wouldn't be right, in a house of mourning!"

Francesca let herself be led indoors. The hall now seemed dark and malevolent to her, waiting for her like an animal in its lair. Everyone was in the drawing room, and she hesitated, unwilling to set foot in there, either. It was where the coffin had stood, a haunted place now. Mrs. Lane pressed another cup of tea and a plate of sandwiches in her hand and led her to the verger's wife, an affable woman who had raised a large family and took most things in her stride.

"Sit down, Miss Hatton, do! A bite of food will do you good," she said solicitously, offering the chair beside her. "You're pale, my dear. And small wonder, with this crowd. But it's a proper turnout, isn't it? Very fitting! Well, now, will you be staying on with us? I do hope it's true; we haven't seen nearly enough of you since this war began." She sighed. "Only last week, we lost three more of our lads from the Valley. Gassed, one of them, and the others maimed and not likely to live. We need to stay close, those of us who are left!" Her Devon accent was pronounced, the a's broad. "Perhaps you can help us roll bandages or knit gloves and scarves for the soldiers. It will take your mind off everything to stay busy!"

"I don't know what I shall be doing, Mrs. Danner. It's early days yet."

"And so it is," she answered with the warmth of a woman accustomed to offering comfort. "Healing must come first— Lordy, look who's just come in! She's always uneasy in company. I glimpsed her at the back of the church, but I never expected we'd see her here."

The woman at the door was draped in half a dozen shawls, as if the autumn air was more chill than she cared for. Thin and angular compared to the plumpness of most of the wives from the village, she had pinned her hair back into a knot, but the tendrils of graying curls seemed to defy capture. It was difficult to judge her age, but everyone knew her. She lived in the cottage beyond the church, and was regarded as being a little touched in the head. Miss Trotter, she was called. Leighton had visited her earlier, Francesca recalled.

Walking tentatively across the polished flagstones to where Francesca stood, she held out a thin hand and greeted her in a reedy voice. "Your grandfather was a good man, child, he had a heart that was pure."

"You're confusing him with Galahad, Miss Trotter," the rector interposed lightly, coming up to join them. "Your visitor has gone, Francesca—he thought it best not to say good-bye."

Miss Trotter said, "The Scot, you mean. *He's* not a nice man, that one. Political, I'd swear it."

"Political?" Francesca asked in surprise. "How on earth would you know that?"

"I can't really say," Miss Trotter answered vaguely. "It's just the way he strikes me."

"Will you have a cup of tea and a plate of ham, Miss Trotter?" the verger's wife asked, coaxing her gently toward the drawing room.

"I don't mind if I do," she answered, following in a cloud of lily-of-the-valley scent. Over her shoulder she smiled at Francesca and remarked softly, "He's at peace, you know. I can feel it."

Francesca felt a wave of warmth reach out to her.

"They always say that people like Miss Trotter see more clearly than most," Stevens commented, watching the two women walk away. "She came to the church the other day, and told me that I ought to think less about what to say over Mr. Hatton and more about the Henley child. And I hadn't even known Betsy was ill!"

"Had Miss Trotter been looking after her?"

"That was the odd thing—no, she hadn't. She just came to me and said what she had to say and was gone. But it was a timely warning. Betsy had a high fever and I sent for Dr.

Nealy." He shrugged. "I daresay Miss Trotter heard the news from someone who came to her for—um—other help."

There was no doctor in the village—Dr. Nealy drove down from Tiverton to serve the people of the Valley. Miss Trotter's store of herbs (and, some claimed, charms) were called upon discreetly from time to time. Stevens turned a blind eye—the help the old woman dispensed had nothing to do with attendance at services or his parishioners' faith in God on Sundays, and he was wise enough, he had once told Francesca, not to meddle.

People began to make their farewells, thanking Francesca for "doing him proud" that day, as "his blood *would* do," suggesting that she had filled her cousins' empty shoes to the satisfaction of the Valley. It was an accolade.

Soon she could grieve in private, she promised herself, her public duty done.

Leighton turned to take his leave of her. "I should like to speak to you on Sunday if I may," he said, glancing at Stevens, but directing his request to Francesca. "It won't take long."

"You're leaving, are you?"

"On the contrary." He offered her what she chose to regard as a nasty smile. "I think I've found what I've been searching for. Good day, Rector."

And he was out the door, leaving her alone there with Stevens.

CHAPTER 8

When Mrs. Lane arrived the next morning, she brought a sealed envelope with her to the small sitting room.

"This was pinned to the front door. I saw it as I came up the drive. Uncivilized way to leave a letter, I'd say."

Francesca took the envelope and examined it. A good-quality stationery—but not posted, instead hand-delivered.

She broke the seal on the back and opened it to find a single sheet inside.

You don't remember me—you didn't recognize me yesterday. I was your nanny before I left to marry my late husband. I wonder if you'd be willing to give me an hour of your time? I'll come to the house around ten this morning, if that's convenient for you.

There was no signature.

Francesca looked up at Mrs. Lane. "Did I have a nanny

when I was a child? I have no memory of her—just of sharing Mr. Gregory with my cousins."

"There was a woman who tended you when you arrived from Canada. Mr. Hatton was at his wit's end, you a baby not yet two and crying most of the time. She was living in Somerset, I do think, and he brought her here looking like a man who'd found salvation. But she didn't stay long; she was young, and there were no eligible bachelors in the Valley to walk out with her. Although Mr. Hunt, over in the next valley, took quite a fancy to her. Your grandfather soon sent him about *his* business! Scandalous, that was. He was *married*, you know, Hunt was, and didn't give tuppence for his wife."

"She's coming to call at ten. What was her name?"

"The nanny? Weaver, I think it was—Miss Weaver."

"She's a widow now. I wonder what she wants?"

"My dear! You've grown so like your mother!"

An attractive woman in her late forties came into the room smiling, her face alight as she held out her hands to Francesca. She had been at the church, but hadn't spoken more than a few words at the reception.

"And of course you'll have no recollection of me! My name is Passmore, now. Henry and I were married for twenty years. It was a happy time!"

"Mrs. Passmore. Please, do be seated. You knew my mother? But I thought—she was killed in Canada with my father, while traveling. An accident."

"Yes, of course, that's true! I must have been thinking of your cousin's mother. Simon's mother. She was a lovely young woman. But tubercular, you know. She went away to Switzerland, for a cure. And sadly never came home." Mrs. Passmore reached into her purse and handed a photograph to Francesca. "She gave me this, before she went away. She asked me to keep it, a good luck charm, you might say, to bring her back again."

Francesca looked down into the face of a woman holding a

baby in her arms. She was fair, slim, and very pretty, her smile warm.

"This is Simon?" Francesca asked, studying the sleeping child. Smothered as it was in a lace cap and a long beribboned gown, it was impossible to tell whether the infant was a boy or a girl. "But, no, Simon had brothers. This must be Harry, then. The youngest."

Mrs. Passmore replied, embarrassed, "Yes, it must have been Harry—of course! I could hardly tell the boys apart!"

Calculating dates in her head, Francesca handed the photograph back to Mrs. Passmore and said, "He was not quite three when I came to River's End."

"And a lively young lad. I asked Mr. Hatton how he would ever manage, with five grandsons and now a little granddaughter. I remember he was amused, and he said, 'Do you know anything about ostriches?' 'Ostriches?' I asked. 'Why, they're a large bird on the plains of East Africa. Their feathers are very fashionable.' And he answered, 'Yes, yes, but there's more to the bird than feathers. The male goes around his territory collecting all the hatched young he can find. Never mind who fathered them, he takes them as his own and rears them. Guards them to the death, and few predators want to risk themselves within reach of his beak or his foot.' I was astonished."

"He most certainly brought us up well. We were happy children."

"Yes. And now those lovely boys are gone! I wept at the news, you know. My deepest sympathies, my dear! It can't have been an easy time for you or Mr. Hatton!" Mrs. Passmore paused, a moment of reverie. "I wonder—do you have any photographs—of your family, perhaps? Or of the boys growing up. I should really enjoy seeing how much they had changed!"

"The only family photograph I know of is one of my parents on their wedding day. My grandfather always kept it by his bed—"

Francesca stopped abruptly. She remembered it by the bed during her grandfather's last illness, and it had surely been there the day after he died. But she had wandered into his room last night, lonely and at a loss for company again, and it hadn't been there. Had it?

Mrs. Passmore was saying, "He loved both of them, his sons. Poor Tristan and Edward! It was tragic that they died within such a short time of each other. But he had living reminders, didn't he?" She glanced once more at the photograph in her hand before putting it away. "Children are such treasures. Mr. Passmore and I were never blessed in that way. But I hope in the course of time that you will be. It will carry your thoughts forward, into the future."

Francesca smiled. "I shall have to choose a husband first."

Mrs. Passmore rose, punctually on the quarter hour, as if she had measured the proper time for a morning call. Or concluded her business there.

"Thank you for seeing me, my dear Miss Hatton. I'm quite devastated for you. I know your grandfather's death has been a great hardship, coming as it did on the heels of losing your cousins."

As soon as Mrs. Passmore had stepped into the drive to walk back to the village, Francesca went upstairs to her grandfather's bedroom.

The photograph wasn't there.

She went to find Mrs. Lane.

Every sign of yesterday's funeral feast had vanished. The extra tables, the silver, the china. The last of the serviettes and tablecloths had been laundered, pressed, and folded. The extra food distributed to the poorer families, the house thoroughly aired. Francesca herself had polished the tea service and the silver platters in the early hours of the morning, much to Mrs. Lane's disapproval. She had also weeded the vegetables, anything to keep her hands and mind occupied.

She said now, "Do you know what's become of the photograph of my parents that my grandfather kept on the stand by his bed?"

"I thought you must have taken it," Mrs. Lane answered. "It was there yesterday morning when I went up as usual to do a little dusting, but when I walked into Mr. Hatton's room last evening, to say a private good-bye, like, I didn't see it." She shrugged deprecatingly. "I know he's gone, but old habits die hard. He always liked his room fresh and tidy every morning, the bed turned down every evening. And he was that fond of flowers."

"Yesterday, after the funeral—those people wandering about the house—you don't suppose one of them could have taken it? But that doesn't make sense."

"There was the Scotsman Mr. Stevens saw off the property. Though I wouldn't put it past *him*, that Mr. Leighton." Mrs. Lane said it tartly. "He's up to no good, accusing people of murder and the like!"

"Yes, well, why would Mr. Leighton take a photograph of my parents? It won't help him in the search for his mother!"

"If I was you, I'd walk around the house to see what else may've gone missing!" Mrs. Lane folded the last of the ironed tablecloths and tucked them carefully in the linen closet. The scent of lavender came wafting out as the door closed.

"I was that surprised by Mrs. Passmore," she went on, locking the closet from old habit. "I quite remembered her as taller, and plump into the bargain!"

"Mrs. Passmore?" Francesca asked, dragging her thoughts back to her visitor.

"Of course I was but a girl myself, and look at me now! Wider than I was, by half!" Mrs. Lane chuckled. "Marriage must have agreed with our Miss Weaver!"

Francesca went to her grandfather's room and searched thoroughly through the chests and the closet shelves. But she hadn't been mistaken. The photograph of her parents had disappeared.

Why had Mrs. Passmore mentioned it? And who would have wanted to take it?

The Tallon family lived over the hill, nearer the moors. Their house had been constructed by the same builders who had created Francis Drake's house at Tavistock, although High Knole hadn't had the good fortune to have been a Cistercian monastery to begin with. Early Victorian owners, recognizing that, had added a mock church tower, to disastrous effect. The present owners had removed the tower and put a walled garden in its place, protected from the winds that swept down from Exmoor.

Mrs. Tallon was delighted to see Francesca so soon. A woman of early middle age already comfortably settled as grandmother to a numerous brood, in private she still called Francesca by the family's pet name for her, Cesca.

Hearing it reminded Francesca of her cousins. They had often played with the Tallon children, drawing them into all manner of harebrained schemes.

"I must say, you carried off the funeral well, my dear! Francis would have been quite proud of you. He was always rather foolish over his darling girl, as he called you. But are you managing? You look so tired!"

"I am a little. Mrs. Tallon—at the service there were a number of people I didn't know. I thought perhaps they'd been friends of my grandfather's, but they didn't introduce themselves. I was wondering if I should have known who they were and spoken more warmly to each of them about their connection with my grandfather—"

"I did notice there were outsiders among the guests, yes. Well, it was to be expected, wasn't it? Francis went to London from time to time. I did try to speak to one of them, but he wasn't friendly. Walsham, I think his name was. But that Mr. Leighton was quite nice. He asked if I'd known his mother, but of course I hadn't."

Damn the man!

"One of the women came to call yesterday morning," Francesca continued. "She was a Miss Weaver when she came to River's End to be my nanny. Do you remember her?"

"Miss Weaver? Well, I haven't thought about her in years! Where on earth did she pop up from? She went to New Zealand as I recall, with a family taking up a sheep station there. I remember thinking at the time how odd it was that she should leave so suddenly, but Francis said she was quite happy and eager to go. He refused to stand in her way."

Francesca described the woman who had called herself Mrs. Passmore, then asked, "Does that sound at all like Miss Weaver?"

"No," Mrs. Tallon replied at once. "But, of course, twenty years can change a person out of all recognition. I'm surprised she didn't speak to me. No one else in the Valley seemed to care much for her, you know, an outsider, and I always did my best to make her feel at home here. Well, I did that for Francis's sake, more than hers. Finding good help has always been a problem with only a tiny village to provide any entertainment on days off!"

"Mrs. Lane didn't recognize her, either. Why would someone come here under false pretenses? If it wasn't Miss Weaver— She had a photograph of Harry's mother, holding him as a baby—a christening photograph, I should think. Do you remember my cousins' parents?"

"Well, I most certainly remember your uncle Tristan. He could talk the birds from the trees. A scamp if ever there was one, and always in trouble! I was half in love with your father—he was older, such a dashing young man, Edward. So handsome, like dear Francis. Infatuation is a good thing, you know—it keeps a young girl out of mischief, mooning about over someone who doesn't know she's alive. And I was most definitely infatuated with Edward! I would treasure the silliest things—a leaf he'd toyed with, sitting at the tea table and no doubt bored to tears by the conversation. He found some excuse to go down to the stables and dropped the leaf as he got up from his chair. I rescued it and preserved it in my keepsake book. And another time, I took the spoon from his teacup and pressed my lips to it. George would call me mad, if he knew, and perhaps I was. But at the time it was the most exciting thing!"

Francesca tried to picture placid Mrs. Tallon in transports of delight over a teaspoon. "Did you meet the girl my uncle married?"

"The wedding was in Hampshire, as I remember. They didn't visit Devon that I know of. If you want my opinion, the Valley had grown far too dull for Tristan's tastes. But then Francis did tell me that your aunt Margaret wasn't the best of travelers. The train made her quite ill."

"Yes, I was told she was consumptive."

"Consumptive? Not at all! Wherever did you get such a foolish idea? Apart from a pregnancy every year, it was my understanding that your aunt Margaret enjoyed excellent health." Mrs. Tallon's face changed. "Did Francis never tell you, my dear?" She clicked her tongue. "I can't believe he didn't think—! But I suppose when he sold Tristan's house in Hampshire, he felt he had put the whole tragic business behind him. Out of sight, out of mind. How like a man. Still, you were bound to find out from strangers, sooner or later. Tristan and his wife were killed, you see. Murdered in their beds. I don't think they ever found the madman who did it."

Francesca drove home with her thoughts roiling. Leaving the motorcar in the yard next to the stables, she strode across the lawns to the back garden and sat down on the Murder Stone, heedless of the hem of her gown.

Was this how the stone had got its name?

From her murdered aunt and uncle?

It was a painful possibility—the cousins might have heard the word when they were too young to understand what it meant and simply liked the sound of it. For they couldn't have known the truth. Not one of them had ever told her that their parents had died so horribly. Children seldom kept such secrets for long.

Another mystery from her family's past. A shameful one, at that.

She shivered. Only a few days before she'd said to Richard Leighton, "It's hardly a common thing, is it, to have a murder in the family!"

Simon, the eldest of the five brothers, had been very young when he came to live at River's End, perhaps no more than six. It might have been possible to keep the gruesome truth from him. But at some stage her grandfather would have been obliged to confess what had happened, if only to give all his grandsons a bulwark against learning the story in a crueler fashion. Children could be heartless. They teased and taunted without any thought of the pain it caused.

Or had Francis Hatton been unable to face the truth himself? Years later, he hadn't wanted to accept the deaths of his grandsons.

Died in disgrace... Those were the words Richard Leighton had used. As if he had been told rumors and half-truths, but didn't know much more than that. Just as well. He'd have used her family history for his own ends.

Was this why the boys had been tutored at home until it was time to go up to Oxford? To keep them sheltered from gossip and taunts? She had never considered that there might be a reason behind the family's isolation!

An angry voice startled her. "So this is where you are. Mrs. Lane informed me that you'd gone out."

It was Richard Leighton. Francesca sprang to her feet, away from the Murder Stone. "But I *had* gone out—to call on a neighbor!" Defensive before she could stop herself.

"So you say."

Angry in her turn, she retorted, "What are you doing in my gardens? Were you asked to wait here?"

"No. I was told you weren't at home. I was restless, I walked back up the hill later, and there was no answer to my knock. I came round to the gardens to see if there was anyone in the kitchen. I don't think Mrs. Lane much cares for my visits. I wouldn't put it past the woman to ignore a summons to the door if she'd seen me on the step."

"Did you take that photograph of my parents from my grandfather's bedroom? How dare you walk about my home as if you had a right—"

"I've taken nothing from your house. I want nothing from your house!"

Over the hill, out of sight, someone fired a shot. Leighton's head came up, eyes instantly alert.

"Someone hunting stoats or foxes. The farmers up the Valley don't know any better," Francesca told him. "Anything wild is an enemy."

Leighton went on, as if the interruption had given him time to digest her accusation, "What photograph? What are you talking about? There was the man who had invaded the upper floors—the rector went to find him."

"Yes, I remember. But perhaps you were there as well—"

"Why on earth should I steal a family photograph! It's not your family I want to find!"

"This is getting us nowhere!" Francesca took a deep breath. "I'm sorry I wasn't here earlier. To tell truth, I'd forgotten you would call! But you've found me now. What was it you wanted?"

"I discovered something of interest on Friday. Would you care to see it? I'd like to hear what you make of it."

Reluctantly she let him lead her back to the drive. But he strode on, down the hill toward the bridge. "Where are we going?" she demanded. "I thought you'd brought it with you—"

"I couldn't. You'll see. Behind the churchyard."

Francesca opened her mouth to argue, and then changed her mind. The first precept of battle, Simon, the warrior, had always drummed into his ragtag army's head, was to lull the enemy into thinking *he* was attacking.

It confirmed his defenses and his weaknesses...

CHAPTER 9

"Hatton," Leighton was saying as they walked, "may have been all that you remember of him as a grandfather. That's not my argument. But a child sees what fits into a child's world. Kindness, love, the small gifts for a birthday, the sense of safely belonging. You grew up expecting nothing more, nothing less. Am I right?"

"He was a good surrogate father, and even a good mother to us—we had no one else to care, my cousins and I."

"But there may have been a darker side to him. Is that impossible?"

Francesca said nothing. He was hardly one to speak of dark sides!

Leighton glanced at her, as if certain he'd struck a chord.

But then she asked, "What do you remember of your mother? I didn't know my own; she was dead before I was two years old. You were eight."

He was quick to pick up the thought behind her words. "And she may have had her own dark secrets? A lover somewhere, a tryst that went awry? I can't tell you that she didn't. But if she was prepared to run away with another man, willingly and with no regard for her child, I never saw it in her manner even on that last day. No excitement, no haste, no sudden, unusual burst of affection because she was leaving me behind. She was herself. I've thought this through, searching my memory each night— searching for any small sign we might have overlooked. For one thing, she wasn't *dressed* to go away. She wore a walking gown that I'd seen many times, and took nothing with her except for the small purse she generally carried. Hardly the behavior of a woman rushing out to meet a clandestine lover."

"She may have been more clever than you gave her credit for!"

"All right. Touché. But let me ask you. Have you ever been in love, passionately in love?"

"No," she responded instantly, stung and surprised. "What does that have to say to anything?"

"Have you ever known anyone who was?"

She hesitated, answering slowly, "A friend. She was madly in love with an officer in a Welsh brigade."

They had reached the main road, about to cross the bridge. The river ran sweetly beneath the stones, and their feet echoed on the boards.

"All right, 'madly' is the key," Francesca finally admitted. "But it only proves that Victoria was older and better able to hide her emotions than my friend ever could. And your mother *was* a married woman. She must have learned to conceal her feelings. Not only from you, but to keep your father from finding out."

They went up the hill past the church and to the broken, ancient Celtic cross that had marked the long-ago sailor's tomb.

Leighton gestured toward it, then stood there for a moment staring down at it before squatting to point out something scratched into the lichen-encrusted stone.

Francesca knelt to examine it more closely.

"V-i-c-t-o-r-i-a..." Leighton spelled for her, his finger marking each letter.

"So it is. Half the girls in England were christened Victoria, during the Old Queen's reign. I shouldn't be surprised to find it here or anywhere else. The children use this shaft for games, sometimes, when the church has an outing. From here to that black gravestone just there is where they run bag races or carry an egg in a spoon. Young girls come here to spy the new moon over their left shoulder and see the face of their love. I did it myself at twelve. My cousins teased me unmercifully."

"And did you see him? Your love?"

She laughed in genuine amusement. "Our gatekeeper, Wiggins, came to find me on my grandfather's orders. As children we were never allowed outside the bounds of River's End, you see—not alone. Poor Wiggins must have been sixty, his hands gnarled and his joints stiff, and he was the first man I saw. It cured me of superstitious nonsense." As the laughter faded, she said, "You've been at great pains, if you found this faint scratching."

"Actually, I didn't. The maid at The Spotted Calf told me about it." He gestured toward the inscription. "She said that it had been there since she was a girl. And look—there are other names scratched here. Marianne. Sarah. Laura. A Roman burial for other women?"

Francesca Hatton had been educated with her male cousins. She knew what he was talking about. If one threw a handful of earth on a corpse and repeated Hail and Farewell three times over the body, in the sight of the gods it was now buried and at peace. Only here the names had been scratched in stone, close by the churchyard, as if to give them peace as well, and keep them—wherever they lay buried—from walking in the dark...

"It could be the names of girls who came here to find their lovers," she answered lightly, shaking off her own morbid thoughts. "You'll never know. Nor shall I. Now, if you don't mind—"

He stared at her, not bothering to disguise his frustration

and anger and impotence. "Did you scratch your own name among them?"

"I was twelve. No. I was afraid my grandfather might learn what I'd done," she replied steadily. "Don't you see, that's the whole point? This Valley is close—and closed. We keep to ourselves, we keep our business to ourselves—and yet we know almost at once if a mouse so much as sneezes under the baker's bed! It would have been the height of stupidity for Grandfather to bring an unwilling woman here, much less murder her here or bury her in the churchyard! The servants would whisper among themselves. Sooner or later rumors and gossip would begin to trickle through the village, and the outlying farmers would hear it at The Spotted Calf. They would carry the tidbit home with them, or to market—"

"Are you telling me that Mrs. Lane would gossip about her employer? I don't believe it!"

"Mrs. Lane has a very—puritan view of life. She might not gossip—but she would leave Grandfather's employ at once, if he did something she couldn't approve of. Screaming captives in the attic might well fall into that category."

"You're making fun of me," he said tightly.

Her anger flared. "No, I'm telling you that you can destroy my grandfather's reputation—his memory—with your prying questions and your insistence that he was a monster," she retorted. "He was the most respected man in this Valley. What if, after all, you've been chasing a shadow? What if, one day, the police charge another man with this alleged crime? The harm will have been done here. How will you undo it? Will you write nice letters to the people of Hurley, explaining that you'd been wrong from the start? That it was all some terrible mistake?"

"It will never come to that—Alasdair MacPherson is a fair man! Do you think he would have told me who murdered my mother, if he wasn't absolutely convinced he was right?"

Absolute conviction was one thing—absolute proof might be another, she thought. MacPherson had lost a beloved daughter—his only child. He would want to see blame squarely placed—he would want to put his hands around the throat of the man who had destroyed Victoria and slowly choke the life from him. She might have been Thomas Leighton's wife, but it was Alasdair MacPherson who was avid for revenge, who hadn't forgotten—who drove the instrument of his hate until he'd distorted the vision of his grandson.

But then, a little voice reminded her, *might it be your own vision that's distorted? Where in God's name does the real truth lie?*

On the heels of that caveat, as if he'd read her mind, Leighton inquired, "Were you ever curious about your own mother?"

"I asked for her when I first came here—my grandfather would show me her picture and tell me how hap—" She stopped, and then said, "As I grew accustomed to this life—to my newfound cousins—the old one faded away." But she and her cousins had been much younger than Richard Leighton when his mother vanished. "At any rate, Grandfather never encouraged us to dwell on the past. I suppose he believed it was for the best."

Because of a murder—his own son's murder?

"My father drank for five years, before he pulled himself together and found another woman to love. She was good, very plain, the antithesis of my mother. I came to value her, if not to love her. As he must have done. There's one other stop, if you'll spare me the time. I'd like to visit Miss Trotter's cottage with you."

"What, again? You don't give up easily, do you?"

"If you recall, she'd told me about the drowned serving girl. But she wasn't quite as forthcoming about your grandfather. Perhaps if you're there, proving that I'm not doing this behind your back, she'll tell us both what we want to know."

"It's you who wants to know! But all right, this one last thing. After that, you'll leave the Valley and leave me in peace."

"It's not a bargain I'll make," he replied grimly.

They walked on up the road to the tiny cottage that Miss Trotter occupied. It was old but well tended, and the walled garden in front was fragrant with herbs and flowers. Chamomile and tansy, horehound for sore throats, foxglove for the heart, and strawflowers that the village girls bought and tied with ribbons to decorate their summer hats.

Miss Trotter appeared happy enough to find two unexpected guests at her door. She shooed the sleeping cat off the chair by the hearth and dusted it with a rag before offering it shyly to Francesca.

Leighton leaned against the stone mantel shelf, tall and out of place in this diminutive room.

"I was just finishing the bottling of my horehound cough syrup," Miss Trotter told them, explaining the aromatic steam coming from a pot on the hob. "It's already in demand, what with this uncertain weather."

"Mr. Leighton has come to speak to you, Miss Trotter," Francesca began.

"Yes, about his mother. He's been here before, and Mrs. Horner at the Rectory told me about him, too." The vague blue eyes, like a china doll's, moved from Francesca to Leighton. "Mrs. Leighton wasn't the drowned girl, I did tell him that. But he thinks perhaps I'd been wrong about it."

Leighton stirred uncomfortably. "You couldn't remember her name. And bodies which have been in the water aren't always readily identified."

"Why should I remember the poor girl's name?" Miss Trotter answered soothingly. "I didn't know her. But someone did. That's all that matters."

"Why did Francis Hatton pay for her burial? Was it guilt?" he pressed.

"It was a kindness. It was the sort of man he was," she replied, turning to set the filled bottles on a shelf. "Your grandfather now, what manner of man is *he*? Would he have left the poor soul to Potter's Field?"

"My grandfather?" he repeated, surprised. "Alasdair

MacPherson is a good man. He loved his daughter very much."

"And spoiled her into the bargain, I daresay. Fathers do, you know! Did she marry the man she wanted, or did Mr. MacPherson choose a husband for her?"

Leighton didn't know how to answer her. "I—don't think it ever occurred to me to ask. I— My father was some years her senior. But it didn't seem to matter to either of them."

"Perhaps she preferred older men. Or thought she did. Spoiled girls sometimes will." Miss Trotter's voice offered no judgment, only speculation.

But her questions had annoyed Richard Leighton. "It's Francis Hatton I've come to talk about."

"I thought we *were* talking about him." She smiled, distracted by the arrangement of the bottles. "It might help to look at a photograph of your mother, if you have one. I see things in faces."

He toyed with his watch chain as if reluctant to answer her. "I—didn't bring it with me—it's in my bags at the inn."

"Yes, it would be." She appeared not to be disappointed. "You loved her memory dearly, I can see that." It was an odd choice of words, and Francesca looked up from stroking the cat on the windowsill as Miss Trotter went on. "And what you're asking me is whether or not she loved you as much. I wish I could answer you. It's a heavy burden for a child to carry alone, you know. I can understand why she haunts you still. It's there in the darkness you live in."

His very silence revealed the old woman had struck home. And he didn't answer her directly. Instead he said, "There isn't much time left. My grandfather isn't a well man. He deserves the comfort of knowing. Was Hatton my mother's murderer? And what did he do with the body? Your own mother worked for the family during that time. Surely there's something you can tell me that will point me to the truth!"

"I doubt he did her any harm, sir. It wasn't Francis Hatton's way. He'd lost someone *he* loved, you see. He knew the grief of that."

"Did you know my grandmother?" Francesca asked, surprised and curious. "Can you tell me anything about her?"

"Your grandmother?" Miss Trotter asked, turning. It was as if Francesca had changed the subject. "She wasn't from the Valley, of course. A Somerset family, I always was told. But her people had lived here more years ago than anyone can remember. And it may be true, for all I know."

"But what sort of person was she?" Francesca persisted.

"Quite a pretty little thing, more than a little vain. It was an arranged marriage. Her sons took after her, which was a heartbreak for Mr. Hatton. Handsome, headstrong. Vain. Easily led."

"Why do you say it was a heartbreak?"

"Did Mr. Francis never tell you? Your father now, Mr. Edward, he took a fancy to card games and was ruined. Your grandfather sent him off to Canada, for his own good. How was anyone to guess it would be the death of him? But Mr. Hatton blamed himself all the same. It was a terrible grief to carry. And Mr. Tristan, he was one for the drink and soon fell into bad company. His wife was leaving him..."

In disgrace...

Francesca hastily moved on, aware that Leighton was listening to every word. "And Mrs. Leighton—Victoria Leighton. What do you think became of her? Have you ever heard whispers that could point Mr. Leighton toward an answer?"

"I know most things. But not that." She bent to sniff another pot that was steaming gently. "I've wondered, from time to time, if Mr. Hatton was a scapegoat."

Francesca, pleased, glanced across at Leighton. "I don't suppose you've ever stopped to consider that."

Miss Trotter hadn't finished. "Still, if I stood in your shoes, sir, I'd look away from the Valley. This is where Mr. Hatton's family lived. He'd not be likely to keep his secrets here, would he? Gloucestershire, now—"

"Gloucestershire?" Leighton asked quickly.

"Happens it's the first county popped into my head. But

you might take your pick of any and have better luck than here."

Francesca stood to leave, satisfied to let Miss Trotter have the last word.

Leighton followed her to the threshold, bending his head under the low sweep of the thatched roof. It was as if he couldn't let it go—but was reluctant to challenge the old woman directly. Finally he said, "My grandfather was always sure the answer lay here. Which of you ought I to believe?"

"I'd have been told, sir, if I was wrong." Miss Trotter spoke the simple words as if she had ears in the village—or familiars—or a sixth sense about life. The cat stretched, yawned, and watched them malevolently as Leighton thanked her and turned to go.

Miss Trotter turned to the shelves and brought down a small glass flask. "Here's more of my dandelion wine, Miss Francesca. You might have need of it again."

Francesca stared at her, stunned.

Miss Trotter closed the younger woman's fingers around the bottle and smiled with kindness. "I know my own wine when I smell it," she said softly. "He didn't mind. It brought back pleasant memories and a better end. A little was on Miss Honneycutt's breath, too. The nurse. It was a kindness to both." And in a softer voice still, certain not to carry as far as Leighton's ears, she said, "If I stood in your shoes, I'd be mindful of what young Master Simon was always saying, that in any battle knowledge is strength."

It was an uncanny echo of what she'd told herself less than an hour before.

"And I'd be likely to stay on Mr. Leighton's good side until I discovered what it was he really wanted." Miss Trotter glanced over Francesca's shoulder toward the man waiting on the path. "He won't make old bones, that one. Mark my words." Then she added, "Better for whatever it is he fears to die with him."

Badly shaken, Francesca turned away and walked through the garden to the path.

Leighton greeted her impatiently. "What is it? What did she tell you? What did she give you?"

Francesca looked down at the flask in her hands. "It's dandelion wine. My grandfather was quite fond of it—"

And to her absolute astonishment, tears began to roll down her pale cheeks. Fumbling for his handkerchief, Leighton looked away.

She was glad that her downcast lashes concealed the agony of guilt.

CHAPTER 10

They walked together back in the direction of River's End, Leighton silent to give her time to recover, and Francesca struggling to overcome a despair that seemed to blot out every other emotion. And then she became aware of the man at her side, took a breath to steady herself, and tried to bring her mind to bear on the present.

"I'm sorry Miss Trotter wasn't more helpful. But I did warn you."

"She knows more than she's willing to say."

"Does she? Or is it that you don't have an open mind, willing to hear what she *is* saying?" Before he could retort with his customary swift anger, she went on, "If it were my family, I'd listen to *every* side of the argument rather than try to force what I do hear into a preconceived notion."

"Aren't you doing the same, in an effort to defend your grandfather?"

"All right, then. A bargain. We'll work together, shall we? I to clear my grandfather's name, and you to find your mother's fate." She waited for a space, remembering that in chess, nothing was rushed.

She had been taught the game well. On rainy afternoons there had been fierce competitions among the cousins, Robin challenging Peter, Simon attacking Freddy. She and Harry, the youngest, had wrestled with their chessmen until one or the other brother was victorious and came to their aid. Her greatest triumph was at the age of fourteen when she conquered her grandfather. Simon had stood silently behind her chair, watching every move, and howled like a banshee when she called out a shy "Checkmate!" Harry had turned a somersault, and Peter brought out an empty bottle of champagne and saluted her. Freddy and Robin, scrutinizing the board, congratulated themselves on being excellent teachers. And her grandfather, grinning, had replaced the empty bottle with an unopened one, as her reward. The champagne had made her dizzy.

"There's always the possibility that your mother is still alive," she told Leighton quietly. "You don't want to believe that, of course, but for a moment, just one *moment*, ask yourself where your mother might have gone if she had had a very strong reason to leave you and your father."

"I confess, I did consider that. When I was fourteen and grown up enough to understand that most marriages have their secrets. Still, I couldn't imagine that she could choose someone as old as your grandfather to take up with." He paused, then added with some restraint, "It was impossible to picture her in bed with a man of that age. Now I know better, that he was as physically capable as a younger man of satisfying a woman's needs. Or taking her against her will." He ran a hand over his gaunt face. "I assure you, there was nothing loverlike in her departure! And if it wasn't kidnap and murder, if it wasn't a passion for another man, what reason *can* there be for going away without a word?" There was anguish in his voice, and long years of wishing. And of hating.

Francesca stopped on the drive, her eyes on the trees that

shaded it. "I don't know. But my grandfather might have known—and felt he couldn't betray her."

"Yes, there's that." His agreement was grudging. "But what would make him side against my father, who believed himself to be a friend? That hurt more than you realize. My grandfather was half mad with grief—and I couldn't imagine what was happening to me or to her. Why leave all three of us in an agony of uncertainty? It makes no sense! It's little short of cruel!"

A sharp report echoed again through the sunlit trees. Leighton swore, then said, "I've come to hate guns. I've seen what they can do to flesh. I wouldn't put an animal through that terror."

Francesca walked on. "Was it bad?"

"The Front? I can't describe it. And you wouldn't believe me if I tried."

"No, perhaps not. But I've seen the wounded, coming through London. What struck me most was their courage, their acceptance. They were so very brave. I know I'd hate the people who destroyed my lungs or took away my eyes and left me helpless!"

"You don't hate the enemy, Miss Hatton. You just accept the need to kill as many of him as possible, before he can kill you, so that everyone can go home. Bravery has nothing to do with it. Bravery is just not making an ass of yourself in front of men who are depending on you to get them through alive. If the whistle blows, you go over the top in a hail of fire, and take what comes."

"That's an odd way of putting it!"

"No, it isn't. No man wants to let his comrades down. It's the worst sin, far worse than dying. Anything but that."

It was the first time the two of them had spoken together in normal conversation, rather than meeting each other as adversaries. Francesca said, "That isn't how my cousins saw war. When they were boys, playing in the back garden."

"Boys have never been to war. It's easy to believe that it's all a game. That the dead will get up off the grass in time for tea."

They had reached the circle in front of River's End. On impulse, Francesca said, "I have no idea what Mrs. Lane has left for my luncheon, but there's generally enough for two—"

"Thank you, but no."

The abrupt refusal, with neither grace nor explanation, brought the warm blood to Francesca's cheeks. She'd been out of line, and he had been forced to remind her of her manners. So much for any expectation of working together! She wasn't certain it was what she'd wanted, anyway.

She said, "I hope you can find the answers you're searching for. I must tell you that I agree with Miss Trotter. I don't think they lie here, in the Valley. You are wasting your time—wasting precious time."

She stepped into the hall and closed the door behind her without looking back.

But she carried with her the anguish she'd heard in Leighton's voice only a few minutes before. That made it all the harder to believe that her grandfather could have had anything to do with Victoria Leighton. He had never been a heartless man—

Yet the rector had said only recently that sometimes her grandfather could be cruel....

The next morning she paced the house in a restless mood. If there was only someone she could confide in—trust with her questions! With her doubts and fears. But where to put that trust?

That was the price of being the last of the Hattons. She could rely only on her own instincts, her own wisdom. Her own courage.

She summoned Bill to drive her into Exeter to call on Branscombe.

The solicitor rose from his desk as she was admitted by his clerk, and said, with some surprise, "Miss Hatton—? Did we have an appointment set for today?"

Francesca took the uncomfortable chair across from him

and replied, "There are several—matters—I wish to arrange. The first is a set of memorial plaques for my cousins, to be placed in St. Mary Magdalene's nave. White marble, I think, with an inscription. A simple one—dates—their names—their ranks and regiments, and where they died."

"Your grandfather was quite certain he did not wish to commemorate his grandsons' deaths—"

"It would have meant accepting that they were lost forever, and he couldn't bear that. Sadly, I've been forced to face up to the truth, and I shall feel better when there's a memorial to each of them," she said firmly, "set up where it can be seen by all who loved them."

Branscombe was too well-bred to frown. "Then it shall be as you wish—of course."

Francesca thought: *You'd much rather ignore me, and deal with my grandfather. But it's too late for that.* Aloud she said, "And there's another matter. A young woman, some years younger than I am, came to the service for my grandfather. A Miss Andrews." It had taken her most of the drive to Exeter to recall the name of the woman she'd encountered during the reception after the funeral. The one in black veils. "She seemed to expect a legacy of some sort in my grandfather's will—"

"On that point I can relieve you of any concern. Miss Andrews came to me, as you had rightly suggested, and I informed her roundly that Mr. Hatton had not seen fit to include her in his will. And that was the end of it."

"Did you know the name? Were you familiar with her story?"

"Not at all. But a small act of kindness is not something a man of your grandfather's stature would have spoken of to me. *If* her story is true, of course!"

"I'd like to settle five hundred pounds on her," Francesca said, surprising herself.

"My dear Miss Hatton—are you aware that this woman may make a practice of turning up at funerals and pathetically making a claim on the deceased? It's sometimes done, sad to say."

"I don't believe she was lying. And I've more money than I know what to do with. A few hundred pounds will make no difference to my life, and it might to hers. Do you have her direction?"

"I made a point of asking for it, in the event she was not what she appeared to be." Branscombe stirred the papers on his desk in a halfhearted effort to locate it.

"Then you will see to this for me, if you please."

"I shall make a note of it—"

"No. A note serves no purpose. I want it done this day."

"Miss Hatton—"

"And there's another matter. The estate in Essex. Do you know how it came into my grandfather's possession?"

"I'm afraid I didn't handle that transaction. He brought me the deeds after the fact and asked me to hold them for him."

"I was informed by a Mr. Walsham that the estate was in settlement of a gambling debt."

"As to that—"

"Could it be true?"

Branscombe paused. "After the funeral, Mr. Walsham asked if he might call on me later. We set an appointment, which he failed to keep. As to what he wished to see me about, he refused to say, calling it a very private matter."

Which meant that Walsham could have lied to both of them...

"Do you know why someone hated my grandfather enough to send him a threatening message—one that my grandfather kept?"

"I know nothing about threatening messages!"

She gestured to a box sitting on his desk. "You held it for him in one of those—in my grandfather's box."

"If it's there, your grandfather placed it in my keeping. I have not read it!" he replied angrily.

Francesca nodded; she believed him. "Could you give an

approximate date on which you received this letter for safe-keeping?"

"That I can do. We keep a log of all transactions." He sent for the ledger, and while they were waiting, Francesca asked, "I don't suppose you can tell me anything about the Somerset property."

"Indeed I can. It's a house called The Swans, in Falworthy, one that had once belonged to your late grandmother's family. Centuries ago, as I understand it. It came up for sale—much diminished now, you understand!—some thirty years ago. What had once been a very fine house in its day was quite small by modern standards, and needed a considerable amount of work. Much of the land had been sold off. But what remained was fair enough, and Mr. Hatton felt it suited his purpose. He ordered our firm to purchase it for him, in confidence."

"What *was* his purpose?"

"He didn't confide in us. But the house was restored and enlarged. There are accounts paid attesting to the work. I have no recollection of a tenant. No rents are collected by our firm. Which is foolishness—a house ought not stand unoccupied, and so I have told Mr. Hatton. But he was well satisfied with matters as they stood. Both in Somerset and in Essex."

"There are a number of charities listed in the will, charities that my grandfather had supported. Could you give me their names again?"

Mr. Branscombe summoned his clerk to fetch the Hatton box, and delved into the contents for the will. He began to read, peering at each line as if he didn't recognize it.

"There's the sum for St. Mary Magdalene's Church, of course. We'd spoken of that at the reading. There's a sum set aside for a monument to the missing of the Somme Offensive. Such a memorial has been suggested in a number of quarters and was dear to Mr. Hatton's heart."

Harry had died on the Somme. He had been missing for a week before they had found his body.

"A bequest to his club in London," Branscombe went on,

running his finger down the sheet of heavy paper. "Quite a large sum—an endowment to be precise—to the Little Wanderers Foundation—"

"What on earth is that?"

"It's to do with children, I believe. There's a bequest to Moresley, where he was at school, and one to St. Mary's Church here in Exeter. Another to the Seamen's Benevolent Society for widows and children of men lost at sea." He set aside the document and sighed. "Nothing of great import, but showing a proper concern for the needs of others. He was always a generous man."

Francesca found herself remembering the unpaid smith, who had looked at the shoe of a horse drawing a carriage similar to her grandfather's.

"Where is this Little Wanderers Foundation located?"

"It's an address in Somerset. Falworthy, in fact."

Another connection with Somerset... *Why was Francis Hatton drawn there? Guilt? Retribution? Or a secret life...*

The clerk had returned with the ledger, opened at the appropriate page.

Mr. Branscombe scanned the entry. "Here we are. 'Letter, Francis Hatton, to be placed with his papers. No action.' And the date—"

It was the year Victoria Leighton had been married. She remembered the date from the marriage lines that Richard Leighton had shown her.

She thanked Mr. Branscombe and took her leave.

But on the journey back to River's End, Francesca asked Bill if he had ever heard her grandfather speak of a Little Wanderers Foundation.

Something flickered in his eyes as he looked back at her in the small mirror. "Did Mr. Hatton never mention it to you, Miss Francesca?"

"No. Never."

"That's odd! But then it was like him not to want praise for his good deeds. He was always such a one!" There was warmth in the old man's voice, as if serving Mr. Hatton had been a matter of great pride.

"What *is* the Little Wanderers Foundation?"

"It supported orphans, Miss. Not any orphans, mind you, but those Mr. Hatton felt deserved a better chance in life. Many's the time I've driven him to look at a child. A good few have gone on to do well—to my knowledge one is a captain in the Navy, another a barrister. Mr. Hatton gave them respectability, you see, as well as education, and that stood them in good stead when they went out into the world."

"Where did he find these children?" Francesca asked, fascinated. Had Miss Andrews been one of them?

"They'd be brought to his attention, in one fashion or another. I never quite understood that part of it. Nor was it my place to ask. But I've glimpsed one or two of the little ones, and they'd break your heart, to see them so happy and well kept."

"I wonder why he never took me with him."

"I couldn't say, Miss."

They were well into the Valley now, the trees flitting across the sun like pickets in a fence. She asked:

"Does Mrs. Lane know about this?"

"I never spoke of Mr. Hatton's business, Miss. If he wished the rest of the staff to know where he'd been or what he'd done, it was his place to tell them."

"Yes, quite right," she answered, absently. It appeared that her grandfather hadn't been a complete ogre after all, with dark secrets shadowing his life. Perhaps Mr. Branscombe had been right, that vultures came to funerals to fight over whatever scraps they might find. And how vulnerable she must have seemed! A young woman all alone and likely to be susceptible to their schemes.

A comforting thought to cling to . . . but it still didn't explain away Victoria Leighton.

They drove in silence for miles, Bill concentrating on the heavily rutted road and Francesca enjoying the beauty of the Valley, as she always had.

And then Bill said, "This Mr. Leighton, Miss. The gentleman who has been coming to the house. Is he a relation of your family's?"

"Mr. Leighton? Not at all! I'd never heard of him until he came to call the day the will was read."

"I see, Miss. Begging your pardon."

But she asked, "Why should you think he's related to the Hattons?"

"I was enjoying a pint at The Spotted Calf the other night, and he came in to sit down for a bit. I could see him quite clear. It'ud been nagging at me, why he looked so familiar. And then it came to me. I've seen that dark, brooding shadow on your grandfather's face, time and again when there was something on his mind. Something troublesome that he couldn't see an end to. And on Mr. Harry's face, for that matter, when he was by himself and thought no one was watching. Deep thinkers, both of them. It set me to wondering..."

He glanced back at her in the tiny mirror by his head. "You're the same, Miss Francesca, if you don't mind me saying so. You take trouble to heart yourself and don't let it out. Two peas in a pod, you and that Mr. Leighton..."

THE COUSINS

Peter . . . the engineer

I was born to build things. Or on occasion to take them apart to see how they worked. It was in my nature—and got me into trouble now and then, when what I took apart was beyond putting back together again.

Grandfather would say that no one in his family before me had ever yearned to build. But he was laughing when he told me that, and I was pleased.

I'd had an insatiable curiosity about the Murder Stone ever since I could remember. It was unusual, that stone, unlike any other I'd seen in the Valley. White and curved, almost human in the way it nestled in the grass, cradled by the earth. Our tutor told us it was immensely old. Older than Rome, certainly, and nearly as old as the pyramids. To my eyes it didn't appear to be native stone, but the logistics of dragging it here and setting it in place must have been incredibly difficult. I was fascinated.

A year later I decided to look at the position of the stars from the stone. I could see Orion swinging overhead, and other constellations I recognized. But what pleased our tutor was my discovery that at the solstice, from the end of the stone nearest the house, the winter sun rose to strike its cold pale surface with a golden light and travel its length until the whole glowed for a brief and glorious moment.

All my wild brothers could think about was Druids—Simon raided the linen closet and we'd dance through the garden, chanting, in the light of the moon.

But I found myself—not usually given to flights of fancy—wondering if sacrifices were ever made there on the stone, to summon the sun north again. To bring back its warmth for the planting season. The Celts, we had been taught, did such things.

Another day I took my notebook out there and made my measurements. I used a trowel from the toolshed to scratch around the edges, to see how deep the stone went down into the earth. There was no budging it. I didn't like digging around it, to be honest. It was like trespassing in some private place. Every time the steel of the trowel touched the stone, I could feel the jolt in my arm. As if I were meddling with things best left alone.

Idle superstition, of course. Simon's fault for all the bloody war games we had played here.

But nor could I chip a bit off the edge to put on the shelf in my room....

Still—as I was excavating the rim of the stone, I saw a fleck of gold shining in the sunlight.

I fished it out, stared at it, and could make no sense of it. A tiny triangle with one raw edge, as if it'd broken off something else. No markings, nothing to tell me anything.

I held it in the palm of my hand and the cool feel of the gold gleaming in the sun was exciting at first. And then strange. As if I'd disturbed something I shouldn't have.

I marked the place of that bit of gold on the chart I was making, and then thrust it back deep into the warm earth again. Out of sight...

I never told anyone about what I'd found.

I often wondered if I'd done the wrong thing... or the right thing.

Wiggins, who lived in the gatehouse, told me that a long time ago, the stone had been called the Witch's Stone. He couldn't say why, just that before River's End had been built on the hill, people had avoided the place, as if it were cursed. No one had wanted to farm just there. Hallowed or haunted, it didn't matter, Wiggins insisted, they stayed away.

Mr. Gregory laughed when I repeated the story, but unlike our tutor, Grandfather listened to me with sober interest. "Stones aren't evil. It's what people do with them that's evil. Build a garden wall—or a catapult for war. You can destroy anything by your actions, even love."

I couldn't think, at thirteen, what love had to do with the Murder Stone.

The image of ruthless sacrifice on a cold, bare winter's morning was far more in line with a boy's bloody imagination.

I often thought about the Murder Stone when I was doing sappers' work in France. Somehow it had become a talisman of boyhood and happiness, far safer for a soldier to remember in the intervals of battle than the people one misses so desperately. I didn't like tunneling underground, in the darkness and wet. It's an engineer's task, and I did it well, but that had nothing to do with liking it.

But I swore that if I survived this war, I would come back to River's End and watch the winter sun touch the Murder Stone one more time. To mark a new beginning.

CHAPTER 11

Deep in the night, Francesca woke with a start. She had been dreaming, and somehow the sound of the dog Tyler scratching at the door of her room had been masked by the dream. But now the noise was persistent, anxious. With a sigh she threw back the bedclothes and felt on the floor for her slippers, pulling them on.

"Yes, I'm coming—" she murmured, flinging a shawl around her shoulders and running her fingers through her unbound hair.

But when the bedroom door was opened, the dog didn't turn straight for the stairs to be let out. Instead he stood in the passage staring toward the room at the end where her grandfather had slept.

"He isn't there," she said softly, stroking his smooth head. "He'll never be there again."

The dog's ears twitched, as if he understood; and after a moment he moved toward the stairs, nose to the polished floorboards. Francesca followed.

The case clock in the hall struck three, and as she counted the strokes, she heard the dog growl, low in his throat.

"What is it?" she asked quietly. "What's wrong, Tyler?"

He growled again, and looked up at her. The hair on the back of her neck seemed to stand on end as the dog's had done. She could feel the animal's stiff fur under her fingers as she gripped his collar. Foolishness, she scolded herself. He was old, confused. But in the dim light from the night candle at the top of the steps, he didn't look confused. Whatever had disturbed him was below—prowling.

Somewhere in the house a board creaked, as if someone had stepped on it.

Francesca felt exposed, alone and with nothing but the dog to stand between her and whatever it was that had awakened him.

Tomorrow night, she promised herself, I shall take Simon's pistol to bed with me! *I swear I will*—

But bullets won't stop ghosts. . . .

Tyler began to move down the steps, his arthritic legs stiff. Francesca followed him. It was better than standing alone in the darkness at the head of the stairs like a cornered animal.

The dog had been taught not to bark. But the growl was steady and ominous, and she could see that he was hunting whatever it was that had caught his ears.

He paused at the landing, head swinging toward the back of the house. Then he went down the remaining steps intently, his paws padding silently, his tail rigidly straight.

Francesca, one hand in his collar, matched him stride for stride, her heart beating heavily now and her breath coming shorter. What would she—they—do, if there *was* someone beyond the door at the back of the stairs? Or standing silently in a dark room, unseen until she had turned her back—

She shivered at the thought. One of the vultures come back to search—for what?

When Tyler scratched at the paneling, she reached out for the knob of the door to the kitchen passage, and they both went through, into the pitch black void beyond.

Relying on the dog's senses and not her own, Francesca let him lead her through the darkness, toward the servants' hall, the pantry, the kitchen. All the doors to either side of her were shut. Ahead lay the last but one, closing off the small stone-flagged space where gardeners and grooms could leave their muddy boots and hang their heavy coats on pegs before meals. Even as she reached for the knob, a draft swept under the frame and across her feet—and then was cut off.

Someone had silently opened and closed the outer door just beyond, the one that led into the kitchen garden. Francesca hurried after the intruder.

The square panes of glass showed moonglow over the vegetables and the cutting garden, touching the tops of trees in the lawns, crowning them with pale, cool light.

Nothing moved out there, no one lurked in the shadows that she could see. All the same she opened the unlatched door and let the dog out into the garden. He disappeared for a time, down the path that led to the stables and the drive.

And then he came back again, tongue lolling, apparently satisfied that he'd seen the villain off.

"It was your imagination all along," she reproved him half-heartedly. And heard the nervous edge to her voice.

She considered waking Bill and asking him to search the grounds, then changed her mind. What could he do, an elderly man alone out in the darkness? An army could be concealed among the trees or hidden in the deep shadows of the shrubbery. And a faint wind rustled the grass like a thousand tiny feet racing across it.

Who had been walking in the night? Ghost or human?

Yet the draft across her feet had been real . . .

And in the house where she had lived so comfortably for most of her life, she now felt afraid.

It was the fault of those vultures at the funeral, she told herself. They'd brought their discontents and hungers and accusations into River's End. They'd stirred up doubt and uncertainty, like old dust.

Walking with Tyler back to the stairs, she said accusingly to the ghosts of her cousins lingering there, "And not much help you are, either!"

Her voice echoed through the house.

There was a torch that had belonged to Robin in his room, and Francesca went directly there to fetch it. With its beam to guide her, she quickly searched the house.

Her grandfather's study was her last stop. The scent of Francis Hatton's pipe tobacco lingered, reminding her too strongly of him. Breathing it in was like bringing him back again. . . .

Here, too, there was nothing out of place, nothing missing as far as she could tell. The beam of the torch swept around again—and this time picked out something on the carpet. It was the pot of autumn crocuses that her housekeeper had brought up that very morning—yesterday morning, it was now. It had fallen from its stand and lay upside down on the floor, damp earth scattered around it.

Francesca searched the bits of soil carefully for footprints, and found none.

Ghosts left no prints—

But the dog sniffed suspiciously at the earth, then moved on to a cabinet of curios that her grandfather had built into the wall beside the hearth.

The glass door was ajar, but whether Mrs. Lane had left it so after cleaning or someone had opened it tonight Francesca couldn't say. The contents appeared to have been untouched: souvenirs of Hatton family warriors over the generations, from a sword used in the Scottish uprisings to the pathetic trophies her cousins had sent home to their grandfather during the brief months they had served in France. Simon had promised, going off to war, that he'd fill the cabinet shelves with glory, but there had been no time . . . no time.

Remembering the missing box that the gruff man at the funeral had been searching for, she made certain that there wasn't an empty square on one of the shelves—she wouldn't put it past him to come again to search.

But all was as it ought to be.

With a sigh she closed the door, only to see it open again a little as if the latch was not as strong as it usually was. Shining the torch on the workings of the bolt, she thought she could detect fine lines, scratch marks, as if someone had used a penknife on it. One of her cousins? In the days when the doors were locked and they were forbidden to play with the cabinet's contents? Drawn to the surveyor's tools, Peter had begged often enough to be allowed to use them....

She left the spilled pot for Mrs. Lane to clear away. As she mounted the stairs, the clock struck four. Francesca paused to count the strokes. Freddy had adored the Westminster chimes, and at the age of three had been discovered in the middle of the night sitting just where she was standing now, absorbed in the clear musical tones. He had, Mr. Gregory confided to their grandfather, perfect pitch. A rare gift ...

The dog, beside her, wagged his tail as if encouraging her to return to bed.

Still ill at ease, she threw the torch's bright beam up the staircase and followed it with Tyler at her heels.

In another part of the house, the roof creaked, and she almost leapt out of her skin. But that was a common enough sound. It was her nerves that were betraying her now.

For the first time since her grandfather's illness, Francesca locked her bedroom door for what was left of the night. And was glad of the dog's snoring presence by her bed.

She dreamed of London and the choking smoke of the engines roiling through the cold station. A train had come in, and she was moving through a carriage, the walking wounded packed together in the compartments, the stretcher cases lying along the corridor wall. They were from the Somme, someone told her, and were very bad. Blood soaked bandages and faces were drained of color, pinched with pain.

There was nothing she could do for them—the pots of tea were empty, the trays of biscuits gone. But she found a flask of dandelion wine in her pocket and began to hold it to the lips of first one man and then another, moving resolutely through the carriage. Behind her someone said, "She's killing them!" She didn't care, she could see that the wine was comforting the wounded. Their eyes were grateful. The flask was empty when she reached the last man in the carriage; there was nothing left for him. Someone said, "He won't make old bones. It's a pity." She lifted the man's head into her lap, watching him trying desperately to drain the last drops from the flask into his mouth. Nothing came.

And she looked down at him, wanting to tell him how sorry she was. How—

The gray face of Richard Leighton stared up at her, accusing and bitter.

Francesca cried out, waking herself and startling Tyler into a drowsy yelp.

Mrs. Lane was dismayed to find her precious bulbs scattered on the study carpet.

"He did like autumn crocuses," she said, carefully lifting the root systems to set them neatly back in the pot. "But that stand has always been unpredictable. I should have remembered..."

Francesca said nothing about what had happened in the night. Watching Mrs. Lane, she said, "Has it? What a shame! Mrs. Lane—I've been thinking. It really isn't wise of me to stay alone in a house that isn't locked. Even with Tyler for company. I've dug out the keys. I doubt if you'd want to carry *that* around with you," she added, holding out the heavy brass key to the front door. "I shall leave it on a hook behind the frame where no one will see it. But this key fits your pocket, as well as the door by the kitchen."

The housekeeper raised worried eyes. "I've said from the start, Miss Francesca, that you oughtn't stay here on your own! But the alternative, to close up the house, would be such a shame. And Mr. Lane needs me to do his breakfast for him, or I'd sleep in myself—"

"No, no, there's no need. But it quite startled me when Tyler woke up so suddenly in the night. Poor old thing, he must have heard the stand overturning, crashing to the carpet, and thought Grandfather had come back. And as I lay there, it struck me as rather silly to latch all the windows each night—and leave the doors unlocked! Wouldn't Robin have had something to say to that!"

"Yes, he was ever the practical one!" Mrs. Lane sighed. "It was a bad night, all round! You won't have heard, but Tommy Higby, who lets out the cows for old Mrs. Stoner, was nearly killed this morning, close to dawn! There he was, minding his own business, you know, talking to the cows the way he does, and there was something brushed past his shoulder, and one of the cows fell dead, shot in the head! And Mrs. Handly's daughter, she had twins, one born yesterday at five minutes to midnight, and the other born ten minutes after midnight. I've never heard of twins born a day apart."

She finished brushing up the earth from the floor and got heavily to her feet. "How will I ever remember a key, Miss Francesca?" she asked as her mistress set the plain iron key into the palm of her hand. "Like as not, I'll walk out of a morning and forget to bring it! Perhaps if you advertise for a companion—"

"I don't want a companion," Francesca told her firmly. "I'll be right as rain. And you need only to tie a knot in your shawl, and it will remind you until you've become used to the idea of locking the door."

Still doubtful, the housekeeper went about her duties. Francesca stood there in the study, looking up at the books that ran round the room, their spines stiff and colorful behind the glass of the doors. How often had she watched from a cushion by the fire as her grandfather sat by the hearth reading—

"Ghosts don't knock over flowers in a pot, do they, Grandfather?" she murmured. "Tell me they can't!"

When Francesca went down to the village in search of the rector, she found everyone she met eager to tell her about the close call that Tommy Higby had had, and how the cow had fallen dead at his feet without so much as a sigh.

William Stevens was on his hands and knees, crawling behind the dark green drapes that hung behind his desk. He looked up, grinned with embarrassment, and with some difficulty rose to his feet, his hand on the back of his chair for balance.

"Sorry! I've lost the last good nib for my pen! Wretched thing popped out and vanished like a wicked soul!"

"You should use a fountain pen," she told him, smiling in return.

"Good heavens, no! They leak. It's good to see you. What brings you into the village at this early hour?"

"For one thing, news of Tommy Higby and his cow."

"It will pass into folklore, mind my words. The Spotted Calf, in another generation, will become Tommy Higby's Cow."

"Now there's a dreadful thought. I'd heard firing, you know. This last week. I thought it was a farmer after stoats."

"And probably was this morning, only in the haze the wretch missed his mark and got the cow instead. He'll go home and behave himself, now, and remember next time not to drink too much, keeping himself warm on his night watches."

Francesca took the chair across from the rector's desk, and said abruptly, "Someone told me yesterday that I looked a little like Mr. Leighton. Dark, brooding shadows in my face. Is it true, do you think?"

"Lord, no! That is, ought I to see such a thing?"

"No, that's the point."

He grinned. "They do say, you know, that one grows to

look like one's dog and one's enemy. You have a choice—Tyler or Leighton."

"He has a way of setting my back up. Worse than my cousins ever could!"

"Leighton said as much of you to me yesterday. And claimed it was his fault." Considering her again, Stevens said, "One can come to love one's enemies, you know. It isn't unheard of."

She grimaced. "Yes, well, in the Christian sense, perhaps!" Then she added ruefully, "I sometimes forget that you're a churchman."

"He's a good man, Francesca. Solid. Fought in France and earned a medal for bravery, was wounded and sent home." It was as if he were testing her. His eyes were hooded as he turned the pen in his hand, shielding his thoughts.

"Yes." *As if that excuses everything*... she added silently. "But you've already told me he may not have long to live." The words brought back vividly the dream she'd had in the night. Wincing, she looked away.

"There's that, too, of course." He dug through the cluttered drawer of his desk and found a worn nib. "Well, you won't be called on to render Christian duty in Leighton's quarter. I expect he's leaving this morning. He told me he was coming along to say good-bye."

Surprised, Francesca asked, "Why? I mean, why is he leaving?"

"He didn't say. It was as if something was on his mind." The rector pulled out his watch. "He's late."

"Changed his mind most likely," she said acerbically. "I for one will be glad to see him gone." Rising from her chair, she asked, "Any reports in the Valley of housebreakings?" It was the question that had brought her here.

"Housebreakings? Not that I have heard. Why?" There was concern in his voice as he accompanied her to the door. "Has there been trouble at River's End?"

"Tyler was restless in the night. It reminded me that I live alone."

"And I remind you in turn that you are always welcome here. I owe your grandfather for many things, not the least his interest in keeping the church roof over our heads!"

"I'm fine. Tyler misses Grandfather terribly, and any noise in the night makes him lift his head in the hope he's come back."

"Trying for you, I should think!"

"Yes—and no. Thank you for your invitation, all the same. It's appreciated. I'll send you Grandfather's fountain pen by Mrs. Lane. He'd like to see it put to use again!"

With that, Francesca said good-bye and left. The rector stood watching her walk down the hill toward the bridge. She turned to wave, and would have sworn she glimpsed a speculative shadow in his eyes.

She strolled back to River's End, enjoying the early morning. The dawn mists had vanished, and the sun warmed the earth, giving the autumn air a quality that she loved, almost tangible where the beams fell golden through the trees.

I don't want to go back to London—

The thought came unbidden. Her first reaction was that it had been unconsciously prompted by her dream. But it wasn't the first time she had said as much.

The dead here she knew. They were her family. And the dying men in stuffy trains were strangers she could no longer bear to send on their journey uncomforted. She hadn't recognized how much of herself had been shut down emotionally until she had reached this Valley and realized that she had no strength left for her grandfather's suffering. . . .

There was such a thin line between surviving and enduring.

She looked up at the house as she came up the drive, thinking how small it had seemed with the cousins running amok along the passages and down the stairs. Now it seemed enormous, and so pitifully empty.

Rather than bring Mrs. Lane to unlock the heavy front

door, Francesca chose to walk round to the kitchen door by
way of the formal gardens on the south front, her shoes whis-
pering through the leaves strewing the path. How long before
the gardens would have proper care again? How many years
before able-bodied men could work here and bring the beds
back to their former glory?

There had been a heavy dew on the lawns, and she held her
skirts out of the wet as she crossed the grass and turned
toward the back of the garden.

I need Harry's teasing—or Freddy's music—to cheer me
up, she thought, paying heed to where she put her feet. Even
Simon's wars would be—

She broke off, staring at the place where the Murder Stone
had lain half buried for as long as she could remember.

There was a body lying there now, still and limp and, from
what she could tell at such a distance, quite dead.

CHAPTER 12

Shouting for Mrs. Lane, Francesca ran heedless of her skirts toward the man lying on his right side, his head on one arm, his face out of sight.

But she was already certain of his identity, and she heard herself exclaiming furiously, "Why couldn't you have gone home to die! You've brought nothing but trouble—"

She reached him and stopped short, staring down at a mask of blood, black now, and already attracting flies.

Leighton lay there without moving, and instantly, training took over. She reached down a hand to feel his throat beneath the collars of his coat and his shirt.

There was a faint pulse, but the flesh was cold.

He was alive, but in dire need of medical help.

Francesca knelt and attempted to turn him. He flopped over on his back like an unwieldy sack.

She spun around and ran to the house. Mrs. Lane wasn't in the kitchen, and calling her name, Francesca finally found her in one of the bathrooms, scrubbing the floor.

The older woman looked up in alarm as Francesca burst into the room.

"I need help, Mrs. Lane—Mr. Leighton is in the back garden, bleeding badly and very cold. We must send to Tiverton for Dr. Nealy!"

"We'll never move him, Miss," Mrs. Lane answered, hastily drying her wet hands on her apron. "Not between us. Tall as he is!"

"Get your coat, find someone in the village who can help us lift him. He ought to be in his bed at the inn, where he can be kept warm. I'll have Bill hitch the horse to the cart."

They were flying down the stairs, the housekeeper breathing heavily, one hand pressed to her chest. "What's happened to him—?" she gasped.

"I don't know—I didn't stay to find out. There are horse blankets in the stables—I'll wrap him in one of those to start with."

"Those filthy things? It will never do, Miss! There's blankets in the chest in the box room—"

"There isn't time."

They'd reached the kitchen, and Mrs. Lane clutched a chair's back for a moment. "I'm not as young as I was—"

"Hurry!" Francesca urged her. "I must find Bill—"

The old coachman was in the barn, mending harness and placidly talking to Tyler, who had taken to wandering out to the stables when there was no other companionship.

"Bill—we must hitch the horse to a cart—and I need blankets. Mr. Leighton has been hurt, he's lying in the back garden—"

"Miss!" Bill dropped the harness and straightened, staring at her. "What's he doing *there*?"

"It doesn't matter. I've sent Mrs. Lane to the village, to find men to lift him into the cart. We can't do it ourselves, and in the meantime, I must keep him warm—"

She ran to the room where tack was kept and pulled up the heavy lid of a sturdy box set against the wall. Taking out two of the horse blankets folded inside, she let the lid fall shut again. As it did, raised bits of wood in a long trio of scratches on the underside nicked the back of her hand. As raw as if they had been made yesterday, the splinters still sharp; they drew blood, but she took no notice, already on her way out the tack room door. The blankets smelled of camphor used to keep out the moths, and she sneezed twice as she hurried on toward the bottom of the garden.

Richard Leighton lay as she had left him, although it appeared that he had tried to shift his left arm over his eyes. She wrapped him in the horse blankets, lifting him as best she could to shove an edge under one side and then the other.

He grimaced as she did so, and then began to mutter something. Francesca rocked back on her heels, listening to the orders he was snapping out to his men, threatening them with mayhem if they didn't keep their heads down. And then, as if he'd heard a whistle blown for the attack, he began to struggle, ready to lead his men in the next assault.

"All right, you bastards, let's go! They're more afraid of us than we are of them, and—" The rest was garbled, and then he seemed to laugh. "Steady as you go—we'll make it—another hundred yar—!"

His lashes fluttered and his eyes opened, focused on nothing.

Francesca waited, and after a moment said, "Mr. Leighton?" in a quiet voice.

His head swung toward her, but there was no recognition in his eyes. "*What are you doing here, woman*—" As if she'd appeared out of nowhere in the chaos of a battlefield. And then the lids shut and opened again. This time there was awareness in his glance. He made an effort to sit up.

Without ceremony, Francesca pressed him down again. "No, lie still, Richard—we'll have you back in your own bed as soon as may be—"

She could see Bill coming with the cart. He clicked his tongue as he led the horse across the lawns, and came to kneel uneasily before the prostrate man. "Best do as she says, sir—"

Leighton said in bewilderment, "What the hell am I *doing* here—"

"You must tell me," Francesca answered equably. "This is where I found you not fifteen minutes ago, pale as death and senseless. There's blood all over your face. From the color of most of it, it's been there a while."

He put up a hand as if in disbelief, then scowled as he looked at the blood on his fingertips, swearing softly.

"Don't touch your face," she warned. "It will just start the bleeding again!"

Two burly men rough-clad in brown corduroy trousers and heavy boots came hurrying across the lawns, calling to her. They manhandled the hogsheads and kegs for Jenny Ranson, the innkeeper's wife.

"Thank you for coming so quickly! This man has been hurt. If you help us lift him into the cart, there, we'll carry him down to the inn."

"No, I can manage on my own—" Leighton protested, and then cursed as his sudden movement sent his head spinning.

"Begging pardon, miss, but the doctor was at the inn, having his morning tea, and he's following in his carriage," the taller of the pair informed her. "We're not to touch the man until he has a look at him."

"Is someone ill?" she asked quickly. Dr. Nealy came to Hurley for only the most serious cases.

"He's just been to see Miss Trotter, if I heard Jenny aright," the other man answered.

"Miss Trotter? What's happened?" She was genuinely fond of the old woman.

"Nothing that I've been told of, miss," the taller man said, eyeing the recumbent Leighton. "She's just finished that syrup she brews up for coughs. And Doctor has spoken for a good part of it—"

Leighton said, "If you'll help me to my feet—"

"No, sir, begging pardon, sir, but the doctor has forbade you to move."

"To hell with the doctor, then, I—"

But they could already hear a carriage clattering into the stable yard, and within two minutes Dr. Nealy joined them.

He cleaned the blood from Leighton's face and examined a long wound that was still weeping. It lay along Leighton's temple and into his hairline, a welt that was ugly and red. Hidden by the heavy bleeding and matted hair, it had been impossible to see.

"Well, now," the doctor was saying, wiping his hands on a bit of cotton and sitting back on his heels. "You were luckier than Tommy Higby's cow!" But Leighton, at the end of his strength, fell back amid the horse blankets, his gaunt face slack and senseless.

Dr. Nealy went efficiently about his work, dressing the wound, and then wrapping gauze strips around the patient's head to hold the dressing in place. "He's staying at The Spotted Calf, is he not? Well, it won't do. Too far. Miss Hatton, my dear, you'll have to provide a bed—"

"Indeed not!" she began indignantly.

But the doctor was already adding, "Mrs. Lane can stay the night here, until he's well enough to be moved. That will be propriety enough!"

Under Dr. Nealy's guidance, the men bundled Leighton into the blankets, forming a rough sling, and then lifted him.

"Don't drop him, men!" the doctor scolded sharply. "Now, in proper cadence, we'll make our way to the kitchen door. Gently as you go—! Miss Hatton, if you will—"

She had no choice but to walk ahead of the trio, and hold the kitchen door wide. The back stairs were too narrow, and they trundled their burden up the main staircase in the hall. Francesca, ahead of them, flung open the door of a guest room. The sheets were damp, but the doctor said, "Light a fire and bring hot water bottles or even a warming pan if you can find one. Now, if you will, my dear, we need to undress him."

She left them to it and went to find hot water bottles in the kitchen cupboard. She had filled them often for her grandfather, wrapping them in flannel to set against his feet as he lay immobile after his stroke. It took time to heat the water, and when Francesca had reached the stairs again, Mrs. Lane was hanging onto the newel post, her face still red from the effort of hurrying back from the village.

"I've had the inn prepare his bed—" she began, and then saw the hot water bottles in Francesca's hands. "Oh, my good Lord, he's not here, is he? And the guest room sheets not aired this month or more—?"

She went hurrying up the stairs, puffing as she went, and Francesca followed close behind.

Events had happened too fast. Francesca felt violated, her house invaded, a man she disliked ensconced in one of her bedchambers, and the doctor giving instructions as if she were ten and in the way! Had he forgotten that she worked with the Red Cross? Or did he remember only that she had vomited when poor Harry's leg had been laid open by the collapsing shed roof? At the door of the guest chamber, Mrs. Lane turned to take the water bottles. "And I'll just be down to fetch the scuttle and start a fire in here," she was saying.

Behind the housekeeper's back, Francesca could hear the doctor speaking in a low voice to his patient, soothing words, meant to put him at his ease. She had the feeling Leighton was still arguing stringently to be taken to his own room. But the stalwarts from the inn had been sent away, and as she turned back to the stairs, Dr. Nealy called to her.

"There's concussion. In addition to the wound, it appears he fell and struck the back of his head on that infernal stone. The last thing he needs is to be rattled about just now. Sometimes he's coherent, at others he's back in the war. He's suffering from double vision and dizziness. You'll have to sit with him and keep him quiet. And if he begins to vomit or falls into a deep sleep from which you can't rouse him, send for me at once. There may be a severe headache, as well. I'll stay the night at the inn if there's no sign of improvement, or here, if need be."

"If you could find a nurse—the one who tended my grandfather—"

"Miss Honneycutt has other work to do, or I'd have sent for her. Now then, nothing solid, until we see where his stomach stands. Water he can have, and weak tea with sugar in it. None of that strong brew Francis preferred! No milk. And I'll see if Mrs. Lane can prepare a broth for the evening—"

"Is Mr. Leighton awake?"

"Yes, I've not let him sleep. I'll leave you to manage his care while I go in search of Mrs. Lane."

She couldn't remember the last visitor who had spent the night in this room. Before the war, at any rate, and most likely friends of the cousins down from Oxford or London.

River's End, unlike many of the houses in the Valley, had never been noted for elaborate entertaining. But the country's prevailing mood of triumph in 1914 had been replaced by depression and austerity as the news from France grew more sobering in 1915. Shortages of food and shrinking staff had changed the nature of grand dinners or lighthearted weekends in the country. Wings of houses were closed, others were commandeered by the Army for hospitals and officer billets. The Valley was too far from the railway to be included in these lists, but the frugality of the war years had not passed it by. Some parties went on, of course, people doggedly clinging to the past or determined to put a happier face on the war. But the King and Queen had set an example of retrenching, and for the most part the nation had followed. Plays and musical events had become charity benefits, and attendance at churches across England had gone up. It was a changed society. For the better or the worse, Francesca thought, no one could predict.

She stepped quietly into the bedchamber. Leighton was lying on his back, eyes closed.

Francesca couldn't be certain whether he was asleep or pretending. Without a word, she moved a chair so that she was not close to the bed but could still study his defenseless face.

His eyes were blue, hers hazel. He was fair, and her coloring was darker. More important than coloring, she could see that his face was structured differently, the chin less delicate, the cheekbones less pronounced.

Although—there were the same smudges of sleeplessness under his eyes as beneath hers. Was that what Bill had glimpsed at that late hour in the smoky lamplight of the pub? How often had Bill also seen her grandfather sleepless and troubled?

She noted, too, the tautness of skin that never relaxed, the lines of laughter washed away by long days and longer nights. The stress of burdens silently carried for too many years. The mark of despair. Throughout her childhood, why hadn't she seen the despair in her grandfather's face? Or had he been more clever at concealing it?

What was the darkness she had sensed in this man? She wondered if Miss Trotter had put a finger on it: Most of his life, Richard Leighton had loved a memory—not a reality. A woman he'd worshipped and put on a pedestal—whether she deserved it or not. If so, he must have been tormented by the knowledge that she'd deserted him—that she had loved him so little that she could walk away without a second thought, with no regrets. In some ways it must have seemed more comprehensible for Victoria Leighton to have been taken away against her will and murdered.

She was beginning to realize that Francis Hatton's guilt was in some ways more momentous to Richard Leighton than his innocence was to Francesca.

They were locked in an impasse and neither could retreat.

Francesca went back to scanning Leighton's face.

What had Bill seen? What had she missed? In either man?

It didn't matter. It was a far fetched notion to begin with, and she was too tired to care.

Leighton stirred, murmuring something she couldn't quite catch.

Against her will, the flask of dandelion wine flitted through her mind. And there was a little of the laudanum left. But of course concussion victims were not allowed spirits....

As if Leighton sensed her presence—and her mood—he

said, "I dislike being here as much as you dislike having me in your house. I have told you before, I want nothing from you or yours."

"I'd heard you were leaving this morning."

He smiled a little. "This Valley has so many secrets. And yet it still manages to whisper about everything that happens."

"There's nothing otherworldly about the fact that I knew your plans. I had stopped in at the Rectory this morning. Mr. Stevens was expecting you to come and say good-bye." She paused. "What happened in the garden? Do you know?"

"Someone shot at me. That I ducked out of habit may have saved my life. The bullet creased my skull instead of splitting it. Although the way it feels at present, he succeeded in splitting it after all—I've the devil of a headache!"

"There was another such accident this morning—only the first victim died. A cow."

At that, Leighton finally opened his eyes. "A cow?"

"You're in good company, it would seem. The shot missed Tommy Higby by inches, and hit the cow instead. Tommy is quite the hero. Everyone is talking about him!"

"Who the hell is wandering about with a rifle!" he asked testily, and then put his hand to his aching head. "Don't you have a policeman in these benighted parts?"

"As a matter of fact we don't have a local policeman, or a local doctor. That is, there's one of each in Tiverton. Or Exeter. Take your pick. We borrow one when we must. There's seldom any need for a constable in the Valley."

"Well, someone should stop this fool before he does kill."

"It's a farmer after foxes or stoats. People have been losing chickens, I suppose. Meat is scarce enough without sharing it with vermin."

There was a faint hint of humor in his question. "Are you equating me with vermin?"

"As you like," she replied, repressing a smile. "Indeed, there've been times when putting you down to stop your insinuations did cross my mind. If Dr. Nealy hadn't arrived in the nick of time, I'd have had you removed to the knacker's yard by now."

"God knows, I feel as if that's where I belong. Where are my clothes?"

"Mrs. Lane is cleaning the blood off your shirt and coat. They'll be returned as soon as they're dry and pressed. You bled horrifically. Head wounds often do."

Francesca thought he had drifted into sleep again. She heard him giving orders, trying to call back his men and beginning to thrash about. Afraid that he might be sinking into deeper sleep than was safe, she went across to the bed to try waking him. Just as she got there he swore violently and opened his eyes.

"Miss Hatton. Will you fetch the doctor, please?"

"I think he's gone back to the village—"

"*Fetch him, please.*" There was no doubt that he meant what he said. His face was chalk white.

Francesca did as she was told, calling to Mrs. Lane as she ran out the front door.

When Francesca returned with Dr. Nealy in tow, she found herself barred from the guest room. Leighton had been sick in her absence, and Mrs. Lane had taken it upon herself to clean the bedclothes and the floor. The doctor nodded at the news and disappeared inside.

"Nausea and dizziness. To be expected, but not welcomed," he reported later, coming into the sitting room where Francesca was waiting, an untouched book in her lap. It was her grandfather's translation of Juvenal, picked to distract her. "I'll finish my luncheon at The Spotted Calf, and then come back for an hour or so until the patient is more settled."

Francesca saw him out, then went in search of Mrs. Lane. She was pouring a can of hot water into the laundry tub; the sour odor of sickness filled the room that had been used for washing as long as Francesca could remember.

"Poor man! Quite sick, he was! And ashamed of it, too."

"Yes, well, it's no more than he deserves, prowling about in someone else's grounds!"

"He explained to me that he was looking for you, to tell you he was leaving," she said reproachfully. "After all, he'd found you there once before."

Francesca said nothing.

With the hot water poured up to the lip of the tub and soap added, Mrs. Lane rinsed her hands. "Let that set a bit, and then I'll finish it up. You should see his back, Miss Francesca! It's so scarred there's hardly any flesh that's whole! A terrible wound and only just healing, angry and red still. No wonder he hasn't been able to return to France!"

"England is full of men who are terribly wounded. It's the price of war."

"Now, Miss Francesca, you mustn't be bitter!"

"It isn't bitterness," she answered. "It's a reality none of us was prepared for!"

When she looked in on Leighton an hour later, he wore one of her grandfather's nightshirts and there was a basin ready on the table by the bed, if the nausea should return. A clean cloth lay beside it. His face was pale, drawn, his eyes shut.

As she took her seat again, he murmured, "I'm sorry to give your housekeeper so much trouble."

"She's changed her mind about you. Now she's beginning to look upon you as a wounded hero, eager to return to battle as soon as you've healed. My cousins never came home. I expect you'll become their surrogate."

"I won't be going back to France." The words were clipped and hard.

Surprised, she said, "Why not? They're desperate for men."

"They sent me home to die. So far I've cheated them."

CHAPTER 13

Dr. Nealy returned in early afternoon, with Leighton's luggage in his carriage and word of the war. "Ward Carlson stopped at the inn, on his way home to Tiverton. He'd picked up the London newspapers before taking the train to Exeter," he told Francesca, excitement in his face. "There's a report that despite the rains, we've made important advances along the Somme. Good news indeed! It's been a quagmire, they say. Impossible to move men or troops through the thick mud. Still, General Rawlinson isn't letting it stop him. It appears that we have a foothold on the Schwaben redoubt, but the Germans are fighting hard to defend the rest of their line. And the French are using their new guns at Verdun. That should put the Bosche to flight!"

But all too often such heady pronouncements were premature—or wrong. The War Office and the Army hoarded news, as if half afraid to believe it themselves. By the time it reached the papers, it was often old or incomplete.

"I'm glad!" Francesca answered, trying to warm to his

enthusiasm. To her, battles meant longer trains of wounded coming through, pathetic victims of the Army's willingness to throw more and more men against the German lines in the hope that numbers would ensure a breakthrough.

Dr. Nealy saw it differently. "You're needed in London, my dear! You ought to close the house and go!" He was rubbing his hands with eagerness, as if envying her the opportunity. "Your grandfather would want you to do your bit!"

"There are more than enough women to do the work I did," she answered. "There's nothing left for many of them except to offer comfort where they can. I wonder if there is such a thing as battle fatigue for *us*, the ones who stay at home and wait."

"I never expected to hear you of all people speak like that, Miss Hatton!" He looked at her closely. "Are you sleeping well? It may be that you haven't fully recovered from your grandfather's illness and death."

"Yes, I'm sure that must be it," she answered, uncomfortable arguing with him. "When will you move Mr. Leighton?"

"Mrs. Lane has agreed to stay the night as chaperone, and Mr. Leighton has been told that it will be a day or two before I'm certain he's out of the woods."

Francesca suggested that the doctor leave the luggage where it was, standing in the hall, until Bill could take it up. And as soon as he had disappeared up the stairs, safely out of sight, she knelt by the two leather cases and swiftly searched through them.

But if there was a photograph of Leighton's mother amongst his belongings, she failed to find it.

Mrs. Lane rested after dinner, agreeing to taking over the charge of sitting with the patient at midnight.

When Francesca went to wake her, the housekeeper was snoring heavily and even shaking her shoulder failed to rouse her. Walking back through the silent house, Tyler's nails clicking at her heels, Francesca returned to Leighton's room.

He had slept fitfully during the afternoon and early evening, but never the dreaded deep sleep that Dr. Nealy had warned about. Nor were there any more rambling regressions to the war. For the most part he seemed to be resting comfortably enough. She sat by the fire, listening to the sound of his even breathing. Tyler, snuffling in self-pity, reminded her that she should be in her own bed and he should be on his thick rug by her. She fondled his ears, but his mournful eyes were enough to fill her with guilt.

Shortly after the clock struck one, Leighton woke. He said into the silence, "Is anyone there?"

"I'm here, and my dog," Francesca replied lightly. "He's the one who is snoring."

A quiet chuckle came from the bed. "Talk to me, if you will," Leighton said then. "I've slept long enough. It's left me unsettled. We won't wake the dog."

"Talk about what?" she asked warily.

Leighton lay quietly, eyes shut, face pale, not speaking.

At length he said, his eyes still shut, "What did your housekeeper mean when she referred to where I was found in the garden as the Murder Stone?"

"It's what my cousins called that white stone when they were young. All their executions and so on took place there."

"A bloodthirsty lot, I'd say." There was an undercurrent of amusement in his voice.

"No more than most, I suppose," she heard herself saying defensively. "Everyone fell in with Simon's games. Because I was the smallest, I was often burned at the stake."

"Joan of Arc in a lace pinafore? Yes, I can see that."

"Sometimes I had my head cut off as William Wallace. Whatever bit of history we were reading at the moment. I rather hated burning."

"Surely these cousins never got carried away!"

"No, they burned twigs in the grass. But the smoke would rise up. It always made me ill afterward...I don't know why. As if I'd actually felt the flames on my flesh."

On his last day in Devon, Simon had taken her out to the

Murder Stone and said solemnly, "Shall we kill the Kaiser here? Bash his brains in, in that silly helmet of his, and be done with this madness?"

It would have been better for everyone, she thought, if he'd done just that. War wasn't at all like playing in the back garden. There all the defeated foes had got to their feet, grinning and filthy, and trooped off to beg treats from Mrs. Wiggins, the cook, before climbing a tree to eat their booty.

I'm learning to accept how it is, Freddy had written his grandfather. *And of course it's what one must do. My sergeant, on the other hand, seems to feel nothing when the man next to him is decapitated, and blood flies. He spits into the unspeakable mud and shoves the body away from the ladder, calling, "Next," as if nothing of importance has happened...*

Leighton's voice broke into her memories. "Simon must have been a natural leader."

"He inherited that from my grandfather, I suppose. If he'd lived, he was sure to become a famous general. Or it might have been one of the others—who knows? Still, name any battle fought in the last three thousand years, and Simon could tell you how it was planned and executed, and what went wrong. God knows, I was swept up in most of them—I could tell you myself!"

"What did your nanny have to say about wild goings-on in the garden?"

Francesca found herself thinking of Mrs. Passmore. "She didn't last very long, apparently. I was turned over to my cousins' tutor early on. We were a mixed lot, you know, my five cousins and I. But we got on well enough." She smiled nostalgically into the fire. "It doesn't seem possible that they're all dead now. Lost at Mons and Ypres, Passchendaele and the Somme. And the Murder Stone is still there, at the bottom of my grandfather's garden, where it has always been." But not for long...

"You loved them, I think. Your cousins."

"More than I ever realized. Harry was as much a leader in his own way as Simon was. And Freddy—he was a composer, as well as an accomplished pianist. Would he have played on the concert stage, if he'd lived? Peter was a wonder with his hands—he designed all manner of things for us to play with, from forts for Simon's soldiers to a house in a tree. What could he have done for mankind, besides digging tunnels under the German lines? And then there's Robin, the explorer, who really wanted nothing more than to inherit River's End. Where would he have gone, what amazing things would he have brought back for museums? He had his feet planted firmly on the ground, he was the one who kept us safe. The steady one, who couldn't keep his own men alive in No Man's Land, try as hard as he would. It must have broken his heart! That's the real tragedy of war, you know. None of us will ever see what the dead might have accomplished with their lives. What their sons and daughters would have grown up to do. It's the waste, not the dying, that's so horrid."

She shrugged, acknowledging the melancholy mood that had swept over her but unable to shift it.

"I can't say that I encountered any of them in France. I wish I had."

"Yes. Well. Speaking of growing up in a family of boys, I can't imagine being an only child."

The instant she spoke the words she wished she could take them back. In an effort to chase away her own shadows, she had inadvertently brought his back. She could see the darkness envelop him, as it had sometimes enveloped her grandfather in his last weeks.

After a moment he answered her, surprisingly without the usual anger. "A daughter was born of my father's second marriage. My half sister. But I was away at school and saw little of her. She's very like her mother and your cousin Robin. Quiet and practical. Unlike you and your cousins, we have very little in common, other than a father. But she's affectionate and bright, and I like her. She cried the day I was brought home on a stretcher to be nursed—or buried. Then she turned to and wore herself down trying to save me. It's one of the reasons I left the house as soon as I was able. To spare her."

The clock in the hall chimed two.

"And the other reason was Francis Hatton's obituary in the *Times*."

"We'd hammered at him for years. Letters. Private investigators. Once or twice we convinced the police to take a renewed interest in the case."

She was reminded of the letter that had cursed the Hattons. Yet it had been written before Victoria disappeared.

"I suppose in his shoes I'd have walked warily, too, and said nothing. But I—we—had hoped that at the end, his conscience might have goaded him into making a gesture. A little peace for a family who hasn't known peace in decades."

And what peace would it bring to Richard Leighton, she wondered, if he finally discovered the truth? He thinks now that knowing will help. But what if it only makes matters worse?

"Have you told me everything I ought to know? About my grandfather and your mother? I still find it hard to believe that your grandfather could be so convinced of Francis Hatton's guilt when there's only the slimmest evidence."

"Francis Hatton wrote to my mother two days before she vanished. I brought her the post that morning, and she read the letter with a frown on her face. Then she burned it. I'd never seen her so angry before, and so I remembered it. But I didn't realize the importance of what I knew. Not for some years, when I overheard a conversation between my father and my grandfather. Then it all fit together. Why should I not believe the evidence of my own eyes? Hatton wrote to her— and she refused to answer him. And so he came after her."

"You said nothing to me about a letter!"

"I was the only witness to that. I didn't think you'd believe me." His voice was weary. "I told you about independent witnesses instead."

"But everything still comes back to the central question. *Why?* What possible motive could there have been?"

"It may be that the only two people who could answer that

are dead. The other factor is that my grandfather and Francis Hatton never liked each other. Hatton was my *father's* friend, if you remember. Thomas Leighton's best man. My father fought my grandfather for months, trying to change his mind about Hatton. And in the end, I suppose, he started to believe the accusations himself. That's when he began to drink heavily. A part of him died with Victoria." And then with a wrenching of the spirit, he exclaimed, *"I'd wager my soul that she would never have deserted us of her own free will!"*

Francesca stared into the fire. "It's unthinkable. She must be dead. But I can't agree that Francis Hatton killed her."

"The letter was addressed to her. To Victoria. Not to my father. Why would she have burned it if it hadn't been some form of—solicitation? Someone had to carry her away from the Downs. She's not buried there. We've searched. And whoever it was couldn't have done that on foot. That means a carriage—a cart. A horse. Planning—not a chance encounter!"

"My grandfather had his failings. Why not your mother? What if she'd written to him first—"

There was silence in the room, the sound of the dog's breathing threading through the snap of flames.

"Then what in God's name became of Victoria Leighton?" her son asked into the stillness. "I won't give up searching. That's all that's left to me now."

"I wish you would show me her photograph. I keep trying to imagine her, what there was about her that could have drawn my grandfather to her." To the woman whose name might well have been on his lips in the last weeks of his life. If she could somehow understand the bond between this woman and her grandfather—

"To judge her character in her face? Like Miss Trotter?"

"It's not her character I want to see. It's what might have attracted my grandfather—"

But the door opened at that moment and Mrs. Lane came in, overflowing with apologies for not hearing Francesca call to her earlier.

Francesca left their patient to the housekeeper and went up to her own bed. But not to sleep.

The next morning there was a knock at the door. Mrs. Lane was resting and Francesca opened it herself.

A rawboned man with dark red hair stood on the steps, hat in hand.

"Begging your pardon, Miss. I was looking for wark in the Valley, and was expecting a sairvant to answer the door. I did knock at the kitchen door first."

"Everyone is busy," she said warily. He was wearing the uniform of a medically discharged soldier. And one eye was hideously scarred. "Have you asked at the inn? Or the Rectory?"

"There's naught to be had. Though the rector's housekeeper was kind enough to gie me a meal."

"What brings you to Devon? Your accent, I think, is north of Glasgow."

He grinned ruefully. "I havena' the coin to travel north. I warked for three weeks in Dorset, repairing a barn roof after a storm brought it down. If I can find other wark, I'll be home by Hogmanay. That's a holiday, Miss."

Francesca thought fleetingly about her own gardens, so neglected and overgrown. But she said, "I'm afraid there's nothing I can offer you. I'm sorry."

"If it's references you're needing—"

He reached into his pocket and took out a letter, the envelope smeared and crinkled from being carried around with him. "My last employment, Miss."

She read the sheet inside, and returned it to the envelope before saying, "This is very glowing. But you'd do better asking at some of the farms over the hill. They're always short-handed."

"Ah, weel. If ye're sure?" There was disappointment in his scarred face.

"I'm sorry." But she gave him some coins, out of pity.

She closed the door, but as she passed a window, she saw the Scot standing in the drive, looking at the house. It was only a small step from that to wondering if he had also taken to housebreaking. But that was not fair to a wounded soldier out of work.

Still, the gruff Scot at the funeral—could he have sent someone to search again for the box he claimed he'd bought from Francis Hatton? What better way to do that than live on the premises and bide one's time?

"I've grown disgustingly suspicious..." she scolded herself, walking briskly to the kitchen to put on a pot of tea. Everything seemed to have hidden meaning, secrets like shadows just behind every action. She found herself swinging from uncertainty to uncertainty. Her grandfather, stalwart and loving, had always stood behind her, and now he was gone. The cousins were gone. She was alone. She would never have dreamt how lonely it would be.

It bit deep into her bones, and it was what had made her say no to the ex-soldier, for fear that she would decide not on the basis of what he could do but what she wanted him to be, an able-bodied man standing guard at River's End, bulwark against noises in the night.

The hot tea and a small slice of stale sponge cake picked up her spirits and she went back upstairs, knocking lightly on the guest room door before entering.

Leighton was standing, clinging to the bedpost. He had managed to dress himself, after a fashion, shirt unbuttoned, trousers unbelted, stockings and shoes on his feet, but the laces not tied.

Clicking her tongue in annoyance, Francesca went to him, putting an arm around him, helping him to the side of the bed again, where he sat heavily.

"I don't particularly want you here," she told him, holding her temper in check. "But if you insist upon being foolish, I'll have you on my hands twice as long!"

"I'm not foolish. I'm tired of lying there. My back aches. Get me to that chair by the hearth, and I'll be satisfied."

"The doctor ordered you to rest in bed—"

"The good doctor ordered me to rest. I can't if I'm in pain."

He made an effort to stand again, this time able to remain on his feet without her support. But he kept a hand on her shoulder as he walked to the cushioned chair by the fire. "That's better," he said. And color had returned to his face, she could see it for herself. He leaned his head against the chair's back, saying, "I can't lie still for long periods. I'm sorry."

Francesca recalled what Mrs. Lane had said about the wound in his back. She asked, "Would you care for something to drink?"

He grinned, a lopsided one. "I'm drowning in broth. It's quite good, but I'd as soon have something more substantial."

"It's broth, until Dr. Nealy tells us otherwise."

"Whatever you can find. I'd be grateful."

Francesca brought him a small dish of the pudding that Mrs. Lane had made for her luncheon.

Leighton ate hungrily, and she left him to enjoy his food.

Tyler woke Francesca with the heavy growls she had heard two nights before. She laid a hand on his collar, but it did no good. He went to stand by the door, impatient for her to open it.

She had no wish to surprise Leighton in the passage on his way to the bathroom. On the other hand, she was not about to give him free rein to explore her house or rummage through her grandfather's desk in search of whatever evidence he suspected might be here.

Catching up her robe and Robin's torch, she opened the door for Tyler and stepped with the dog into the dark passage. Down at the far end, another figure stood on the threshold of the guest room, dressed in shirt and trousers.

She heard the soft "Shhh!" and stopped herself from speaking. For Tyler had turned the other way.

Moving into the passage, Francesca followed the dog, and moving just as quietly behind her, she could tell that Leighton had come to join her.

"Go back to your room!" he hissed at her shoulder, but she shook her head.

Tyler went to the top of the stairs. After a moment, he lumbered down them and turned toward her grandfather's study.

She felt a surge of fear as his hackles rose, his nose pressed to the knob. *Oh, why didn't I look for Simon's pistol when I had the chance!* she chided herself. For the room beyond seemed to be alive with something—

And then Leighton stepped around her and flung open the study door.

Francesca flicked on her torch, sweeping the room. The long drapes were billowing in the cold wind pouring in from an open French door. Tyler was already there, sniffing at the low sill.

Then the dog lifted his head and growled, this time with ears pricked. She caught his collar to hold him back.

Leighton crossed to the opening to stare out into the night. Beyond the terrace lay beds of perennials bordered by flowering shrubs that hadn't been trimmed for two years. The long pendulous branches cast heavy shadows where the starlight failed to penetrate.

Francesca demanded softly, "What do you see? Do you want the torch?"

After a moment, Leighton turned and said, "No. I was wrong. There's no one out here. But I would have sworn   "

"Are you sure?" She stood in his place, peering out. The sensation of being watched crept over her. She cast the torch beam around the gardens twice, but could find nothing to explain her sudden uneasiness. And then an owl flew silently out of the trees beyond, startling her before it vanished among the overgrown beds.

She chided herself for an overactive imagination and

moved away with the reluctant dog to let Leighton push the curtains aside and swing the door closed.

"Careless," he said, as if explaining the door opening by itself in the middle of the night. "But no harm done."

"These French doors were latched—they're always latched, ever since my grandfather took ill. We haven't used this room since then. Besides, Tyler wouldn't have growled just because they'd blown open. He smells something here! Look at him! For that matter, what brought *you* out in the passage just now?"

She wished she could see his face in the darkness, but it was a pale shadowed blur, and she couldn't bring herself to turn the torch into his eyes.

"I heard something as well. I'm not quite sure what it was. I thought perhaps you couldn't sleep, either, and I came to see if you wanted company."

"I was soundly asleep, until Tyler woke me. It's the second time he's done that." Shivering in the unheated room, she added, "I might as well make tea. Now that I'm wide awake." She smoothed the dog's head, encouraging him to follow her to the kitchen. "I don't know whether there was really someone here or not—"

But Tyler knew the sounds of the house as well as she did, and he had sensed *something*—a noise, a scent. A step—

The kitchen fire had been banked for the night. As Leighton blew it back to life, Francesca said, "Ought you to be out of bed?"

"I'm not a model patient," he said tersely.

Francesca put on a kettle and then searched in the cupboards for cups and saucers and the sugar. "Mrs. Lane won't care for our meddling in her domain. There's more pudding, if you care for it."

They sat at the cloth-covered table where Mrs. Lane took her own meals when she was in the house, and when the water had boiled and Francesca had stirred the tea leaves a second time before pouring, Leighton said, "The pudding was very good, but no, thank you."

Francesca smiled in spite of herself. "You'll be ravenous by morning."

"Very likely." He gestured around him, and asked, "Are you comfortable, living alone like this in such an empty mausoleum of a house?"

"It *is* a mausoleum," she acknowledged. "There are more dead souls here than living. But it's where I grew up, and I feel comfortable enough. Except when something like this happens. Where do you live?"

"I've a flat in London. My father has settled his present house on my half sister. We discussed it, and it seemed the wisest thing to do. I was going off to fight, and she had the better chance of living to inherit it."

"What do you do, when you're not soldiering?"

"I'm a solicitor. Or was. My practice will be nonexistent now. And I haven't been well enough in the past few months to take it up again."

"You were wounded on the Somme?"

"With thousands of others—it started with a bloodbath, and even the Army doesn't know how many died there. I lay under the wire—No Man's Land—for half a day before anyone had time to dig me out from under the corpses of my company and the Germans they'd killed. That was the worst of it, lying there in the heat and hearing men crying for help, and no help coming. There were so many wounded that the doctors only worked on those they could save. They held out little hope for me, patched me up, and sent me back to England. I've never seen such human misery. Dante could have used it for his vision of hell.... Most of us have nightmares. At night in hospital I could hear screams that went on and on, until someone woke the poor bastard—sorry."

"Do you have nightmares?"

"I'm told I do. I don't know. Mercifully. Sometimes they'd give us something to help us sleep when we couldn't. When the Sister came round with the little tray, I used to pretend I was asleep. I had had so much morphine I was afraid I was growing addicted. Men did."

Francesca shivered in spite of the warm cup she held between her palms. "The wounded I've seen seldom have much to say. They're so grateful for a kind word—a cigarette—a mug of tea. It's the most appalling thing when they make light of their pain or their fear. 'It's nothing, Miss—I'll be right as rain in a week or two. Wait and see!' I was always moved to tears! And the ones who'd been gassed—you could hear them as soon as you stepped into the carriage. One man was so blistered I couldn't have told you what he looked like. They thought he might not live."

"It isn't a sight for women."

"On the contrary, I think it's what women do best, to offer comfort and a sense of home. Many of the soldiers called me 'ma'am,' they were so young. I wanted to hold them until their mothers could come and take them back."

Tyler, who had been lying quietly beside the stove, suddenly growled again. And in the same instant, the door knocker resounded through the house.

They stared at each other.

"Stay here. I'll see who it is," Leighton said.

Francesca was about to argue with him, and he cut her off. "I may be injured, but I can deal with whoever is there."

"The key is just by the door," she called softly after him as he disappeared into the shadows.

But it was only Dr. Nealy, come to see his patient and put out to find him opening the door. Francesca, standing just out of sight in the passage, could hear every word. She had caught up a knife from the worktable, and now sheepishly tucked it behind the voluminous folds of her robe.

"I was called out by a case of shingles," Nealy was saying, "and as I came back I turned up the drive to see if all was well, and found there was a light burning in your room, Leighton. What are you doing, answering the door?"

"I couldn't sleep," Leighton replied. "Which you tell me is a good thing. And Miss Hatton was kind enough to make me tea. Step in, it's bitter out there."

"I could do with a cup!" the doctor said, rubbing his hands together as he took up the unspoken invitation.

He came through to the kitchen to find Francesca seated decorously in one of the chairs, Tyler at her feet.

"Miss Hatton! I'm sorry you've lost your sleep on my patient's account," Nealy said, setting his case on the worktable where the knife lay peacefully once more. "But I'd be grateful for something hot. I'd been wondering if I could rouse Mrs. Ranson at the inn!"

Francesca took down a third cup and filled it for the doctor. He added cream but no sugar and sipped appreciatively. "I've a thermos for my carriage and never think to fill it ahead of time. Well, then, Leighton, how are you managing?"

"I expect to leave in the morning."

"Early days yet to be deciding that. Your color hasn't come back as well as I'd like, and I want to have another look at your eyes. There's still some double vision, or I miss my guess!"

Leighton neither confirmed nor denied it. But Francesca had seen how he seemed at times to blink as if trying to clear his sight. She said, "I'll leave the two of you to talk. Mr. Leighton, if you'll see Dr. Nealy out and bank the fire afterward?"

She escaped to her room, taking Tyler with her. As she climbed into bed, she wondered why she had picked up the kitchen knife and what she would have done with it if Satan himself had stood at the door.

It was as if she couldn't let Leighton walk into danger alone—

It had been an unsettling response, one she was glad that neither Leighton nor the doctor had witnessed.

Was it also a measure of her growing fear?

CHAPTER 14

By afternoon Leighton was pronounced well enough to return to the inn. And as soon as the sheets had been washed and pinned to dry, Mrs. Lane was eager to return to her own cottage. Francesca was left to walk through the empty house and admit to herself that she had liked the company, however much she'd pretended otherwise.

Leighton had proved to be less of a burden than she had expected, and perversely she was ready to believe that he was pretending to feel worse than he did. Refusing to lower her guard, she had brought in his breakfast tray and left him to feed himself, unwilling to ask what the doctor had decided about his condition. The deep gouge along his temple was still inflamed, bruising already darkening the skin around it.

And so it had been a surprise when she had found him standing in the hall, his luggage at his feet, waiting for Bill to bring around the motorcar.

As the early dusk of autumn began to fall, leaving the

house dark and silent, Francesca went to the sitting room, where a fire burned on the hearth. From her grandfather's room she'd taken the small book that Francis Hatton had been translating before his stroke, hoping to find comfort in it. But she was turning the pages without really seeing them.

Before Mrs. Lane had left, they had made the rounds of the house, seeing to the doors and window latches. Everything was as it should have been and there was no reason last night for the study doors to have come open on their own. *Had* there been an intruder? She didn't want to believe it.

Or had Richard Leighton gone down the stairs quietly, opened the French doors for reasons of his own, and then, coming back to his room, unwittingly roused Tyler?

Had he been hoping to frighten her by staging the scene as proof there was an intruder in the house? But surely he knew nothing about the earlier instance! Or by leaving the door ajar, had he been intent on covering his tracks after searching the study? And if he had been searching, it could mean only one thing—that he still refused to believe that there were no secrets in this house to find.

And yet—there may have been one secret she'd kept from him.

Victoria. Victoria...

Victorious. Victorious...

What had her grandfather been trying to say to her? If she could only sort that out, she would be on safe ground challenging Leighton's suspicions.

Or had he even been aware that his granddaughter was there in the room with him? For all she knew, he could have been responding to some deep emotional suffering, and the name had slipped free, despite his iron grip on the past.

And that, thought Francesca, would change everything. If he had remembered Victoria Leighton at the end of his life, then there must be a reason.

The uncertainty was a burden that grew heavier with each passing day. And she had to carry it alone.

She dared not trust even the rector with such explosive evidence. That camaraderie between soldiers—that bond of male sympathy and understanding which had come out of serving in France—would in the end divide Mr. Stevens's loyalty. And he was a priest, for whom murder was a deadly sin.

If Francis Hatton hadn't touched Victoria Leighton, why had a man of her grandfather's integrity deliberately concealed information he might have possessed about the woman who had deserted a grieving husband and child? Surely by doing so, Victoria had placed herself beyond the pale!

But if there had been some wild attraction between the two of them—strong enough to have lasted for years, through Victoria's marriage, through the birth of her son—would it have ended in murder? Not perhaps love . . . but lust. Surely it could be just as devastating.

Had there been, God forbid, liaisons over the years that had been masked as visits to London—to the dentist—to lunch with friends?

What if Victoria Leighton had planned her own disappearance? What if she'd come here and thrown herself at Francis Hatton? What would he have done? He needn't live with her openly here—there were other places they might have gone.

Even her grandfather might have been tempted by a brief and passionate affair. After all, his wife had been dead for years.

And what had Victoria done when the flames had burned to ashes? If Francis Hatton hadn't killed her—and it was still impossible for Francesca to think of him as a murderer!—had she killed herself?

Suicide . . . It would explain so many things!

And it would be an answer that Richard Leighton would never accept.

Another ghost to walk the halls of River's End . . .

Or did this one walk in Somerset? Or Essex?

Surely better settings for a rendezvous than River's End, where small grandchildren ran underfoot and the Valley would have been alive with gossip.

It's time to visit these two houses, Francesca told herself. *As soon as possible. If they went there, I want to know. It's like an exorcism—if I can discover what happened, I can begin to cope with it. I want to see for myself why my grandfather never told me about Somerset and Essex—why he never found tenants for these two houses—and what he did when he went there on his own!*

She could still hear her grandfather's voice saying that name over and over again. And it was beginning to weigh on her mind.

No. It's not the name—

I'm afraid of her, she realized, surprised. *I'm afraid ... and I don't know why!*

The next morning Francesca asked Bill if there was sufficient petrol available for a journey to Essex and then home by way of Somerset.

"If there isn't, I know where to find it," Bill assured her. "If you'll give me an hour or two, Miss. You'd do better to use the carriage."

"The horses shouldn't be rushed. But I can be there and back in a matter of days, if you'll drive me." She didn't tell him she was afraid to leave the house empty and unguarded for longer than that.

Francesca was just carrying her small overnight case out to the motorcar when Leighton was driven up to the door by the doctor.

"Hello, where are you going?" Dr. Nealy called. "Back to London, is it?"

"Only a brief visit. There are things I need. Things I never thought to bring when I expected to be here only a week or two. I had no idea Grandfather—" Francesca broke off, realizing that she was babbling to cover the lies she told.

"Then it's fortuitous that we've come," the doctor responded with his customary high-handed cheerfulness. "I was going to ask you to drive Mr. Leighton here as far as Exeter or Tiverton, where he might find a train to London. If you're willing, it would be a kindness to take him as far as London with you."

Something in Leighton's face told her that the doctor had been equally high-handed with his patient, and that the latter would welcome any excuse to stay where he was.

Her mouth open on the point of refusing, Francesca closed it sharply and nodded. "Why not?"

There was a flash of annoyance in Leighton's eyes at her words.

But better by far to have this man on his way to London than left behind in the Valley in her absence. Meddling. She was never sure how far she dared to trust him.

"That's settled then," Dr. Nealy replied breezily. "Don't tire him, will you? Stop if he requires to rest! I'm not at all convinced he's well enough to be out and about!" And turning to Leighton, the doctor added, "I *do* have your promise that you'll see the Army surgeon straightaway—I'd feel better if he kept an eye on you."

Leighton impatiently agreed, got down from the carriage, and took his place beside Francesca in the rear of the motorcar. The doctor saw them off, and Mrs. Lane, standing in the doorway of the house, waved as if they were lovers on their way to a happy ending.

Leighton said quietly, "I've trespassed on your kindness again."

"You seemed to have made a habit of doing it," Francesca answered lightly. "I'm not actually driving to London. I'm going to Essex."

"Ah. That explains your quandary when the doctor insisted on hanging me about your neck like an albatross. What takes you to Essex?"

"A property in the family. Have you ever been there?"

"A time or two. I had friends near there before the war. Geoffrey had withdrawn from Cambridge and was set on writing a history. Then he met his future wife and that was the end of the history."

They rode down the Valley in silence, and then Leighton said, "This is a sudden decision, I think. On your part. As precious as petrol is, why not go by train?"

She couldn't tell if he was making polite conversation—or probing. "Bill suggested I travel by carriage."

"No, I'm afraid I agree with you about taking the motorcar. You'll be away a week, even so." He paused, and then added, "A constable came to The Spotted Calf this morning. To ask me questions about the shot that was fired in my direction."

"I doubt it was intended to be in your direction. Still. What were his conclusions?"

"That he would make the rounds of the Valley and warn everyone that guns fired indiscriminately were dangerous. He had other matters on his mind, I think, and this business of killing a cow and wounding a man weren't high on his list of urgent affairs. In his opinion that was all the shooter, as he called him, warrants. A good talking-to."

"The Tiverton police have always taken little enough interest in us!"

"I also asked him about your housebreakings."

"Indeed!" She didn't know whether to be pleased or annoyed.

"He told me that there had been no problems in that line for six months or more. He suggested perhaps it was a case of—nerves." Leighton smiled to take away any offense, capturing the Devon accent of the constable as he said, "'Likely she's not accustomed to staying in the house alone after dark. And old dogs dream. If nothing was taken, and no harm done, I'd put it down to a lady's—um—anxiety.'"

"I wish he'd come to speak with me as well—"

"I told you, something else was on his mind. He wasn't interested in your Valley's petty problems."

Beyond Exeter it was a stormy journey. A sweeping misting rain left everything it touched damp. The bad weather continued for the first three days, and the smell of wet wool permeated the motorcar. Although he never asked, when the tenseness around Leighton's mouth warned her he was in pain, she felt obliged to stop on whatever pretext and allow him to stretch the cramped, abused muscles of his back. Sometimes they took shelter in the warmth of a hotel, a tearoom, a pub. When the rain held off, they simply walked up and down a village street until he felt some relief.

Their relationship was stormy as well. Francesca exclaimed in the heat of one argument, "If you want my own opinion—for what it's worth!—your grandfather is the villain of this piece. It's Alasdair MacPherson who has driven you—and driven himself—to the brink of obsession over a family tragedy that might just as well have been no one's fault. I'd like very much to meet him, in fact! One of Simon's military dictates was 'Know your enemy.' "

Leighton smiled crookedly. "I'm not sure my grandfather is aware of your existence. Much less sees you as an adversary."

"If he hates Grandfather this much, you can be sure he would have no love for me!"

"What if I said that I love him as much as you loved your own grandfather? Respect him—trust him. Does that seem strange? Yes, I can see it does. Yet when my father drank to forget what had happened, it was Alasdair who looked after me. I was doubly orphaned for over five years."

And he used the opportunity to indoctrinate you, Francesca thought. *Repeating his lies until you believed them!*

How twisted that was—to take a vulnerable child and shape him to one's own ends, like a smith forging a weapon at the anvil. In her view, only someone bitter and possessed could do such a thing. How it must have galled Alasdair when Thomas Leighton pulled himself together and got on with his life, putting his late wife behind him! Had that simple act of survival been viewed as betrayal? Had it served to reinforce the older man's determination to keep his grandson's memories raw and painful?

"Was he a solicitor, as you are?" Francesca asked one afternoon. "Your grandfather?"

"His family owned factories in Manchester and mines in Lancashire. But he lives in Surrey. South of Guildford. In his day he was a famous cricketer. That's where he met my father—at a match. As far as I know he'd never met Francis Hatton until the wedding, but years before they'd exchanged a heated correspondence in the *Times* on several political questions."

"What sort of questions?" She was intrigued.

As far as she knew, Francis Hatton had never expressed strong opinions on political issues. Any discussions at the dinner table had been tempered, well considered rather than heated.

"My grandfather believed in the dignity of work so that the poor could feed and clothe themselves," Richard Leighton was saying. "Hatton called that exploitation. Alasdair countered that his factories were a model of modern thinking on the subject of child welfare and labor—and had been even before the Berlin Conference on that issue. Hatton all but called him a liar. Alasdair responded that Hatton was a wealthy man dabbling in social matters to assuage his conscience. Hatton replied that bread on the table and clothes on the back hardly amounted to dignity. These were necessities, whereas education gave a man the tools he needed to spring beyond his station in life. Not simply to survive but to grow. Alasdair allowed me to read several of the newspaper cuttings."

"Heated? Vitriolic is more the word."

"Yes, well. It was hardly the best beginning for a wedding party when they came face-to-face."

Francesca smiled. "Hardly."

But she was thinking about the Little Wanderers Foundation. "He did more than dabble, you know. My grandfather. He tried to help where he could."

Still, Francis Hatton was arrogant enough to look down his aristocratic nose at what he must have considered this social upstart, brash new money built on trade, trying to assume the moral high ground about his workers. And MacPherson would have angrily resented the suggestion that land and a long family tree made the gentleman.

So these two men had been adversaries long before Victoria had cluttered up the picture. Had that had any bearing at all on later events?

She said, to shift the subject, "South of Guildford, you say? It's not too far off our route. Isn't that true, Bill? Shall I drop you there?"

"No——" Leighton quickly shook his head, and then said, "I have nothing to tell him. It's what he's waiting for. News. Hope has kept him alive far longer than his doctors expected. His will is remarkable."

"I should think you'd want to be with him now. Especially now."

"I'm afraid to sit by his bed. He knows me far too well. I couldn't lie to him. I wouldn't try."

There was a sadness in his voice that touched her.

As the motorcar neared the turn for Guildford, Francesca insisted that they pause for half an hour, long enough for her to meet Alasdair MacPherson.

And Richard Leighton was equally adamant that it was too great a risk, given the old man's state of health.

The next morning Francesca, still angry at being thwarted over Guildford, broke suddenly into the ensuing verbal battle and said, "Look, if we must share this motorcar, can't we at least carry on a civilized conversation? Otherwise, I shall be forced to put you out here and let you make your own way back to London!"

For she had noticed that Bill, silent, his eyes on the road, shifted uncomfortably during the worst assaults on Francis Hatton's character. He had revered his lifelong employer, and she thought it must be difficult for him to listen without the privilege of saying a single word in her grandfather's defense. It was unfair.

"Dr. Nealy will have something to say about abandoning me," Leighton was answering. "All right, then pick a topic. Religious life in ancient Mesopotamia, for starters. Or how to grow coffee in unsuitable African climates. We'll manage to quarrel about that, too, sooner or later!"

And she laughed in agreement.

But in the back of her mind she kept asking herself why Francis Hatton had refused to clear his own name from the start. If he wasn't guilty, why had he never spoken out? Silence was almost an admission...

What did he know about Victoria that he couldn't tell?

She was back to that single word: suicide.

There was one thing that Francesca hadn't bargained for when she agreed to share the narrow confines of the motorcar with Richard Leighton.

More than any of the cousins, he reminded her of her grandfather.

The boys had inherited the family height, the athleticism that had marked Francis Hatton's own youth, the shape of the jawline, the coloring—physical attributes passed on through their father. But sometimes she could shut her eyes and hear the timbre of her grandfather's voice as Leighton became absorbed in their discussion.

She tried to convince herself that it was a trick of her imagination, but when the anger had been set aside and Leighton appeared to have forgotten who she was—an enemy—she could hear nuances that struck her at once. So like her grandfather when he was well launched on a favorite theme: warmed by enthusiasm, vibrant and enthralling.

And the darkness that drove this man at her side—the fearful intensity of his need to find answers—was all too reminiscent of Francis Hatton's moody introspection as the war moved into early 1915 and Simon was killed.

What answers had her grandfather searched for, without her knowledge? What had driven him into an isolation that shut her out?

Had he somehow been trying to protect her—had he believed that, for her sake, silence was better than confession?

There was something else these two men had in common. Both knew they were dying. Her grandfather had lain in his bed for weeks, his iron will alive until the end, but his body helpless to obey it. He had not found it easy to endure mere existence when he had always been accustomed to shaping his life. Francesca had watched him day and night, and seen the passionate hunger for peace. What she hadn't realized until the end was that peace was beyond him, and what Francis Hatton relished more than life was oblivion.

When Richard Leighton failed to find the answers his grandfather wanted to hear about Victoria Leighton, when his own body had forsaken him, would he take the sleeping draughts he'd refused in hospital and finish what the war had begun?

As she had held the cup of dandelion wine laced with laudanum to her grandfather's lips that dreadful night, he had opened his eyes, smiled at her, and drunk it down with such relief that she had wept with his head in her lap, overwhelmed by grief. The guilt had been hers—it still was. But that haunted desire for an end of suffering had been his. How could she have pretended not to see it?

It would never do to let any memory of Francis Hatton color her feelings toward Richard Leighton. The latter was dangerous. She had told the rector, Stevens, as much. It would never do to let sympathy for the man blind her to the truth—

that he would ruthlessly sacrifice her family if he could find his dead mother.

A truce there could be, to see them to London. But even the simplest friendship was out of reach.

In the small hotels where they lodged each night, they dined together and then sat by the firelight of the lounge, sometimes not talking at all but listening to the soldiers on leave. Accustomed to a houseful of men, she felt at ease there.

Francesca vowed not to let the companionable silences lull her into confidences—or even worse, trick her into trust. The unresolved grief for her cousins and her grandfather was a raw wound—and loneliness had become a hurting that wouldn't go away.

I could like this man, if I'd met him in different circumstances—if I were not a Hatton or he were not a Leighton.

But it didn't matter—even if she fell head over heels for Richard Leighton, there was nothing she could tell him about his mother's fate.

It's a quarrel we had no part of, but we're caught up in it as surely as if we had been there, shaping the events. It's as if Victoria Leighton is alive and vindictively bent on destroying all of us....

Or worse still, was she dead, leaving a curse as her legacy, like a living presence?

What would she say if she could know that her own son had been dragged into its vortex, too?

Late the third day, they found the road to London clogged with military vehicles, troops, and lumbering wagons of fodder, shells, and weapons, their lumpy canvas coverings roughly defining what lay beneath as the rain weighed them down. The roads to and from the Channel ports as well as the southern ports, one weary officer informed them, were hopeless, mired in mud.

"Fighting at the Front has been heavy. Everything's in short supply," he said. "And the trains are packed."

Frustrated, Francesca said to Leighton when the officer had gone back to unsnarl a tangle of harness and horse from an overturned wagon, "We shan't get anywhere near the city. Not tonight, not tomorrow."

"We could turn north and make better time," Bill recommended. "While you were speaking with the officer, a supply sergeant told me the north roads were clear enough. But that won't help Mr. Leighton here reach London."

"I can stay with my friends outside Cambridge. And it's on your way."

"All right, then."

Assessing the tiredness in Leighton's face, she wondered if he was in need of more care than even Dr. Nealy had judged. On the other hand, she didn't think he was in any mood to return to his father's house and his half sister's nursing. There was a restlessness in him now, as if he sensed time growing shorter, and he didn't want to die before his quest was finished.

It *was* a quest, this search. She knew that even when he was at his most charming. Yet somehow it was changing, going far beyond his grandfather's obsessive insistence on vengeance, perhaps beyond Leighton's own need to prove that his mother hadn't callously abandoned a small boy. It was becoming something that kept the pain at bay, that made the struggle to go on living worth the effort. The darkness that she had seen in him when he first came to River's End was still there, but now it had a different quality—as if he was clinging to it with a fierce tenacity to shut out another approaching darkness.

She had come to know, too, that he wasn't a man to ask for quarter, however much he might be in need of it. Like Simon. Or Harry. Even her grandfather. It was a trait she could unequivocally admire.

But blood was still thicker than water. Or anything else she might feel.

CHAPTER 15

They ran into a Zeppelin raid just north of London. The rain had returned, a thin veil that fell from a dark smudge of a sky. The great airship was invisible coming across the tops of the heavy clouds, the deep *whump-whump-whump* of its engines marking its relentless progress. Bill switched off his headlamps and pulled the motorcar off the main road into a churchyard shadowed by yews.

It was coming closer—the rumble of the engines louder—

"I think it's dropping down," Francesca warned over the noise. "They sometimes do, when there's no visibility! Looking for a landmark, something to guide— We ought to find cover, *now!*"

They scrambled out of the motorcar and crouched in the rain in the shelter of the stone tombs, anxiously scanning the sky.

Leighton called out, "Bombs—!" and threw his arm across Francesca, pushing her to the ground before she could hear them fall.

The night was suddenly orange and gold and blue, unbearably bright. The force of the blasts stunned them, hurting her ears. The hail of falling masonry and roof tiles and chimney bricks scything through the streets was terrifying, and flames leapt high, feeding on the gas mains. Something came rattling down from the church tower and fell with a crash only feet away from them. People everywhere were screaming, running out of houses, calling to one another. The stench of burning filled the night wind, making Francesca nauseous.

Bill was swearing, sailor's oaths, learned in his Cornish youth.

Francesca, her nose in the wet grass, realized she was crying, her hands pounding the earth beside her. Leighton shifted, drawing his arm back from her body.

People were still running through the streets, coming out of houses, staring in fright up at the sky, mouths opened, faces blanched in the queer light. Children wailed and somewhere Francesca heard a man shouting obscenities at the invisible airship as the fires boiled up.

And then in a single moment the brilliant light caught the Zeppelin's sleek gray hull, sliding obscenely through the clouds.

Bill was saying roughly, "You've no business going back to London with those things about, Miss Francesca! They're the devil's work. You ought to stay well out of it!"

But she was already on her feet, her training overcoming the first shock. "We must help—"

The bombing had stopped. The ship was gone.

Bill had the motorcar in gear, and they were quickly in the thick of the damage. The fires had turned the bottoms of the clouds an angry, flickering red, the smoke rolling upward, seeking escape.

On the other side of the square, two streets had taken the brunt of the attack. Hardly a building on either side was still standing, rubble flung about with the force to kill, making it impossible to tell what was roadway and what was not. Impossible to take the motorcar any closer.

Dust was rising in virulent clouds, and the fires were still producing volumes of heavy smoke.

People were already frantically digging out victims with their bare hands and whatever tools they could find, mostly splintered boards and lengths of railings. Coughing in the unspeakable air, Francesca threw herself into the line, frantically heaving aside the hot rubble, scorching her face, burning her gloves. They found two children, scratched and bruised but otherwise unharmed. Francesca wrapped them in the blankets someone passed to her, soothing them and holding them close.

Beside her a constable and another man were pulling another victim out of a ruined stairwell, lifting a table off her legs. The woman's face was a mask of blood and plaster dust, her body limp. The constable shouted and someone, a doctor, came leaping across the debris to bend over her and lay a hand on her throat. He began to give swift orders, pointing toward a section of the road that was clear and already becoming a makeshift surgery. The woman was alive.

Francesca hugged the children tight and told them.

Leighton, heedless of his own injuries, was suddenly beside her. He pulled out a whimpering dog, who crawled to the children and began to lick their faces, his tail wagging with joy. Singed but unhurt, she thought, except for a cut near his shaggy ear. She led the children out of the way of the rescuers and took them along with the dog to a group of other children, handing them over to a badly shaken gray-haired woman who gathered the newcomers warmly into her brood. Francesca touched her shoulder and then returned to the digging.

It was two hours or more before all the victims, alive and dead, had been accounted for. Townspeople, coats and shirts and trousers thrown on over their nightclothes, were already passing out tea to the workers and making the wounded comfortable. Someone had laid out the dead under sheets. The white line of bodies seemed somehow pathetic in the destruction all around them. A priest moved among them, touching each and briefly praying. The damage was shocking. Francesca saw an elderly woman wandering about in a daze, trying to find her own front door. Someone came to lead her away, and she began to sob.

Francesca, weary to the bone, stood by the motorcar, drinking hot tea and speaking with the doctor. Leighton looked ghastly as he came toward them, and the doctor gave him a searching glance.

"Old wound," Leighton said tersely, and the doctor let it go. He was too tired to do more.

Leighton moved to stand next to Francesca and without fanfare put an arm across her shoulders, as if they had just come through a hard-fought battle. A comradely gesture that was intended to comfort both of them. She leaned against him for a moment, grateful. Peter would have done the same, she told herself. But Peter was dead, like the rest of her cousins. She ached for human warmth to fill the void.

"Where are you heading?" the doctor asked Francesca. "Not too far, I hope! You're not up to it."

"To Essex," Leighton answered for her. "Any chance of a place to stay here?"

" 'Fraid not. Any spare rooms will be needed for those poor devils." He gestured with his teacup to the survivors, still milling in the street, as if lost. "And there weren't that many extra to start with. Sorry, you've earned a bed—"

Francesca thanked him and opened the motorcar's door. "I'll drive," she said, thinking of Bill's age. But the old man shook his head and got behind the wheel. It was an hour or more before they found rooms in a small inn where it was possible, nearly, to pretend the war didn't exist. But for their bloody clothes and streaks of dust and ashes across their faces and smearing their hands. The owner went down to the kitchen and made thick sandwiches. Famished and weary, they sat there with him, telling him about the raid in exchange for his hospitality.

At the top of the stairs, as they were about to go their separate ways, Leighton paused, then took Francesca's hand. He said nothing, as if waiting for her reaction. She stood there, startled and unable to think what to do, trying to read his eyes. Remembering the warmth earlier of his arm across her shoulders, she realized she wanted to be held. Even if he still hated her tomorrow. It would wipe away the images of death and despair. Was that what he wanted as well? But when she didn't respond, he let her hand go.

She felt utterly bereft.

"Good night," he said brusquely. And walked on down the dark passage to his room.

She waited, hoping he might look back. But even as she did she realized that it was something a woman might do. Not a man...She listened as his door opened and then closed before turning to her own room.

The next morning, as the sun was struggling to pierce the clouds, they found the house of Leighton's friends locked tight, the shades drawn. No one answered his knocks.

But a neighbor, opening her door to peer out at them, said with some relief, "Oh, it's just you, Mr. Leighton! They've gone away to Wales, you know. An aunt isn't well, and they were summoned."

"Did they tell you when to expect them back again?" he asked, taking off his hat and turning to smile at her.

"They couldn't know that, could they? I'd be happy to let you in, but they didn't leave me the key! The little dog went with them. I expect it will be a while yet." She looked back at the motorcar standing before the cottage gate. "Did you drive all the way from London? What a pity! They say there was a terrible raid at Marbrook last evening. People killed. I hope it wasn't too bad, coming through today!"

Leighton thanked her, and turned away.

Something in his face—was it satisfaction?—made Francesca wonder if he had counted on this man Geoffrey and his wife being away. Had he already been told that they were summoned to Wales—?

She sat there watching him stride back to the motorcar. He

was saying to Bill as he stepped in, "You can drop me at the nearest station. There will be trains back to London."

"We haven't the petrol to turn back," Francesca said. "As you well know. There may be a railway station later on. Even if you must change in Cambridge."

"It doesn't matter."

She was sure now it didn't . . . Suspicions began to rise and simmer. Once he learned she was going to Essex, he'd never had any intention of stopping in London! He believed she would lead him to—what? How could she have been so *blind*?

They found Mercer half an hour later, and asked directions at a smithy on the outskirts of town. Bill turned the bonnet of the motorcar east, and near a bend in the road a mile on they saw the drive marked "Willows."

Whatever Francesca had been expecting, it wasn't the house that came into view. Built of old rose-colored brick, it was set among broad lawns that ran down in the back to a winding stream bordered by a wood. A solitary bench had been placed where the sun would rise directly over the stream and through a break in the trees, etching the water and the east front with golden fingers.

It spoke of something that touched Francesca on the raw. Of love and protection. Of permanence.

Who had sat there, side by side, watching the morning come awake?

And what had lain between them?

She walked about the grounds, looking up at her grandfather's house from different angles, noting the trim gardens that ran up to the south terrace, the smooth lawns that spread like a carpet around the eastern approach, feeling the warmth and beauty that surrounded the property, the grace of the architecture, the sense of welcome that seemed to reach out from the dark wooden door with its elegant brass knocker in the shape of a pineapple. On either side of it stood urns that held small topiaried trees, and a flight of graduated steps curving down to meet the drive.

So different from the Valley! With the wide, bright sky of Essex arching over the land, embracing the trees of the park, clouds banking high in Constable fashion, and the late sun gilding the glass of the west windows, it was—

"Why did you never tell me?" she asked her grandfather under her breath. *"It's—I would have loved to visit this house..."*

But something had drawn Francis Hatton here. Something—or someone—had persuaded him to keep this house a secret even from his own family.

Tragedy? Happiness? Bitterness?

Leighton was speaking to her, but Francesca ignored him, the hurt she felt going too deep to listen.

Bill was standing by the motorcar, staring at the house with no expression on his face.

Francesca went to him and asked, "Did you bring my grandfather here? Did you know about this place? Please, tell me!"

"I never came here. Nor heard of it from him." He turned to look at her, something in his eyes. "I don't know why, but it reminds me of my sister Bethie. Somehow."

"Your sister?" Francesca hadn't been aware that he had a sister. "Did she live here?"

"Lord, no, Miss! She died at eighteen." He was silent, then said, "There's too much sky here. I don't think I like that." The countryman in him spoke as he added, "But then, it's not River's End, is it? Nor like Cornwall, neither. Although at a guess, I'd say the soil is rich enough, and not stony ground."

She walked up the steps and lifted the brass knocker. There was no immediate answer. Yet someone had kept up the gardens and the lawns. Someone had maintained the drive and prevented the shrubs from encroaching, someone had polished the window panes and ironed the linen drapes hanging in the room she could see to her left. The roof and the brick, the outbuildings and the stables were in good repair, unlike those in the Valley. Here there was help, and someone who worked hard to maintain every blade of grass.

Leighton said dryly, "Have they, too, gone to Wales to visit a dying aunt?"

Before she could answer, a coverall-clad man appeared around the side of the house. Middle-aged, he was limping from what appeared to be a clubfoot. He said roughly, "It's Mrs. Perkins's day off. She's the housekeeper."

"Who are you?"

The dark face grinned. "I'm Mr. Perkins, when I've left my Wellingtons outside and scrubbed the earth from under my nails. Out here, I'm called Ben. Who may you be?"

"I'm Francis Hatton's granddaughter. I've come to see the house."

He studied her for a moment, not with insolence but curiosity. "I was wondering when you'd come. I said you would. Mrs. Perkins has gone into Cambridge to spend the day with her sister. There's no one to take you through the house." The words were colder, as if she threatened a very comfortable life, intruding like this. "And I can't let you in myself, can I, because I haven't a key. There's a room in the stables I use when the housekeeper's not here."

"What's the size of the property? Can you tell me that?"

He shrugged and answered reluctantly, "The house and the land around it. Three good-sized farms. A dairy. Not large, but prosperous enough."

"I'll come again tomorrow," Francesca told him, turning on her heel. "You may send word to Mrs. Perkins to expect me!"

In the event, she wasn't sure she really wanted to return to Willows.

The house and the land had been restored with such loving care that she was jealous of it. As if in making Willows beautiful, her grandfather had shut her out of something so powerful in his life that no one, not even his granddaughter, was allowed to share in it. But where was the need? Francesca would have taken an oath that so much beauty had to do with a woman. Why couldn't her grandfather have said so? Was it because the woman he'd imagined walking the passages, touching the flowers in the gardens, sharing that bench by the stream with him was already wed—to someone else?

I wish I could have come here free of ghosts—my own and Richard Leighton's. Why couldn't I have walked through that door and rejoiced for Grandfather's happiness? Instead she had been shown only shadows of something she could feel and not understand. She felt somehow betrayed.

Taking rooms at the tiny hotel on the High Street in Mercer, Francesca discovered that Mrs. Perkins had another sister, this one the innkeeper's garrulous wife. The establishment was small, nearly empty, and Mrs. Kenneth was happy to spend the dinner hour chatting with her only guests. Rumor must have already told her that someone had been asking about Willows, and she was no doubt as curious about Francesca's party as Francesca was about the house.

Francesca asked Mrs. Kenneth if she knew how long the estate had been in Mr. Hatton's possession.

"Not quite a quarter of a century, I'd say. My father always told me it was the best thing could happen to it, that house. The previous owner, a Mr. Walsham that was, being a man who cared for naught but money and London, let it go something terrible. It was in a grievous state, according to my father, before Mr. Hatton took a liking to it. But you'd never guess that now, would you?"

"I understood there was something about a gambling debt of the previous owner's?"

"As to that, I'd have no idea, Miss. My father never said. I don't think he cared much for the Walsham family, father or son. And I wouldn't put gambling past either of them—they were always up to no good! Two-faced and sly!"

Having seen Willows, Francesca thought it was no small wonder that the Walshams were eager to reclaim it. How much money had her grandfather lavished on the estate, over the years? And why—if he never lived there?

Francesca, remembering the gardens at River's End, observed, "My grandfather was fortunate to find people like your sister and her husband."

"My aunt was the housekeeper then," Mrs. Kenneth replied affably. "And now my sister. There's those of us who say Ben married her for Willows—he was that taken with it. And he works hard, there's no mistaking it. Mr. Hatton could drive up to the door any day he chose, and the house was always ready to receive him. My sister kept everything neat as a pin, but if he sent word ahead, we'd turn out the cupboards, beat the carpets, change the beds, order in food—it was a whirlwind, I can tell you. But she's that particular."

"Did Mr. Hatton sometimes bring guests with him?" Francesca asked.

"Not as a rule. He'd come alone and stay for a few days, then be gone. But there *was* a lady one spring, 1895 or thereabouts. Oh, I must have been no more than fifteen at the time! Mr. Hatton hadn't sent word he was bringing her. My aunt was that surprised when she stepped out of the carriage. She'd been crying, and pulled her veil over her face to hide the tears. They stayed nearly a week, mostly sitting on that bench down by the stream when the weather was fair, or by the fire in the sitting room. Mr. Hatton introduced her to the staff, but somehow my sister didn't think it was her real name."

Francesca was silent, digesting what she'd been told.

Leighton asked, "Where did they go when they left?"

"Back to London. She told him one morning she wanted to go to London. She seemed a bit happier that day. As if making up her mind had been hard, and now it was done, she could be comfortable again."

"Are you sure of the year?" Francesca asked.

"I remember it well, because it wasn't more than a month later that Mr. Hatton's daughter-in-law was found murdered in her bed, along with her husband. A tragedy, the newspapers called it. And the police never to my knowledge discovered who had done such a terrible thing!"

THE COUSINS

Harry ... the charmer

I've heard people say I've lived a charmed life. It's
most likely true. I've been happier than most. But
there's a dark side to that, shadows that spread
across the face of the sun sometimes and leave their
stain.

As if I'd be called to pay one day for the luck that
had come my way.

I never knew my parents. I was barely toddling
when they died, and so there was no empty place
where they'd been. Not even a faint echo of a voice,
soft silks against my cheek, a special scent. Just—a
blank—that was more than filled by the family I did
have. My brothers, my grandfather. Cesca. I never
pined—I don't suppose any of us did. Neither my
grandfather nor the servants ever spoke of my
parents, or Francesca's, come to that. Later I was to
wonder if my mother or my father would have
wished us to know about their childhoods—how

they had come to meet—how they might have planned for our futures. But it had never been a pressing question, and so it was never asked. I accepted life as it was, with a smile, because unpleasantness had never touched it. I even escaped the measles that sent my brothers to bed for ten days.

It was our grandfather who brought us up. We were urged to make the most of everything that came our way. I thought sometimes that Grandfather wasn't as pleased with Simon's war games as he might have been, though the Hattons have a long history of battle honors over the generations. But Grandfather tolerated them, and encouraged us as well to study our lessons and look at the world as a place where we could take any path we chose.

Simon yearned toward the Army, and Peter read everything he could lay hands on about the Suez Canal, Hadrian's Wall, the pyramids, the railroads across the American West—he was afraid sometimes that there would be nothing left to build by the time he was a man. Freddy would have been happy enough composing for the piano and playing his own works. Robin was drawn to the land, and although not the eldest, he would have run River's End with the care and love that any good estate deserved. But he wasn't the eldest, and so—ever practical—he had decided to become an explorer.

I was the only one who was never certain just what it was I wanted to do with my life. I sometimes had the feeling that it didn't matter, that I'd not live to any great age. As if the legacy from my parents was a brief life, never intended to bloom and grow.

Those were the dark shadows behind my happiness.

Grandfather listened when I told him I had no great expectation of living to his age. I was all of twelve at the time. He assured me quite sternly that illness had killed my parents, not a curse . . . although that word hadn't really crossed my mind. But it had crossed his, I could see that.

Still, I'd never known him to lie to us.

When I stopped and thought about it, his own life had been filled with loss. His wife, Sarah, my grandmother, had died young. As had both his sons. He had been lucky to have grandchildren to carry on the family line. The six of us, my brothers and my cousin, would more than make up for his griefs, I hoped.

It buoyed me, that thought, for a very long time. It gave me a sense of purpose in my life, as if in some small measure we could repay all Francis Hatton's care and love.

But the war came, and then Simon was killed. As if as soon as we left the sanctuary of the Valley some jealous god had remembered us and pointed us in other directions from those we'd expected to take. A silly notion for a grown man to harbor!

And then Freddy was killed. And Robin. I never served with them; I wasn't there when they died. Although rumor claimed Freddy had been cut down crossing No Man's Land, Robin had been gassed, and Simon was caught in an artillery barrage, I knew it was leaving the Valley that had killed them.

Peter and I were the only ones left.

Then Peter died with his sappers when the tunnel came down on top of him.

And I was the last one standing.

I was glad that Francesca was a girl and safe. She'd never witness the horrors I'd seen. She wouldn't watch men die and know that the next

shot might find me or the man next to me—or the
third down the line. *My* men, and I couldn't save
them.

I shut my mind to dying, and did what I'd
been sent to France to do—defend my country
and protect as well as I could the men fighting
under me.

Then 1916 broke to find me still alive, and six
months into the year I was wounded—and
survived. A long, nasty crease across my ribs that
cracked three of them. They patched me up, joking
about the luck of some men, forced to lie in the
comfort of hospital with pretty nursing sisters at my
beck and call. Lucky Harry...

Then word filtered down that there was a
big push coming. I knew long before my orders
were cut that most of us in hospital would be
hurriedly pronounced healed and sent back to our
units.

I left on the first of July with a dark sense of
doom. I was certain I would die, but not of the
place or time of dying.

It was as if the curse that had cut down my
brothers had got around to me at last.

I wrote to Grandfather, telling him that I was
filled with dread—and then tore up the page.
Instead I wrote a letter thanking him for his
guidance over the years, his strong faith that had
become ours, his courage in the face of the blows in
his own life, and promised that I, the last of the
Hattons in France, would stand bravely and come
through the looming battle covered with honor and
glory, more than enough to share with my fallen
brothers....

I carried that letter with me on the first day of
the Battle of the Somme—and on the second day,
had it sent behind the lines to be posted.

By that time I knew that there was no hope. And all that was left to me was to show no fear and to give those around me all of my own experience to bring them safely through without me....

And wait for the curse.

CHAPTER 16

"What I can't understand," Francesca was saying the next morning after they had settled their account with Mrs. Kenneth and were following their luggage out to the motor-car, "is why *you* would wish to go back to Willows. You heard what Mrs. Kenneth told us. The woman who arrived there was in some distress, yes, but free to come and go about the house—free to choose to return to London. Hardly a terrified, weeping prisoner! I don't see Mrs. Perkins putting up with *that*, if she's anything like her sister. She'd have had the constable in!"

"It's true, I grant you. But whether the woman was a prisoner or not, I want to find out who she was!" Leighton had been tense all morning, short and taciturn.

Was he afraid that he'd stumbled on a truth he wasn't prepared to hear?

"You're intent on making every bit of information you find into a case for your own obsession, aren't you!"

"The timing is *right*."

Francesca shook her head, but there was nothing she could say that would change his mind.

She herself didn't want to go back to Willows. She had always been so sure that River's End had been the center of her grandfather's life. That his grandchildren were his joy. It hurt to think that the Valley had only clung to the fringes of his real world. How many of the visits to Willows had been disguised as journeys to London? And above all, she couldn't bear to think that it was Victoria Leighton who had lured him there from his family!

But in the event, the journey back to Willows was unsatisfying for both Leighton and Francesca.

When Francesca asked to see the housekeeper, Ben Perkins informed them that he'd sent no message to his wife. "She isn't here. Make of that what you will."

"Willows is my property now, if you remember. I have the power to have you removed from your position," Francesca told him, angry with everyone.

"It won't do me any harm," he answered. "A man like me can find work anywhere these days. But the house will suffer. You'll find no one to care for it as we did. No one you can trust."

Leighton broke in. "Do you remember Francis Hatton coming here with a woman? They stayed a week. It was the only time he brought anyone to Willows."

Ben stared from one to the other of them, arrogance in his manner. "Oh, yes, I remember her. Everyone knew about her in the village. My wife tried to put a proper face on it, saying she was his son's wife. But she warn't. I saw her eyes, they looked me over for all I had this foot. He'd brought his whore, you see, to tell her there was an end to the affair."

Leighton snarled, "Watch your tongue!"

The caretaker considered the taller man in front of him and added in a less aggressive, almost whining voice, "I heard her *say* if he deserted her she'd kill herself. I expect that's exactly what she did. Go ahead to Cambridge and ask my wife, if you don't believe me! I'll give you her direction, if you like."

"What was her coloring? I don't suppose you'd remember that?" Francesca asked.

"Fair. Like him," Perkins said, jerking his chin toward Leighton. "Slim. Tall for a woman."

They found Mrs. Perkins in a cottage on the eastern edge of Cambridge, in a quiet street where the houses were a generation older than most in the city but kept well enough until the war. The white fences around front gardens were in need of paint, and the trim was flaking. A huge plane tree, white and moss green, stood by the street, angular limbs spread out in a canopy. Dead leaves clustered around the gate and carpeted the flagstone walk.

Mrs. Perkins's other sister was a widow and the two women had just come in from doing their marketing. It was hard to tell them apart, and Francesca thought perhaps they were twins.

Something in Francesca's face struck Mrs. Perkins as introductions were made, and she said, with anxiety, "My Ben was rude, wasn't he? It's the foot, you see—I am so sorry I wasn't there to greet you properly, Miss Hatton, and show you round the house. It's what you came for, isn't it? I can't think what Ben was about, not to send for me at once! I'll just ask Lydia to put the teakettle on . . ."

"There isn't time, Mrs. Perkins," Francesca said. "And besides, we've only come to ask about a visitor that my grandfather brought to Willows, years ago."

"Did Ben tell you about her? He's got it all wrong, Miss Hatton, if he said unkind things about her! She was a quiet lady, and in trouble. I could tell—there were shadows under her eyes, and I heard her weep a time or two when there was no one to hear. Mrs. Merrill was her name. Mr. Hatton was good to her."

"How—kind?"

But Mrs. Perkins was still anxious about the impression

her husband had made, and it took some patience to turn the subject back to Francis Hatton's guest.

"He was always kind, Miss. Toward everyone. And I heard him say once that what her husband had done was unforgivable. That he ought to be taken out and horsewhipped! But Mrs. Merrill said he'd been good to her, too."

"Was Mrs. Merrill her true name, do you think?" Leighton asked, breaking a grim silence.

"I don't know, sir. But there were times I'd speak to her, and the poor thing wouldn't answer at first. As if her mind was far away and she didn't hear me use the name. It did make me wonder. Whatever was upsetting her, Mr. Hatton couldn't find a way out of her dilemma, and in the end they left."

"If you saw a photograph of this woman—after all these years, would you remember her face?" Francesca asked.

Mrs. Perkins shook her head. "I'd doubt that I could. After all this time. But Ben might remember. He's good with faces. You aren't thinking of selling up the house, Miss Hatton? Or letting us go because of Ben? He's a hard worker, I promise you, in spite of his rough ways!"

Francesca sat looking out the window as they drove away from the house. She was thinking about Ben Perkins. She hadn't liked him. He was arrogant—rude—deliberately insulting. *Had* he seen something in the behavior of the houseguest that Mrs. Perkins had been blind to? He had relished insinuating that the woman had been attracted to him.

On the other hand—depending on who the woman really was—it could have been true.

How had Mrs. Perkins put it? *Mr. Hatton couldn't find a way out of her dilemma, and in the end they left.*

Her dilemma. What had it been? The fact that she'd left her husband and couldn't go home again?

She thought, *That's assuming it was Victoria!* If the houseguest was Margaret Hatton, she might well have sent for her father-in-law, most especially if her problem had concerned her husband's behavior. And he would have come. It was even likely that he'd have brought her here, where she could work out her dilemma in privacy. The house was quiet, secluded.

Leighton was saying with satisfaction, as he glanced at his pocket watch, "It wasn't Victoria after all. For one thing, she wouldn't have flirted with a caretaker. And she certainly hadn't been mistreated by my father. It was a wild-goose chase, coming here."

"Well, you needn't have," Francesca retorted, pettishly.

And then it struck her.

Simon's second name was Merrill—*how could she have overlooked that?*

Because she'd been too busy expecting to find the body of Victoria Leighton!

And that was foolishness. No one could have successfully buried a murder victim under the willful, inquisitive, malicious eye of a man like Ben Perkins! He would have leapt at the opportunity to blackmail Francis Hatton! He would have bled him dry of every penny he possessed!

But something there was, here.

Francesca struggled to bring the pieces of the puzzle together. If Willows had been made into a shrine—then to whom? Certainly not to her uncle Tristan's wife, Francis Hatton's own daughter-in-law! Perhaps there was a logical explanation. Perhaps Margaret Hatton, in distress and needing a sanctuary for a few days, *had* come here, using her maiden name to stave off gossip. And Francis Hatton had seen no conflict in that.

The true mistress of Willows might never have come here at all. Because she couldn't. Because she was dead.

And that turned full circle back to Victoria Leighton.

CHAPTER 17

In a desperate attempt to rid herself of her own demons, Francesca turned to Leighton and said, "I want to meet your grandfather. I want to hear what he has to say—why he's been my grandfather's enemy for so many years. I think he's hiding something about your mother's disappearance. I think there's something that was never talked about, something that you were never told! And I believe it's time to hear the real truth about this affair!"

"Are you mad? I told you. He's dying. He won't see you, and trying will only serve to upset him."

"It's convenient, isn't it, that he's dying! It spares him from visits by anyone he doesn't want to see."

"He's a lonely man, sitting in his room, living with his memories. I had wanted to bring him a measure of peace, enough peace at least to quietly die. This isn't the way to do it!"

"Tell me about him. Is he tall and fair—like you?"

"He was. His shoulders are a little stooped. His hair is still thick, and remarkably fair for his age. And his eyes are so blue they seem to see straight through you. It wouldn't do any good to lie to him. He would know before the words were out of your mouth."

"Why should I lie to him! Perhaps a dose of truth would rid him of this mad obsession—"

"He's not a madman. He was one of the finest cricket players in the south of England. He was an angler, with endless patience. There was more to his life than anger. Even if it was the anger that I saw most often—"

"Exactly my point! And there's something you haven't considered—"

He waited, silent.

Francesca said, "Whatever you may think, you saw a child's version of events. It's possible that your father could never tell you the whole truth. He may not even have told your grandfather. Don't you see? You both were the innocent victims of whatever it was that had happened—and for that reason alone, he'd have fought to protect you! Even lied to your grandfather for his own sake— Better to leave you in the dark than to destroy something precious."

"Damn it," he answered coldly. "I was eight years old—"

But what did that have to say to anything, Francesca wondered. She had been twenty-three when Francis Hatton died, and she was only now discovering all the things he had never wanted her to know.

Luncheon in a small town just north of London was an ordeal. Leighton was still silent and moody. As he shoved aside his plate, he looked up at Francesca and said, "Very well. I'll take you to visit my grandfather."

It was such a surprise that for a moment she was speechless, the last bite of food on her fork forgotten. Why had he changed his mind?

Or was it what he had planned from the start?

Had he simply waited to take her to Guildford until she

was convinced that it was her decision to visit Alasdair MacPherson? She would never wittingly let herself be lured into such a trap.

It would have been a very clever move . . .

And now she was committed.

He can't do anything to me, Alasdair MacPherson. No matter how much he hates the Hattons.

Can he?

Another shower of rain peppered the windscreen as they turned toward Guildford.

"Why will you never show anyone your mother's photograph?" Francesca asked.

Leighton answered, "It's all I have left of my mother. That and a book she read to me in the evenings. My father allowed me to keep both of them. Everything else he destroyed one night in a drunken rage. I don't care to hear what you read in her face. I don't want to look at her likeness for the rest of my life with a thousand people at my shoulder, staring, inquisitive, insensitive. Why should I take any pleasure in that?"

"Even," Francesca persisted stubbornly, "if it helped you find her?"

But he had no answer to that.

CHAPTER 18

It was late in the afternoon when the motorcar pulled up the steep hill that led to the gates of Alasdair MacPherson's house.

It was neither grander nor larger than River's End, but there was a pretentiousness here that mocked the severe style of the house in Devon.

As if Alasdair MacPherson, unlike Francis Hatton, felt free to flaunt his social position, his wealth, and his place in the world at large.

Ornate. That was the word, Francesca thought, looking at the imposing gatehouse, so unlike the Wigginses' simple cottage, and again at the almost Gothic portico over the drive, where visitors could arrive and descend in any weather. The stone was creamy, as if it had come from Dorset, and the lawns were smooth.

Richard Leighton studied it with warmth in his eyes, and then he glanced at her as if to see how she had responded to his family's home.

I'd rather live at River's End than here....

And then another thought followed. *Alasdair MacPherson is as alone in this great house as I am in River's End.*

We have that loneliness in common.

An elderly man greeted them at the door. "Welcome home, sir!" His eyes lingered on the bruised wound on Leighton's forehead, but he was too well trained to comment.

"Hallo, Carter," Leighton replied. "How is my grandfather today?"

"Not well, sir. A little agitated. He's been waiting to hear from you."

"Yes. Well. There's been no news to send him." He led Francesca into a drawing room done up in cream and a soft spring green. "Wait here. I'll go and speak with him. Carter, see if you can find some tea for my guest."

And then he was gone, up the curving staircase in the hall, disappearing down the passage at the top.

It was all of fifteen minutes before Leighton returned. Francesca had barely touched her tea.

"He won't see you. I'm sorry. And I dared not press."

That was unexpected. "Did he tell you why?"

"It—isn't one of his good days. He's in bed."

Disappointed, she said, "And it wouldn't do to go up to him, would it?"

"No. He enjoys his helplessness as little as your grandfather must have done."

Rising from her chair, she gathered her coat and her gloves and followed Richard Leighton out into the hall. Carter was waiting to see them out, and Leighton stopped to say something to him.

Francesca turned to look up the staircase, as if it called to her somehow.

And then she saw why. At the first landing, nearly out of sight in the shadows, stood a man. She could just pick out the white of his shirt under the smoking jacket he was wearing, and the gleam of his fair hair.

In bed Alasdair MacPherson was not. Whatever he'd told his grandson to say.

Francesca stood there, riveted.

And from the top of the stairs, such a wave of hostility seemed to wash over her that she took a step backward. It was as if she were the living embodiment of Francis Hatton, and the man looking down at her was damning her for all time.

She was a Hatton, and not to be intimidated. She returned his stare measure for measure, her chin high. And it was Francesca who broke off contact first, turning her back on Alasdair MacPherson and walking out of his house as if he had been a rude host and she wanted no part of him or his.

Richard Leighton hadn't seen the exchange, and she said nothing to him as he handed her into the motorcar.

But she felt herself shiver, even in the warmth of the sun. *I saw his eyes,* she told herself, even though she knew it was impossible. *I saw them, and they were as cold as death....*

Proof, if any was needed, that MacPherson was convinced beyond any possible doubt that Francis Hatton was a murderer.

"Where to now, Miss Francesca?" Bill was asking her.

She wished she could tell him to drive directly to Devon.

But there was one more thing left to do.

CHAPTER 19

The house in Somerset was set back in broad lawns at the end of the town of Falworthy. The whitewashed and handsomely thatched cottages ran out at a copse of trees, and just beyond that stood tall stone gateposts capped with swans. The rain had stopped and the air glistened with moisture, adding a soft golden glow to the sunlight.

Bill gestured with a gloved hand. "That should be it, Miss. The Swans. Just where the postmistress said."

Leighton got out to open the gates, and caught his breath as he turned back to step into the car. He motioned Bill to pass through, but when Francesca turned, she could see that he was holding on to the gate with one hand as if in need of support, his face tight under the brim of his hat.

Aware of her scrutiny, he said only, "I'll walk to the house."

She agreed, needing this private moment to prepare herself.

The drive was not long, and two large beeches graced the sweep that ended before the steps.

She could see now what the solicitor, Branscombe, had told her earlier. The Swans had once been a sizable manor, but was hardly more than a comfortable dower house by the time her grandfather had bought it. He'd added graceful wings with an eye to doubling the space as well as making the building better proportioned. Behind the house, there rose an old tithe barn, which had also been restored, next to a stone stable that must hold half a dozen horses. Not as pretty as the house in Essex, with nothing of the air of lovers about it. Still, a very attractive estate and fairly prosperous.

Who lived here, then? And what did the occupants have to do with the Little Wanderers Foundation?

She had walked around the side lawns and then back to the main door before Leighton had caught up with her. His face, still strained, was grim.

In answer to her knock a young girl with her hair pulled back by a green ribbon opened the door and said in pleasing accents, "I'm sorry. There's been a small accident, and Mrs. Gibbon has gone to see to it. If you will come in and wait in the drawing room, she'll be with you shortly."

Francesca thanked her and followed her into what was called the drawing room but was actually a comfortable room with chintz covers on the chairs, polished tables, and landscape paintings on the walls. It spoke of family warmth and contentment.

Leighton said, as soon as the girl had gone, "This house, at least, is inhabited."

"Yes . . . I wonder who the girl may be. My solicitor told me there had been no rent paid on the property. And yet a family lives here." In the distance they could hear other children's voices, singing together.

A woman swept in, dressed in gray that matched her hair, blue eyes tranquil behind a pince-nez on a gold chain hanging to her ample bosom.

"I'm so sorry to keep you waiting! One of the children had cut himself in the barn and I was called to attend. I'm Mrs. Gibbon. How may I help you?"

Francesca gave her name and was immediately over-whelmed by an outpouring of sympathy.

"Francis Hatton was a wonderful man, my dear! I have to tell you, we have cried our own tears over his passing. If my duties had allowed, I would have come to the service. But we had three little ones convalescing from measles, and I didn't like to leave them. It's a pleasure to meet you at last—your grandfather loved you so dearly!"

But there was a wariness behind the effusive greeting that caught Francesca's ear. Mrs. Gibbon was not best pleased at all. And even after Richard Leighton had been introduced, the older woman glanced his way several times as if his reasons for being there were still a mystery.

And you are no less a mystery for us, Francesca thought.

She chose her opening accordingly. "I've long wanted to come and ask about the Little Wanderers Foundation—"

"My dear, of course. I'd like nothing better than to show all that we've accomplished! Mr. Hatton's generosity has been repaid a thousandfold by the children who have come through these doors over the years. And we've always been proud of each of them. But you must see for yourself, not take my word."

"This, then, is an orphanage—" Francesca commented in surprise.

"Indeed, no, Mr. Hatton insisted we never call it that. Our children live as in a family, you see. Just as any other child might do. It promotes a sense of worth, rather than obliga-tion."

Mrs. Gibbon conducted her guests through the rooms where her charges slept, a classroom where lessons were in progress, the dining room where they took their meals, and a nursery for the very young. The children Francesca could see from the doorway were well behaved, smiling, indeed almost like a large family that got on well together.

"Where do these children come from? How do you find them?" Leighton asked, following the women.

"It doesn't take long for word of us to reach the ears of

those who find themselves in trouble. Or in need." Mrs. Gibbon turned to face him. "Sadly, since the war we've seen more than our share of tragedy. Young men dying before they could even be told they were fathers. And young mothers with nowhere to turn for money, giving up their children because the Army refuses to accept their legal existence. Or come to that, doesn't want to know! There is only so much we can do, without being overwhelmed ourselves. We take the most promising, to give them a chance. And pray others will be speedily adopted into a good family. We've been lucky, I can tell you. Much of the credit for that went to your grandfather, Miss Hatton. He worked tirelessly on our behalf. Everything is handled quite discreetly, you see. That's our hallmark."

"How did my grandfather come to take an interest in orphaned children?"

Mrs. Gibbon hesitated. "I don't really know the answer to that. Although he did say once that an unfortunate death had shown him his way."

Francesca was immediately alert. A suicide? Suicide was a disgrace, something a family swept under the carpet. Like murder...

Moving on to another classroom, Francesca asked, "There was a young woman—Elizabeth Andrews. Was she one of your charges? As I remember, she felt she owed my grandfather for his care of her."

"As a rule, I don't discuss our children, but since you already know about her, I can tell you that was true. Mr. and Mrs. Andrews had just lost their only child to diphtheria, and Elizabeth was so shy and sweet-natured. A perfect match. Poor as church mice, the vicar and his wife were, but such a loving home! A Mr. Chatham knew of their situation, I believe, and that's how Mr. Hatton came to hear of it." Mr. Chatham had been rector at St. Mary Magdalene before William Stevens had come to the Valley....

"And this is a working farm," Mrs. Gibbon continued, gesturing to the outbuildings they could see from an upstairs window. "We grow most of our food here, and the children are taught to help. No task is too menial, but the point is not labor so much as understanding that working with one's hands is not a disgrace. Even those who go on to public school or university are taught this way. It wouldn't do, in Mr. Hatton's opinion, for a child to look down on those less fortunate. Education and respectability. Those were his watchwords."

They were passing a small room that had been set aside as a chapel, and here Mrs. Gibbon paused. "Religious training is fostered as well. And you'll note this table in the back of the chapel. Here we keep our 'family,' our collection of photographs. Mothers with children, fathers and mothers together—grandparents—happy faces, loving faces. We put them here so that our little ones might feel that each has had a family, and look upon that as a natural progression—"

But Francesca was no longer listening. Among the photographs was one she instantly recognized. It had, until only a matter of days ago, been standing on the table by her grandfather's bed—

CHAPTER 20

She went directly to the collection of photographs. Picking up the silver frame that held that of her parents, she said sharply, "How did this come to be here?"

It wasn't a duplicate—she recognized the design of the frame, the feel of the silver filigree, the weight of it.

Mrs. Gibbon said, "It's strange that you should ask. We don't know. Last week, when one of the senior girls was dusting in here, she noticed that it was new and she spoke to me about it. I'd never seen it before. But another photograph *was* missing, and we have no idea what's become of it or even when it was taken."

"This is my grandfather's. It was in his room when he died. And then it disappeared from there—"

She looked up at Leighton. She had even suspected him at the time....

"Good heavens, Miss Hatton! Are you quite sure? You must by all means carry it home with you! I don't know how such a thing could have happened—it's terribly odd—!" Mrs.

Gibbon looked distractedly from one of the framed photographs to the other. "I have no idea—and where has *ours* got to? We've never had problems of this nature before—!"

Francesca turned to Leighton. "The photograph you have. Will you fetch it now? Please?" It was the only excuse she could come up with to send him away while she held a brief private conversation with the older woman.

To her relief, he didn't refuse her request.

Mrs. Gibbon was still apologizing profusely, but Francesca said as they moved on in Leighton's wake, "No, please, it isn't your fault. But I should like to have this again, if I may."

Then, when Leighton was out of hearing, she changed the subject. "I'm glad to learn that Elizabeth Andrews was one of your successes. She came to my grandfather's funeral, you know. It was kind of her."

"Elizabeth's adoptive father wrote regularly every year until his death, giving us reports of her and expressing his gratitude to Mr. Hatton. It doesn't surprise me that Elizabeth was brought up to revere him."

"Do you keep records of all your children? How they came to be here, who their parents were, where they went to live if they were placed? What became of them when they grew up? Who was on the staff? That sort of thing."

"Yes, of course, that's so important. I have the current ledger here, but Mr. Hatton sent for the rest of them in July. Just before we learned he was taken ill."

"Did he? Didn't that strike you as odd?"

"He was always content to keep them locked up in our strong room. I was considering writing to you and asking if we might have them back—at your convenience, of course!"

"Did he leave anything else for safekeeping in your strong room? Letters, family documents—" Confessions or last words...

"I don't think such a thing would ever have occurred to him!" Mrs. Gibbon smiled. "He was such a private man, wasn't he? But he did have a remarkable way with children.

He called himself an ostrich, taking all the hatchlings under his wing."

Mrs. Passmore had said something about ostriches....

Nodding her head toward the motorcar, just visible outside the entry, Mrs. Gibbon was saying, "Do you believe this photograph Mr. Leighton is fetching is the one we're missing from the chapel? But how did it come into his possession?"

"I'm quite sure it isn't yours. I wanted an opportunity to ask you about a woman, a Mrs.—"

Leighton was near enough to hear them now, and Francesca was forced to break off.

To her surprise, in his hand was not a frame but the pocket watch he sometimes wore. As he came up to them, he flicked open the gold case. And in the back, where the rim had been designed as a miniature frame, a young girl's face looked out at them, smiling. The photograph had been professionally tinted, and had the luminous quality of a painting on ivory.

Victoria was captured much earlier than Francesca had expected. Her expression was spirited, a little quizzical, more mature than the still unformed features. Life hadn't yet touched her. Her hair was as bright as the sun, held in place by a pale green ribbon that accentuated its fairness. Her eyes were very blue, with darker depths.

You couldn't tell here, Francesca thought, what Victoria Leighton might have become. A loving mother—a wandering wife—a terrified woman.

Yet somehow the eyes weren't as innocent as the face....

Francesca looked up from the smiling gaze to Leighton's eyes.

His were harder. He had seen a cold and bitter world, and he knew he was dying.

Mrs. Gibbon was examining the likeness with interest but shook her head. "No, this is quite lovely, of course, but it isn't the one that we're missing. I'm so sorry to have troubled you for nothing." She handed the watch back to Leighton, and then said to Francesca, who was moving on toward the door, "It's interesting, all the same. The shape of the face reminds me of the child we were just speaking of. Were you possibly suggesting that they could be related?"

Francesca, who was just a little behind Leighton now, had the chilling feeling that Mrs. Gibbon's next words would—however unwittingly—destroy every illusion that Richard Leighton treasured.

She made a sudden movement, intent on catching Mrs. Gibbon's eye. When she did, she shook her head vehemently and only once.

It was all going wrong—! Instead of a private moment to discuss her grandfather's past, she was finding herself thrust into Richard Leighton's!

"Child?" Leighton's voice was tight with tension. "*What* child?"

Mrs. Gibbon frowned, uncertain. Her glance faltered and slid back to Francesca for guidance. "We were just discussing—a case where a child had been brought up to revere Mr. Hatton for—for his care of her. I found that rather—touching. I didn't intend to suggest—"

She was stumbling over herself in an effort to mend whatever damage she might have done with her comment—and was unaware of the pit she was still on the brink of falling into.

There was such anger in Leighton's face that Francesca impulsively touched his arm. "We've taken enough of Mrs. Gibbon's time—"

"*What* child?" he asked again, not moving.

Mrs. Gibbon stiffened. "I really can't give you names, Mr. Leighton. It's against our policy. But it was intended as a compliment—I hope you'll take it as such. She was one of our dearest charges."

He turned to stare at Francesca, who was firmly thanking Mrs. Gibbon before she could say any more. Behind him Mrs. Gibbon, noticeably upset, begged Francesca with her eyes to explain.

But that would be impossible in front of Leighton.

"We'll be on our way now—"

"But the disposition of the house—" Mrs. Gibbon began.

"I see no reason to change anything that my grandfather has done. I only wish he'd brought me here sooner."

"He often said he wished he had brought his sons here before they died."

"Can you tell me about the photograph that's missing? Was it a family—a woman—"

"It was a mother and a child. Very lovely, both of them, and quite a favorite of the little children. We were so sorry to discover it had gone—"

"Has a Mrs. Passmore come to this house recently? Or perhaps she called herself Miss Weaver. An attractive woman in middle age?"

"We have visitors from time to time, and that description could fit any of them. Frequently they're mothers hoping to learn what's become of their son or daughter. But I don't recall meeting a woman by either name. Sometimes, of course, the name they give isn't their own... We are used to that as well."

In the motorcar, Leighton said furiously, "Did you put her up to it?"

"Up to what?"

"That hint that a child in that house might have been my mother's? To see a resemblance between my photograph and one of the orphans?"

Francesca allowed herself a count to ten before answering, thanking whatever gods there were that he hadn't known the background of the conversation. More than anything, Elizabeth Andrews didn't deserve to be caught up in the coils of the Leighton family's wretched affairs, and it was important not to bring her name back to this obsessed man's attention.

Instead she said, "This quest of yours—it might be the only thing on *your* mind, but the rest of us aren't absorbed by it! Mrs. Gibbon has a very responsible position at The Swans, and she's hardly likely to suggest to a stranger that the young girl in the photograph in his pocket watch later became the mother of one of her charges! She merely said there was a resemblance—*she* thought I was suggesting more than that! And I *hadn't*—"

"Then why did you ask me to show the photograph to Mrs. Gibbon?"

"All right—I'll tell you! I wanted to ask her questions about my grandfather. Personal questions that had nothing to do with you. It was a ruse, for God's sake!" Her quick sympathy earlier had been trampled in his anger. And she wondered why she had even felt the need to protect him from disillusionment.

Did they truly look anything alike, Elizabeth Andrews and Victoria Leighton? Had Mrs. Gibbon seen something there...?

Francesca doubted that Leighton had glanced twice at Miss Andrews on the day of the funeral. She herself was finding it hard to recall the girl's face. There had been vulnerability in it, and shyness, the softness of adolescence. A touching innocence, so real in Elizabeth Andrews—and belied in the photograph by knowing eyes. Surely all these two women had in common was an English fairness and, purely by chance, youth.

"Besides," she said aloud, casting about for straws, "your mother was dead long before this child was born. Resemblance or no resemblance."

Leighton wasn't satisfied. Finally she touched Bill on the shoulder, asking him to stop the motorcar.

"Shall we turn around and get to the bottom of this business? I don't mind. It will prove to you that we weren't conspiring behind your back."

But the truth was, she did mind. She couldn't bear to have someone like Alasdair MacPherson, filled with such hatred, coming here on a wild-goose chase and disrupting the serenity and happiness of the Little Wanderers home.

"No. She'll lie through her teeth to protect her precious

orphans—" Then he stopped. "I'm sorry, that's not fair. Who was the child you were discussing while I was out of hearing? Will you at least tell me that?"

"You heard the beginning of the discussion yourself; it wasn't behind your back! The rector in Hurley at that time, a Mr. Chatham, knew of the case."

The anger seemed to be subsiding, but the shoulder just touching hers in the narrow rear seat of the motorcar was still stiff with resentment and uncertainty.

She thought, *He's been different since the night of the Zeppelin raid.* Or was something else bothering him? Had the foundation of his search been shaken by something he'd discovered—and she hadn't?

"What I'd like to know," Francesca went on, shifting the direction of the conversation, "is how *this* photograph was taken from River's End!" She held up the one she'd retrieved from Mrs. Gibbon. "And why?"

"The house is never locked. And you were away for the reading of the will, the funeral—"

"Not the funeral, Mrs. Lane and Mrs. Horner were there most of the morning, preparing the meal." But not all of the morning. "Unless it was one of the mourners— And if that's true, how did it end up here?"

It had to be Mrs. Passmore...if she hadn't been to Falworthy and this house of the orphans, how had she heard that tale of the ostriches?

"To other matters—what am I to do with you now?" Francesca asked him. "Dr. Nealy will very likely have my head if I bring you back to Devon."

What she read in his face was an admission that he was going to do just that—return to the Valley.

Before she quite realized how it would sound, she exclaimed, "But I don't *want* you there—"

"No." He forced a smile. "I don't suppose you do."

They had reached the village of Falworthy again, driving down the High Street. Bill was saying, "There's a tea shop just there, Miss Francesca. It's well past noon, and we ought to stop."

She ate with relish, but Leighton morosely drank his tea and had no appetite.

"You don't remember your mother. You can't know," he said after a time, "what it's like to wonder if she's safe—if she's hungry or cold or lost—if it was something that you did that drove her away. If she's ever coming home."

Francesca said softly, "I used to wonder about the accident that killed my parents. Why I survived and they didn't. Whether my mother was holding me and protecting me with her body. Whether my father or my mother died first—or if either of them survived long enough to know that I was safe. I wondered a thousand times what they felt, when the lorry bore down on them—if they had time to be afraid, if they were in agony before they died. It's what people do when there are no answers."

Yet another part of her mind was still wrestling with the question of whether Elizabeth Andrews could have been the love child of Victoria Leighton and Francis Hatton. It would have meant a liaison between them that had lasted longer than anyone had realized. Ruin would prevent a woman from returning to her family; it needn't have been murder. And when the affair was over, she might well have killed herself. It would explain so much.

And with the help of the old rector, Chatham, Francis Hatton had found a safe haven, a loving home for Elizabeth Andrews.

No, it couldn't be true—there had been no provision in his will for the girl. And Francesca was certain her grandfather would have seen to that.

Turning to Leighton, her own appetite vanished, Francesca said, "If you're coming back to the Valley, I warn you—I intend to press on. I'll spell Bill at the wheel, if need be."

"I won't hold you up," Leighton answered. "And I should

drive. Bill has done enough. Besides, I need the distraction!"
He went to pay the reckoning.

It was Francesca who needed the distraction. Fifteen minutes later as she sat looking out the window, but blind to the
rolling landscape of Somerset, pretty, huddled villages in the
cup of hills, she was beset with doubts.

Why did Victoria Leighton follow her like a malevolent
spirit everywhere she went? Doggedly, as if with intent to dis-
rupt her memories and her security at every turn? It was as if
she had come back from the dead to revenge herself on the
last of the Hattons...

It was well after midnight when the motorcar reached the
turning for River's End. Bill was slumped in the passenger's
seat, deeply asleep. Francesca had taken the robe from the
boot and made herself comfortable in the rear seat while
Leighton drove, and the only conversation between them was
a query now and again about a turning.

Francesca let herself drowse, making an effort to close her
mind to everything. But the image of Alasdair MacPherson's
shadowy, hate-filled figure, standing on the landing watching
her, crowded out oblivion, bringing her awake again with a
start. She could feel the heat of his ferocious anger still, a living thing that had shocked her. Even though she had done
nothing to him, he would gladly have seen her in hell because
she was a Hatton.

And each time her eyes flew open, from where she sat she
could see the outline of Leighton's profile as he concentrated
on the muddy, rutted roads.

Why had he decided to return to the Valley, ignoring Dr.
Nealy's urgent instructions to see the Army surgeons? Was he
afraid to hear what they would tell him about his injury? The
stiffness that dragged at him seemed to grow worse each
day—although she couldn't tell how fiercely sitting for long
periods in the motorcar might have aggravated it. He was the

kind of man who would prefer death to the helplessness of paralysis. . . .

Theirs had become a confused relationship. Adversaries—enemies—and yet she had felt safer the nights he was at River's End, even though she half suspected him of being the intruder. She had felt more comfortable making this long journey with him sitting beside her in the motorcar, as one of the cousins would have done, even though he had infuriated her at times and she had wished him at the devil. The murky depths of Victoria Leighton's fate swirled about both of them, threatening to engulf them. She couldn't imagine the fear that invested his moody silences at times.

Perhaps Miss Trotter had best described it. A fear that his mother had deliberately walked out of her son's life. He would sacrifice her grandfather to prove that it wasn't true.

She wasn't even certain now that he reminded her of her grandfather—it was *surely* superficial at best, a trick of the mind. And yet there *was* something of Francis Hatton in this man that she recognized more than any physical likeness. A wounded spirit . . .

Unless Richard Leighton had played on her loneliness and vulnerability. Unless it was all a charade, and she had fallen easy prey to such devious plotting.

There had to be *something* of Alasdair MacPherson in his grandson, if only the single-minded will to destroy the Hattons.

They had picked up rain shortly after leaving Dunster, and the downpour was intense as they went up the drive at River's End, the tires splashing to a halt by the steps.

"Give me your key," Leighton said, "and I'll open the door for you."

In the light of the coach lamps she dug into her handbag for it. "It's the key to the kitchen door. You'll have to go round to the stableyard." She reached over his shoulder to put the key into his palm, afraid one of them might drop it in the darkness.

But when he got to the stableyard, he couldn't step out of the driver's seat, biting off a cry of pain as he tried.

"You were foolish!" Francesca scolded, tired herself and in no mood to be sympathetic. "You should have told me—"

Somewhere in the Valley a gunshot reverberated, and then echoed again. Francesca, startled, jumped.

Leighton sat there, his teeth clenched, his face turned away from her. But he did not move. Bill, awake now, took his own time climbing stiffly down from the motorcar, and between them, Francesca and her coachman managed to extricate Leighton from behind the wheel.

They were wet through, all three of them, by that time. Francesca sent Bill into the kitchen to rake up the fire, and she herself took a moment in the servants' hall to divest herself of hat and coat and shoes that were heavy with water. She found a pair of Mrs. Lane's slippers and put them on, throwing one of the housekeeper's shawls over her shoulders.

The old dog was staying at night with Mrs. Lane as arranged. Francesca missed his wriggling welcome, the busy tongue trying to lick her face.

Bill had stoked the fire, set the kettle on to boil, and disappeared to his own quarters in the stables. Leighton, left in a chair in the kitchen, was shivering as Francesca came in to help him out of his coat. She could tell she was hurting him, but he made no complaint.

The kitchen was just beginning to warm up again, as Francesca got Leighton back into a chair nearer the stove. He sat there, braced and silent, while she made a pot of tea and put the first cup into his clenched hands.

He drank the hot brew with gratitude, saying at one point, "Thank you!" in a voice not yet quite his own.

"You'll have to stay the night," she told him with resignation. "I haven't the energy to drive you to the inn, and frankly I doubt if you could make it that far. You've slept in the guest room before. It won't hurt to use it again. Or there's the great armchair in my grandfather's study, if you don't want to face the stairs."

Bill came back into the kitchen, furling his umbrella. "The motor's under cover, Miss, and I've left your baggage by the hall door. I'll just have a cup of that tea, if you don't mind, and then be off. Unless Mr. Leighton is going on to the inn?"

"He can't, not tonight," she answered. "Sit down, the pot is ready."

"Just as well not to take the chance," Bill agreed, and took his place on the far side of the table. "Thank you, Miss Francesca."

He looked tired and old, and Francesca realized that she had pushed him as well as Leighton and herself. It had been unfair. But Bill had served her grandfather and would serve her as long as he could. It was his nature to be faithful.

Leighton was less gray as he finished a second cup of tea. She had laced it with a little whiskey.

"A wild-goose chase," he said for a second time, as much to himself as to his silent companions.

"Yes." And then she said, "No, it wasn't. I've seen the house in Essex. And I've learned about the orphans. I told you before, my grandfather has done some good in this world, and I'm sorry I couldn't tell him so when he was alive!" She thought of Miss Andrews, and was glad now that she herself had provided for the girl. Mr. Branscombe hadn't approved, but Francesca had felt it was right.

She collected the tea things and set them in the sink. "Well, we needn't discuss it tonight! Can you make it up the stairs, Mr. Leighton? Or shall we try for the study?"

In the event it took Bill's strength as well as hers to get him up the steps and onto the high bed. While Bill lit the fire already laid on the hearth, Francesca managed to take Leighton's wet shoes and socks off, setting them by the fire, and then said, "I'll bring up your luggage—"

"Don't. I'll wait this spasm out, and see to it myself. You've done enough."

"Heaping coals of fire on your head," she agreed, and followed Bill out of the room.

Looking back at the door, she could see his face, shadowed by the candlelight. Eyes hooded, dark planes for cheeks, nose and chin highlighted, he looked like a villain in an ancient play, masked and painted to portray evil....

It was not a pleasant image to carry with her down the passage.

By the time Francesca awakened, Leighton had gone.

Mrs. Lane had no idea where. "He came through the kitchen in his heavy coat and asked to borrow my umbrella and a pair of your grandfather's Wellingtons. Then he was off, and when I asked him where to, he told me he was going *hunting.*" The last was said doubtfully, as if Mrs. Lane wasn't sure whether he had been serious or not. But she was full of news of the shooter, and how last night Mrs. Tallon had lost a goose to his marksmanship.

It was mid-morning when Leighton returned. Francesca heard him calling her name as she sat at the little walnut desk in the sitting room, going through the mail that had arrived in her absence.

She answered and he appeared on the threshold.

He looked as if he had been digging through the briars and climbing across muddy terrain. The Wellingtons had been left in the entry, but the trousers he wore and the heavy sweater were filthy. Francesca exclaimed, and he said, testily, "I won't soil the upholstery. But I need to talk to you."

She gave him the straight-backed chair from the desk and sat down on the sofa near the fire. "All right, I'm listening."

"It's hard to tell where the shots we keep hearing are coming from. Echoes in this Valley mask sounds well. And there's been rain, wiping out most traces of him. Still, I went to see if

I could discover any tracks this man's made, before someone is killed."

"Did you have any luck?"

"There were no tracks to be found. My first thought was he'd come from one of the farms. But I kept searching and finally I found a lair. A place where someone has been living rough. Our shooter isn't a local man."

"The Scots soldier who came here looking for work?" she asked, thinking back.

"I can't answer that; I never saw him. The place he chose, however, is high up among some boulders a few miles from here. The way they're set, they could act as a shallow cave with ease. Heavy boots—his tracks everywhere in front of the opening. Snares for rabbits, to feed himself. The remains of a fire. A little tea and a tin to heat water. Some sugar. Other odds and ends, indicating he'd been there for some time. But no sign of him, or what kind of weapon he might be using. He keeps it clean enough. I found oiled rags in a crevice in the driest corner of the cave."

"Now that you've discovered this place, he'll know, and move on!"

"I left no tracks of my own. He won't know I've been there. Not unless he saw me—or sensed me. It's something you learn at the Front to survive. That odd feeling that someone has crossed your path."

"I felt it," she acknowledged, "the two nights someone got into this house. Do you think it was the same person? I don't particularly like the sound of that! It's time to call in the constable, I should think!"

"The constable won't waste his time on a homeless man hiding in the hills. But the Army might, if he were a deserter."

"Deserter!" she repeated, appalled.

"He wouldn't be the first. But I'm reluctant to turn him in. They're harsh with deserters. God knows I can sympathize!"

"Well, there's not much sympathy for a man prowling the hills shooting at people and breaking into homes. It's just a matter of time before someone is seriously hurt. You were lucky, you know. And Tommy Higby as well!"

They went to speak to Mrs. Lane, but she swore nothing was missing from her stores. "I keep a close eye on the pantry, Miss Francesca, you know I do. I'd notice at once if there was food taken. But with the evenings coming down earlier I'm beginning to feel uncomfortable walking back to the village alone. If you wouldn't mind having Bill drive me, I'd be that grateful."

"Yes, of course, you need only ask him when you are ready, Mrs. Lane." Francesca had been standing with one hand behind her, the framed photograph hidden in her skirts. She brought it out now, and showed the housekeeper.

"Look what's turned up!"

Mrs. Lane stared at it. "My stars! Now where on earth did you find that!"

"In my desk in the sitting room, of all places. I don't have any recollection of it, isn't that silly?" Her eyes met Leighton's over the housekeeper's head. "It was quite a shock to put my hand in the drawer and touch the edge of the frame."

"Well, it's not too surprising," Mrs. Lane answered, offering comfort. "You were that distracted in Mr. Hatton's last hours. I've never seen you as upset as you were! But no harm done, and I'll be happy to carry it upstairs again."

"No harm done," Francesca agreed.

Back in the sitting room, Leighton asked, "Why did you lie to her?"

"You're used to London, you don't know how these people think. She'll be afraid to come here, even in daylight, if there's a housebreaker about, in addition to that man with his gun. And I can't manage the house without her. If I try to explain how I'd found it in a home for orphaned children in Falworthy, the story will be all over the village before the week's end. It will just add to my grandfather's legend, and somehow I don't think he'd care much for that. No, what's more important is the fact that nothing is missing from the pantry—which means our intruder wasn't here foraging for bacon and salt—or picture frames, either!"

"He might have come to take whatever he could find, and sell it. But the dog frightened him off."

"I don't know," she said, "what to believe anymore. Will you send for the constable or shall I?"

To her surprise, he said, "I will."

But she wondered, afterward, if he would do anything of the sort.

They hanged deserters . . .

When he returned to the inn that afternoon, saying dryly that once more he had trespassed on her hospitality, Francesca loaded the pistol she had taken from Simon's cupboard, and laid it by her bed next to the torch, ready for the night.

Tyler was on the floor by the bed as she tried the weight of the barrel and the grip.

She had never fired a pistol, but Simon's war games had taught her enough to know that a steady hand mattered more than good aim. A wavering muzzle was the surest way of showing herself to be a novice. . . .

The night passed uneventfully. And as she finally fell asleep in the first light of dawn, she remembered thinking that marriage had something to be said for it, if only for the comfort of hearing another person breathing quietly next to one when one woke in the night and was frightened

To her surprise, Francesca learned over her breakfast that Leighton was gone from the Valley. He had been driven into Tiverton at first light, to take the early train from there.

He's gone back to Falworthy and the orphanage, Francesca told herself. *He can't leave it alone, this obsession of his.* She felt a flare of anger at the obstinacy that seemed to rule him. But that soon drained away.

He might have said good-bye, was the next thought. *He must have made up his mind yesterday afternoon—*

And on the heels of that—*I won't see him again.*

It was such a strong certainty that she felt a wave of desolation. Even hours of heavy labor, weeding the flower beds, dragging sacks of debris out to the compost heap, digging out young sprouts of trees that had taken root in the spring, she couldn't shake the bleak mood that had settled, like an ache, in her very bones.

THE COUSINS

Robin . . . the practical one

They tell me I'm practical. It's rather like calling a person stodgy, dull.

But I can't help myself. I see the solution to problems while there's panic all around me and nobody seems to think straight. The best course of action is to remain calm and think the situation through. I'm good at that.

Not the most romantic of qualities, but then I've never felt much like sweeping a girl off her feet with poetry and flowers and florid speeches. If she likes me, she likes me. And if she doesn't, there's not much I can do about it.

Growing up with four lively brothers gave me more than enough opportunities to learn practicality, I can tell you that. More often than not, they'd rush headlong into whatever game they were playing, and it was left to me to remind them that leaping off the shed roof wearing an old coat for a cloak was silly, unless you were in the market for a broken neck. I had to keep an eye on Francesca, too. Fearless, clever, ready to follow us into whatever mischief was afoot—I'd often have to catch her pinafore strings and hold on tight, to prevent her from drowning herself in the pond or tumbling headlong out of a tree or running herself on the stick swords we'd made for ourselves. She never played a damsel in distress. Simon recruited her to be lionhearted, and she was, even when she got herself bruised more times than I'd like to count.

I'd always loved her as much as if she'd been my own sister. Her parents died young, like ours. And so we became orphans together and came to live with Grandfather. I couldn't remember my father and mother. I couldn't even remember where we'd lived before. Simon said it was flatter and greener, but he was only six and I expect he made up the story. I always intended to ask Grandfather about that, but it never really seemed important enough when the thought crossed my mind.

Part of being practical is being observant. I was generally the first to notice when one of us was coming down with measles or chicken pox or mumps. I could see the tiredness around the eyes and the lack of spirits. I could tell when one of the servants was unhappy. And sometimes when Grandfather wasn't aware that I was looking, I'd see a terrible loneliness in his face. I sometimes wondered if that was because we were such a pack of wild beasts and he'd had to put aside his own life to look after us. But his love never was grudging, so I expect I was wrong there.

Practical doesn't mean one's omniscient.

That there was something worrying him I was certain. And so I tried to keep an eye on my unruly

brethren and my little cousin. To help make
Grandfather's life more bearable.

I listened, too, which is sometimes hard when
you're young and feeling the tug of audacity and
rebellion.

At least twice to my certain knowledge letters
arrived in the morning post that abruptly sent
Grandfather into his study with the door locked
behind him. It would be hours before he emerged, his
face strained, and his voice clipped. He would leave
for London, then, restless and driven. I thought
perhaps it was money—I'm sure we six ate
prodigiously, and we outgrew our clothes at a
shocking rate.

Later, as I grew older, I learned there were
pressures besides money that drove a man. To my
way of thinking, Grandfather appeared to be in his
twilight years. I was fearful that he might die soon,
and then what would become of us? Robin, ever
practical . . .

But he couldn't have been more than fifty then,
and vigorous. Now that I'm twenty, I realize that he
was more than Grandfather to a band of unruly
children. He was a man involved in various business
matters, his club in London, the charities he
supported. He had close friends who valued him,
judging from the letters and invitations that arrived
for him. I wondered, sometimes, if there were
women as well. If there were, he kept that part of his
life closed to us.

I asked him once why people pitied us when they
learned we were orphans. I'd been happy enough at
River's End; it hadn't occurred to me that I might
have missed the love of a father and mother.

"Bill Coachman was an orphan, you know," he
told me then. "His father died at sea, and his
mother was never well. When he was ten, he and his

younger sister were sent here to earn their living. His mother couldn't care for them, you see, and in fact she died shortly afterward. They were alone in the world, except for two cousins who were fishermen. My father saw to it that Bill learned to read and write. To do his numbers. He explained to me that education gave even a stable boy dignity, and we who had more were bound by duty to see that those without were cared for."

"Did Bill share your tutor?"

"No, he was sent to the village school."

"Did his sister go with him?"

"For a time."

"What became of her?"

He cleared his throat. "Unhappily, she died." And then he added with bitterness, "She hadn't been born a lady, you see, and the English are sticklers for breeding, however learned you are. It's rather like horse racing—you must know the dam and sire if you're to value the colt. When she fell in love, the match wasn't considered—suitable. And so she was destined to become a nursery maid, not a wife."

"Was she our nursery maid?" I asked.

"It was long before your time, I'm afraid. I was barely older than Simon is now. Seventeen, perhaps. Old enough, I thought, to know my own mind."

He changed the subject then. As far as I know it was the only time he ever spoke of Beth Trelawny. To me or anyone else.

I was a child, a practical child at that, and I wanted to hear the end of the story. But I could see it was no good asking Grandfather. Instead I asked Bill about his sister, one evening as we stood by the gates and watched the long shadows descend across the hilltops and bring the day to an end. The smoke from his pipe climbed into the trees over our heads. I liked the masculine fragrance of it.

For a moment I thought he hadn't heard me. Then he said, his face barely visible in the gathering dusk, "She was such a pretty little thing, my sister Bethie. And spirited. Everyone at the house adored her. Mr. Hatton—your grandfather, that was—cared for her particularly. And when she—died—he saw to it that she had a proper burial, as if she were a lady. Then he went away for a time and didn't come home again until his own father was dead. They'd had a falling-out of sorts. I never knew what it was about. I wouldn't speak of Beth to him, if I were you. It's not a time of his life that he cares to remember.

"But I'll tell you something else. I can't get it out of my mind."

All ears, I was prepared for some exciting secret.

Bill tapped out his pipe and prepared to walk back up the drive. "That young cousin of yours—Miss Francesca. She has much the same spirit as my sister Beth. The same little ways. I look at her sometimes and find my heart turning over. I wonder Mr. Hatton hasn't noticed it as well. It's like after all these many years Bethie's come back to us. You must promise to look after her, now, and guard her. Miracles like that don't happen twice."

Disappointed, I promised. I was too young to understand what love was.

But when I was twenty and saw a young French girl on a road outside Abbeville, I found myself wondering if my grandfather had loved Beth Trelawny and hadn't been allowed to marry her. Because that French girl's face had stayed in my mind for weeks afterward. And for the first time, I knew what it was to want something—someone—who was beyond my reach.

I was a soldier then, and couldn't go searching for her.

And being practical, I told myself that she didn't deserve to become a young widow, if anything happened to me.

CHAPTER 21

A week of weeding and trimming the gardens had not spent the nervous energy that drove Francesca Hatton.

As the sun began to slide over the western hills, she bundled the last of the leaves and pruning debris into an old sack and dragged it to the compost heap that had lived behind the barn for as long as she could remember. Once the rich dark soil had filled pots and perennial beds, but it had not been turned over since the first year of the war and Harry's departure for his training. Beyond Bill's ability, beyond hers, it had stagnated like the rest of the gardens, waiting for the peace that never came. Everyone had kept up appearances in the first weeks, the first months, and then the first year of fighting. But the depressing events of 1916, from the bloody Easter Rebellion in Ireland to the heaviest casualty lists yet in the first days of the July Somme offensive, had left everyone dispirited and worried.

She emptied the last sackful and in the fading light went back for the rose canes and saplings she'd set aside. A thorn in her finger made her swear, and she was trying not to drive it deeper into her flesh as she lugged her armful to the heap and wearily stacked it to one side of another pile. *Tomorrow,* she thought—*tomorrow I'll rake it over the top, where it belongs. It's too dark tonight…*

But not too dark, apparently, for the shooter.

A *crack!* startled her so badly that she tripped over the rake and went down hard, scraping her hands and face against the rough edges of pruned wood.

She scrambled to her feet and shouted, "Damn you! If you want to kill someone, go shoot the *Hun!*"

There was silence from the wood that ran along the top of the hill, and not even the snap of a twig to tell her whether anyone had been standing there to hear her or not. Certainly the shot had not been aimed at her.

Her arm was beginning to sting rather fiercely, and she pulled at the sleeve of her old sweater to see what was wrong.

Her hand came away with a smear of blood, and she thought for an instant that she'd been shot after all. Her breath stopped in her throat for a moment, and then let go in a long sigh. No, she'd torn her arm on the sharp point of a branch she'd just cut. It lay upended like a spear and she had fallen on it.

"I'll have the constable on the idiot—or the Army!" she fumed.

The cut would have to be seen to. Well, she'd finished for the day, at least.

Walking back to the house, she could feel a warm trickle down her arm, and she began to hope that Mrs. Lane had waited for her to come in before leaving for her cottage in the village.

But there was no one in the kitchen and Mrs. Lane's wool shawl was gone from its hook by the door.

The room was still warm from the banked fires, and a lamp had been lit, so that Francesca could readily find her dinner on its covered tray.

She had no interest in food. Her arm was burning fiercely and she was still a little shaken from the sudden shock of her fall. It was a wonder she hadn't been more seriously hurt.

Now, she thought, *I know how Richard must have felt....*

She drew some water and heated it on the stove while she tried to strip off her shirtwaist and gauge the damage.

An oval-shaped bleeding cut ran at an angle just above the elbow.

She could see bits of debris in the wound, caught in the ragged skin.

"Oh, bother!"

Washing it awkwardly, she cleaned it as best she could, and then wrapped a tea towel around it to keep the blood off her undergarments.

Until now she'd been too preoccupied to notice that her fingers were trembling. Sitting down clumsily in one of the kitchen chairs, she thought, *Good Lord! I'm going to faint—*

She put her head down between her knees until the dizziness had passed.

When she could think clearly again, she was surprised. The arm didn't hurt terribly; the wound wasn't all that deep. Half the force had been absorbed by her sweater sleeve, and there hadn't been an inordinate amount of bleeding—

Yet the red patch of scraped and torn skin and welling blood had made her physically ill.

Every time she pictured it in her mind, the dizziness returned in force.

This is ridiculous! she chided herself. *After all the ghastly wounds I've tended.* It wouldn't do for Mrs. Lane to come in tomorrow morning and find her mistress lying unconscious on the floor from such a minor scrape!

Yet it was several minutes before she could calm down enough to gather up her clothing and make her way upstairs. It wasn't until she had completely dressed again that the dizziness abated. But she could sense that it lurked at arm's length. She lay down on the bed, where Tyler soon found her.

The sound of the door knocker rising and falling on its brass plate brought her up sharply. Who on earth would call at such an hour—?

She slipped into Simon's room across from hers and looked down at the front steps.

Miss Trotter stood below, her shawls and scarves like ghostly garments in the pale twilight.

Feeling a wash of relief, Francesca went down quickly to admit her.

Miss Trotter came wafting in in that fashion of seeming to drift rather than walk.

"I heard another shot as I was walking home—I thought perhaps someone had been hurt again—" she said, and looked closely at Francesca.

"Well, I wasn't shot," she answered, summoning a smile, "but I'm afraid I've cut my arm."

Miss Trotter had her in the kitchen in short order and was soon examining the injury. She removed the tea towel, tut-tutted under her breath, did much better work of cleaning the area, and applied a cool salve before taking out bandages from another pocket somewhere in her garments.

"That should do," she decided at length. "Such wounds tend to get infected if they aren't seen to." Glancing at her patient's face, she said, "Does it hurt? I can give you a little something to ease that."

Francesca said, "It doesn't hurt all that much—I just—don't like looking at it—or—thinking about it."

"Hmmm." It was a noncommittal murmur. It was hard to tell whether it was meant as sympathy, understanding, or disbelief.

"How did you know that I needed help?" Francesca asked after a moment.

"I heard the shot. My hearing is quite good, you know. I could tell the direction. And there was Mr. Leighton, of course."

"He's gone back to London," Francesca replied to an unasked question.

"I know," Miss Trotter answered with simplicity. She cleared away the tea towel, setting it to soak in cold water, and rolled up the rest of the bandages with the little pot of salve.

"How do you know everything?" Francesca asked, looking up at her, the vague eyes meeting hers. It was not the first time she had wondered if this omniscience was true, or an affectation.

Miss Trotter smiled. "I always have. It's just—there."

"My grandfather—"

"I laid him out, you know. Before the undertaker's men came. Miss Honneycutt asked me if I would. And I smelled the dandelion wine on his breath. It was on Miss Honneycutt's, too. I knew then what you'd done. Put them both to sleep, and only Miss Honneycutt was allowed to wake up."

Francesca, her fingertips pressed to her lips, couldn't speak.

"Is he at peace?" Miss Trotter said as if reading her mind. "I expect he is. He hated being bedridden, you know. It was a hate that went deep."

"I didn't mean to—to—"

"No, that's true, you didn't wish him harm," Miss Trotter said quietly. "It was a kindness that took a Hatton's courage."

She washed her hands, dried them, and drew on her ancient gloves, preparing to leave. "You never gave that man any of the wine. I wondered if you would be tempted."

"Mr. Leighton?" Francesca shook her head. "I couldn't—"

"No. But when the courage is there...And you never cared to see anything suffer. Even as a child." She gathered up her shawls. "Just as well. That one needs to heal before he dies."

It was an astute remark. "Yes. I rather think he does," Francesca replied. "But I don't expect we'll witness the change."

"Mark my words. You haven't seen the last of him. If that's what would please you."

Francesca found breath enough to thank her and then saw her to the heavy door, locking it after the frail figure that seemed to vanish into the night.

That night she dreamed that the wound was alive, writhing and tormenting her like a burn that wouldn't heal.

She got out of bed, to walk the passages of the house, Tyler trotting doggedly in her wake as if duty had triumphed over sleep, but only just.

The house seemed different.

Francesca couldn't put her finger on what it was. She went through the rooms, looking at the latches on the windows, touching the photograph of her parents in their wedding finery, sitting once more in its accustomed place, smoothing the covers on each of the beds where her cousins had slept.

She had once found comfort in that—but tonight there was none.

It was as if the ghosts had left. . . .

He's at peace— But had he taken the boys as well?

Her cousins no longer seemed to haunt the foot of the stairs, mourning for lost youth. And her grandfather's bed was just a bed. There was no sense of the man's presence lingering to touch her spirit.

It's time to return to London, she thought sadly. *Time to go back to the trains and the wounded and the women who try to offer comfort.*

It's the mood I'm in, she told herself, hoping to lift her spirits. *It's the wound in my arm, reminding me of the past—*

That brought her up short.

Why should the cut on her arm touch a chord of memory?

I'll be fine once I'm back in my old life—I'm depressed, that's all.

Mrs. Lane would take in Tyler again, and the old dog could come each day to the house he knew best, until he was buried in the back garden. Even he wouldn't miss her, for he belonged heart and soul to her grandfather. As had her cousins, she reflected.

Francesca went back to her room and slept well enough for the rest of the night. But her decision had been made, and tomorrow she would tell Mrs. Lane that she was leaving.

When Bill brought up the post the next morning, there was another half-dozen black-edged cards of condolence from people who had known her grandfather. They were penned with sincerity and often with affection, as if the writers truly regretted the loss of a friend. But Francesca seldom recognized the names, and knew nothing of the relationships between Francis Hatton and the members of his club or other circles of friends. It was kind of them to write, she told Mrs. Lane. He would have appreciated the gesture.

But one letter in the post was not a card of condolence. Francesca opened it without any warning that she might regret it.

There was no date, and no salutation.

> *You don't know me, of course, and have no reason to believe what I'm about to tell you. But your grandfather's sons had no children by their wives. Both died violently—and without heirs.*

She stared in dismay at the sheet of stationery and the words that ran in a thick black scrawl across it.

Who on earth would have written such a cruel thing?

Her thoughts flew to Richard Leighton. It was not the sort of thing he would do—but she wouldn't put such viciousness past Alasdair MacPherson. And what of the men who had attended the funeral—Walsham, angry over the land his father had gambled away; the Scotsman, who had looked more like an undertaker's man, come to search for a promised box?

This letter attacked her *personally*. A change of tactics?

Remembering the message cursing the Hattons, the one that her grandfather had kept in the solicitor's box in Exeter, she considered the sheet in her hand again.

That same venomous spite. She shivered. But from whom?

I thought I'd reached the end of the catalog of Francis Hatton's crimes—she thought for a second time.

Apparently not yet. Not yet...

She balled the sheet of paper up and tossed it in the fire.

If rattling her had been the aim of the sender, he—she—had succeeded.

There was much to settle before leaving for London. She had no idea when she might be given leave to come back to the Valley.

At the end of the second day she accepted an invitation to dine with the rector. Stevens seemed unusually quiet, introspective.

Smiling, she asked him if he was sorry to see her go, and was shocked at the expression on his face as he lifted his eyes to hers. There was longing, and regret, followed swiftly by resignation.

All his kindnesses, his concern for her, his care, flashed through her mind. Only partly for her grandfather's sake had this man watched over her. He loved her. And she had not realized it because William Stevens had concealed his feelings too well.

Cursing her stupidity, Francesca wished she could call back her words. Then she said with a lightness she was far from feeling, "Well. I shall be back when the war is finished. I don't like London all that much. Of course I have another choice, the house in Essex. But Grandfather never lived there.

I don't suppose I ever shall either." She explained briefly about the two properties.

"I don't believe Hatton ever wanted to live anywhere but here," Stevens answered thoughtfully. "He never really wanted to see his grandchildren face the world. I think the early deaths of his sons made him overly protective, unwilling to let any of you find out what was outside the Valley. Like the German fairy tales, he kept you bewitched in his castle. But children grow up. I don't expect he'd ever looked that far ahead. Or dreamed it would be war that deprived him of his grandsons. It was sobering to watch them march away—and devastating to see them die."

Francesca found herself thinking of the letter that had come two days ago. And the other that had arrived only this morning.

It had said, *"Who was your mother? If he was your father?"*

It, too, had gone into the fire.

"Did you know about the orphanage in Falworthy, Somerset?"

He shrugged. "I'm one of their bright stars. I never knew who my parents were. I was taken in before I had any memory of a life before that. I had a leaning toward the church. Or so I thought then. And it was cultivated."

Surprised, she asked, "You were one of the orphans?"

"Oh, yes. It wasn't as bad as you might think—"

"I've seen it for myself—"

She studied the well-shaped head, the long, slender-fingered hands. A child with a good heritage, perhaps. Or born on the wrong side of the blanket . . . More important, a kind man, compassionate and sometimes wise. She might have come to care for him in time. His scars made no difference.

Stevens was saying, "That's how I came to be here, after I was wounded. Your grandfather arranged it. The man before me, Chatham, was probably just as glad to find himself on his way out of the Valley. He was well past retirement. But for me this was a haven. I needed peace and quiet, time for wounds to heal." He gestured to his scarred face. "Hardly the best appearance for a fashionable church, do you think?"

Uncomfortable talking about himself, Stevens went on. "I hear by the usual means that you took a turn at stabbing yourself the other evening. Why on earth were you working in the gardens?"

"I don't know——" she began, aware that she was lying. "An excess of energy, I suppose. I was tired of watching them languish."

"How is the wound?"

Francesca frowned. "It hasn't bothered me particularly. Miss Trotter dressed it. Yet every time I change the bandaging, I feel a little sick. As if it were something—horrid to look at. And it isn't—instead, it's healing nicely." It made her uneasy to talk about it and she told him so. "Odd as that may sound!"

He set his teacup aside. "Perhaps it touched a real memory. I expect you were bloodied often enough as a child, playing with those wild cousins of yours. Or you may've been sent off to bed without your dinner a time or two. As a warning to take fewer risks." A smile took any sting out of his words.

As if a door in her mind had swung partly open, she could see herself, small, frightened, staring at a terrible wound on someone's arm. It hadn't bled although it was ugly and red . . . blistered. She could tell it hurt very badly. Then she was crying, sobbing into the skirts of a woman who had picked her up and carried her away from all the people staring at the burn—

Not a cut—a burn! And it hadn't happened to her, but she had seen it.

Francesca said, "You're nearly as good as Miss Trotter at mind reading. There *was* something."

"Would you care to talk about it? Would it help?"

"There isn't much to tell you. It's hardly more than a confusion of images—and it probably seems worse because of that. But I know now the wound wasn't mine. I *saw* it, and something about it—the circumstances surrounding it—badly frightened me. It probably explains why I was always uncomfortable with open fires. Somehow I associate the two. Strange as that may sound."

She could see herself standing in tears before Simon, stubbornly refusing to let him burn her at the stake again.

"You did, only this past Wednesday," he pointed out for the third time. He was running out of patience.

"But it hurts. You never warned me that it hurts! It made Freddy cry—"

"It's only make-believe smoke, and a handful of twigs. Not real fire."

"Promise not to light the fire, and I'll do it."

"That's silly. If there's no fire, how can you burn at the stake?"

In the end they piled the sticks at Francesca's feet and sprinkled ashes from the drawing room hearth over them. It wasn't the same, Simon kept telling her, and she mustn't make a habit of complaining.

But try as she would, she couldn't recall what had made Freddy cry. That memory was locked away somewhere, hidden even from herself.

Rousing herself from the past, she said, "I'd been wondering only this morning if the memory was somehow associated with my parents' accident. This fear of burning, I mean. But now I don't think so—" She shrugged. "Well, it doesn't matter."

Yet in an unpleasant way, it did.

She had no memory of that motorcar crash. She had been far too young. But to see Freddy—who never cried—in tears of pain must have shocked her deeply. She hadn't ever wanted

to hurt that way herself. Even though she hadn't at all understood what had happened to him.

"Sometimes knowing the source takes away the terror,"
Stevens was saying.

"Yes," she agreed. "Sometimes." But not always.

A message arrived from Mrs. Gibbon. It was a gentle reminder
that Francesca had promised to return the Foundation ledgers
to Somerset. And it ended with an apology.

> *I assure you I didn't mean to upset Mr. Leighton. I*
> *thought, since you spoke so freely of Miss Andrews,*
> *that my comment would be of interest to you. Was the*
> *young woman in the photograph inside the watch his*
> *mother by any chance? I was appalled that I might*
> *have touched on something best left buried in the*
> *past . . .*

Francesca put aside her packing for an hour or
more, to search through the house for the ledgers Francis
Hatton had taken from the Falworthy orphanage in early
summer.

But they were not in his study, not in the closet of his bedroom, not in the small estate office. She did find under his
bed a wooden crate with the name of a Falworthy greengrocer stamped on it.

The resourceful Mrs. Gibbon? Offering him a box in
which to carry the ledgers safely? How many were there? And
what had he done with them?

Had those ledgers been the magnet for whoever had invaded the house on two different nights? And had whoever it
was found them and removed them?

It was a blow.

"But you didn't tell me about the orphans—you never told
me the ledgers were here—! How could I have protected them if

I didn't know—!" she demanded of the silent bed where her grandfather had slept—and died.

Francesca asked Mrs. Lane, who was peeling carrots for dinner, if she knew anything about a box of ledgers, but the housekeeper shook her head.

"Lord, no, Miss Francesca, he'd never talk to me about such things!"

"But there was a wooden greengrocer's box under his bed—surely you knew that?"

"Of course I did! He told me he'd put it there, and I left it where it was!" She looked up from the carrots as if she thought Francesca had taken leave of her mind.

But then if Francis Hatton had told her he had put a bit of the moon under his bed, Mrs. Lane would have dusted around it without complaint until he decided to remove it.

"Was the box full—empty?"

"I never looked, Miss Francesca! Why should I?"

The knocker rang through the house. Francesca said, "No, finish your cooking. I'll see to it. The rector, I should think!"

She unlocked the door with the heavy key and opened it instead to the man who looked like an undertaker's assistant. The Scot.

He said, without greeting, "The funeral's done with. I've come for what's mine."

"Then you must speak to the rector in Hurley or to Mr. Branscombe in Exeter," she answered coldly. "I don't deal with people I don't know."

Before she could shut the door, he said rapidly, "The name's Campbell. I'd think twice about that, if I were you! I handle tasks for gentlemen who don't wish to be seen to act on their own behalf. It's not a matter I'd want bruited about, and nor should you!"

Francesca stopped short. "What are you saying? That it wasn't aboveboard? Your agreement with my grandfather?"

"Aboveboard? You have to be daft, woman! He knew what he was getting himself into, well enough. He knew how I intended to use the information."

"*What* information?"

"It was mine. I paid for it, didn't I? He set a steep enough price, by God! And then he kept the bloody money and never sent what I'd bought!"

"You said something at the funeral about a box—what sort of box? Describe it for me!"

"How in hell's name am I to know?" He was staring at her in frustration. "He put the damned lot into a box. That's what he said, and that's what I'll have!"

Francesca would never have leapt to such a conclusion if the message from Mrs. Gibbon hadn't just arrived. And if she hadn't just seen the empty crate under Francis Hatton's bed for herself. "Box— You *bought* the *ledgers* from him?" she asked, stunned.

"Oh, yes, and I have a right to them now! By God, I do. I told him I'd have the newspapers down on that house in Somerset, if he didn't agree to work with me. And I would have done that. My masters would have been pleased to repay him for his stubbornness."

"That was blackmail!" she cried.

"And perhaps it was. But we understood each other, and in the end, he gave me what I wanted. At a price. It was worth it—in my line of business!"

"How were you planning to use the ledgers—to harm anyone important whose name you found there? To search out children who might have left the home and gone on to do well?"

There was stark antagonism in Campbell's face. "It was a political matter—so I was informed."

Miss Trotter's words suddenly came back to Francesca—how had she known that the Scot had a political connection? Or had Campbell been here before, pressuring Francis Hatton to do what he wished? With Miss Trotter, separating fact from fancy was never easy.

"Thank you for clearing up the matter!" Francesca retorted sharply. She was furious that this man had badgered her grandfather, furious that Mrs. Gibbon and the Falworthy children should have been put at risk. "As for the ledgers, before he died, my grandfather took them all to the moors and threw them down one of the old mine shafts. You're welcome to search for them there! At a guess, the ink will have run in the water at the bottom of the shaft, and the paper will be rotting away to scraps by now. But you may find legible bits, if you look hard enough. And if you come here again, my solicitor has been instructed to inform the police to look into your—affairs."

She broke off, shocked to hear herself tell him such bald-faced lies. And yet if someone could steal a photograph from the house in Falworthy, Campbell might well break into the strong room there—or threaten Mrs. Gibbon and her young charges. Just as he had threatened Francis Hatton.

Was that why Grandfather had insisted on taking the ledgers back to Devon, and then purposely failed to return them?

All the same, the lie had come so easily to her lips, swift and believable, as if her grandfather had stood at her shoulder, urging her on. And that frightened her almost as much as the man standing on her doorstep.

When had her childhood vanished and this grown woman taken little Cousin Francesca's place?

The day Francis Hatton's will had been read.

Before Campbell could retort, she had slammed the door in his face and locked it.

Still breathing hard, she leaned against the wood, listening to the fury of pounding fists hammering on the other side and the strident voice shouting, "Which mine shaft? Where? You must tell me *where!*"

But what did my grandfather do with those ledgers? If he sold them once—had he been offered a better price elsewhere?

No. Not Francis Hatton!

CHAPTER 22

Francesca set out on the fourth morning after taking her decision to leave. There had been two more of the anonymous letters, but this time she had shoved them into her desk in the sitting room, refusing to open them. Whoever was writing them, there was malice in the words and an intent to hurt. If they continued to arrive—or followed her to London—she would take the matter up with her solicitor. And these would be evidence.

She was dressed and in the hall, ready to leave, when she felt compelled to walk out to the gardens and stand for a moment by the Murder Stone. She couldn't have said why; it was an instinctive urge that went back to childhood and a happiness that had seemed limitless.

Harry. Peter. Robin. Freddy. Simon.

She whispered their names as if reaching out to them, calling them back one last time.

What would she do, after she'd carried out her grandfather's wishes and somehow transported this familiar lump of stone to far-off Scotland? Could she bear to part with it? For the life of her, she couldn't see any necessity for taking it away from here, where it had belonged for centuries. In this one thing, she was tempted to defy her grandfather.

Why, at the end of his life, had he suddenly turned against the Murder Stone? If she could understand that, his request would seem more reasonable.

Francesca pulled off her glove, wanting to reach out and touch the familiar, cool surface. Then withdrew her hand, hesitant. Finally, after a deep breath, she stooped and laid her fingers against the stone.

It seemed to quiver under her touch. Or was that her own flesh trembling? She rose to her feet.

She was doing the right thing, leaving here. Even the stone agreed.

And who is superstitious now? she asked herself as she walked back to the house.

The Valley was wreathed with heavy fog when Bill drove her in the carriage to Exeter, where she was to take the train for London. She had smoothed Tyler's head and scratched behind the old dog's ears, and tried to keep the tears out of her voice as she bade him farewell. Mrs. Lane had pressed a tin of freshly baked biscuits into her hand "for the journey." The rector had waved to her from the bridge but hadn't come to the house.

At the station, Bill clasped her gloved hand without a word, his face saying what he could not.

"I'll be back soon, I promise," she told him. But both of them knew it was a lie. Nothing would bring her back before the war's end.

Except, she told herself, unanswered questions. Yet the break-ins had stopped with the departure of Richard Leighton, although the shooter had fired again at first light. She had heard the echo as she was dressing.

The train was over an hour late. Exeter was blanketed by a

sea mist, the red sandstone dark with wet, streets so murky that lights from shop windows hardly penetrated the gloom, casting an eerie glow as if they were at the bottom of the sea. As soon as Bill had disposed of her baggage, she urged him home again before visibility grew even worse.

"I know the city, and I shall be safe as houses at the station," she reminded him. "And God knows when we shall see the train. Mr. Branscombe's office isn't far, I can call on him if I need anything! I'd rather know you were safely in the Valley before the daylight fails entirely."

In the end he put her into the charge of the elderly station master and reluctantly left.

Shortly before noon, when the train still hadn't arrived, Francesca, famished, finally went in search of the station master and asked when the train was to be expected.

The old man pursed his lips. "There's been a storm to the east and debris on the line," he confessed. "I'm told it'ul be another three quarters of an hour before we can hope to see the train."

"Then I shall have time to find something to eat."

He directed her to a nearby shop where she could find tea and sandwiches, cautioning her to have a care in the fog.

The tea shop seemed to swim alone, an island in a gray sea. Its coziness was welcoming as she stepped inside. Other refugees from the railway station were already being served, and it was nearly a quarter of an hour before she could place her order. As she was finishing her potted ham sandwiches, the whistle of the incoming train startled her. She hurried to pay her reckoning and went out into the street.

If anything, the fog was worse. Sounds were muffled, confusing. She was just skirting crates stacked by the roadway when the man behind her missed his footing and stumbled. Trying to catch his balance, he jostled her into someone else and the next thing Francesca knew, she was in the street. She could hear a cart coming at speed, looming out of the mist, and leapt toward the walkway, but the crates pinned her in the road.

As she cried out, the lead horse struck her hard on the shoulder, spinning her first into the crates and then, in a hard rebound, directly in the path of the oncoming high rear wheels. She managed to roll beneath the cart in time, and then as the carter shouted curses at her for being in his way and tried to rein in his team, another vehicle crashed into him and a hoof caught her leg with a glancing blow.

A laborer ran into the road and dragged her to her feet to push her to the safety of the walk. One of the horses, startled by his sudden appearance almost under its feet, reared, sending the laborer and his burden reeling across the walk. Francesca struck her cheek hard on the damp stone of a building.

The train's clanging bell echoed in her ears as darkness came down.

It was quiet when Francesca opened her eyes. She tried to think where she was. The bed was too hard to be hers at River's End, and a shielded lamp burned at the end of the room on a table where her windows should have been.

Her throat was parched. She moved a little, thinking to go downstairs for a glass of water, but there was something heavy and clumsy pinning her leg to the bed. Trying to shift it hurt too much and she stopped. Lying there, searching for familiarity in her surroundings, she fell asleep once more.

A woman's voice woke her, asking her name, wanting to know if there was someone who should be contacted on her behalf. Francesca answered fretfully that there was no one left—her family was dead.

When another woman asked the same question much later, Francesca was beginning to think more rationally.

"My name is Hatton, Francesca Hatton," she replied. "I don't think I know this place."

"The casualty ward at Queen Victoria Hospital, Miss Hatton."

"Yes," she answered, for some reason annoyed. "Many little

girls were named for the old Queen—" Then the words broke through the confusion and she repeated, "Hospital?"

"You were found at the scene of a road accident, Miss," the nursing sister told her, kindness in the soft voice. "Rather battered and bruised, I'm afraid. We've let you sleep and heal."

"I don't remember anything!" Her head was aching. The sister turned to speak to someone out of sight. A cup of tea appeared as if by magic and she was lifted against pillows to drink it. Every bone in her body complained vociferously. "Mrs. Lane?" she called to the shadowy second figure, and then was too busy drinking thirstily. "What's wrong with my leg? There's something in its way—"

"It's broken, Miss, and in splints. Does it still hurt? I'm afraid it's too early to give you anything more for the pain."

The tea was soothing. Francesca answered drowsily, "Have I been here long? I mustn't miss my train."

She never heard the answer or felt the cup removed from her hands.

Hours later she woke again, this time clearer-headed and hungry. Her body still ached, but the pain was more bearable as if bruises were subsiding.

The staff was kind, but she learned that she hadn't been the only victim of fog-related mishaps, and the small hospital had accepted the worse cases, mostly broken bones.

"Luckily," a middle-aged sister informed her, "in your case it's not the weight-bearing bone. But see the older woman across the way? Compound fracture," she explained darkly. "Ah, here's a tray for you. Can you manage? I've more mouths to feed than I have hands!"

Francesca stopped her as she turned away. "I remember— I was taking the train this morning."

"Not this morning, my dear!" Sister answered with amusement. "You've been here nearly two days! What do you think of that? If there's anyone you want to come and fetch you, tell Matron. She'll see to it."

Mr. Branscombe, Francesca thought immediately, and then changed her mind. She wasn't up to his fussing over her, commandeering a private room and making the overworked staff wretched. She wanted to go home. If Matron would send word to River's End, she told herself, Mrs. Lane and Bill would come at once and take her home.

They had sedated her again as the leg began hurting. That reminded her of Richard Leighton, and she wondered if he had seen the Army surgeon as he'd promised.

Someone came to set pillows under her leg to support it, and she finally managed to drift into sleep.

She woke to the sound of Francis Hatton's voice, and his strong hands holding hers. The ward was dark save for the night lamp on the table by the door.

"Oh, you've come!" she exclaimed, tears filling her eyes. "You don't know how I've longed—"

The sedative had fuddled her wits. Grandfather was dead—yet she could hear him saying, "Dearest girl—I've been frantic!"

"No, you mustn't worry, I'm much better," she assured him. "Just terribly drowsy. My eyes feel as if there were pennies weighing them down."

"Sleep then. I'm here. I've asked to sit by you for a while. They won't throw me out—"

His lips brushed her forehead, and then she heard him moving away. He came back with a basin of cool water and began to bathe her face and hands, the sponge moving gently over her skin. He was saying something about a telegram.

"Harry's dead, isn't he?" she demanded forlornly. "The telegram said he was."

"Yes. Your cousin is dead." The voice was low, careful not to disturb the patients on either side. Its warmth seemed to make Harry's fate less unbearable, because they were sharing this last enormous grief.

Tears slipped out of the corners of her eyes, and she could

feel her lip tremble. She was so very tired—there had been no one to comfort her for so long.

"You won't leave me, will you? You won't let them throw you out!"

"No. I'll be here when you wake, I promise."

But when she woke at first light, there was no one in the chair beside the bed. "Grandfather?" she called softly, thinking he might be somewhere just out of sight.

As the last dregs of sleep faded, she remembered that Francis Hatton was dead and would never come again.

It was Richard Leighton who came striding through the ward half an hour later. He was freshly shaved, his clothes pressed. And his fair hair was damp as if he had just bathed and was too much in a hurry to brush it fully dry.

"You're actually awake, I see!" he said cheerfully, in a mood so different from the darkness that usually held him in a tight grip.

Startled to see him, she exclaimed, putting a hand up to her disheveled hair. "Where did you come from?"

"The hotel. They threw me out in spite of my pleading. Matron told me six, and it's barely two minutes past."

She remembered that his watch held Victoria's photograph, but said, "Whatever are you doing here?"

"I've come to take you home. I expected to find your solicitor here, but Matron informs me you've had no visitors."

"I didn't care to see him, if you want the truth. I sent word to the Valley as soon as I could."

She told him about the fog and her accident, but he already seemed to know the details.

A sister, young and pretty, came down the ward toward her, bringing flowers in a glass jar. "For you!" she said, her eyes sliding to Leighton's face.

"How lovely! Where on earth did you find violets at this time of year!" she asked Leighton as the young woman set the jar on the table and went away with a last lingering glance at Francesca's visitor.

"There's a shop Matron told me about. Not a great selection, but fair enough. I've spoken to someone at the hotel—about arrangements to drive you to River's End."

"Bill should be here soon. You needn't go to so much trouble!"

"It isn't trouble. Ah—there's Matron. I'll be back shortly. Where is your luggage?"

"I don't know!" She frowned, trying to think. "I suppose—it must have been sent on to London. I left it at the station when I went to the tea shop. How awkward!"

"Then I'll see what can be done. Sister will help me. She's just going off duty."

An unaccustomed flare of something—jealousy? Impossible!—raced through Francesca. She could see the pretty young woman waiting for Leighton at the ward door. The smile on her lips.

She said, to change the subject, "I dreamed about my grandfather last night. It was—comforting."

"Matron tells me the clothes you were wearing were in no state to be saved. I'll ask at the railway station for your luggage before seeing what's to be had in the shops."

Taking Francesca's hands, as he had done the night of the Zeppelin raid, he said, "I won't be long." Once more his eyes were on her face as if expecting a response. When she didn't reply, he added, "You'll be home by teatime, if I can manage it."

She had been bathed and her hair washed before Leighton came back.

This time Bill was at his heels, lines of strain marking his face. But he smiled when he saw Francesca, saying only, "Miss?"

She watched his gnarled hands twist his cap through his fingers as he came to stand awkwardly by the bed.

"It's not serious, I promise you," she said, gesturing to the splints, just visible under the coverlet. "Did you bring Mrs. Lane with you?"

"No, Miss, we didn't know where you were! The station master sent word by one of the carters that you hadn't got aboard the train, and no one had any idea where you'd got to. We were that worried! Rector, he went to London, but you weren't there. Gave us a terrible fright, that news did! But Mr. Leighton, here, saw me on my way to Mr. Branscombe's office and hailed me. A bit of luck that was, to be sure!"

"But I sent word—" She remembered giving one of the Sisters her name and could have sworn she'd spoken with Matron about a message to River's End! Had it really happened? Or, like her grandfather's visit, was it only another drugged dream? They had kept her quiet with sedatives, and her wits were still so muddled— "Never mind! All that matters is that you're here. And Mr. Leighton is here. Now I must think what to wear home!"

"Your luggage is in the boot of the motorcar, Miss. The station master held it for me. Tell me what you need and I'll fetch it. Is it that gray case?"

By late morning Francesca was nestled among cushions in the rear of the motorcar. Leighton was beside her, just as he'd been on the journey to Essex.

Miss Trotter had been right, she told herself, ignoring the nagging ache in her leg. Richard Leighton *was* coming back to the Valley. She refused to examine the question of why it mattered.

She could feel his shoulder next to hers, his body bracing hers behind the shield of cushions against the jolts of the badly rutted road. The passenger's seat had been shifted forward to allow room for the cumbersome splints on her leg, covered now by a rug.

They had given her something at hospital to ease the pain of the journey. She was content to sit quietly and listen to

Leighton talking with Bill as they drove out of Exeter and turned north to the Valley.

"... Miss Hatton sent me a telegram," she heard Leighton explaining to the old man at the wheel. "From hospital. I took the next train out of London—"

"A telegram? But I never sent you any telegram! I can't imagine what you're talking about." She tried to turn and look at his face.

But she could feel a physical withdrawal in the man at her side. As if he had shut himself off from her without warning.

And after that, he spoke only when he was directly addressed, his coldness so apparent that even Bill subsided into silence.

She wanted to explain that she hadn't had his London direction—that it would have been impossible to reach him. That she was glad that he had come to her, however he'd learned about the accident. But something in his manner made it impossible to confide in him.

Her violets, wilting in the cold air, seemed to mock her as she looked for a way to break through the impenetrable barrier that had so unexpectedly been thrown up between them. After a time she set the flowers aside and pretended she wasn't hurt by the abrupt change in Richard Leighton.

Why had he lied to Bill about a telegram? And how had he come to find her? Why was it that every time she warmed to this man, he cut her overtures short and shut her out?

Had his grandfather taught him only hardness and cruelty? Or was he afraid that if he set down his burden even for a little while, he could never lift it up again?

Mrs. Lane had opened the house again and was in the kitchen, cooking, when the motorcar turned into the drive. Mr. Lane and two brawny men from the village were summoned to bring down a bed and set it up in the sitting room, so that the patient wouldn't have to manage the stairs. A cheerful fire already blazed on the hearth. Tyler was there, to wag a ferocious welcome, his stiff, thick body corkscrewing in delight.

Mrs. Lane also found a boudoir chair in the box room, dusty but in good repair. That was brought down and cleaned. Ensconced on that, her leg propped up before her, Francesca leaned back and said with a sigh, "It really *is* good to be home!"

The rector, who had heard the motorcar and hurried to the house for news, said, "I'll be on my way and let you rest. I'm glad you're safe! Leighton, shall I bespeak a room for you at the inn?"

"Yes, if you will. I'll be there on your heels."

Francesca thanked the rector warmly for traveling to London for her sake and wished him good night. Then she turned to Leighton. The house was quiet around them, the dog asleep under the bed.

"I have you to thank as well—"

He was standing at the window, not looking at her. "Why did you deny sending that telegram? There's no one here but the two of us. You can tell me the truth."

"But I have told you—I never sent a telegram to you or anyone else. And if you think about it, I couldn't have known how to reach you."

"I gave my card to Mrs. Lane. Or you could have asked at The Spotted Calf."

He turned and held out a telegram form.

Francesca read it with rising indignation.

Am seriously injured. Please come as soon as possible. Queen Victoria Hospital, Exeter.

And it was signed *Francesca Hatton.*

"But who could have done this? I never spoke of you to the staff—"

He considered her for a moment, and then said flatly, "It doesn't matter. You had no reason to summon me, I can see that. Perhaps it's on a par with these. One was waiting for me at the flat, and the other arrived just after I returned." He reached into his pocket and withdrew several envelopes.

Before he had even put them into her hand, Francesca recognized the writing on each of them.

"What do they say?" she asked with trepidation, her eyes going to his grim face.

"Go ahead. Read them."

She opened the first. The sheet contained no salutation and no signature. But the words that had been written there in black ink leapt out at her.

If you find the proof you are looking for, what will you do with it?

"What proof? About your mother? Or my grandfather?" She looked up at him. "Do you know who wrote this?"

"Proof of murder, I suppose. I have no idea who may be behind it. Someone from the Valley? Someone in Sussex who knew my mother? Read the second."

Francesca opened it. This message was as straightforward as the first.

You have so little time left. Will you waste it—or use it wisely?

She looked up at Leighton. "What does this mean?"

"I never told you. There's a bullet lodged next to my spine. The military doctors disagree on the prognosis—whether it will cripple me first or kill me outright. They do agree I don't have a long and productive life ahead of me. It's pressing on the nerves."

It was true, then. The rector had suspected it . . . but that was not the same as hearing it from Leighton himself. She could think of nothing to say, and he made no effort to help her.

"How many people would know such a thing?" she asked.

"A handful. But I shouldn't think it would be difficult to learn I was invalided out of the Army. Or why."

"It still doesn't explain why *you* should have received such letters. There have been others—similar ones—sent to me. And I thought perhaps it was—" She stopped, unable to say that she could almost believe they'd been sent by his grandfather. She had sensed the intensity of Alasdair's hatred, there in the shadows of the stairs. Who else would have hated Francis Hatton enough to write them? And why send them to his grandson? To remind him of his duty? Trying for a moderate tone, she continued. "—was something to do with my grandfather. The first two I burned. You should have done the same with these!"

"First two? You kept the others?"

She gestured to the desk. "In the top drawer. Under the stationery and that book of household accounts."

Leighton opened the desk and looked where she had indicated. He took out letters identical to his own.

"May I?"

Francesca nodded, then thought better of it. "No, let me open them."

She did, and read aloud, " *'You are surrounded by enemies. Trust no one. Not even the solicitor!'* "

"A warning then," he said. "Whether a friendly one or not, it's hard to tell. And the other?"

Francesca opened that, and didn't immediately read it aloud.

"What does it say?" Leighton prompted.

" *'If you find your brother,'* " she read slowly, " *'you will understand everything.'* I don't have a brother. I never did. Well, it shows us, doesn't it, that this is nothing but ridiculous nonsense!" She set the letters aside with distaste.

"Is it?" Leighton asked. "What about the two you burned? What did they say?"

"I— They were about Grandfather—my family." She didn't want to tell him the truth, that they had questioned her paternity.

"Strange how everything comes back to your family. My mother's disappearance, the vultures who attended the funeral, whoever it is who has walked with impunity into this house at night. Secrets that have no answers. Small matters, apparently. All of them. But there *has* to be something behind what's happening—or someone."

"The vultures came because of the *Times* obituary—just as you did. And the man shooting in the Valley is a deserter, you suggested that yourself. He probably doesn't even know

Francis Hatton existed. Next you'll tell me that my accident on an Exeter street was somehow my grandfather's fault!"

He smiled briefly. "No, that needed no human agency. A storm cut a swath of damage across a good part of southern England. That's why your train was delayed. We'll grant you the storm and the shooter, then! But I have a feeling that the telegram and these letters are of a piece. Why were they sent to you? Why were they sent to me? My mother is the only tie between us!"

Too weary to argue any longer, she replied, before she thought, "My grandfather is dead and buried. There must be someone else who knows—or believes he knows—what became of your mother. And the only two people I can think of who could tell us are your father—or your grandfather. But that brings up the question of how either of them could have discovered I was in Queen Victoria Hospital?"

Richard Leighton stared at her for a moment. "Yes," he answered slowly. "You bring up a very good point!"

CHAPTER 23

Francesca's leg ached in the night, and the sitting room was stuffier than her bedchamber. Getting down from the high bed was possible—climbing back was not. And she hadn't had the foresight to stock the table beside her with books to read. As the hall clock struck one, she even found herself seriously considering taking up the needlework she'd abhorred as a girl—it would help pass the time.

Mrs. Lane, who had stayed the night, was upstairs and out of reach, out of hearing. Nothing less than a scream would rouse her, and Francesca even had her doubts about that.

The old house seemed to creak and stir with different voices from those she was accustomed to in her own bed, and a gusting wind rattled the windows and touched the sitting room door, as if someone had tested the latch.

At long last Mrs. Lane came bearing a tray of hot tea and a pitcher of warm water for bathing. Francesca sat up, brushed

her hair out of her face, and answered the housekeeper's subdued greeting.

"Did you sleep well, Miss?"

"Not at first. Oh, this tea is lovely—"

"I've got a little bad news for you this morning, Miss."

Francesca stopped stirring her tea and looked up.

"It's old Tyler, Miss. I found him lying just outside
your grandfather's door. Already cold. He hadn't wanted to
come downstairs, you know. The poor old creature seemed
to be set on staying in your room. And I left the door ajar-like,
so that if he needed to get out, he could, without waking
us all."

"He's dead? You're sure—" Francesca set her tea aside.

"Oh, yes, Miss. I asked Bill to come and fetch him,
and bury him in the bottom of the garden. It's what
Mr. Hatton had always said he'd do, if the dog went first. 'He
likes the garden best,' he'd say. 'And I think I'd like to be
buried there as well, if it was all the same to the rest of the
world. But it's the churchyard for me, and the garden for dear
old Tyler.' "

The boys, her grandfather—the dog . . . all gone.

She felt like burying her head in her hands and weeping.

But the dog had missed her grandfather dreadfully. Had he
finally given up waiting for his master to come back again . . .
and decided to join him?

"I'm glad," Francesca said, "that you remembered. Thank
you, Mrs. Lane." But she could see that Mrs. Lane hadn't finished. The housekeeper busied herself in the room, tidying
here and there.

At length she said, "Somehow I'm not comfortable staying
here of a night, Miss Francesca. Not with that shooter about.
And when I come down this morning, I found doors open
that I'd swear I'd closed. It's fair to giving me the willies."

"But if you aren't here to help me—"

Mrs. Lane turned to face her. "It's time you went to the
Rectory, Miss. Mrs. Horner could help care for you, and the
rector could lift you and carry you where you needed to go.

His foot's not so bad that it'd hurt him. I can't do that. And it makes Mr. Lane uneasy when I'm not there of a night. It'll be a while before you're walking well again, Miss. And I'm not up to doing for you and for him, day and night. I'd come every day to see to the house, mind you. While it was light. Wash and dust, and set out a meal for Bill. But I don't quite see myself sleeping another night here, what with the dog gone now and you not able to move."

"But I don't want to leave," Francesca protested, feeling as if the world was collapsing around her. "And you'll see, I heal quickly, I always did."

"Not with that leg broke, Miss. No, it's best. I thought it through while I was making your breakfast, and I feel it's the best thing for both of us."

The housekeeper was adamant, tension in her face. She was afraid . . .

Francesca said without committing herself, "We'll talk about it later. I think, if you could help me—I desperately need to find something to read, and my torch, if you please. My comb and brush—a small mirror."

"Yes, Miss, I'll see to them."

The housekeeper was gone, before Francesca could add to her list.

What am I to do? I wish I'd gone on to London.

But she knew she didn't mean it.

When Leighton came, Francesca told him sadly, "Tyler is dead. My grandfather's dog. And Mrs. Lane refuses to stay here at night again. She wants me to move to the Rectory."

Leighton frowned. "Is that a good idea? The rector, after all, is not a married man." He didn't seem best pleased.

"He has a housekeeper. Mrs. Horner. I can't walk, I can't manage on my own. And who'll come from the village to stay the night, if Mrs. Lane won't? The women are a suspicious lot; they'll be sure something is wrong here."

"You could try Miss Trotter," he suggested. "The healer."

Francesca brightened. "Yes. She just might come."

"There's news of the shooter," he went on, taking the chair next to the bed, for all the world like a visitor in a hospital ward.

"Indeed! Mrs. Lane heard him again this morning. Have they caught him?"

"No. But the Army thinks it has a line on him. A patient went missing from a military hospital in Hampshire some weeks ago. And he stole the night guard's rifle and belt. The man was asleep at his post."

"It's a long way from Hampshire to the Valley," she remarked skeptically. "He'd have done better, if he'd come this far, to make for Exmoor. Or Dartmoor."

"It's possible he may have lived near here. That he's trying to make it home."

"Near the Valley? Who is he?" she asked quickly.

"The Army didn't give a name. It could mean they themselves don't know. Or aren't prepared to say."

"If he was a patient, there ought to be records—! Who told you this story?"

"It came with a milk cart returning up-valley. The carters are better than a newspaper. I heard it at the inn this morning." Leighton paused. "The hospital in Hampshire takes difficult cases. Officers mainly. Head wounds. Shell shock. Troubled men. The refuse of war. I visited a friend there once, when I had leave. He sat twitching and jerking like a broken puppet. He had no idea who I was. Come to that, I nearly failed to recognize him. A fortnight later, he slashed his wrists with a broken glass. It was reported that he'd died of his wounds, peacefully and honorably. They often lie in such circumstances. To spare the family."

"An officer? But the only officers from the Valley—" Francesca felt cold. "Not—not Harry, do you think? Or Robin? Not—one of the cousins!"

"No, of course not!"

But he had spoken too quickly, Francesca noted, and she wasn't comforted.

"I'd wanted to see him caught—taken away from here," she confessed. "Now—I'm not so sure. If he's one of ours—anyone from the Valley—but I'm tied to this bed, I can't do anything to help!"

"Whoever he is, he can't go on living rough with winter coming. And if he's in need of medical care, he won't get it out in the hills. The Army won't shoot him—"

"You don't know that!"

"If he's not a deserter, Francesca, there's nothing to fear."

"If only I could *walk*—!" But it would be weeks before she could expect to see that much improvement.

Dismissing the subject of the man in the hills, Leighton said, "Shall I call on Miss Trotter and ask if she's willing to come?"

"Yes, please! I don't want to go to the Rectory—especially not now! And there's a pair of field glasses in the cupboard in my grandfather's study. Could you bring them to me, before you go? I can at least amuse myself a little, looking out the windows." She was afraid to ask him as well for Simon's pistol.

But she hadn't misled him. He said, "No. Stay away from that man, Francesca! He's dangerous, even though he hasn't killed anyone yet. He isn't one of your cousins, and he isn't someone you know."

Who had come into the house at night?

Francesca remembered what Leighton had said earlier: *"He's trying to make it home."*

"I've been lying here until I'm ready to go mad! Can you help me to the boudoir chair?"

"I'll even move it to the window, if you wish it. But no glasses."

He did move the chair, and then gave her his shoulder to help her limp to it, saying, his arm around her, "They were reported dead, remember that. The Army seldom gets the count of its dead wrong."

"Mr. Stevens told me once that sometimes bodies were only so much flesh, hardly recognizable as human."

"He had no business telling you that." He settled her in the chair, and drew a rug over her feet and limbs. "Are there books I can bring to you?"

"Yes, but they're beside my bed upstairs. Mrs. Lane will have to fetch them." She smiled. "If she caught you rummaging around in there, it would shock her no end."

"I'll go in search of Miss Trotter, then. To set your mind at ease about staying on here."

"It's kind of you—"

"No. Not kind." He gave her an odd smile. "Perhaps I'm only trying to get on your good side."

"I don't have a good side," she answered ruefully. "Not anymore!"

But as he reached the door, she asked for a second time, "Why did you come back to the Valley?" He had brought her home . . . he needn't have stayed in the Valley. He was such a contradictory man. She wished she could understand him.

He looked at her over his shoulder, hesitated, and then said, "I thought I knew. Now I'm not sure."

When he came again, Francesca was finishing her luncheon on a tray in her lap. Beside her were some half-dozen books, set in a tidy stack.

"What news?"

"Miss Trotter was difficult to persuade. I asked her to come this afternoon and give you her answer."

Francesca sighed. "That means no. She's so reclusive—always has been."

"Do you think Mrs. Lane would stay—if someone else spent the night here as well?"

"You?" she asked bluntly.

"I was here for two nights, when I was concussed."

"You were in no condition at the time to threaten my maidenly virtue. The doctor probably told her as much."

He grinned. "The way the woman slept, I don't think your virtue weighed too heavily on her mind."

In the event, Miss Trotter did not come, although Francesca had told Mrs. Lane that she expected her before dark. Uneasy about leaving, the housekeeper lingered until the light began to fail, then scurried off down the hill as if all the devils of River's End were at her heels.

Francesca had asked her to leave the kitchen door unlocked, and as the hours ticked by, she began to think about that. There was no way to reach it and lock it again—and Miss Trotter wasn't coming.

The house seemed noisier in the wind. She had always watched Tyler, when the floorboards began to creak or the ceilings cracked and settled. If he raised his head to listen, she took note of it. But when he slept on, twitching with his dreams, she'd known there was nothing to worry about.

Now she was aware of every sound, not precisely afraid, but feeling claustrophobic in this small room where there was nowhere to run.

I'd give anything now for Simon's pistol—!

Mrs. Lane had settled her in her bed again, with her dinner on a tray within reach, a pitcher of water to hand, and books close on the table.

It was a little before seven-thirty when the door knocker's heavy *clang* rang through the house. Francesca, sighing with relief, waited for Miss Trotter to walk around to the kitchen door. Surely she'd think of that, even if Leighton hadn't thought to tell her.

The knocker rang out twice more. Francesca waited. It was useless to call out, no one could hear her— She had only to be patient.

But time passed without an appearance by Miss Trotter.

Leighton, then. It had been Leighton who had come to see if she was all right. Or the rector, concerned that Miss Trotter was frail company for a woman unable to walk. Perhaps Mrs.

Lane was right, that staying in the Rectory made more sense. But she hated giving up her independence, even for a matter of weeks. And if the rector was in love with her, it would be uncomfortable for both of them.

She leaned back against her pillows, her mind now on the kitchen door.

Twenty minutes later, Francesca looked up, startled. Surely—surely someone was moving quietly down the passage toward her—

Ah. Miss Trotter, bless her! Either she'd gone down to Hurley to ask Mrs. Lane which door was unlocked or she'd thought about the kitchen door on her own.

Francesca had opened her mouth to call out when the door opened tentatively and a stranger stared at her, as shocked as she was.

Even as she was reaching for the knife on her dinner tray, Francesca realized she knew the frightened woman standing in the doorway.

Mrs. Passmore, who had claimed to be Francesca's nanny for the first months of her life here at River's End—the woman who had stolen a photograph from the house in Somerset—

"What do you want?" Francesca asked, her voice cold and hard, but her hands were shaking so much that she dropped the knife and hid them beneath the bedclothes.

"Oh—oh, my good God—I knocked—I knocked, truly—no one came—I thought the house was *empty*, that you'd returned to London—"

"What do you want?" Francesca repeated, recovering first. "My dog is under the bed, I have only to give him the signal—"

"Please—no! I'm not here to harm anyone—" Mrs.

Passmore began to back out of the room. "I'm terrified of dogs—I'll just go—"

"Move to leave again, and he'll attack. Who are you?"

"But—I told you before—I was your nanny—" She was haggard.

"You're a liar. The real Miss Weaver is in New Zealand. I have written to her."

The woman's face seemed to crumple, tears filling her eyes. "Truly—my name is Mrs. Passmore. I didn't lie about that. And I did meet Miss Weaver once. Years ago. In Somerset. And truly my husband is dead..."

"Then why have you come here—*twice!*—under false pretenses!"

Mrs. Passmore fumbled for a handkerchief. "When my husband died in 1914—we had no children, you see. I always thought perhaps that was because of what I'd done years before—" Her voice trailed off, her eyes unable to move away from the shrouded foot of the bedstead.

"Go on!"

"I had had a child out of wedlock. Before I was married— by another man. I taught his children, I thought he lov—he cared for me. But I was wrong. I took my child to that house, The Swans, in Falworthy. Someone had told me— And I left my son there!"

She was crying in earnest now, the threat of the dog forgotten.

Francesca said impatiently, "Sit down and pull yourself together."

The woman obeyed, creeping in and casting frightened glances at the bedclothes that hung to the floor, concealing whatever was underneath. She sat by the fire, perched on the edge of the chair that Leighton had used, and said, "I *tried* to put what I had done out of my mind. And when—when Mr. Passmore asked me to marry him, I never found the courage to tell him about my baby. I was afraid he would walk *away*."

"And now your husband's dead, you want to find this child of yours?"

"I have to *know*—don't you see? They're killing so many young men out there in France! I look at the casualty lists, thousands of names, and it's no use, because I have no earthly idea what name they might have given my child in that home. And he could be dead—wounded—or alive—there's no way of telling."

"But why come to me? I know nothing—"

"Because your grandfather owned the house in Falworthy. That's what Miss Weaver told me many years ago—she was teaching the little ones there when I—I was a client. And you must have inherited the responsibility, since he had no other survivors. I hoped you might know where the records are kept, and if I could look through them for my boy."

"You'll have to speak to Mrs. Gibbon. As far as I know she's always had sole responsibility for the orphanage. Not my grandfather."

"She appears to be avoiding me! I went there before Mr. Hatton's funeral, and I was told she was occupied with an outbreak of measles in the house. I did manage to persuade a young girl to show me the public rooms, but that was all. When I called again, Mrs. Gibbon was reluctant to answer my questions. It did make me wonder if she was hiding something—that perhaps it was true your grandfather had adopted my son. I've heard the whispers, you know! If he found a child to his liking, he'd take it for himself and raise it as his own. There were five boys, and I thought the one they call Harry down in the village—I thought he might be the right age—"

CHAPTER 24

Francesca stared at Mrs. Passmore.

The woman could read disbelief in her face, and searched quickly in her handbag, bringing out the photograph of a woman and child she had shown Francesca before—the one she had most certainly taken from The Swans in Falworthy.

"Please! Look at this photograph! *Was* this Harry? I studied the collection on the table in the chapel, and the instant I saw this one, I knew it had to be my child! He looks just as my brother did at that age! I have this to prove it—"

She drew out another frame but wouldn't approach the bed for fear of the dog beneath it. Francesca had to reach out to take both of them.

Looking at first one and then the other of the infants, she could understand what Mrs. Passmore was saying. There *was* a resemblance between the two babies, but in her opinion it didn't go beyond the wide eyes, plump cheeks, and tentative smile all children that age possessed. In fact, Francesca couldn't say with any certainty if both were boys.

But then Mrs. Passmore was blinded by her own convictions.

"Who is the woman in this photograph? My late aunt?"

"Oh, no, I'd swear that's Miss Weaver holding the child. She was the one who told me that fascinating story about the male ostriches, you know. I found it very consoling over the years. And the only reason I can think of for her to have done so was because my son was to be given to your grandfather! I was so grateful that someone—I'm sure it was Miss Weaver!—had been kind enough to leave this photograph where I could find it one day, if I came back." She smiled sadly. "It was wrong of me, I know, but I slipped the frame into my bag when the little girl showing me around on my first visit was distracted. And when I went back again, I left the one I'd taken from this house, hoping it might somehow find its way back to you."

"But why on earth did you take a photograph of *my* parents?"

"I didn't know who they *were*," Mrs. Passmore cried. "Not then! And it was the only photograph I could find in this house. I couldn't ask—you'd only just buried your grandfather! I simply took it, thinking it wouldn't matter to you but in some way it would help me. I can't explain—I was so hungry for something—anything that might lead me to my son!"

"Harry couldn't have been your child," Francesca told her bluntly. "He was born to my aunt and uncle—"

"No, no! I have evidence!" She held out a yellowed cutting from a newspaper. "Look!"

It was an obituary notice, Francesca saw, for Tristan and Margaret Hatton. Dead by an unknown hand . . . She scanned the short column quickly. It listed as survivors only Francis Hatton, father, and Edward Hatton, brother, of Canada.

"This can't be right," Francesca told her firmly. "There were five sons—my cousins." *How had Grandfather managed to keep their names out of the newspaper? Bribes—to protect his family from brutal gossip?*

Ignoring her, Mrs. Passmore said, "I tell you, I've spent

months looking for answers. And the only one that fits is that my child was adopted into this family. I came tonight to search for other photographs—of Harry in his uniform or at school—something that would show me how his face changed as he grew up. Something that would tell me that I'm right! I didn't want to steal anything—I wasn't doing any *harm*—"

"Housebreaking is a serious offense! Have you come here in the night before this?"

"I promise you, I never did any such thing!" Mrs. Passmore exclaimed, as though affronted. "But I'm desperate—I couldn't think of another way to *ask*!"

"I'm sorry. Whether he was truly your son or not, Harry is dead—buried somewhere in France."

"That doesn't change anything. I need to see what kind of man my child grew into. I need the peace of mind of knowing that my abandonment didn't ruin his life, that he went to a good home, was loved—cared for—"

Her face was a mask of grief. "I want to mourn," she said, through her tears. "I want to leave flowers somewhere and think about him as the man I never watched grow up. I want to *mourn*!"

After a time, Francesca said quietly, "I don't believe there are any photographs of the cousins growing up. My grandfather always called them a waste of time and an embarrassment later in life." But had that only been an excuse—?

"There's the one of your parents—the one I took at the time of your grandfather's funeral—"

"My father sent it to him. My grandfather refused to own a camera!"

"I can't believe—"

"There *are* no photographs."

The ravaged face lifted, studied her. Then Mrs. Passmore tucked the photographs and the cutting back into her handbag as if tucking a child into its cradle. "You grew up with Harry," she begged. "What was he like?"

"He was sweet-natured and fun and, oh, I don't know, just *Harry.*"

"His father—the man who seduced me—was a charmer. There was a lightness in his manner, as if nothing bad had ever happened to him. As if the gods had promised him nothing bad would ever happen. If your Harry was like that, I don't know how he bore the war. How he could watch the killing and not go mad from horror."

Francesca, too, had asked herself if his laughter had been stilled, his spirit dead long before his body died....

"You mustn't torment yourself this way," she told the older woman. "You can't go about looking for children who might resemble your son—there will be hundreds who could be him. And no assurance that this or that one is truly the child you're looking for."

Mrs. Passmore said spiritedly, "You have never borne a child. You don't know what it is like to carry him in your body—"

"But you preferred to marry Mr. Passmore and pretend this child never existed," Francesca pointed out.

"He existed in my heart," she replied simply. "And I told myself I'd done all I could for him. But then the war came, and my husband passed on soon after. I began to wonder about my own boy. They say dying soldiers call out for their mothers—I could hear him in my dreams, and I'd wake up weeping. If there was a young man you loved, you'd surely feel much the same. Wondering if anyone was with him when he died, if you could have comforted him, if he called your name..."

With dignity she got to her feet. "I'm sorry if I frightened you. I didn't intend to do harm," she said for a third time, as if she truly believed it. "I only wanted to see young Harry's face."

"You told me," Francesca said, "that my aunt had gone to Switzerland, that she was consumptive."

"It was a lie. I didn't want to mention murder. I wasn't sure how much you knew."

"What happened?"

"I don't think anyone knows, really. There were rumors that the truth had been hushed up, and as far as I'm aware, no one was ever apprehended for the crime. A tragedy. I followed the story all those years ago, you see, having heard Miss Weaver speak of Mr. Hatton. It took me a very long time to find this cutting, but I managed." She walked to the door, wary of what lay beneath the bedclothes. "He won't bite, if I leave now, will he? I'm staying at The Spotted Calf, if you should wish to press charges. But I beg you not to!"

On the threshold she stopped. "Are you here all alone? Except for your dog?"

"Tyler's all the protection I need."

"On your word of honor—there are no photographs?"

"You could ask at Oxford. Surely there were house photographs, or sporting events—"

"I've been there," Mrs. Passmore said. "They couldn't help me. Or wouldn't. You are my last hope."

"I'm sorry. I can't help you."

Mrs. Passmore nodded and was gone, shutting the door gently behind her.

Francesca lay there listening for another hour, wondering if the woman had truly gone—or if, with no one to hinder her, she had taken the chance to quietly search the house anyway.

Mrs. Passmore's words lingered in her mind. She refused to think that Harry, darling Harry, might not be her cousin by blood.

Of course the woman had lied again and again; it was impossible to sift fact from fancy. The dead husband and the illicit affair could all be of a piece with the portrayal of herself as Miss Weaver. Who was she and what did she want?

Yet, surely, there'd been such vehemence in her story....

I should have sent her to Mr. Stevens, Francesca told herself. *He'd have known what to do. What to say—*

Unable to lie there in the bed any longer, she managed to swing her splinted leg over the side and drag it to the boudoir chair. It was still by the window and too far from the dying fire. Shivering, she was sorry that she'd made the effort. And the bed was too high to clamber into as easily as the chair had been. If the fire went out, she would be cold indeed!

Perhaps Mrs. Lane was right, and she was being unreasonably stubborn about staying on here.

There was a scratching at the door, for all the world like Tyler begging to be let in.

"Who's there? Mrs. Passmore?"

"It's Miss Trotter, dear Miss Hatton. May I come in?"

Miss Trotter refused to go upstairs to one of the bedrooms.

"I won't be able to hear you if you call. And I shan't sleep for wondering if you need me. No, if you don't mind, I'll just search out a few pillows and blankets and make myself comfortable here by the fire. Your chair will do just fine. I'm rather like a cat, you know. Happiest in the chimney corner where it's warm."

It was strange to share the sitting room with someone. To listen in the fire-glow to someone else quietly breathing. And yet there was a comfort in it.

Despite the fact that Miss Trotter could see into her soul.

It was after three when Francesca came awake and couldn't go back to sleep. And as if Miss Trotter had sensed it, she said, her voice muffled in the quilt she had pulled up over herself, "Miss Francesca? Is there anything you need?"

"No," Francesca answered softly.

She lay there, thinking about her grandfather and all that had happened to her since she had first come down from London to care for him. The secrets. The questions. The ugly glimpses into another life. It brought a sigh.

And I'm no better, lying to that man Campbell!

But how else could she be rid of him? For that matter, where *were* the ledgers, with all their secrets? She would have liked to examine them herself. To silence the insinuations in those anonymous letters. To silence Mrs. Passmore, too.

She stirred again, restless.

"Is it Mr. Leighton who is troubling you?" Miss Trotter spoke softly.

In the darkness it was easier to talk. Francesca said, "Mr. Leighton? No, why on earth would you think that? I was wondering—I don't think I ever knew my grandfather. Not really. How could I, with so much of his life hidden away from me? Were my cousins in the dark as well?"

Across the room there was a listening silence.

"I know that he won a house in Essex gambling—but not why. I know that he bought a house in Somerset as a home for abandoned children—but not why."

"He hated the Walsham family," said the soft voice, surprising Francesca. "He punished them by taking away their house."

"Hated them? But why?"

"He said once that they were vermin, and he wanted to see them brought down. He couldn't forgive them for what they'd done to his son. Mr. Edward, your father. He blamed them—he said but for their schemes, Mr. Edward would still be alive. Here where he ought to be, not buried across the sea."

Francesca asked, "Was that why Grandfather never lived in the house? It reminded him of my father?"

There was only the sound of the fire in the room, and Miss Trotter's steady breathing. Francesca decided she must have fallen asleep.

When she spoke again, the old woman's voice was light as a thread. "I've always believed it was *her* house. If she hadn't died as she did. And therefore no one else should ever have it. I wouldn't have been surprised to learn he ordered it burned to the ground before he died. But I expect there wasn't time."

"*Her?*" Francesca's first thought was of Victoria Leighton.

"He loved her more than anyone in his life." There was an implacable sadness in her voice now. "Except for you."

"Who? My grandmother?"

"If he'd wanted you to know, I expect he'd have told you."

"I don't understand! Why didn't he marry this woman?"

"There were reasons. I sometimes wonder if the two of them would have been truly happy. But they never had a chance to find out. 'What might have been' is always better than what is."

"Are you telling me this woman was married to someone else? Was that what kept them apart?"

"Go to sleep, Miss Francesca. Let the past bury its dead."

In the morning, Miss Trotter was gone before Mrs. Lane arrived.

When Mrs. Lane was changing the sheets on her bed, Francesca asked her if her grandfather had ever been in love with someone else, before or after her grandmother's death.

"Lord, Miss Francesca, don't ask me! I never poked my nose in his business, and you know that."

"It was a long night. I couldn't help but wonder—"

"If Miss Trotter is filling your head with nonsense, you'd be better off at the Rectory!"

Francesca rubbed her eyes. "I'd be better off if I had some answers!"

"It was his life, Miss, not yours. If he'd wanted you to know the whole of it, he'd have told you!"

"Did my cousins visit here with their parents, before they were orphaned?"

"He and your uncle were estranged," she answered with reluctance. "They'd had words."

"You never saw them—before they came to live here?"

"I told you, there was hard feelings. Now, I've got to put the potatoes on, or you'll have none for your luncheon!"

"Where are the letters they wrote from the Front? They aren't in his desk, I've looked."

"He burned them. As soon as he'd read them. I saw the ashes when I cleaned the grate."

"But why? You'd have thought—he never showed most of them to me!"

"You weren't here. You were in London."

It was an accusation, and it stung.

"I never questioned anything he ever did, Miss. Nor should you. It isn't right!"

And she was gone, the sheets bundled in her arms, her mouth in a tight line.

THE COUSINS

Freddy . . . the musician

It was a day that enticed small boys to roam.

I remember it that way, at least. I was nearly
seven years old, and beginning to believe I was
invincible.

Simon's fault, of course—we had done battle
in wars everywhere in the world, and won. (If
History said we might. Simon was a stickler for
getting it right.) That day I was tired of playing
William the Conqueror. I'd never much liked him
anyway, because he'd tricked King Harold at the
Battle of Hastings. To my way of thinking, it wasn't
an honorable victory. We'd just finished reading
Marmion, and I liked that story much better. But
Simon had made new swords and he was set on
Hastings.

I dug in my heels.
Simon and I argued.
In the end I stalked away in a huff.

We had been warned for as long as I could remember not to walk beyond the gates of River's End. But the River Exe ran some fifty feet from them, passing under the bridge where the ghost of the spotted calf was said to appear.

And I was all for seeing ghosts. It would be a grand adventure, I was sure.

I hadn't wandered far downstream—only far enough from the gatehouse that there was no danger of Wiggins spotting me—when a frog splashed noisily into the water.

Frogs and little boys...irresistible.

I took off my shoes and my stockings and waded in with gusto. The river ran swiftly just here, but by God, I nearly caught him twice.

Off-balance and laughing, I didn't hear anyone coming.

The next thing I knew there was a voice at my back, calling to me. Not by name, but I turned all the same.

Someone was standing near my shoes, holding the reins of a bay horse with black markings. The sun was behind her, and I couldn't see her face clearly.

"Yes, ma'am?"

"I saw you leave River's End. Do you live there?"

"Yes, ma'am. I'm Frederick Louis Talbot Hatton."

"Indeed."

I could hear the voice, low and warm, but the sun was still in my eyes.

I was turning back to search for the frog when an odor of something sweet rose in the air. I squinted and saw that she held a long stick in one hand, a match in the other. And as I watched, she set the stick alight. Quite leisurely, as if she did it all the time and knew it would catch. And it did.

"What are you doing here, all by yourself,

Frederick Louis Talbot Hatton? Are your brothers about as well?"

"No, ma'am. I'm quite alone. They're playing at war."

I heard her laugh. "Yes. I could hear them from the woods on the ridge, where I was riding." The voice had changed, grown harder, and that made me uneasy. "You are an unexpected find. I feel as if I've been lucky after all."

I began to pick my way across the river, back to the bank. Suddenly afraid, although I couldn't have said why. My feet, wet to the ankles, seemed to belong to someone else. Cold and numb now, and hardly able to balance on the stones. I'd forgotten utterly about the frog I was pursuing.

She turned the stick in my direction. She had wrapped her handkerchief around the end, I could see that now. And the flames were gobbling at the cloth, turning it black, burning into the dry wood. She had thrown the first match into the grass and held another in a gloved hand, ready to use. By her boots I could see where she'd dropped a small, pretty bottle. I thought it might be perfume. Or ointment. The sweetness had mixed in with the smoke, an unpleasant combination, changing both.

"Frederick Louis Talbot Hatton." She gave each word an ugly emphasis. "How would you like to die, this morning?"

Frightened, I stepped back, slipped off the stone I had been standing on, and felt the cold, rushing water move up the legs of my trousers. There was white ash now on the stick, around a red core of coals. I'd never known sticks to burn that quickly.

"No, you mustn't fall in the water, Frederick. I

don't want to see you drown. I want to watch you burn."

And with that she lifted the flaming stick and brought it down on my head and then laid it against my arm, almost the way Simon knighted us when he was king. But this wasn't a make-believe sword, it was a brand, and I could smell my hair singe and then the cloth of my shirt catching, scorching the flesh beneath.

The heat seared into my skin. My sleeve vanished in curls of white linen blackened at the edges, just like the handkerchief. Beneath it a terrifying pale streak was growing on my arm beneath red-hot coals. A lick of flames darted up and the patch turned a fiery red.

Mesmerized, I stood there, unable to move. The stick veered toward the front of my shirt. I screamed then, and flung myself into the river, dousing the flames and sending a shock of cold water through my body. Even though the smoking wreck of my sleeve was extinguished, I could still feel the pain. My arm seemed to be afire from my wrist to my neck. And I rolled in the water, heedless of my clothes, trying to put it out.

When I stood up, dripping, crying, more frightened than I'd ever been in my life, the woman was gone. Her horse was gone. The little bottle was gone. There was nothing there on the riverbank except bruised grass and droppings from the bay.

I scrambled wildly out of the river, fearful that she might come back before I could escape. Stumbling over my shoes and stockings, I didn't stop to put them on but ran barefoot, as hard as I'd ever run to win a competition against my brothers. Once I looked back over my shoulder, and I could have sworn I heard her laughing. But I didn't care. I was blindly racing for the gates of River's End, and safety. Home. Grandfather...

I ran without thinking, ran in desperation, heedless of stones scraping my feet, my heart beating so heavily I could barely breathe. Past the gatehouse—Wiggins had gone to his dinner, and there was no help for me there.

Up the drive, and as the drive curved, I turned toward the stables and the back garden. I was in no state to reason, but dripping and filthy, I was aware I wasn't fit to come through the front door.

I had nearly reached the Murder Stone, where Cousin Cesca was being burned at the stake. I could smell the twigs that Simon had lit in the grass. Nausea hit me like a wall.

And then I slammed into someone—booted feet, rough hands—

Bill, our coachman, already old to a child, but sanctuary.

He caught me, held me away from him.

"Here—what's this, what've you been up to, my lad!"

He carried me, wet and dripping, into the house, and told one of the maids to fetch my tutor from his room. My brothers had trooped after me, eyes solemn, mouths open. Cousin Cesca, smaller than Harry, had a torn pinafore, and one sash was dragging. Her face mirrored mine, horror followed by tears of shock.

Mr. Gregory, the tutor, arrived, his face darkening as he caught sight of me. "What have you been up to, young man? Look at the state you're in—disgusting!"

I didn't know how to tell them. About the river, about the woman, about the stick that had sent me headlong into terror.

"I fell in," I said, hiccoughing, and Mr. Gregory

began to lecture me on leaving the bounds of
River's End while the cook, Mrs. Wiggins, was
examining the blackened cloth of my shirt—

"He's been playing with matches, from the look
of him!" Mrs. Wiggins was saying. "And serves him
right to be burned like that! If I've told those boys
once, I've told them a dozen times—"

I stood there, trembling, dirty and wet with tears,
and silently let the accusations wash over me.

And then my grandfather was there.

He lifted me in his arms, river water and all, and
I flung my own around his neck, crying again.

He sat down and held me on his knee, looking
me over. The reek of singed hair and blackened
cloth was heavy in the room and made me queasy
again. Grandfather saw the burn soon enough, and
the blood. Francesca saw it, too, and gave a little
gasp. Then she, too, began to cry. My wound looked
ghastly—I could just see myself.

"What's this?" Grandfather wanted to know, his
voice gentle. I just sat there, dumb and trembling
with cold.

Mr. Gregory was all for dire punishment, but
Mrs. Trotter and her daughter came to clean and
dress my arm, taking away my burned shirt and
bringing me a new one. My grandfather sat there,
silent, holding me on his lap all the while.

Then, as the women were herding me up the
stairs to my room, my grandfather disappeared
through the kitchen door.

When I awoke, my missing shoes were standing
neatly side by side at the edge of the bed, a pair of
clean stockings beside them. I knew then that he
had gone searching the riverbank to see what had
happened.

Grandfather never said anything more to me.

And it was years before I brought up that day to anyone.

It was the first time I'd ever experienced cruelty. I realized when I was older that whoever she was, the woman by the river would never have set me alight. She was taunting me, which in some way was more horrifying. But to a child, it was not logic that mattered, it was primeval fear, and she knew that.

Yet that day, as he sat at the kitchen table holding me, it was possible that my grandfather understood far more than I had been able to tell. I don't know why I believed that, except that his mouth was a grim line and his eyes were as cold and green as the sea. Anger directed not at me but at something I didn't understand. And why else would he have gone to the river straightaway, to search?

It was three weeks before my arm was well enough to play the piano again. I'd always played the piano, long before I knew note from note and could barely reach the keys. It was anguish to be denied music.

As boys will do, I delighted in thrusting the ugly wound on my arm under Francesca's nose, terrifying her. It was cruel of me; I realized that when she cried when we next wanted to burn her as Joan of Arc. And I felt ashamed then. Yet somehow her fear made my own less—personal. As if by sharing the horror, it became bearable.

Over the years the memory of the woman and what she'd done faded into the past. And then I was in the trenches, the first time the Germans used a flame thrower.

For a black and appalling instant, I lost my nerve. I was without warning a small boy again, and the burning stick was as real as the woman and the horse. And it had nothing to do with war. The stink of blackened wool and flesh choked me.

I have wondered, from time to time, if she was real—or a ghost. But my scar is real enough, and so she must have been as well—

CHAPTER 25

Leighton arrived with a pair of crutches under his arm.

Overjoyed, Francesca was determined to try them at once.

"It wasn't my idea," he confessed. "I must give credit where it's due. Stevens found them in an attic. He'd used them in hospital. We've cleaned them up, and lowered the armrest. Do you think you can manage?"

"Oh, yes, just watch me!" As she adjusted to them, she said, "I had an—unusual—visit last night: the woman who had been here before, posing as my nanny. She's the one who took the photograph of my parents, the one we discovered in Falworthy. Her child was adopted from The Swans. It seems she believes Harry could be her son. Is she staying at the inn?"

"There's another guest. A woman," he answered absently. He was watching as she moved awkwardly around the room on her crutches, slowly gaining confidence. "Francesca?" The change in tone made her turn to look at him. "I may not have long to live. Which makes me rather poor stakes for a husband. The truth is, I've fallen in love with you. God help me—it was never what I'd intended!"

She fell then, tangling feet and the crutch's tips in her astonishment. He caught her, hands holding her briefly before setting her safely on the chaise. She stared at him, searching his face.

"But you hate my family!" she blurted, and bent to retrieve her crutches.

When she looked up, in his eyes she could read an astonishment that matched her own. As if the confession had been unplanned.

"I've hated your grandfather as long as I can remember. I tried to hate you. I'm afraid I've made you despise me. Francesca—it wasn't Francis Hatton who comforted you during the night in the ward! It wasn't a dream. Don't you remember?"

She did remember the hands that bathed her face. The voice that wrapped her in contentment as she fell asleep. *"Dearest girl..."*

Richard?

He moved away. "I've made rather a fool of myself," he said. "Forgive me."

She said then, "I'm afraid to care for you. Every time I've come close to you, you've pushed me away. Even on the drive from Exeter! If it was you in the hospital ward, why were you so cold afterward?"

"I thought you'd changed your mind. I believed that telegram, you see. I was frantic to reach you. I had to plead with Matron to let me in the ward at that hour. I needed to see with my own eyes that you were safe. And then you denied sending it. You *were* glad to see me in Exeter! I couldn't be mistaken about that!"

She had spent hours weeding the flower beds, the last time he'd gone away without a word. To root out caring. She said, "I don't know what to feel."

"We've got off on the wrong foot—"

"No, we haven't," she cried. "That's the trouble, don't you see? There's always Victoria—your mother—standing in the shadows between us as surely as if she were still here. How can you love me, when your life has been devoted to proving that someone in my family drove her to her death! If I let myself love you—and someday you discover what happened when you were eight—I'll be left to choose between you and Francis Hatton. How can I do that?"

"I don't expect you to choose—" He sat down beside her at the end of the chaise. "For the first time in my life, I've found something—someone—who matters more to me than what happened all those years ago. Will you believe that? Will you believe that when I walked away from you, all I could think about was coming back? I'm here with you, and all we seem to do is quarrel. I reach out to you—and you give me nothing in return. No sign of what you might be feeling."

"I'm afraid to love you!" she said again. But she remembered her silence that night after the Zeppelin raid. When he had held her hands and she had not known how to respond.

"Which makes me believe you could."

She closed her eyes. The words she wanted to say were swallowed in the numbness inside her. How could she tell Richard that she had killed the man she had adored more than anyone, and that she couldn't betray his memory now by marrying the very person who accused him of murder?

He may have given up his quest—but Richard Leighton hadn't given up what he had been taught to believe.

There was a difference.

And into the silence he said, "They're dead, Francesca. My mother. Your grandfather. The time has come to let them go. While there *is* still time. I love you. And I want to spend what's left of my life with you."

But there was a painful knot in her chest and she couldn't answer him. From her grandfather she had learned how to keep secrets.

Long after he had gone, Francesca sat where he'd left her, her crutches in her lap.

If she had thought at all about falling in love, she would have pictured laughter and joy, her grandfather smiling broadly, her cousins teasing her, a sense of the rightness of her choice.

Not hovering on the edge for weeks, reining in her feelings until she barely recognized them. Not confused by anger and uncertainty and even fear. And how had they managed to survive, these feelings? Because they had. In spite of everything. Growing deeper while she wasn't looking.

If Richard proposed again, how could she hold out a second time?

As he left the room, Richard had asked, "Isn't it a risk worth taking? To marry me? We'll have a little time. It could be enough.... Will you at least do me the honor of thinking about what I've said?"

And before she could remember to thank him for the crutches, he was gone.

CHAPTER 26

An hour later, Mrs. Lane came to the sitting room to announce another visitor, her mouth tight and her expression hardly welcoming.

It was Mr. Walsham.

Annoyed, Francesca wished him at the devil.

Entering the room, he said without greeting, "I'm told you paid a visit to Essex. What was your opinion of the property there?"

"The villagers in Mercer tell me that my family has been a better steward than yours," she answered him bluntly.

"You must see that it's a goodly heritage. And understand why my father and I were angry to have it stolen from us."

"Hardly stolen!"

"My father was drunk. He was tricked into playing cards."

"So you say. But as I don't know my grandfather's side of the story, I'm not about to be swayed by yours." She recalled what Branscombe had said—that there were always vultures at funerals looking for opportunities.

"I tell you, that man cheated us out of our heritage and he did it out of sheer vindictiveness!"

"Why should someone like my grandfather dislike your family so much?" she retorted. "What had you done?"

There was surprise in the fair, Viking face. "Don't you know? Hatton always blamed us for what happened to his precious son. He swore it was our fault Edward got himself into debt, our fault that he had to flee the country, our fault that he killed himself on some Canadian road and never came home. Well, I can tell you Edward Hatton joyfully made his *own* reputation! He'd cheat if there was no other way to win. He'd borrow money and never pay it back. Gambling was in his blood. He got out of England only a step ahead of the bailiffs, even though his father tried to hush up the scandal. Money can always buy silence in some quarters. If you've got enough of it. And when there was no recourse in law to punish us, Francis Hatton took the law into his own hands!"

"I refuse to believe a word of this!"

"I don't care whether you believe it or not! The Hattons never care for the truth, do they?"

His anger and bitterness seemed to feed on itself. Before she could order him to leave, he went on in that harsh, hurried voice. "Did the old man tell you about his other son? No? If a man can't hold his drink, he should stay away from the bottle. Tristan couldn't; it was like a madness with him. He got himself into bad company, and in the end he brought the pox home to his wife. When the doctor told her why she'd miscarried, she shot her husband and then herself. Hardly a family tree to be proud of, would you say? The high-and-mighty Hattons fall as hard as ordinary men!"

So that was why the newspaper cutting Mrs. Passmore had shown her had little to say about the deaths! *Dead by an unknown hand*... Why the police hadn't vigorously pursued a killer. Why neither she nor her cousins had ever been told the truth. Syphilis—and a miscarriage.

Was that what had brought "Mrs. Merrill" to the house called Willows in Essex? *I heard him say once that what her husband had done was unforgivable. That he ought to be taken out and horsewhipped!* Mrs. Perkins had told Francesca. *Whatever was upsetting her, Mr. Hatton couldn't find a way out of her dilemma, and in the end they left Willows. . . .*

No wonder he'd found no way out! Even her grandfather couldn't have changed what Tristan had done. Yet at the end, he must have blamed himself for the murder and suicide of Tristan and Margaret Hatton. It was impossible to imagine what anguish Francis Hatton had suffered then.

Francesca could feel her fury like a hot lump in her mind, and she hated this man standing so self-righteously in front of her.

The words of the letter cursing the Hattons came back to her: *May you and yours rot in hell then—it is no more than you deserve!*

It had come true beyond the writer's wildest dreams. For it had been aided and abetted by human cruelty and viciousness at every turn.

No wonder her grandfather had chosen this quiet backwater in which to protect his precious grandchildren from gossip and a shocking revelation.

"I never want to see your face again," she told Walsham, revulsion in her voice. "In this house or in this Valley. Do you understand me?"

"You're not your grandfather! *You* can't stop me. And you won't like hearing such stories as I might choose to spread abroad. I suggest you come to terms with me. Worse things than a broken limb can happen to a woman alone, with no family to protect her." The venom in his voice matched that in his pale eyes.

"My grandfather left a considerable sum of money to build a memorial to the men missing in the Somme offensive. I'd bear that in mind, Mr. Walsham. Touch me or mine—tarnish my grandfather's name and reputation in any way—and I'll turn Willows into a burial place for widows and orphans of this war. *And put that land out of your reach forever.*" It was quietly said, but with such a ring of passion that Walsham involuntarily stepped back.

"You'd never do it. The property's too valuable!"

"I'm Francis Hatton's granddaughter, remember? What do I care about the cost? Now I suggest you leave before my fiancé hears of this conversation. Unless you wish to be exposed for what you are!"

Without a word he turned and walked out of the room.

Francesca reached for her crutches and followed him to the hall door, left standing wide in his wake. She turned the heavy brass key in the lock, almost on his heels. Outside she could hear the hired carriage start off down the drive.

She leaned against the wooden panels, cold comfort for her reeling thoughts.

I don't know if I've made matters worse—or frightened him off, she thought. *Still—there's an enemy for life!*

It was on her way back to the sitting room that Francesca had calmed down enough to recall exactly what she'd said. Her *fiancé*—

She had made the claim in anger and self-defense. Not in love.

The realization shook her.

Over Mrs. Lane's protests, Francesca changed her clothes and summoned Bill with the motorcar. She made it as far as the steps, and then with difficulty scrambled into the rear seat, although her splinted leg felt as if it weighed more than she did.

The rector stood as she came hobbling through the study door, admitted by a hovering Mrs. Horner.

"Well, well!" William Stevens said, surveying her skill. "I'm happy to see you're managing. But—er—ought you to be here?"

"That's what everyone asks me." She sat in the chair he

pushed forward for her, and leaned against the back for a moment to catch her breath.

"What can I offer you?" he asked. "Tea? A little sherry?"

"I'd like some of that hoarded whiskey of yours, if you don't mind."

"The last time you drank whiskey, it was yours, and your grandfather had just died."

"I know."

He dismissed Mrs. Horner and added water to a small amount of whiskey in the bottom of the glass. "That's all you're allowed, with those crutches."

Francesca nodded ruefully. "I shan't make you watch as I break the other leg."

"No." He sat down across his desk from her, and after a time said, "Is this in the nature of a pastoral call?"

"In a way," she admitted. "Mr. Leighton has told me that he'd like to marry me."

"Good God! Is that what the whiskey is in honor of?"

"I don't think I gave him an answer. But soon afterward, I told someone—in anger—that we were engaged!"

She spilled out the whole story of Walsham's visit, adding, "Could it be true about my father? Was he careless at the wheel because he wanted to kill himself? Didn't he care about my mother and me in the motorcar with him? And when did my aunt contract syphilis—after Harry was born? *Were* the cousins my cousins? Did my grandfather keep their names out of the obituary to protect them from curiosity and nastiness? Or didn't they exist?"

"Walsham, damn and blast him, was probably lying, hoping to frighten you into selling up. But there's one way I can help. Shall I write to the rector at the church where your cousins should have been baptised, and ask for a copy of the birth records?"

"Would you? I'd be so grateful!"

"I don't know the truth of your uncle's death. Or your father's. Mr. Hatton never confided in me—after all, it was something that happened years before my tenure here. Even if Walsham spreads such rubbish about, people are bound to consider the source—the man can't have a very savory reputation. If I were you, I'd ask your solicitor to warn him off. I've told you before, Francesca, you oughtn't stay in that empty rambling house all alone!" The words were clipped, angry.

"I shan't be alone—if I marry."

"You know nothing about Leighton! His situation, his prospects—"

"He's told me. They aren't very good. I shall probably be a young widow. Oh, damn, look, it's your whiskey making me cry! I'm so very *tired*—"

"You're crying because you're confused about this whole damnable business. Tell me the truth, do you love this man? You *are* a considerable heiress, you know. You must take that into account."

"Bother the money!"

"Do you want me to have a talk with Leighton?" he asked. "I'm willing, if that will help."

"You can't see into his heart any better than I can. And it's my heart I'm not sure of. How is it possible to love a man who called Grandfather a murderer? You're a priest, talk to me about forgiveness!"

"Francesca, your grandfather was a human being, not a saint. He'd done things he was ashamed of—and things he was proud of. You saw what he wanted you to see, and it was enough for you. If Leighton found no proof in all these years, *is* there any?"

She remembered the lines around the Somerset Brass in the church:

For the sins of my youth, I have paid. God accept my soul and grant it peace....

"Everything has been too muddled since he died. What am I to believe? He may not have been my grandfather, for all I know. What if, like you, I'm another of the orphans he took pity on? And Harry as well, as Mrs. Passmore is trying to tell me. Did I have a brother? I don't know. Perhaps he was one of the cousins—or you—or someone I've never met, taken away when I was too young to remember him. Was that why my grandfather brought you here? To look after me when he was gone? Who knows what was in his mind!"

The scars across his face were white with a tension that she had never seen there before. "*Francesca*—" He stopped and turned away to search for something on his desk, as if to give himself a chance to recover.

She realized that she had burdened him with more than he could bear. She had already seen how much he cared for her. She hadn't stopped to think how hard it must be for him when she asked his advice on marrying another man.

Guilt swept her.

"I'm not your brother," he was saying tightly. "And that isn't why I came to the Valley!" Then, in a more normal voice, he drew on his priestly role once more. "What brought on all this soul-searching?"

She took the letters she'd received out of her pocket. "There were two others. I burned them, thinking that that would be the end of it."

He read them through quickly and said, "I shouldn't let these weigh with you. They're unkind, and meant to be. Walsham is very likely behind them."

Yet she'd had the strongest feeling they'd been written by Alasdair MacPherson. She finished the whiskey. "I'm troubled, all the same."

"Would it make any difference to you if you—or Harry—were adopted?"

Tears filled her eyes unbidden. "You don't understand how much I loved my grandfather. My cousins. What if I don't belong at River's End after all? What if—" She stopped, hearing the whiskey speaking, knowing she'd said enough. "Oh, bother, I'm not good company for anyone! You've been kind to listen to me ramble. I'll be all right. But I shall have to find myself another dog. The hound of the Baskervilles might do." She gave him a rueful smile.

He suggested gently, "I think you ought to stay here

tonight, Francesca. Miss Trotter is hardly a suitable companion—she's more frail than you are."

"You haven't told me what to say to Mr. Leighton."

"I'm the last person to tell you that," he said quietly. "Follow your heart."

"That's the problem. I'm not sure I know where it is."

As the rector was seeing Francesca to the door, she turned to him and asked, "Where is Mr. Chatham? The rector who was here before you? Is he still living in that little house on the water, beyond Exmouth?"

"Yes, I believe so. He hasn't been well. He was glad enough to lay down his responsibility and rest."

"I'd like to go and see him—"

She broke off as the sound of lorries came down the narrow, rutted road, sending the ravens swooping up in raucous objection. And around the bend swept a pair of Army vehicles filled with men.

CHAPTER 27

"What on earth—?" Francesca began, watching the lorries.

They didn't speed on down the road as she'd expected, heading north to Minehead or Dunster. She could see they were slowing, braking for the village of Hurley.

She turned anxiously to the rector.

"Are they here to find the shooter, do you think? Oh, gentle God! You'd think he was a division of German infantry!"

"The Tallons were adamant that something had to be done before he killed someone. I expect they're behind this."

"Well, you must stop the soldiers. I don't want them to take this man, whoever he is—whatever he is! Not just yet." The sergeant would have listened to her grandfather. But not to her. "Not until we find out if he's a Valley man."

The lorries had drawn up by the small green, and a sergeant got down, looking around him with interest. Middle-aged, a rough face. If there was compassion in it, she failed to find it. The men behind him stared out from under the lorry's tarpaulin, rifles upright between their knees, for all the world like a firing squad.

"Francesca, it's not in your hands. This is Army business."

"They believe he's a deserter—they wouldn't go after a man who was ill, armed like this. It's inhuman!"

How would she feel if it was Harry they were after? What if they hanged him, and he was in no fit state to defend himself? He deserved a chance—

"Go and ask them—" she commanded, her hand gripping his arm. "Go and find out what they intend to do—"

But before he could reach the lorries, Mrs. Passmore was flying out of the inn, to stop the sergeant as he was about to order his men to dismount.

Francesca could hear the woman from where she was standing at the Rectory door, Mrs. Horner looking over her shoulder.

"Sergeant! Please—someone just told me at the inn—he's my son—I've come to find him and help him— Please—don't do anything rash! Let me speak to him and ask him to come back quietly to hospital—"

The intensity of grief in the woman's voice reached Francesca where she stood. The rector had caught them up and was speaking quietly to the sergeant, while Mrs. Passmore was standing almost on tiptoe, waiting to hear the response.

Mrs. Horner was saying, "Her son—the *shooter*? Bless me! What's he been doing here in the Valley, then?"

Now Mrs. Passmore was in tears, her hands over her face, and Stevens was offering her comfort. The sergeant had his men out of the lorries and was giving them instructions, gesturing up the hill toward River's End and the long, wooded ridge.

"Aren't they a rough-looking lot!" Mrs. Horner was exclaiming. "I'd not like to be in that poor soul's shoes."

The soldiers had fallen in and were preparing to march toward the bridge.

Francesca had all she could do to stop herself from shouting to the rector, asking him what was happening.

And then, with his arm around Mrs. Passmore's shoulders, he led her back to the Rectory and handed her over to his housekeeper.

"I didn't know he was her son!" Stevens was saying, shocked. "She's been in Hurley since yesterday, but she'd said nothing about a son—nothing about this man on the hill! Not in my hearing."

"She's searching for a child. Her son would be of an age to fight, you see. She'd convinced herself he was brought up in the Valley. Now she's heard about our man up on the hill, and I expect she's afraid he might be her son."

"No wonder she's beside herself!"

"She feels terribly guilty for abandoning him. She wants to make amends. I think she needs him as much as she hopes he needs her. Look, when they bring this man in—if they do!—I want to see him!"

From the sitting room behind them, Mrs. Passmore called, "They aren't going to harm him, are they? Miss Hatton—do you trust them to keep their word?"

Lowering his voice, Stevens said to Francesca, "I was told they were going to try to flush him out of wherever he's hiding and take him back to hospital. There will be no trouble. The sergeant's done this before, I'm sure! He must know what he's about. Francesca, come back inside—"

"You must see to Mrs. Passmore. If there's any news, you'll send word straightaway?"

"Yes, but—"

Bill was coming back, hurrying.

"Help me into the motorcar, if you will." And as Stevens did so, she remembered something else. "Ask Mr. Leighton not to talk to the Army. If he cares for me at all, he won't speak to them!"

"I don't know where Leighton is—"

"He should be at The Spotted Calf. Will you do that for me?"

"Gladly, as soon as I've seen to Mrs. Passmore. Francesca—"

"No, there's no time. Just remember to speak to Mr. Leighton."

And she tapped Bill on the shoulder as soon as he had turned the crank and stepped behind the wheel, urging him to hurry.

Stevens looked after her, then turned back to the house.

He failed to see Leighton standing in the doorway of The Spotted Calf, also staring after Francesca's motorcar.

The Army was up in the hills until nearly dark, searching. Francesca, sitting by the window in the boudoir chair, her field glasses and the pistol that had belonged to Simon on the sill in front of her, listened for any sound of gunfire, and waited. Her leg ached abominably, and she ignored it.

Leighton came in the afternoon. He said nothing more about marriage. She asked if he'd told the Army where to look for the shooter.

He shook his head. "It's their job to find him, not mine. If he's as clever as I think he is, he heard them coming up the Valley in those blasted lorries, and is off to another safe haven. Good riddance, I say. I don't fancy being shot."

"I shouted at him once—told him to go fight the Hun. It's not something I'm proud of." Absently she put a hand across the healing wound on her arm, easing it gently.

"You saw him?" he asked, surprised.

"No. But I heard him. And I thought perhaps he was near enough to hear me."

"Is it true that he's Mrs. Passmore's son? Everyone at The Spotted Calf was speculating."

"I'm sure she'd like to believe he is. Maybe it's true; who knows? But I think not. I'm afraid it might even be Harry." She gave him a rueful smile. "Her fear is contagious..."

But the night came on without news from the rector, and

the Army withdrew to The Spotted Calf and liquid consolation.

Miss Trotter arrived with that report a little after dark, and settled in with the knitting that she was doing for the soldiers in the trenches. "They need so much. Gloves and scarves and sweaters." She lifted the needles to show her work. "This khaki is so ugly! I wish I could use gay colors, to lift their spirits, but I'm told it would make them an easier target for the snipers."

"Are you certain there's no word of the shooter?"

"None. I hope he's gone away from here. I have a bad feeling about him, poor lad."

"Bad feeling—in what way?" Francesca asked, suddenly wary.

"I don't quite know," Miss Trotter replied, considering. "I'm afraid he'll die out there, cold and hungry—afraid and alone. It would be rather horrible, in my opinion. But maybe not to him. Death sometimes comes as a friend. . . ."

Francesca, not wanting to think about the man's dying, quickly changed the subject.

The next morning, as the Army deployed through the Valley, Francesca sat by her window again, resting her leg on a chair and waiting.

Leighton came again in the afternoon, with no news.

Again he didn't repeat his avowal of love—nor did he ask if she had decided to marry him. It was as if the proposal had never happened. She was beginning to think he might have regretted his impulsiveness.

Yet she found comfort in his presence. A male voice again in the house, male footsteps down the passage. And he seemed to be in no hurry to go.

She had spent the greater part of the morning, after Miss Trotter's departure, knitting a scarf for the soldiers, and it was already half finished. The verger's wife had sent the yarn to her by way of Mrs. Lane, promising more soon. Weary of knitting, she had read a little, and always she kept an eye to the ridge beyond the gardens for signs of the soldiers out hunting.

Now they sat without speaking, as they had done in the evenings during the journey to Essex. The afternoon cast long shadows down the hill, and then faded behind a bank of clouds. When Leighton got up to leave, Francesca wanted more than anything to ask him to stay another hour—perhaps two. But he had promised to walk Mrs. Lane down the hill.

It rained later, a cold and unforgiving rain.

As darkness fell, Francesca waited for Miss Trotter and listened for sounds of anyone approaching the house on other business. Would the shooter come here seeking sanctuary? And what would she do, if he turned out to be Harry or Simon or Robin? Would she try to hide him somewhere in the house? Or would she send him back to hospital—a traitor to him and not a savior?

Odd, she thought, how personal this dilemma of the shooter had become, once the suggestion that he might be a man from the Valley had taken root. Like Mrs. Passmore, was she so desperate for someone of her own blood to come back again? Would she have felt as much compassion for a man whose identity and face she didn't know? She hoped the answer would be yes.

Outside on the hills, the Army was being thorough, she thought. Both she and Mrs. Passmore would have an answer to their question soon.

Miss Trotter brought the news that Mrs. Passmore had taken to her bed, and Dr. Nealy had been sent for.

"Nervous collapse." She nodded wisely. "A pity. She's pinned all her hopes on the sergeant failing. And now the Army has said the shooter must be gone away, to elude them as he has for two days. There was talk of the search moving on to Exmoor."

The next morning, filled with foreboding and unable to sit knitting in her room, Francesca sent for Bill and the motorcar.

They drove south of Exeter and down to the watery world where the River Exe broadened into an estuary and reached the sea.

Budleigh Salterton was a residential seaside town with a pebbly beach and no reputation for bathing, but from the top of the cliffs, the view was magnificent.

Bill, slowing to look at it, said, "Reminds me of growing up in Cornwall. You could always smell the sea. And hear it, too, if the wind was right."

The elderly Mr. Chatham had built himself a cottage as near the cliff path as he could manage, and his hobby of bird-watching was evident from the drawings and prints of birds filling the small, stuffy room that served as parlor and study. Francesca, ducking under the lintel and watching where she set her crutches among the books cluttering the floor, greeted her host with a tired smile. The journey had been exhausting and cold.

Mr. Chatham at once offered his condolences and added, "I wasn't up to traveling to the Valley for the services, I'm afraid, but I have said my prayers for the peace of your grand-father's soul."

He picked up an array of unframed prints and moved them to the table, offering Francesca the chair nearest the warmth of the fire.

"The cousins are gone as well," she told him. "It doesn't seem possible."

"Your grandfather wrote to me about young Harry. I'd stopped reading the newspapers by that time, you know. I'm too old to see the end of this war, and I can't bear to carry the weight of it any longer. But there are my birds, and they give me a little happiness."

At length, when Francesca had warmed herself by the fire and accepted a cup of tea, Chatham smiled at her and said, "I'm saddened to find you on crutches!"

She told him about her accident, and when he had com-miserated, she moved on to what had brought her to

Exmouth. "I've come about a Francis Hatton that I never knew. Not the grandfather, the man."

Chatham's face had changed as she spoke, and he bent to retrieve a volume that had fallen to the floor from a stack beside his chair. As if rescuing it—or buying time for himself to think.

"What in particular worries you?" he asked slowly.

"A house in Essex," she said, listing them on her fingers. "A man named Walsham. A home for orphans in Somerset. The murder of my aunt and uncle. A child named Elizabeth Andrews . . . who my cousins really were."

Chatham sighed. "I argued with Francis Hatton more times than I can remember. I told him that sins would one day come home to roost! But I always prayed that I was wrong."

"Why did he die with so many secrets on his conscience?" Francesca asked, her voice strained. "Why couldn't he have *warned* me?"

"I daresay he wanted your good opinion, at the end. People do, you know. You were the last child. You loved him. He valued that."

The rector had told her much the same thing. It seemed to be a clerical stock-in-trade.

"I can understand your concern about your cousins," he went on soberly. "If by that you mean that Francis Hatton never explained to them how their parents died. They were already living at River's End when I came to the Valley to take up my duties at St. Mary Magdalene. Still, I begged Hatton to tell the boys the truth, before they heard it somewhere else. But he said they were happy, and they weren't old enough, experienced enough, to cope with a tragedy of that magnitude."

"You didn't know them before the Valley? Or their parents?"

"Sadly, no. Your grandfather told me the story, of course. That your aunt had killed her husband and herself. He said the sins of the father had been paid for, and perhaps it was true."

"It must have cost him a great deal of money to hide the truth."

"Oh, yes, I'm sure it did. The inquest brought a verdict of death by person or persons unknown, I'm sure to spare the family any further grief. Still—"

"When my father died, what did my grandfather do?"

"I was appalled when he took matters into his own hands. His response was that the law couldn't touch the men who had ruined Edward. I warned him that vengeance was the prerogative of the Lord. He replied that the mills of the gods grind too slowly, and he didn't have time to wait on them." Chatham took a deep breath. "And so your grandfather got his revenge. I never knew who it was he blamed."

"Walsham was his name."

"Oh. I'm afraid Edward had an unfortunate taste for cards. Your grandmother's side of the family was rather reckless by nature. There have been other instances, other examples of Hatton's insistence on settling matters his own way. People came, sometimes, to the Valley." His face seemed to have aged. "And sometimes to me."

Francesca said, "They have come to me. Since his death."

But he didn't answer her. Instead, as if to be fair to the dead, he continued, "Elizabeth Andrews, now. She was one of his good deeds. I don't think a child of her temperament would have survived long without a loving home. I applauded him for that."

"And Victoria Leighton?" Francesca had intentionally left that question until the last.

She saw the shock in his eyes before he could hide it. "*How did you learn about her!*"

"Someone—came. To ask if my grandfather had left behind a letter for the Leighton family."

"Dear God! He—never revealed what had become of her.

Her husband wrote twice asking me to use my influence. It came to nothing."

Beyond the windows Francesca could hear the gulls calling and the sound of the sea. It was a mournful backdrop to her mounting fear.

"Then you're telling me that he *knew*—that he may have been responsible—"

"Oh, yes, I could see that in his face. The guilt. He wasn't the same for months after her disappearance. A man walking in his skin without feeling it or knowing what he did. It was terrifying, I didn't know what to say to him, how to reach him. Nothing in my experience as a priest had prepared me for it. It was as if his soul had been ripped from him."

"But why?" she pressed. "Did he love her so deeply? What had he done to her? Why had he taken her from her family? There has to be a reason behind even the most heinous crime! Are you certain you weren't mistaken?"

"It was there in his *face,* I tell you!"

"But the police never charged him—"

"There was—gossip—when Mrs. Leighton disappeared," Chatham told her with reluctance. "Nasty rumors. I heard them—many people must have. It was even suggested that her father, Alasdair MacPherson, had spread them. I can't tell you whether that's true or not. I do know Mr. MacPherson did everything in his power to point a finger of blame at your grandfather. The police interviewed Mr. Hatton on several different occasions. Nothing came of their investigations. Certainly it was all most unpleasant. Mr. Hatton was stoic. I wish I could say the same for myself." He got up to take away the tea tray, a signal that the conversation was over.

She stopped him before he could disappear into the tiny kitchen, shutting her out. "If there was murder on his soul, why didn't my grandfather say something at the end—to me—to his solicitor—to the rector—to redeem himself?"

"Most likely the stroke prevented him from resolving the past."

"He could have confessed to you or Mr. Stevens. For absolution. Without fear of judgment or the police."

"A man like Francis Hatton wouldn't. He always argued that it was the weak who need absolution, not the strong."

"You were rector when I was brought to the Valley. Do you remember?"

"Oh, quite clearly. Your grandfather went to Southampton to fetch you, and came back with you in his arms. A frightened little thing, all eyes and dressed in a pretty burgundy coat with a collar of dainty white feathers. A lovely child!"

"Are you quite sure he brought me from Southampton—and not from Somerset?"

"He told me you had come from Canada. I saw no reason to doubt him." His eyes watched hers.

"I'm—on the point of becoming engaged to Victoria Leighton's son."

He was thunderstruck.

"You don't know what you are doing! Of all the sins that lay at Francis Hatton's door, Victoria Leighton was surely the worst. And if you marry her son, it would be—a travesty. I beg you—!"

"Why? Neither Richard nor I are guilty of anything—why should we be punished for the past?"

"Her family would have destroyed Francis Hatton if it had been in their power. And it's as likely that I'd sail to the moon as it is that a Leighton would fall in love with Francis Hatton's granddaughter. For your own soul's sake, walk away from this man!"

He set the tea tray aside and said, "You must leave now, Miss Hatton. I'm an old man; my heart is not what it was. I mustn't allow myself to become so upset."

"But you must help me," Francesca replied. "You've known me from childhood! What are you keeping from me?"

He all but turned on her. "If you came to me for advice, I

have given it. *But you don't know what you are doing if you meddle in this wretched business!"*

Shaken, Francesca asked Bill to take her home.

As he helped her into the motorcar, the coachman said, "Miss Francesca—are you all right?"

"It was a more difficult journey than I'd expected. I'm—just very tired."

"It was good to see the old rector so well," Bill said over his shoulder. "He never judged any soul. That's a rare thing in a man of the cloth."

And yet Chatham had judged Francis Hatton, she thought. As well as Victoria Leighton. *What had these two done to be cast outside the pale?*

She didn't know what to believe—but his words rang in her ears.

"It's as likely that I'd sail to the moon as it is that a Leighton would fall in love with Francis Hatton's granddaughter."

CHAPTER 28

Francesca's leg ached, keeping her awake. Miss Trotter was curled up in the boudoir chair, sleeping peacefully.

Just as her body badgered her, Francesca's mind gave her no peace.

What had Mr. Chatham been afraid to tell her? What else did he know about the affairs of the Leightons and the Hattons? There was something behind his aversion to the woman that she couldn't put a name to.

And if Mr. Chatham had been shocked at the thought of a Leighton marrying a Hatton, what would Alasdair MacPherson have to say?

She turned restlessly, trying to find a comfortable position.

Another worry clawing at the back of her mind was the fact that there had been no news from the Army's search. The shooter, if he was still in the hills above the Valley, had so far been cunning enough to elude his pursuers. For that matter, even she had heard their heavy boots crashing through the undergrowth like cattle on the move, and surely the shooter could follow their progress, too.

Francesca turned again, this time pummeling her pillows into shape.

Miss Trotter's thin voice breaking the silence startled her.

"Miss Francesca, are you asleep?"

"No. Yes."

In the fire's fading light, Francesca could just see Miss Trotter's face, an oval embedded in the shroud of shawls and quilts that mummified her.

After a time, Miss Trotter went on. "I heard from Mrs. Lane that you'd visited Mr. Chatham today."

"He lives in a cottage overlooking the sea. He seems quite happy there."

"He always did like the water. I've never seen the sea. Someone told me once it was noisy."

"It can be. When the waves are crashing ashore and the gulls are calling. Sometimes it can be soft and rather soothing. Early dawn. Or late in the night before the tide turns."

"I was born in the Valley. I'll die here."

Francesca said, "Mr. Leighton has told me he'd like to marry me. Should I believe him?"

"I don't know, and that's the truth."

"Yes. Well, I don't know myself," Francesca answered forlornly.

The silence lengthened again.

And then somewhere in the Valley a shot echoed through the night, sharp and clear.

Francesca had thrown off the bedclothes before she remembered that her crutches would take her through the house and no further. "Oh, *damn!*" she swore at her helplessness.

But Miss Trotter said, "I wouldn't worry if I were you. They're edgy, the soldiers. Most of them come from cities, you see. They don't like walking through the shadows at night, and jump at the rustle of a mouse in the leaves. It was safer at The Spotted Calf of an evening, and then off to their tents afterward. The sergeant, he's out to show he's efficient and so he's got them hunting at night now. His men don't like him very much."

"How do you know all this?"

"Oh, well, there's talk about. And I listen. People forget I'm there."

"What do they say about Richard Leighton, in the village?"

"They've reserved judgment. We don't warm to strangers, as a rule. That Mrs. Passmore, she's got the sympathy of the village, if it's true the shooter is her son. It would be such a tragedy."

"It's a tragedy whoever he is," Francesca answered, thinking of Harry. There was nothing she could do tonight. Even with two good legs. Walking out in the dark into a line of nervous men would only get her shot as well.

Miss Trotter was breathing deeply again, slipping into sleep as easily as a child. But Francesca lay awake, listening to the night sounds.

In the morning Mrs. Lane brought the news that one of the soldiers on the hill had shot himself in the foot during the night, tripping over a trailing vine he hadn't seen until too late. The sergeant was fit to be tied. Mrs. Passmore was feeling only a little better but had eaten her breakfast. As for the shooter, no one knew where the man might be.

But Mr. Leighton, she added, had asked her to tell Francesca he would be coming to call at ten, if that was all right with her.

"He was walking back over the bridge when I came up the hill this morning. He said he'd found it hard to sleep. He could hear Mrs. Passmore weeping in the room next but one to his."

Leighton arrived as promised, his face drawn with fatigue.

"I went early this morning to the rocks where the man has been hiding." As she was about to protest, he held up his hand. "No, the Army had come down to the village, and I wasn't followed. There's no one there, no sign of anyone there. He cleared away his tracks, the snares, the ashes from the fire, everything that would have signaled his presence. It's my opinion he's moved on."

Francesca smiled in relief. "I heard the shot last night! I thought—but Mrs. Lane tells me it was one of the soldiers."

"Silly fool. A London man, with no experience." He sat down as if his back ached.

She said, "Thank you for telling me. I wish there was some way I could reassure Mrs. Passmore. But it could do more harm than good."

"It's my belief the Army will pull out today or tomorrow. No harm done. That will comfort her. But you must realize this shooter could kill someone before he's caught. That will be on our heads, if we conceal information about him—or where he can be found."

With a sigh she nodded. "I know. All too well."

He looked down at his shoes as if studying the shine. "Francesca. You've never given me an answer. Will you marry me?"

"What will your grandfather say?"

He met her eyes squarely. "He will understand."

"No, he won't. He'll be furious with you. You made a promise to him. He'll expect you to keep it."

"I did promise. But one man can only do so much. And for years I tried."

Francesca said, "And your father?"

"He'll value you for yourself. He's a fair man."

Then why hadn't Thomas Leighton come to Devon to ask Francis Hatton face-to-face what had become of Victoria? Because he didn't want to know?

"Tell them first," she said gently. "Before I give you an answer. For my sake."

Mrs. Passmore came to call. Her face ravaged by tears and fear, she said contritely, "I want to tell you how sorry I am for

The Murder Stone   301

all the trouble I've caused. When I came to the funeral, it was for my own ends. Everyone has photographs, paintings—I expected I'd see your cousins' likenesses in every room of the house. It wouldn't be necessary to disturb you in a time of grief. Sadly, I was wrong."

Francesca smiled. "For your sake, I'm sorry." And found that she meant it.

"I ran into so many stone walls. Here—at the house in Falworthy. You and your grandfather were my last resort. I don't really bear a grudge against Mrs. Gibbon—I can see why the children must be protected, no names named. How horrible it would be for some bedraggled slut or drunken vagabond to arrive at one's door claiming to be one's kin! I *did* understand—only, it broke my heart to be so close to the truth—and to be denied."

"My grandfather never spoke to me of records that had been kept on the children of the Little Wanderers Foundation. I can't tell you where they are, or who might have them. But as you say, that's as it should be," Francesca assured her, wondering where this visit was leading.

"Yes, so one would think . . ." Her voice trailed off. Then she said with a sigh, "There was a rector here before the present one. Do you suppose he might know something about Harry's birth?"

"Oddly enough, I called on him yesterday. When he came to Hurley to take up the living at St. Mary Magdalene, my cousins were already in residence here. And the man before Mr. Chatham can't possibly be alive. He retired at sixty-two."

"Yes, I see that— Oh, thank you more than I can say, for asking on my behalf!" She smiled warmly, happily.

Francesca decided to leave her with her illusions.

"One can always hope . . ." Mrs. Passmore went on, picking at a thread on one finger of her spotless gloves. "I'll be leaving with my son when they find him and take him back to hospital. I didn't want there to be hard feelings between us, you and I. We are—in a sense—*family.*"

Francesca opened her mouth to deny it. Then she was silent, knowing it would be unnecessarily hurtful.

"And I would hope that you'd visit him, too," Mrs. Passmore went on.

"If it's my cousin," she said, "of course I will come often."

"Isn't life odd? I wanted news of my boy, and here he is! Not dead in France after all, but alive and searching for something he had never had before. A mother. It's the most amazing thing!"

Francesca pitied her. Simple need had become obsession. "I hope he'll recover, be whole again!"

"Of course he will, don't worry about that, my dear. Love works wonders, they say. But pray for us, if you will!"

She stood to go, still prompt to her quarter of an hour. "I regret only one thing, that we met under awkward circumstances. I should have trusted my first instincts and come to you openly. But I had a feeling it would be difficult for both of us. Will you say you forgive me?"

"Yes. Of course I forgive you."

And if it turned out to be Harry the Army was hunting—

Mrs. Passmore left, her spirits seemingly uplifted.

But Francesca sat there thinking about the two women—Mrs. Passmore, desperate to believe she had found her lost child, and Victoria Leighton, who might have willingly walked away from her own.

And yet Mrs. Passmore had walked away as well. She had married and said nothing, and she had found a measure of happiness until her husband's death. It was only then that she had remembered and gone in search of her child.

Would the same thing be true of Victoria Leighton—if she were still alive?

Would a day come when Victoria appeared at her own son's door, wanting to be forgiven?

It was not a comforting thought.

Better her ghost, Francesca told herself, *than the living woman.*

What story could a living Victoria Leighton tell, to excuse what she had done? And would it be the truth? Or lies?

I'm glad she's dead. . . .

CHAPTER 29

Leighton had left the Valley, Miss Trotter informed Francesca when she came for the night.

Another departure without saying good-bye. It was getting to be a habit with Richard Leighton!

Yet her head, arguing fiercely with her heart, reminded her that it was she who had asked him to speak first to his father and grandfather....

"But he has kept his room at The Spotted Calf," Miss Trotter prattled on. "Much to the dismay of the village gossips. At first they had pegged him for a wounded soldier trying to find peace and quiet while he healed. Prone to wander the Valley day and night, after all he'd seen at the Front. Like the rector. Now they aren't sure what to make of his comings and goings."

"Day *and* night?"

"It's likely he can't sleep. You can see that in his face, if you look."

"What else do they say?"

"That he's handsome enough to displace the rector in your affections." Miss Trotter smiled quizzically. "I told you once, to hold your enemy close—"

"You must be joking!" Francesca retorted, startled.

Miss Trotter replied quite seriously, "The village would have preferred a Valley man, of course, but most of the eligible bachelors in our part of Devon are dead in the war. Still, Mr. Stevens is almost like one of us."

"What else do they say about me?"

"That you're haunted. It's what brought you home again."

"Breaking a bone in my leg brought me home again!"

"Yes, well, that's only God's hand in helping you know what's best."

"Do they know that Mr. Leighton came here to accuse my grandfather of murder?"

"No, Miss Francesca, and it's just as well. In the village they'd tear him limb from limb, if he offered you harm. For the sake of Mr. Hatton."

Francesca could feel the tears rising to fill her eyes. "I didn't know..." she said. She had been too busy listening to her grandfather's cruelties, his victims.... She'd forgotten he had his defenders as well.

In the early morning light, after Miss Trotter had crept away and before Mrs. Lane had walked up from the village, Francesca again picked up the volume of Latin verse that Francis Hatton had been translating before his stroke.

He had had this volume in his hand in August when his body failed him, leaving his mind to follow in the weeks ahead. And he had never been well enough to come back to it, even though it had lain on his desk waiting.

There were notes in the margins by many of the poems. His translations were crisp and clear, with a knowledge of language and a beauty of expression that lifted her heart.

I knew I ought to have read them before this—

But somehow there had never been a right time.

The notes in his bold and vigorous scrawl would have interested scholars, but his enthusiasm was in the challenge and elegance of the work itself.

Turning a page, she found where his pen had faltered, a word ending in a jagged black streak of ink that ran raggedly across the printed lines and off the paper entirely.

It hurt her to see proof of the blinding pain that had struck him down—caught him in mid-word. Which had in fact killed him in the end.

Gently shutting the book, she set it aside, as if she had pried into something private.

But her eyes had caught a word on that page, and it echoed in her head. After a moment she opened the book again and tried to find her place.

Here was an obscure poet, writing about the British hero Caractacus—telling through his eyes the story of a warrior's capture and his final humiliation as he was paraded in chains through the streets of Rome to stand before the emperor Claudius.

Francesca read the translation and bit her lip in pain.

For a great curse has been laid upon my house
By dark gods who sit in splendor above the
    ashes of my people,
And I am dragged, bound and scorned, before
    my enemies.
A murderous stone weighs on my heart, and
    they who put it there
Frivolously wait to see me beg for release.
But I will die instead and leave only a hollow
    victory—
The white shell of my bones. And
The curse shall be lifted with the stone,
For it has no power over my dust.
Yet I will bargain with the Lord of Hell to
    send it

Winged and flying into the night,
Curse and stone lost together,
Beyond the Pillars of Hercules...

And in the margin, Francis Hatton had written painfully, his hand seizing with the power of the stroke—"*To Scotland—and even that is not far enough from Fran*—"

Francesca reread the words, her heart beating heavily.

At last she understood.

Somehow in his mind—as the stroke gripped hard and the words of the poem still echoed through his damaged brain—Francis Hatton had bound up together the Murder Stone and the sealed letter he had kept for so many years in the solicitor's strong box. And to protect her, the last of his family, he had ordered the stone removed as far away as it could be carried in time of war—not into the depths of the Atlantic, beyond the Straits of Gibraltar, as in the poem, but at the farthest reaches of British soil. Taking the curse with it.

The very tip of Scotland...

"*For a great curse has been laid upon my house... Yet I will bargain with the Lord of Hell to send it/Winged and flying into the night,/Curse and stone lost together...*"

Francis Hatton had believed it was his granddaughter's only salvation...

Who could say but that he was right?

A shiver raced through her, and she hastily closed the little leather-bound volume, feeling as if she had unwittingly touched her grandfather's soul.

CHAPTER 30

Two nights later, Francesca awoke to harsh, discordant sounds of a bell rung hard. She had been counting the strokes in her sleep, knowing it tolled for her grandfather, each year a deep and throaty note.

But as she sloughed off sleep and began to hear the sound in earnest, she recognized the stable bell's iron voice.

Fire—

Francesca rolled out of her bed, reaching for her crutches as she called to Miss Trotter.

But the woman wasn't there. The boudoir chair was empty, the door to the sitting room standing agape.

In the darkness she couldn't find her slippers, but she could feel the edge of her robe at the foot of her bed. She dragged it on, fumbling to tie the sash, and then went swinging through the open door on her crutches.

A burst of brilliant light filled the room behind her, and she whirled to see one of the outbuildings engulfed in flames.

They soared upward in the night sky, fingers of bright orange reaching high into the blackness.

Not the stables, thank God—was her first thought.

Turning awkwardly, she moved down the passage as quickly as she could, making for the kitchen.

By the time she threw open the passage door, she could feel the heat filling the cold night air, and hear the hungry crackle of the fire feeding on hay and dry wood.

It was the shed nearest to the barn, but at the rate it was burning, sparks soaring and flying well above her head, there was no telling what would be the next outbuilding to catch. Even the house was not out of reach—

Hobbling down the path through the cabbages and beets, she could see figures arriving in haste, men from the village wearing trousers pulled on over nightshirts, leather buckets in their hands. Someone was already working the pump, sending water splashing into the horse trough. Bill was there, and Miss Trotter.

The pump was being dragged round from the drive, pushed by men and women whose faces garishly reflected the flames.

The stableyard was filled with people now, and yet the fire was hopelessly beyond their ability to control it. When the pump was ready, they began to hose down the stables and the barn, some of the men looking anxiously in the direction of the house. Stevens was there, and Tardy Horner, for once in his life on time. Other faces she knew, and people were still arriving.

Cursing her crutches for the second time, Francesca could do nothing but watch. Mrs. Lane was there, gray hair flying out of its net, her face already streaked with soot. And Mrs. Horner had forgotten her spectacles.

Someone shouted to Francesca, and she raised a hand in acknowledgment. A man had just been badly singed by the flames, and she saw him coming toward her, one side of his face an angry red.

It was one of the soldiers, and she hurried him into the

kitchen to clean the wound and put salve on it. The smell of singed hair and skin sickened her, reminding her of her arm....

As soon as he was bandaged, he thanked her and was gone. A villager came in with a burned hand, the knuckles raw, and she did what she could for him. There was no time to look for bandaging. Instead she offered him a tea towel to cover the wound. He tore the cloth in two with his teeth, grinned at her, and wrapped the hand. She tied the ends of the towel and he, too, hurried away.

Francesca's stomach was churning.

"It's shock and nothing else," she told herself under her breath. "The sudden shock of the fire." But there wasn't the luxury of stopping to consider the question.

Another patient was brought in, overcome by the smoke, and Francesca ministered to her, listening to the rasping cough, offering cool water for the raw throat. It was the iron-monger's wife, middle-aged and energetic. Now she struggled for breath like an old woman.

The night dragged on, and the shed still burned furiously, while the silhouettes of people working against time seemed to dance around it like witches circling some ancient bonfire. Watching from the window, she saw the first flicks of smoke rising from the barn roof. The horses had already been taken away, rearing with fright. The carriage and cart had been dragged out as well, and other machinery. The motorcar had been moved to the drive, out of reach, with the petrol cans sitting on the house steps.

One of the women came to help make great pots of tea and cut cheese and bread for sandwiches. It was exhausting work, men fighting fatigue now as hard as they still fought the fire.

Francesca glimpsed Leighton more than once, organizing teams to rake burning debris away from other buildings, pointing out sparks settling on roofs, helping wherever he was needed. Later she could just pick him out, sitting on the Murder Stone, hands on his head in despair as if his body had failed him.

By the time a first glimmer of dawn touched the Valley, the shed had collapsed in a blizzard of golden sparks, and then the ruins continued fitfully to blaze up and die back, as if reluctant to give up.

Men stood around in clusters watching, hands hanging as if the muscles in their arms had turned to water. The women were sitting on overturned buckets and rescued bales of hay, on chests from the barn and even an array of saddles thrown haphazardly out of danger. Faces and clothes streaked with soot and dark with water, they looked like survivors of some terrible disaster, waiting to be rescued.

But the house hadn't caught, nor had the stables. The other outbuildings were safe as well, singed and charred in places but whole.

Francesca had organized a half-dozen young girls to help her prepare pans of eggs and rashers of bacon, more tea, stacks of toasted bread. Plates were taken out and passed around, and the tired firefighters accepted them gratefully, eating hungrily.

She hobbled out to thank each of the villagers personally. She knew this hadn't been done for Francis Hatton's sake— fire was the enemy of every household and the only hope of beating it was to fight it collectively. When one was in danger, everyone else rallied round. But her gratitude was no less sincere.

Slowly, people began to wander back to their homes. A few stayed on to watch the smoldering ruins. Leighton came to the kitchen and slumped in a chair, wincing as he did so.

"You should have been more careful—" she began.

He shook his head. "You don't stand by idly I did what I could."

Mrs. Lane was collecting the dishes and pans. Francesca turned to her. "Go home. You've done enough for today. These will wait until tomorrow."

The housekeeper left, promising to be back by early afternoon.

Francesca glanced around at the disaster in her kitchen,

then said wryly, "It has looked better." And she began to laugh. Worry and fear and exhaustion combining to make her feel light-headed.

Leighton looked down at her filthy feet and said, "Where are your shoes?"

Surprised, she stared at her bare feet. "I couldn't find them. And I suppose afterward I just forgot about them."

She wanted to ask him where he'd been and when he had come back to the Valley. If he had spoken to his grandfather—or his father.

There was a tap at the kitchen door, and she went to admit the sergeant. His fair hair was standing up in spikes, and soot had turned his face black.

"Miss Hatton? Sergeant Nelson. I thought I ought to say something—"

"You and your men were everywhere. I can't thank you enough!"

"Duty, Miss, that's all it was. What I wanted to say is that the fire was deliberately set."

"Deliberately?" She stared at him, and then looked over her shoulder to Leighton, who was still sitting in the kitchen, listening. "Come in, Sergeant. You know Mr. Leighton, I think?"

"Yes, Miss. From The Spotted Calf." Nelson nodded to him as he followed Francesca into the room.

"We found signs that the fire was started. Old rags and petrol. You could smell it when I first got here. Do you have any enemies?"

She wanted to laugh, thinking of the people who had hated her grandfather—whose hatred she had apparently inherited. She met Leighton's glance and answered quietly, "My grandfather did."

Leighton's eyebrows rose, as if she had accused him.

The sergeant was saying, "If I had to make a guess, I'd say it was the shooter."

"But why?" she demanded. "What reason could he have to do such an abominable thing? He had no grudge against us!"

"On the contrary, begging your pardon, Miss. A diversion, d'ye see, drawing us all up here while he made good his escape. We was getting too close. I was saying as much just last night."

"No, you're quite wrong! I know who did it. A man named Walsham! He threatened me only days ago—"

"That's as may be," the sergeant answered. "If you can show proof of such a threat, of course you must call in the police. Fire-starting is a serious matter, Miss, it can't be overlooked. But for my money, it's our shooter."

"No, you don't understand—" Yet she could see that he didn't want to understand.

"To put it plainly, Miss, some of these patients are deranged," he told her kindly. "Suffering strikes different men in different ways. When it's unbearable, there's no saying how the mind is twisted by it. Men do things they would never think of doing in their right senses, and become a danger to themselves and others."

"I've seen men suffering," she snapped, irritated by his attempt to coax her around to his viewpoint. "I've seen them crying in pain and begging for morphine. I don't believe the shooter would come here and deliberately burn down my buildings for no better reason than a diversion."

"Well, Miss, there's no better way of proving the matter than catching the shooter and asking him." He nodded to the silent Leighton and walked to the door. "Miss," he said, and went out into the morning.

Francesca sat down in one of the kitchen chairs. "What am I to do?" she asked Leighton. "I'm too tired to think."

"There's nothing you can do. Sergeant Nelson will redouble his efforts now. I hope to hell the shooter is well out of it."

"Then who set fire to the shed?" she demanded, and shook her head. "I'm certain it must have been Walsham, trying to frighten me into returning the Essex property to him."

"He would be mad to do such a thing."

"No, he's arrogant enough to think he can get away with

it." She remembered what Miss Trotter had told her about Leighton walking in the night. "Where were you tonight?"

He stiffened. "Do you think I tried to burn down your house?"

"I simply wondered if you had *seen* anyone. I've been told that when you can't sleep, you walk."

"No. I never saw anyone," he answered curtly, and rose from the chair. "I'm going to bed. It's been a long night. You should do the same."

And without as much as touching her shoulder in affection as he passed her chair, he was gone.

CHAPTER 31

Francesca slept heavily for two hours. Then after bathing her feet in water still warm from the stove, she went to the door to look out at the damage. The ashes were still smoking, charred timbers raising stark fingers to the sky. She crossed over the churned-up earth to see for herself what the cost was.

It was a warning. She could feel Walsham's message: *Next time it could be the house, with you in it. Unless you give Willows back to me.* She wouldn't put it past him to do something as cowardly as burn out a woman.

Impossible to prove, though. And the shooter would no doubt take the blame. The Army would be harsh and unforgiving.

She wondered what her grandfather would do. And then she knew the answer. Walsham hadn't believed the first warning. She'd have her solicitor draw up papers to donate the property to the National Trust, then send copies to Walsham. *Another act of violence and these will be signed.*

Francesca thought, *I'm beginning to understand my*

grandfather better. I'm beginning to learn. Such people had underestimated Francis Hatton, to their regret. His granddaughter must have seemed an inviting target, young, alone, inexperienced in the world. They had forgotten she was also a Hatton.

She was about to turn back to the kitchen, when she realized that Richard was sitting on an overturned box, nearly invisible behind stacks of gear and tools and harness that hadn't been put away again.

He must have seen her.

But he didn't call to her.

When Leighton did return to the sitting room, he looked like a man who hadn't slept at all.

And Francesca could easily guess what he was about to tell her. It was not just the fire that had kept him awake.

"I spoke to my father," he began. "He was very clear. As I expected him to be. 'If you love this woman, marry her. I have long since outgrown any animosity I felt toward that family. Your happiness means more to me than anything.'"

"How kind of him!" she said, and yet it was a strange way of putting his feelings... *outgrown*... As if with age had come some sort of understanding. "And—your grandfather?"

Leighton's face hardened. "He was beyond reasoning with. He can't forget—he won't forgive. He tells me I've forsaken my duty."

"Yes, he was bound to say as much," she answered quietly, responding to the grief she could hear in his voice. It pierced her to see his suffering.

"I remind myself that she was his only child. All he had in the world. He was in torment all those years ago, hounding the police, driving himself and my father to the point of exhaustion. You can't imagine how it was! And that anger—I could see it, as fresh as the day he heard the news. I was told, when I went away to war, not to get myself killed. I was needed more here. In England. It was a bracing good-bye."

She found herself making excuses for a despicable old man selfish to the end. "How can he forgive? It's all he has left, this bitterness, and he can't live long enough now to change. He wants to believe that after he's gone, someone will take his place. Without considering the cost to you."

"I've realized on the journey back to the Valley, what a barren life he's lived. The house is a shrine to his hate, cold and dark and empty. I'm surprised you didn't feel it."

"I suppose I was tired that day—" She couldn't explain that it was the man on the stairs, not the building, that had absorbed her attention. "I wish I hadn't insisted that you speak to him."

"Yes, well. I was in honor bound. He has loved me in his fashion."

They stared at each other, neither of them certain what to say next.

She was reminding herself that she had failed to recognize, in her fierce defense of her own family's honor, how strong the force of conviction was in Richard's. Would that change anything?

She remembered Chatham's words, about the guilt that had seemed to shatter her grandfather at the time. What role had he played in the tragedy of Victoria Leighton? What had he known? What had he done—or not done—to prevent it? But she must leave it there, now, and not look back. Better never to know.

Yet it had been easier, when she could throw his accusations back in Richard's face, to believe herself that they were false.

If I care at all for this man, I must also find a way to put the past behind me. And never look back. Grandfather—

She steadied herself on her crutches and said in an effort toward lightness, "We've had a rather bumpy road to romance, haven't we?"

"I wish so much of it hadn't been my doing."

She held out her hands. "Richard. Marry *me*. Not Francis Hatton's granddaughter!"

He crossed the room to her in two swift strides, taking her hands and then pulling her into his arms.

"It will be different," he said against her hair. "I promise you, it will be different."

She moved her cheek against the rough tweed of his coat.

It wasn't happily ever after, and she knew it as well as he did.

And yet in his arms she found a safe haven she hadn't known since July. A stark loneliness seemed to drain out of her, and Francesca swore to herself she would fight for their future together with all the strength she possessed.

Nothing, not the ghost of Victoria Leighton, nor the virulence of Alasdair MacPherson, nor the deeds of her grandfather would ever come between the two of them again.

She was a Hatton. That was courage enough to build with.

It was three days later that the Army got their man.

Sergeant Nelson, with a determination expressed in cursing his company on to greater effort, had set out this time in earnest. No longer tramping through the hills looking for signs and returning after dark to the tiny pub in The Spotted Calf—no longer hounding his men through trees and undergrowth at night, where they fought shadows and tripped over their own feet. Instead he began by sending the lorries away and keeping his men under close cover. Then he put out spies, stringing them along the trails animals took down to the river, sending them up trees to perch through the long, cold hours, lying in wait in damp brambles, until something moved. He called it training for the trenches, and his men cursed him in turn with renewed energy.

Mrs. Lane, reporting on the second day that the village of Hurley had had enough of occupation, added, "Every mother with a girl over the age of twelve is locking her in of a night, and Mrs. Ranson is tired of broken glassware and spit on the floor. But if that shooter started our shed fire, then it's likely he's far away. He'd be a fool not to go when he could!"

Francesca, remembering what Mrs. Passmore had believed—that the shooter had been drawn back here because somewhere in his tormented mind there was a memory of the Valley—wasn't as easily convinced.

If he had gone to such effort to come here, why would he leave?

Her worry clouded her happiness, and she made Leighton swear he would let her know if the Army flushed out the man.

Miss Trotter, offering what comfort she could, said to Francesca, "If he's eluded them this long, he won't be tricked by the likes of Sergeant Nelson. Mark my words."

But Francesca had sat by the drafty window long into the night, listening for sounds even though the hunt had moved north and south of River's End. Behind her, Miss Trotter seemed to sleep contentedly.

Late on the third afternoon she heard the lorries on the road below the gates and sent Mrs. Lane running for Bill and the motorcar.

They met Richard on his way up the hill to report.

"Francesca—they've got him," he said breathlessly, climbing into the rear seat beside her. "I don't think it's anyone you know—"

"I want to see for myself! Have they hurt him?"

"He put up a fight, the sergeant said. Bruised, but not badly hurt."

"Oh, God, what a terrible thing to do to a man who isn't in his right mind!"

"He led them a merry chase. They want their revenge. It's not the first time."

"No."

As the motorcar clattered over the bridge, Francesca could see the throng of villagers gathered at the back of one of the lorries pulled up by the inn. Her heart stood still in her throat and then beat with a force that hurt.

Was the man in that lorry one of hers? Or a stranger—

Knowing had become as essential to her as to Mrs. Passmore. If it was one of the cousins—*if*—he might perhaps be well enough to give her away when the time came. Someone of her own. Something given back by the war that had taken away so much.

It seemed forever before they reached the scene. She could hear everyone talking at once as they came within earshot. Mrs. Passmore was there, begging to be lifted into the truck to be with her son. As the motorcar swung just beyond the lorry, someone had taken pity on the woman and set her in the back of the vehicle. Francesca, impatient for her crutches, practically fell into Leighton's arms as she got out of the motorcar and was steadied on her feet. Then she began to elbow her way through the mob of people, villagers and soldiers, staring at the sight of the elusive shooter.

One more step and she could see him. Forgetting Leighton, forgetting everything, she leaned toward the tail of the lorry.

And there he was.

Barely a man—filthy, thin, ragged, his face curtained by long matted brown hair and a thick beard.

Tall like Harry and Robin, she could tell that at once, even though he was sitting on a makeshift mound of haversacks.

She could make out scrapes and bruises on his cheekbones, and around the cage of his eyes, the blood still bright red. And his knuckles below the torn sleeves of his coat were raw. He had given a good account of himself.

Mrs. Passmore was kneeling beside him, one hand on his shoulder, the other on his bent knee, and Francesca could hear her, crooning, promising that he wouldn't be alone again; she was there. He seemed not to hear her. His head was bowed as if the burden of lifting it was too great.

The sergeant was asking him in an aggressive voice whether or not he had started the fire at River's End.

The man was no one she recognized.

It was a blow.

Francesca moved a little away from the lorry, letting the villagers surge past her for a better view. As if it were all a Roman spectacle. Pity welled up for the poor man sitting there, defeated. Had hunger drawn him from cover? Or had he just grown weary of struggling to survive on his own?

I don't suppose we'll ever know, she thought, *unless he can remember all this, once he's well enough.*

She wished someone would show a little charity toward the wretched man, and offer him something to drink, a bed in which to rest, and quiet. Out on the hills, he hadn't been faced with such clamor. It must be unnerving now.

Mrs. Passmore reached up a trembling hand to brush the thick hair from his face as the man finally lifted his head.

A pair of weary, bloodshot eyes looked out without emotion or recognition at the circle of people surrounding the lorry. And then as they wandered aimlessly from one face to the next, they met Francesca's.

And sharpened.

Francesca thought for an instant that she would faint. Her blood seemed to have nowhere to go because her heart felt as if it had stopped.

Her grandfather's eyes had been that very shade of green—!

It wasn't Harry after all. His eyes had been hazel, like her own.

Stunned, she met the haggard glance. It fixed itself on her where she stood a little apart from the others, as if she had been there waiting to be recognized.

Only one of the cousins had inherited Francis Hatton's remarkable eyes: Peter, the engineer.

The thought staggered her. But what had happened to the contours of his face, what had become of the familiar lines?

For one thing, the heavy beard concealed the underlying bone structure, and the thinness altered the shape.

Was it Peter? This scarecrow who had aged, not in years but in spirit? He could pass for forty-five, not twenty-five.

Peter had become a sapper, although he had loathed the tunnels. It was unreliable, claustrophobic, perilous work. He had set Yorkshire miners to dig under No Man's Land to the German trenches, and then he himself packed charges where they'd do the most damage. And he'd set them off, watching the blossoming cloud of earth as men were torn apart. He had burrowed to lay mines under machine-gun nests and blown up the pillboxes. He had killed as many with his skill and uncanny sense of direction in the dank, stinking tunnels of clay as others had done with their rifles. More than once his tunnel had collapsed around him, the damaged earth no longer able to support itself. And sometimes the uncertain charges had failed him and exploded prematurely. By his own account he had nearly smothered to death twice. It had been a terrible and harrowing existence. He had written only a little to her about it. But she had read between the lines.

It would be no wonder he hadn't survived with a whole mind. Yet they'd said he died when a charge hadn't gone off on schedule, and he had had to crawl back in the tunnel to find out why—

Burning hot tears filled Francesca's eyes. Whoever this man was, she wanted more than anything to leap into the lorry and hold him in her arms, to tell him that she was here, he was safe now. For the first time, she knew what Mrs. Passmore had felt, a fierce protectiveness and the need to comfort.

Could it be Peter?

But even as she opened her mouth to call him by name, something in the pain-ridden eyes altered. As if pleading with her, begging her not to speak.

Peter had also inherited his grandfather's fierce pride—

Whatever had happened to him, whatever he had become, he had managed to conceal his identity. Somewhere in the darkness that clouded his memory and his mind, he had been determined not to bring shame on his family. Better dead than like a tree stricken at the top, hardly living.

Like Francis Hatton, his grandfather.

Francesca stood there, listening to what he seemed to be silently telling her, swallowing the words on her lips. *If only she could be sure—!*

Or—like Mrs. Passmore, was her need to believe one of the cousins had survived so great that she would see only what she wanted to see in this man?

If she could only speak to him—hear his voice—spend five minutes in his company, she might *know.*

She saw the rector watching her. He was between the lorry and the sign of The Spotted Calf that swung on an iron arm above the inn doorway. Stevens was waiting, pity in his face, for her to make the decision. He was no more certain than she was...he had barely known the cousins.

And then Bill, the old chauffeur, said quite strongly, "That's not the man who fired the shed! I'd swear to it!"

The sergeant, swinging around, was angry. "I was told that nobody—"

Bill, standing his ground, said, "You never asked *me,* did you? I only glimpsed him—but he was fairer, thicker. Older. That's not *him.*"

There was such conviction in his voice that the sergeant demanded, "You're willing to swear to that under oath?"

"I am."

The rector stepped forward. "Sergeant, this wretched man has been a spectacle long enough. If you'll clear out this crowd, I'll speak to him. And those cuts need to be seen to. Some clean clothes found. Now."

The attack from an unexpected quarter silenced the sergeant. Then he said gratingly, "He's *my* prisoner."

"Argue with me, and Captain Leighton and I will have a word with your commanding officer," Stevens retorted coldly. "This man is a wounded English soldier, whatever else he has been through. Now get rid of these spectators, and one of you help Mrs. Passmore back to the inn. Mrs. Horner, if you'll find hot water and some cloths. Miss Hatton, if you will, some decent clothes are in order. I'm sure your cousins must have left behind something that could fit."

"I—yes! I'm sure!"

Tearing her eyes away from the shooter's face, she hobbled through the throng back to the motorcar. Bill was already turning the crank, his face red with emotion. And then they were out of the village, heading toward River's End.

"Bill?" she asked the stiff, straight back in front of her.

"Don't say anything, Miss. For God's sake, don't say anything. And you mustn't cry, it won't do for you to go back with a red and swollen face!"

"No—"

It was difficult getting up the stairs at River's End. She sent Bill ahead to bring clothes from Peter's room.

"No, Miss, it won't do if they fit! Something of Mr. Simon's!"

"Yes, you're right. Go, I'll come as quickly as I can."

They pulled out underclothes and stockings, shoes, a shirt and sweater, corduroy trousers, and a warm coat. A case to carry them in.

Unable to take the stairs fast enough, Francesca tossed her crutches after Bill and then slid down, her splinted leg bumping ahead of her.

By the time they arrived at the village, Mrs. Horner and Mrs. Passmore between them had cleaned up Sergeant Nelson's prisoner, although nothing could be done about his unruly hair and his beard.

Francesca said, pitching her voice to carry as she handed her bundle up to the waiting rector, "These are Simon's clothes. I'm not sure they'll fit, but they're clean and warm."

"Well done," he approved.

Mrs. Ranson had lured the sergeant and his men, except for two guarding the prisoner, back into the inn for a celebratory drink. From doors and windows all over the green, faces watched the lorry, intent and anxious.

As she waited, Francesca wished she knew what they were thinking. Had any of them guessed—had someone seen any small indication, any sign that there was something familiar about this man? The villagers knew the cousins well enough. Or had they been too absorbed in Mrs. Passmore's drama?

From behind the flap of the canvas, she could hear grunts as the rector and the two women got the prisoner into fresh clothes. Then Stevens ushered the women out, holding the flap high long enough for Francesca, standing at the lorry's tail, to see the man clearly.

He looked ready to drop from exhaustion, but he was more presentable and seemed to hold himself with a little more dignity. Mrs. Horner was leading Mrs. Passmore into The Spotted Calf. She, too, looked near to collapse. Francesca heard her say, through her tears, "He must have known who I was! Did you see how he let me bathe his dear face?"

Stevens said peremptorily to the guards, "Step away from the lorry. I've been asked to pray with him."

Reluctantly they dropped back. Someone—Leighton, she realized—brought pints out to them, and they drank thirstily, joking about their prisoner. But Francesca was trying to hear the low murmur of Stevens's voice as he spoke rapidly and carefully to the man imprisoned in the lorry.

And finally, in a voice that sounded rusty from disuse, there was a reply.

The sergeant came out the pub door, ordering his men into the vehicles. Francesca, eaten up with the need to hear, wished them all at the devil.

Stevens lifted the flap again and got down with some difficulty. But his face showed nothing.

"I'm going with you to Hampshire, Sergeant," he said, then came to where Francesca was standing. "Will you be all right, here alone?" His hand cupped her elbow, his face strained. "I don't like leaving you! But there's his need as well—"

She nodded, then asked, "What did he say?"

"Sometimes he can't remember whether he's in France or back in England. He thought he'd somehow been separated from his unit, trying to make it back to his lines. He won't tell me his name. I don't know— He needs care, Francesca. More than anything else right now. *I don't know—*"

"I have money...a private clinic—doctors—whatever he needs! Will you see to it for me?" She tried to keep the despair out of her voice. "Will you do that? Whoever he is! It doesn't *matter.*"

"Trust me. Yes." He added, "I had a feeling he recognized you." But was there conviction behind the words? Or was he simply offering her a measure of hope and of peace? She herself was uncertain now, flustered by the sudden turn of events, unable to think clearly.

And then he was off, limping back to the rectory, to pack a valise.

Francesca stood there on the green even after a light rain blew in across the river. She wanted to lift the flap, defy everyone, to put her mind at rest. Then she remembered the begging in the man's eyes.

She didn't see Peter again....

Leighton stepped out of the inn and crossed to where she was standing.

"They didn't hurt him," he told her. "Just roughed him up a little. It's what happens. Francesca, Mrs. Passmore doesn't have the money to travel to Hampshire. I've given her what she needs. She hopes to take the train tomorrow morning. If you can spare Bill to carry her to Exeter?"

"By all means! How kind of you to think of it. Is she still convinced this man's her son?"

"I don't know whether she is or not. She needs him to be. That's what matters. Did you recognize him? I thought perhaps you had. And then you said nothing."

"I don't think he wanted to be identified. But it seemed— he might be Peter. I'm afraid to hope! I've lost so much. Whoever he is, I pitied him," she said, her eyes on the road where the lorries had vanished around the bend beyond the bridge. "I didn't know how to help—I wanted to cry. He belongs to someone, surely!"

"I saw your tears. I wondered if Stevens had as well. If that's why he went with the prisoner."

"The rector will see he's treated properly. A voice of sanity in the midst of frenzy." Then she asked, "Did you hate that man for having shot at you?"

"I never hated the Germans," he answered, stung. "I can't hate a damaged soldier who doesn't know what he's doing."

Mournfully, Francesca said, "I want to go home and not think about this anymore. It hurts to think about anything—"

He got her into the waiting car and kissed her lightly on the cheek. "Do you want me to come with you?"

"I'll be all right. Truly."

He hesitated as if uncertain how to comfort her.

Bill had cranked the motor and was climbing into his seat. His face was gray.

They were nearly at the bottom of the drive when Francesca said to him, "Do you think they believed you? That he hadn't set the fire?"

"It wasn't him, Miss, I'd swear on my sister's grave it wasn't. But there you are. He was to hand, you might say. Why should they look any further?"

"I'm convinced it was Walsham! But no one will listen."

"What's to become of him, Miss?"

"Mr. Stevens will see to him for us now. With proper care and help— Who knows? I'll be going to the clinic to visit him as soon as I can manage the journey. I'll bring him back then, if it's Peter. In time for the wedding."

But that night she dreamed over and over again of shots fired on the hills above the river, and that when they found Peter this time, he was dead.

CHAPTER 32

In the morning, well before Mrs. Lane had walked up from the village, there was a loud knocking at the front door.

Fog had wreathed the Valley. Trees loomed out of the chill white mist like disembodied creatures, now visible, now swallowed again. Sounds were muffled, the world wrapped in cotton wool, and the knocking seemed to shock the senses.

Miss Trotter, already awake and preparing to leave for the day, went to answer the summons for Francesca.

There was a woman standing on the threshold, the drive nearly invisible behind her, the insubstantial light a contrast to her substance. It was as if she had been deposited on the step by unseen means. No horse stamped in the mists and no carriage's outline was sketched in the swirling whiteness behind her.

Without hesitation she presented her card to the unlikely-looking parlor maid and asked for Miss Hatton.

Miss Trotter, without a qualm, shut the door in her face while she carried the card to the sitting room.

Alice Woodward, Francesca read there in elegant script. The name seemed familiar, but she couldn't place it.

"I don't believe I know her. Where is she?"

"I left her on the doorstep. I didn't *like* her." It was a warning, as if whatever other senses the old woman relied on had awakened with urgency. "You'd best let me send her about her business!"

"It's an absurd hour to pay a social call!" Francesca agreed. "Still—there may be a reason for it. In the drawing room, Miss Trotter, if you don't mind. And—don't go too far away!"

As she flung open the double doors of the drawing room, she could feel the airlessness rush out at her. She hadn't set foot in here since the day her grandfather was buried. Now she unconsciously steeled herself to find the undertaker's black crepe still hanging from picture frames and the tops of the long mirrors. Even though she had ordered it dismantled on the evening of the funeral, the image seemed burned in her memory.

Miss Trotter saw that Francesca was comfortably settled, and then brought Miss Woodward to the room. Francesca surveyed her frankly, not knowing quite what she had expected.

A tall woman, slim, with thick fair hair and brilliant blue eyes, elegantly dressed in a traveling suit of black trimmed with silver embroidery. She, too, surveyed Francesca, noting the crutches lying beside the velvet upholstered chair. Then, without invitation, she sat down.

"I'm afraid I don't know you," Francesca began, "or why you should call so early!"

In a rich contralto voice, the woman replied, "Good morning, my dear. I'm your mother."

Francesca stared at her.

"I beg your pardon!"

"No, it is I who should beg yours!" she said. "You've turned out quite well, I must say. Your father must have been very proud of you."

Fumbling for her wits, Francesca kept her voice level and without inflection. "You're mistaken. My mother died abroad—"

"No, I'm seldom mistaken. I was never the motherly type, you know. It was boring. Francis, when he got me pregnant, thought it would bind me to him. He should have known better."

"Fran—I don't believe you!"

The woman replied philosophically, "No, of course you don't believe me. But there it is."

Francesca fought to keep a rising revulsion under control. "Come to the point. Who are you—and why have you come here? What do you want?"

A belated vulture... like the others. Even Mrs. Passmore, in her own fashion, had wanted something.

"You're a very wealthy young woman," the rector had reminded her.

"It's not for anything sinister, my dear, if that's what you fear. I rather enjoyed my liaison with Francis. He was a far better lover than my husband. No, I came to tell you that you are about to make a rather serious mistake. I'm broad-minded, but even I have my limits. It wouldn't do for you to marry your half brother. However much you may fancy him!"

CHAPTER 33

"Half— *What* half brother?" Francesca's voice was tight with anger as she looked straight at the woman sitting across the thick carpet from her. "Where is this brother? Who is he?"

And then she could feel her anger turn into something else, an icy steadiness that was startling. As if Francis Hatton had rested a firm hand on her shoulder and guided her.

One of the anonymous letters had said something about a brother: "*If you find your brother, you will understand everything.*" This visit was about more than a clever attempt at blackmail.

She looked more closely at the lovely, serene face, and she began to see beneath the superficial smoothness of the skin, the erect carriage, the elegant clothes. Those blue eyes were familiar, and although the shape of the face had changed, matured, begun ever so slightly to age, something in the expression—quizzical and self-contained—brought back the memory of a girl's likeness in the round frame of a gold pocket watch—

And then she knew.

Victoria Alice Woodward MacPherson Leighton...

Alive, well, and in her drawing room. It was so unexpected that Francesca drew in her breath. *Alive*— Alive. Not murdered, not dead—

Before she could absorb that, Mr. Chatham's words seemed to ring in her ears...

"You don't know what you are doing if you meddle in this wretched business!"

He had spoken them after she had told him she was going to marry Richard Leighton.

Was this what he had meant? That it would be *incest*?

For a moment Francesca was very still, her mind racing through the last weeks, scrambling through tiny scraps of fact, trying to glimpse a pattern of events.

As if following her thoughts, Victoria Leighton smiled. "Yes. You *do* know who I am now, don't you? Certainly not that silly little fool who married Edward Hatton and died with him in Canada!" Self-possessed, she sat there watching Francesca with interest.

This—*this* was the woman who had let Richard believe she was dead—who had blackened Francis Hatton's good name. Who had caused so much misery, done so much harm. Francesca said, "I'm not sure who you are or what you want of me. And I don't really care. Please leave."

Mrs. Leighton looked about her at the long, handsome room. "Is this where he lay in state? I would have come to the funeral, but I was away visiting friends in Northumberland and hadn't heard. Yes, I'm sure you'd be happy for me to go. But the truth is, I can't. Does Richard believe I'm dead?"

"Your family believes it."

"That's why I came at such an ungodly hour, before that prune-faced housekeeper of yours usually climbs the hill. I thought it best not to encourage gossip. Can you trust the old hag who let me in?"

"Far more than I can trust you," Francesca retorted.

"No doubt that's true! Miss Trotter, is it? She was always especially fond of Francis. I used to tease him about her."

"A cruel thing to do. It was a worse cruelty to let your family grieve for years! I can't understand how anyone could do such a thing!"

"I didn't care much for children. And most certainly not for a tedious existence in a remote country village where the harvest festival is the most exciting event of the year! Tom was a fool; he thought that what he loved I should love. And so I simply walked away one afternoon."

"There was blood on your shawl—hardly 'simply walking away one afternoon'!"

"Yes, well, if you're going to disappear, the best way is the most dramatic way."

"And my grandfather was left to take the blame for what you did!"

"I should hope he did! I spent enough money in bribes to make everyone believe it was true! A small measure of revenge. And it *was* his fault in a way." She smiled, reminiscing. "The truth was, I was still half in love with Francis. And when I wrote to him, telling him I was leaving Tom, asking if he'd take me in, he refused. He found me in London, and it wasn't long before I'd brought him around to my way of thinking. He would never bring me here, of course. He feared a scandal, and he didn't want it to touch those precious boys of his, even though they were all adopted."

"Peter wasn't," Francesca answered her harshly. "He had my grandfather's eyes."

"My dear child, Francis was no fool. The boys had the proper coloring and a tendency toward height. His sons had disappointed him. Bad company is often ruinous. And so after Edward and Tristan were dead, he started over."

"Daughters are often equally disappointing. Where did *your* wild strain come from?" Francesca snapped.

A peal of laughter filled the room. "Well, well, the child has spirit! I didn't particularly like my father. He's selfish, a grasping, narrow-minded man with a temper. Haven't you discovered that? He drove my mother to an early grave, and I felt no compunction about letting him suffer in his turn. As for Tom, I only married him because he promised to take me to London when no one else would. And then just before the wedding I met Francis. Alas, too late."

"You've left such appalling wreckage in your wake. Do you ever consider that?"

"No, why should I? It's *my* life, the only one I shall ever have. I prefer to enjoy it. And I have."

"So far I haven't seen any proof for your claims." It was difficult, with the woman's seemingly open and frank manner, to tell when she was lying—and when she was not. "For all I know, you aren't who you say you are."

"Yes, of course, you were bound to be hardheaded, like Francis. I've got this—and this—" She took several papers out of the slender purse she carried. They were documents signed by the vicar of a church in Gloucestershire, one giving the date of Francesca's birth and the names with which she was christened. The entry from a parish record book had been copied as well.

"These are forgeries. I was born in Canada."

"That's only what everyone was told. When I grew tired of being tucked away out of sight—and so far from London!— he agreed to take you and set me free. You became the pathetic orphan from Canada. A pretty child, with those lovely eyes, and a sweet nature. Still, there's more of Francis in you than of me. Just as Richard is more like Tom. Did you kill him, at the end? I would have done, rather than watch him lie there in a stupor, scarcely able to lift a hand!"

Francesca's face flamed. "I won't listen to any more of this!"

"We must all pay a price for what we want. Which brings me back to the reason I came here." Glancing at the watch pinned to her lapel, she rose up. "I must go. I'd rather not encounter Mrs. Lane on the drive. She's a gossip—my visit would be all over Hurley before the day was out. And I don't think you would care for that. I know Richard wouldn't."

Glancing around the room, she smiled again. "It was really quite fortunate that those wretched boys died in France. Or this house wouldn't be yours. It will console you for losing Richard. I met one of the cousins, by the way. Frederick Louis Talbot Hatton, he called himself. *He* had good reason to remember me. I'd written to Francis, asking him to meet me in London, and he never came. I was forced to travel down here, and in the end, to make him come out of his lair and speak with me, I had to frighten the child. He ran home, screaming, and Francis came storming out the gates to avenge him. He accused me of cruelty, but it was his fault, not mine. I wondered, afterward, if the burn healed or if Frederick carried the scar to his grave."

Francesca stared at her in disgust.

She was beginning to take the measure of her uninvited guest, who used shock and a cool urbanity to throw a younger, less sophisticated woman off guard. But behind that seemingly impervious facade was something else.

Certainly not the ferocious hatred of Alasdair MacPherson...

Then—what?

As she reached for her crutches, Francesca said, "Did you send those letters to me? And the telegram to Richard when I was injured? How do you know so much about this Valley?"

"I bribe the carters who come through here. Nobody pays much heed to them. And they collect gossip at every stop. It's how I intercepted Matron's message to your housekeeper."

Francesca answered thoughtfully, "I was afraid of your father physically. Yes, I did go to see him! The carters couldn't tell you that, could they? And if he'd had the strength, he'd have taken his cane to any Hatton who crossed his threshold, including me. I don't think violence would satisfy you—you much prefer to let your victims suffer. Alasdair MacPherson is filled with anger, a long-standing, bitter wrath bordering on madness. On the other hand, you're eaten up with jealousy, and it's filled you with cruelty. You always wanted to be mistress here, didn't you? To prove Francis loved you. What stood in your way? Was it me?"

Something flared briefly in the blue eyes so like her son's and then was gone. "I don't feel very motherly, so you needn't worry about my visiting often. But it's important not to allow what standards we do possess to slide. Don't marry Richard— it just won't do, my dear." There was a threatening note in her voice.

She opened the door and went gracefully through it. Not a beautiful woman but one who riveted attention. Francesca felt gauche in her presence, overshadowed by something she couldn't define. But a man could—

"I won't be staying in Hurley, of course. I'd rather not run into Richard. And if you're wise, you won't tell him I called. It will only upset him. And it could very well kill my father. Not that I care; he spent enough money searching for me, and there were times when he came precariously close to finding me. I think the only person I ever truly cared about was Francis Hatton. You didn't know him then—"

And she was gone, heels clicking across the hall floor.

Francesca could only stand there, staring at her empty chair.

Leaning heavily on her crutches, Francesca took stock.

If Victoria was still alive, her grandfather couldn't have murdered her! It was such an overwhelming relief, she felt light-headed.

On the heels of relief came despair. If Victoria was telling the truth about her passionate affair with Francis Hatton after her disappearance, it would be impossible for any marriage to take place. And that would mean giving up Richard—

She tried to think. How *could* Victoria be alive? When all the searchers had failed to find her? Yet Francesca had sent Richard to tell his grandfather about his marriage. Was this Alasdair MacPherson's revenge? Had he found an actress, well tutored, superbly trained—and instructed to put up the one objection to a wedding that Francesca dared not ignore?

That she would be marrying her half brother...

MacPherson's thirst for vengeance went deep, and it respected no rules.

And such a ruse was damnably clever—

But as a little of Francesca's shock faded, she remembered the miniature in Richard Leighton's pocket watch...

And it was very like the woman who had sat in this room not five minutes before!

How—on such short notice—could MacPherson have managed to find someone with the same bone structure, the same expression in the eyes? That same cool audacity? And the unmatchable—coloring—stature—manner.

The truth was, he couldn't have done.

She had to be real!

And if Victoria was real, what shall I do without Richard?

Francesca sat down in the nearest chair, and looked into the bleak future that had just been handed her.

I wish the rector was here—

Then she realized that he couldn't possibly see this nightmare in the same way she did. For one thing, he hadn't felt the personal assault of Alasdair MacPherson's anger. He hadn't listened to Victoria Leighton's callous references to her son or to Freddy. He hadn't heard the woman's casual announcement that she was Francesca's mother.

Stevens would insist that Richard be told—whatever the cost. To the rector, truth was more important than its impact.

But I can't let him tell Richard! I can't let his faith in his mother's goodness be destroyed. He's dying—and he's found a measure of peace, now. I'd rather walk away from the wedding myself—tell him I don't love him after all.

Yet if I do that—am I any better than Victoria, deserting him at eight?

What am I going to do!

She's a woman with no scruples—no shame. She'll stand in the back of the church and tell everyone whatever she wants to tell them, and there's nothing I can do about it! Richard will be shamed—I'll be shamed. And I can't even guess why she'd go to such lengths. Why is she willing to come back to life—why should we even matter to her now?

There's no way I can prove I'm not her daughter! Not with a war on—

I'd have to travel to Canada. And by the time I could reach Devon again, who will believe me? My word against hers?

Francesca said aloud, "I'm afraid of her alive just as much as I feared her dead!"

And was Victoria Leighton counting on that very fear to keep Francesca's mouth shut?

What had happened between this woman and Francis Hatton?

Even the old rector, Chatham, had read guilt in her grandfather's reaction to Victoria Leighton's disappearance. For months afterward, he'd been a hollow man.

But in the end, had he overcome his scruples and gone to her, in lust if not in love?

Francesca was slowly beginning to realize that the identity of the woman who had come to River's End in the rolling morning fog wasn't really the issue. It was how much of the real truth she had told.

Miss Trotter peered into the drawing room. "I heard the door shut behind her. And good riddance, I'd say!"

Francesca looked up. "Why did you ask me to send her away without speaking to her?"

"I told you, there doesn't have to be a *reason*, Miss Francesca. It's in here." And she touched her chest with one blue-veined hand. "It's just a sense I have sometimes. Down deep inside. And that one's trouble. Twisted."

"But you *must* have seen her before—she knew my grandfather," Francesca argued. "Now she calls herself Alice Woodward, but she's really Victoria Leighton. So she says. And I can't ask *Richard* if she's telling the truth!"

"Mr. Leighton's dead *mother*? God help us, Miss Francesca,

if he ever comes to hear of this—it will kill him, Miss! I told you, he revered her so—he'll blame you and not her, she'll see to that!"

She was remembering something else. "Freddy—when he was small, did someone hurt him? Frighten him badly?"

"What kind of hurt?"

"I don't—no, she said a burn. It must have been a burn."

"One morning he'd disobeyed the rules and slipped away to play by the river. I never knew the whole story. He was too frightened to tell anyone. You were playing at Joan of Arc in the garden..."

Uncertain, Francesca shook her head. "I wish I knew—" She rubbed her left arm, where the skin tingled. "You mustn't say anything—not to anyone!"

Why would Victoria Leighton want to stop her wedding?

Even if the story was true, why should her son's marriage mean anything to her? She had cared nothing about him for most of his life!

And then Mrs. Lane arrived, complaining of the fog, and how she would have sworn she heard the sound of a horse's hooves passing by the gates, as she crossed the bridge.

CHAPTER 34

When Mrs. Lane settled to her work and Miss Trotter had walked down the hill to her cottage, Francesca went out to the Murder Stone and lowered herself to the wet grass.

She kept coming back to something else Mr. Chatham had said. *"If you marry her son, it would be—a travesty. I beg you—!"*

Not a proper marriage...

Why wouldn't he come straight out and tell her the truth, if he knew she was Richard Leighton's half sister—Francis Hatton's bastard—? Why had his distaste outweighed duty?

Was it also true that the cousins were adopted—?

The questions tore at the fabric of Francesca's belief in herself, her childhood, her family. Everything that mattered—that she had cherished. She didn't want Francis Hatton to be her father—he was her grandfather, always had been!

How much did she dare believe? How much did she dare ignore?

There was another explanation: that Victoria Leighton didn't care for *any* relationship between Francesca and her son, incestuous or not.

"I'm broad-minded, but even I have my limits."

And that made no sense, either. One didn't abandon a child and then feel a sudden responsibility for his choice of bride!

No, it came down to stopping the wedding. To preventing Francesca from marrying a man she loved: It was *her* happiness that Victoria Leighton resented—and she was prepared to sacrifice her son to harm Francesca.

But why? Why should it matter so much to Victoria that she would willingly come out of the shadows?

And how could her grandfather have refused to tell Victoria's family that she was still alive? Why had he left them to years of uncertainty and grief?

Unless he had believed that a much-loved wife and mother dead was the lesser anguish.

This was not something she dared discuss with anyone. Not until she understood what harm any revelation might do.

Once more she was truly alone.

When Richard came, the mists had vanished in the sunlight like wraiths. He had seen Mrs. Passmore to the train. Now he sat down in the chair near the bed where Francesca lay resting, and said, "God, I'm tired! The fog lasted nearly to Exeter. I think my back has come to know every rut in the road—every rock—every depression. She's on her way; she'll be all right."

"I'm glad. Richard. I'd like to ask you something. Just for the sake of argument! I couldn't sleep last night— I—was thinking about your mother."

"Let's not talk about her. We've agreed: The past is the past. Let it go."

"But how would you feel if you discovered she was still alive?"

He answered pensively, "Even after all these years I'd almost say that it would hurt more to know that she'd deserted us, than to believe she was dead." He considered that for a moment. "If my mother was still alive, I'd have *known* it—and all I've felt since the day she walked out the door has been...emptiness." He roused himself to smile. "A morbid subject for a fair morning. Is it the shooter who is troubling you? He's in good hands! Stevens will look after him. He's used to the way the military works."

"Perhaps that's it. The shooter." Even as she spoke the words, she could hear how false they sounded.

He took her hand in his. "Something is wrong. Do you miss London? Do you want me to take you there?"

She shook her head vehemently. London was Victoria's city—"I don't think I could bear to go back now. I belong here, I always have. Miss Trotter is right, it took a broken limb to open my eyes. It was only a sense of duty that made me volunteer in the first place." And that was only partly true. She'd gone to London not only out of a sense of duty but to watch the trains of the wounded for her cousins. To help and comfort them. And they'd never come home after all.

Richard kissed the fingers of her hand, one by one. "I thought perhaps you preferred the house in Essex."

"No!" she said too quickly. And then she added, "Perhaps someday we'll visit for a week—who knows? I'll be safe here at River's End."

"Francesca. What is it?"

"I don't know. I'm afraid to be happy—I've lost everyone; I'm terrified I'll lose you!"

"How can you lose me?"

But she was unable to tell him that.

When Stevens returned from Hampshire, he came to see Francesca as soon as he'd stopped at the Rectory for a list of pastoral calls collected in his absence.

He said, settling into the chair by the hearth, "I think

we've missed Saint Martin's summer. It's getting colder, not warmer."

"What happened at hospital?"

"They were glad to get the poor devil back again. But there are so many men in need of help and only a handful of doctors. I spoke to Matron about private care. She felt his record of escape might preclude that. I told her I'd cover any charges, and gave her the name of your solicitor. She'll see what she can do."

"Did he remember anything while you were with him? His name? Where he'd fought? What he'd done in the war?"

"I don't think he spoke a dozen words, all told. And there were always other people about. Francesca, don't pin your hopes on this man. He's very ill, and it may be months before good care can break through the shadows in his mind. It may be years."

"If he's one of the cousins," she said, "then it must be Peter. He's the only one with my grandfather's green eyes—"

"You know I hope for your sake it's true. But you must be prepared if it turns out he's someone else. Be ready to step away gracefully." His eyes probed her face. "What's wrong?"

"Inactivity," she lied. "I'm tired of these splints, I'm tired of those crutches, I want to be *whole* again."

"Patience!" he chided, as if to a child. Then he added, "Leighton left a message at the Rectory. He's eager to set a date for the wedding. Francesca, are you sure you're doing the wise thing, here?"

Alas, she was not.

Then she heard herself say, "The sooner the better. For both our sakes. There'll be no finery. Not with the war—and I'm in mourning. As I remember, my grandmother's bridal veil is in one of the trunks upstairs. That will have to do. I won't wait until I can travel to London to look through the shops. Still—I'd like very much to walk down to the altar under my own power. Perhaps you can suggest that to Dr.

Nealy. He'll never listen to me—" She was babbling, and caught herself.

I'll go through with the wedding! What can she do to stop me? I don't believe her—I won't believe her. She has no right to do this to her son!

And on the heels of that a certainty: *She must never know how much I've come to love him—she'll use it against me!*

"If that's what you wish. Would you prefer to have Mr. Chatham officiate—"

Not Chatham, please God, no! "I should like it to be you. If you will."

But she had the feeling he wanted no part in the ceremony.

"Promise me?" she heard herself plead.

"I promise," he said, this time with resignation.

And then he was gone to make his rounds.

In the week that followed, Francesca spent more time in the chilly room where her grandfather had died than she did in the sitting room. In her hands she clasped the leather-bound book of Latin poems. As if to summon the dead back to a time of living.

Mrs. Lane remonstrated, then laid a fire there every morning.

It was a struggle climbing the stairs each day, but she needed the comfort she hoped the room could give her. If her grandfather's spirit had walked, she would have welcomed it to question it. But whatever was left behind after his death, that presence, that force, it was unreachable.

Even the Murder Stone seemed lifeless and cold. As if it knew it was destined for Scotland, and why.

"For a great curse has been laid upon my house—"

Francesca couldn't stop that cool, clear voice echoing in her head.

Victoria Leighton filled her dreams, scolding her, driving

her—toward what? And the doubts that the old rector, Mr. Chatham, had raised, rang through her head until it ached.

Sometimes she dreamed of Richard as well. Loving dreams, happy dreams, but always ending with her running in fear from something in the shadows. Surely a foreboding of what was to come...

Stevens asked her again what was wrong. And Richard sometimes watched her face with silent concern, as if he wondered whether she was having second thoughts.

Was there any truth in Victoria Leighton's words?

Could she, Francesca, actually be the love child of Francis Hatton and that woman? Was she in reality a half sister to the man she was marrying—and no relation at all to the cousins she'd loved?

She couldn't feel the way she did and be his sister.

But there was the old saying—half brother, half lover....

The wedding was set for the fourteenth of December. She had agreed to it.

She searched her own face in her mirror.

It was all lies. It had to be. Some sort of warped vengeance.

What if I marry him and later—when it's too late—we find out it was true?

There was the entry in a church record in Gloucestershire...
Proof? Or forgery?
It's all lies—
But what if it isn't?

On the first of December, with barely two weeks left until the wedding, Francesca went to find William Stevens.

She couldn't keep her counsel any longer. In the mirror her face was thin and strained. At night she slept poorly. Sometimes when Richard Leighton touched her, she flinched, as if it was not right....

Francesca waited until Mrs. Horner had gone home for the day, when the Rectory was empty, no hopeful ears lingering to catch the occasional word. This was not a matter for Hurley's gossip.

But when she arrived at the Rectory and was seated in the tranquil parlor, with its Victorian furnishings and paintings of Devon scenes, she lost her nerve.

Stevens was patient, waiting, talking about whatever came into his mind, and allowing her time to work through her reluctance.

He is a good man, she told herself. *Why couldn't I have loved him, the way he deserves? He doesn't remind me at all of my grandfather—he doesn't have that darkness within him that I saw in Richard—and Francis Hatton.*

But love wasn't something planned; it waylaid you and took you by surprise.

Finally she said, "I had a visitor some time ago. She claimed she was Victoria Leighton."

"My God!" Stevens exclaimed, staring at Francesca. "Are you sure?"

"No, I'm not sure. That's why I haven't said anything."

"Are you going to tell Leighton?"

"No—"

"But you must! He has a right to know!"

"No," she said again. "He was only a child. He wouldn't even recognize her. And she isn't the mother he *remembers*."

"You have no choice but to tell him! This isn't your decision. Leighton—his father—however hard it may be for them to hear the truth, they deserve to know if the woman is still alive. It changes everything! It frees your grandfather of suspicion, it lifts the cloud over this marriage. You must go to him and tell him!"

Yes, it would change those things, she answered silently, *but you don't know how it would change the rest— And then what will I do, when I've lost him?*

Aloud she said, "You haven't met her. You can't judge what a disastrous experience it could be."

"I refuse to believe that. However low she's fallen, whatever she may have done, she's his flesh and blood! No,

Francesca, I say again, you can't make that choice for the Leightons." And then he saw the other side of what he'd just been told.

"Why did she come to you? Why not to her son? Where has she been all these years?"

"I've just told you. She didn't want to see him. She herself asked me not to tell him!"

"She's ashamed—it's a cry for help—for peace—she's asking you to mediate—"

"You weren't there!" Francesca cried. "There's no shame, there's no sense of guilt! She's done what she has done, and there is no *shame*! That's what's so terrible."

"What has she done?"

"She—took a lover," Francesca said desperately. "It was what she wanted to do."

"But why should she come to you?" he repeated, watching her face.

"I don't know. But if I tell Richard— He's made his peace with the past. *I don't want to stir it up again.*"

"I warn you, it's not your choice to make."

"Yes, it is, she asked me not to tell him—"

"Probably feeling certain that you would."

Francesca shook her head. It was worse than she'd thought. Stevens, from the churchman's point of view, saw the prodigal daughter returning to the bosom of her family.

But Francesca had read the same scripture, and remembered that the prodigal son had returned only after he'd spent his inheritance and had nowhere else to go. Desperation, not a heartfelt desire to be forgiven?

If she was certain of nothing else, she was certain that Victoria Leighton did not seek forgiveness.

"You're blinded by the teachings of the church," she told him wearily. "Just stop and think for a moment. Think how you'd feel if your mother came here one day, out of the blue, to tell you she'd sinned—and enjoyed it."

Without hesitation, he said, "I'd forgive her."

"Yes, I'm sure you would. That's your nature. But how would you feel when all of Hurley took one look at her and knew what she had been—and what she'd done."

He grinned. "Sticks and stones—"

"Oh, do be serious! Not even you have enough forgiveness to stomach standing in the pulpit week after week, reading pity and speculation in the eyes of all your parish! In the end, you'd want another living. It would wear you down. Try to tell young girls the wages of sin, when they already know, because the gaudily dressed woman living upstairs here in the Rectory was once a whore and still came home to forgiveness. Not perhaps the best example."

"All right. I understand what it is you're trying to say. But it comes down to the same question: What do you intend to do?"

"I wanted to tell you everything—and I wanted you to tell me it didn't matter. I wanted—I don't know, I wanted—absolution—"

"Absolution isn't mine to give. Will you tell Leighton?"

"If she wants him to know she's alive, let her find him and explain for herself!"

"If he loves you—"

Love has nothing to do with an incestuous marriage, she wanted to shout at him.

But even as the thought formed, she knew that Richard Leighton meant as much to her as her grandfather and any of her cousins had. *And I shall always love him—whatever happens now. There'll never be anyone else. If he dies, I'll have done my best to make him happy while I could. It's what I can offer him. A lifetime of love for whatever time we have left to us! A sanctuary for him. Just as my grandfather provided a sanctuary for me.*

It was almost a relief to admit it to herself. She felt better, stronger.

And what if it turned out not to be true, what Victoria Leighton has claimed? What if I believed her lies, and walked

*away from Richard just as she had done all those years ago?
Without a word of explanation.*

*Was my grandfather locked into silence, too? Unwilling to tell
Tom Leighton and his son what a monster Victoria was?*

But what revenge will she take if I defy her?

FRANCIS HATTON . . .

I'm dying.

That fool of a doctor cheerfully tells me otherwise, and I'd like to throttle him.

It's a daily struggle to keep my wits about me. I can hear your voice, Francesca, and sometimes in the shadows I can see your face. I must tell you what's been left unsaid. But I've trained myself to silence so long that now it's hard to break it.

Can you hear me, Francesca?

Victoriaah...

God help me, have I left it too late?

Listen to me! When I met her, Victoria was engaged to marry Tom Leighton. Her father, MacPherson, held a weekend party to introduce Tom to their family and friends, and I was included among the guests. His daughter waylaid me in the garden that afternoon, and for a time I played her game of light flirtation. She asked what flower I liked best, and I told her autumn crocuses. I added—it was true—they matched her gown. She asked if I thought she was beautiful, and I told her she was. God knew, I thought Tom was a lucky man. And then she asked me to kiss her and let her see if Tom's kisses tasted as sweet. I could have had her. She made that clear. There among the flower beds, with the sun warm on our backs.

Thank God, Tom was too besotted with her to see. But MacPherson realized what she was up to. I think any excuse to disparage me to his friends and Tom Leighton's pleased him, and he put the blame for his daughter's wanton behavior squarely at my door. When I made Victoria cry on her wedding day, Tom set it down to bridal nerves. I couldn't tell my closest friend that as we danced together, his bride begged me to take her away to Italy.

I avoided his house and his company after that.

It's true I lusted for her. Which must have fed her vanity. But she was Tom's wife and I was beginning to realize that what she wanted most was what she couldn't have. If I'd slept with her then, what followed would never have happened. Instead she damned me on her wedding night. I have the letter somewhere ... Branscombe's box.

When she tired of marriage, she did her best to see that I was blamed for her disappearance. She'd warned me if I came forward with the truth, she would swear that I'd done unspeakable things to her, there on the Downs. She's a remarkable actress. Everyone would have believed her. Especially Tom. Her father had already been convinced that she was afraid of me. He turned on me with vengeful spite, giving me no peace.

And neither has she.

It was surely her hand behind that gambler in Essex making your father's disgrace public. I was obliged to send Edward out of the country until the gossip died down. My son's death sentence, as surely as if I'd killed him myself. And she wrote to your uncle Tristan's wife, blaming her miscarriage on syphilis. That had diabolical consequences.

Listen to me! Victoria has a genius for discovering weaknesses and using them to hurt. You must never forget that.

I know why she tried to kill herself on the Murder Stone—she hated River's End, because I refused to make her its mistress. I wished she'd died then. When Simon turned the stone into his battlefield, I thought, he hasn't been harmed by discovering her there. There was no way of foreseeing that the stone's wars would send your cousins to France and a real one. I should have dragged it away long ago, as far from River's End as I could reach. She gloated, you know. After each telegram.

The only person she hasn't touched is you. She's tried, but I always managed to block her. When I'm dead, don't put an announcement in the *Times*, do you hear?

Francesca—do you understand what I'm trying to say to you?

Believe me.

I never loved Victoria Leighton.

CHAPTER 35

The days slipped by. Francesca found it impossible to eat, and Mrs. Lane accused her, laughingly, of being lovesick.

Mrs. Horner brought her a small gift, a beautiful lace-edged tablecloth. When Francesca thought of the hours spent in making it, she embraced the woman, too grateful for words.

Mrs. Tallon, hearing the good news, wrote to ask if Francesca needed anything for her trousseau. "For we must all share, in such times. I have some nice bits and pieces I've kept in a chest all those years. French silk..."

And Mrs. Lane, like a girl, was filled with suggestions for the wedding feast. "I've put by a bit of sugar, and some butter from Mrs. Handly's cows, and there's sultanas and Mrs. Danner's hens are laying well, just now..."

Everyone sought to make a contribution. Three of the women in the village had volunteered to help Mrs. Lane clean the house from attics to cellars.

And Mr. Ranson, at The Spotted Calf, had put in an order for beer and ale, and whatever else could be found.

Tommy Higby's mother sent a cheese.

In London these would have been scorned as country gifts, but to Francesca they were priceless.

But it was all for nothing.

A travesty, Mr. Chatham had called this marriage.

And Francesca went on carrying her burden in silence.

Richard Leighton came daily, offering her his love in many small ways. To pass the time he read to her, he played chess with her, he told her tales of his military training. And he brought news of the war. It had become a slogging match, he said, neither side able to make significant gains and declare a victory at the Somme. She was reminded more than once that Harry had died in vain, over inches of ground.

"We haven't the men to make a clean sweep of it," Richard said another morning, in low spirits himself. She could tell that he longed to go back to his company, that he felt he'd deserted them. It was a bond between soldiers no woman could understand. But it went deep, and she honored it.

"For a great curse has been laid upon my house..."

The lines of the Latin poem often came to her in the night, and Francesca was reminded of the anguish that must have followed her grandfather into his last hours.

It must have been in the back of his mind for years, that ominous letter sent to him anonymously. But he hadn't needed a signature to know who had sent it. He must have watched over the years with a niggling but growing fear that the curse on paper was only a pale reflection of the hatred directed at him by Alasdair MacPherson, and then his daughter's destructive jealousy. But what had he felt about Victoria? Had it begun as love?

Sometimes she hobbled down the passages at night, the

rubber tips of her crutches making soft thudding sounds on the polished wood. Or lay in her bed, trying not to wake Miss Trotter, watching the shadows change across the ceiling above her head as the fire on the hearth slowly died.

If Victoria Leighton is telling the truth, I can't marry him....

What does she really want from me?

I'm not his sister! It's a lie, a trap!

On the third night, she decided there was nothing else she could do until she paid another visit to Mr. Chatham.

Bill drove her to the cottage outside Exmouth in a cold and implacable rain that matched Francesca's mood. Halfway to the sea, she almost asked him to turn back, not sure she was prepared to hear the truth.

She had heard nothing more from Victoria Leighton. She wondered if she ever would. Plainly, Victoria had done what she had set out to do: spoil Francesca's joy in her marriage.

They reached Budleigh Salterton, the sea curtained in rain and heavy clouds, and found the turning for Mr. Chatham's cottage.

The stones in the path were slippery with wet, and she concentrated on where she set her feet before lifting the knocker.

Chatham was not happy to see her.

She thought for an instant that he would turn her away. And then he opened the door wider, and reluctantly invited her in.

Removing her wet coat, she handed her dripping umbrella back to Bill. He nodded to the rector from the entry and then was gone, boots splashing through the puddles as he made his way back to the motorcar.

As before, the rector had to clear a chair for her to sit on, and as he did, he said, "I'm afraid to ask you what has brought you here again."

"Victoria Leighton came to River's End—some weeks ago, now."

Chatham stared at her as if she'd told him the devil had danced on the chimney pots. But all he said was, "Indeed?"

"At least she claimed she was Victoria Leighton! She was— not what I'd expected."

He was silent, waiting for her to go on. A gust of wind rattled the cottage windows and roared down the hearth, sending sparks up the chimney.

"She told me she'd purposely abandoned her husband and her son. And that afterward she'd taken up with my grandfather."

His face was grave. "I always feared that might be the way of it. But I had hoped he was stronger. There was an evil attraction there, had been before she was married. She was the kind of woman, he said, who got under a man's skin. It was a power she enjoyed, he said. She had no shame."

"Her family believe she's dead. What should I do?"

"They would prefer to believe she was dead. I myself believed it. It was always in my mind that she had killed herself when Francis Hatton walked away from her."

It was not the way Victoria Leighton had told the story.

"Why do you say that?"

"There was a woman who cut her wrists on that white stone in the back garden of River's End. The old housekeeper, the one who preceded Mrs. Lane, told me as much on her deathbed. It had weighed on her mind over the years. She never knew what had happened or what became of the body. Only that there was a great deal of blood, and from the upstairs window she could see the woman lying there, white as a corpse. Young Simon was standing near, not ten feet away. By the time the housekeeper reached the gardens, they were empty. She was distressed over it, but never spoke of it except at the end."

"Gentle God! Victoria, then?"

The storm seemed to veer a little, rain striking the windows now, drumming hard on the glass. The roads would be mired in mud—she mustn't linger.

"Self-destruction is an offense against God," Chatham was

saying. "I felt Francis Hatton must bear some guilt for what she did."

"And my cousin Simon? Is it possible he had seen it all?"

"He was very young at the time, scarcely six. I've always prayed the boy didn't understand what was happening."

Yet it had been Simon who had always called the white stone in the garden the Murder Stone...He'd played his bloodiest games there.

"But why should Victoria Leighton come to my door?"

"How should I know?" he said, his voice strained and bitter. "It was an immoral relationship from start to finish, whatever it was she shared with Mr. Hatton. And in one way or another, its evil has spilled over on to the rest of us."

"I need your help!" she urged him. "Why has Victoria come back? Why now?"

"Have you told Richard Leighton about this visit?"

"How can I? He's spent a lifetime searching for her, believing she was torn from a loving family—she's a victim. Should I say to him, 'No, that's wrong, she was tired of you, and wanted my grandfather instead. She didn't love you, you see—she thought she loved him.' He would be destroyed!"

When he said nothing, she went on earnestly, "My dilemma is this: To answer my questions, I must hurt him far more than he deserves. And if all she has said to me is true—I'm going to lose him!"

"Sometimes God puts burdens on us for our own sakes. I saw Victoria Leighton only once—that was in the railway station in London. I heard someone call to her and turned, because I recognized the name. She had a quality—God help me, priest or not, I envied the man she was with! And for years afterward I dreamed of her at night—" The words were wrung from him.

"Please—!"

"Do you really want me to answer you?"

Francesca waited.

"If you are asking me if you are Francis Hatton's child by this woman, I don't know. I can only say it is—possible. Why did your grandfather love you with such intensity, why did he guard you—and at the end never tell you? Because you were *her* child? I thought she was dead, you see. I thought you were all he had. I disapproved of Francis Hatton, and I disapproved of you! She taints everything she touches, Victoria Leighton. I wouldn't put anything beyond her."

Francesca stared at him, speechless.

"My advice is the same as it was before. Walk away from this marriage and don't look back!" He set a tea towel to soak up the rainwater creeping under the door. "You'd better go, before the storm worsens."

"It's Richard who will be hurt a second time, if I turn my back on him without a word. Is that kinder than telling him why? What must I do about Richard!"

"I can tell you only what I suspect. And such speculation is unwise. I repeat, I have never seen any man love a child as Francis Hatton loved you. I never understood it. What was there about you that drew him so unaccountably? Was it the connection to *her*?"

"Why does Victoria Leighton hate me so much, if I'm her daughter?"

But he wouldn't give her a direct answer. And thus she left, unsatisfied.

As they fought the rain on the long drive home, Francesca asked Bill about the woman who had died on the Murder Stone.

He seemed unwilling to answer at first. "It was a long time ago—"

"You must tell me! Who was she? And did she die?"

"I don't know who she was. I helped your grandfather put her in the barn until dark—in that old wooden blanket chest—when it would be safe to take her away. When I came back later, she was gone. I never asked him what he had done with her. But there were long scratches in the lid, as if she'd tried to lift the lid and couldn't."

Long scratches—Francesca had once nicked her own fingertips on them, and never suspected—

"Didn't it worry you? Didn't it seem odd that a woman had died in the back garden and then disappeared?"

"It was Mr. Hatton's business, Miss Francesca. Not mine. If he had ordered me to bury her, I would have done it. And asked no questions. I trusted him to know what was best."

"Could it have been Mrs. Leighton?"

"I don't know, Miss. I have wondered sometimes. Listening to you and Mr. Leighton talk as I did, on that journey to Essex. I did wonder."

"Did Simon see her body?"

"Yes, Miss. But he didn't understand. Mr. Hatton told Master Simon it was a game and took him away so that the lady could rise up and go home."

"Almost a fortnight ago, a woman called at the house. Quite early in the morning, before Mrs. Lane had come up the hill. She claimed to be my mother."

"I'd not let it bother me, Miss. You're Mr. Edward's daughter, right enough."

"How do you know?"

"Mr. Hatton said so, Miss," he answered simply, and turned his attention to the traffic out of Exeter.

When she reached River's End, Francesca walked out in the rain to see the stone at the bottom of the garden. Was it possible Victoria had flung herself here, dramatically daring Francis to let her die, blood spreading across the ground and marking the white surface?

Careless of the child watching, bent on her own histrionics and their effect on her audience . . . Had she hoped the servants might see, and take her side?

Would he have let her die? *Did* he allow her to die? Or had he merely done the expedient thing and got her out of sight, leaving her in the barn while he comforted Simon?

Victoria, furious and thwarted, might well have walked

away. Injured, perhaps, but not dying. Had the scars on her wrists been a constant reminder of failure... ?

That night Francesca dreamed of Victoria Leighton again.

Dr. Nealy came and pronounced the fractured bone healed sufficiently for Francesca to walk down the short length of the church nave, if she gave her solemn word to use the crutches afterward.

Mr. Branscombe arrived at the church one morning with a mason, and a chest heavy enough to require three men to lift it out of the motorcar.

It held the five memorial tablets she'd commissioned for her cousins, white scrolled marble with deeply incised lettering, giving the names of Simon, Frederick, Harold, Robin, and Peter Hatton, their ranks, their regiments, and the dates of their brief lives.

Why had Francis Hatton never ordered them? Out of grief—or because none of the boys had been his? The Hattons had always been arrogantly proud of their long bloodlines.... Surely the cousins deserved their memorial—

Francesca ran a finger over Peter's name, wondering if it was wise to put that up with the rest. Silly superstition! Yet, if he was still alive—

Already Branscombe was asking why she had taken it in her head to spend money on an ex-soldier in a private clinic in Hampshire. She was wasting her inheritance, he scolded—

He had assumed it was someone she had met in London, on the night trains full of wounded. She didn't refute it.

She did ask the solicitor if her grandfather had left a box of ledgers in the care of Branscombe and Branscombe. "To do with the Little Wanderers Foundation," she added.

"It's possible, Miss Hatton, that his health broke before he could see to it. He was still clear in his mind when I wrote the Codicil about the stone, but soon afterward he began wandering."

Francesca sat in one of the nave chairs to watch the mason chisel and fit each tablet, then seal it in place in the church wall.

The cousins would be here to watch her marry Richard Leighton. It was somehow a comforting thought. They'd taken to teasing her, when she was sixteen, about the man she would marry. If she smiled at the baker's son, he was soon mocked unmercifully, until they were all falling down laughing. Peter had fashioned a piece of cheesecloth into a veil, and Harry had been the vicar, while Robin walked Freddy down a make-believe church aisle, swooning with happiness. It had been ridiculous, and the Tallon sons had begged the cousins to do it again. Francesca had vowed to remain a spinster, if she didn't run away to enter a nunnery first, and the cousins had invented a dozen ways of tormenting her imaginary groom.

When the work was finished, Francesca gave her approval and then Branscombe paid the mason. It was, she thought, as if the boys were now officially dead. . . .

The man hurried off to The Spotted Calf to drink up his profits, and Branscombe escorted her home.

In his case he had brought papers relating to the marriage, and a new will for her to sign.

Francesca shook her head.

"Call it foolishness, if you will," she said. "I don't want to sign it now."

"It would not do to die intestate. You are a very wealthy woman. Property and wealth should be disposed of properly."

"Yes, I understand. But I don't want to sign anything." If Peter was still alive, she must provide for him. And if the marriage fell through—

Branscombe tut-tutted, but in the end, she had her way, and he left with the case under his arm and nothing signed.

There had been no more anonymous letters. There had been no other visits from Victoria Leighton—or anyone else with ill will in mind.

Richard was away for a few days, settling his affairs in London. She missed him terribly.

That was surely not a sister's love!

She wondered if he'd stop on his way to London and talk again with Alasdair MacPherson. . . .

The afternoon before her marriage, the rector climbed the hill to River's End and was admitted to the sitting room, where Francesca was testing her leg without its supporting splints. Mrs. Lane was urging her to be careful and not dare rest her full weight on it.

When the rector walked across the threshold, she said, gaily, "Look! An ordinary foot!" She indicated her shoe. "I can even wear my slippers."

She looked up at him, and saw at once the grim expression on his face.

"What has happened?" she asked, filled with a sudden dread.

"It's the man in the hospital," he said, as Mrs. Lane and Miss Trotter stood listening. "I've just received a telegram. Francesca—he killed himself yesterday. The doctors called it severe despondency. I think it might have been despair that he would ever be well again."

She had been standing by the wall, holding on with one hand as she prepared to practice her first steps. "No. It can't be true."

"Here's the telegram. You can see for yourself."

"Telegrams can be sent by anyone." Even Victoria Leighton. To spoil her wedding day. But even as she thought it she knew it wasn't true.

He helped her back to her bed.

"Find someone who is going into Exeter tomorrow. Send a telegram to ask what's become of Mrs. Passmore—"

I never really had him back, did I? Then why does it feel as if I've lost him twice? Dear Peter . . .

Miss Trotter, in the corner of the room behind the bed,

whispered something under her breath. It sounded to Francesca as if she'd said "Hanging is a hard way to die." Their eyes met, and Francesca saw the compassion in the old woman's face.

To Stevens, she said, "I want him brought to the Valley. She can't afford his funeral. Tell her it's for the best, since he liked it so much here. There's no one else to care."

"I'll see to it. Never fear."

"Thank you. Now then, Mrs. Lane, we'll walk once across the room again, and then rest. If Mr. Stevens will give me his arm."

Shortly afterward, Mrs. Lane asked the rector to walk her home, as it was nearly dusk and she was anxious not to linger.

"Miss Trotter can do those splints as well as the doctor can," Mrs. Lane said. "And your dinner is in the cupboard, Miss Francesca. It needs only to be warmed a bit."

When they had gone, Francesca sent Miss Trotter to the stables to find Bill and tell him.

She couldn't have borne to do it herself.

CHAPTER 36

It was just after dawn when Victoria Leighton came back.

"You ignored my warning," she said, following Miss Trotter into the sitting room where Francesca was waiting this time. "The marriage is going forward."

"I decided it was all a lie," Francesca said, facing her down from the bed. "Your son may be dying. He wants to marry me. Why should you throw an impediment in the way?"

"I'd hardly call incest an *impediment*."

"I have only your word for that. And papers that any good solicitor can show to be forgeries."

There was a flicker of shadow in Victoria's eyes. "Do as you wish, of course! I expect to be in attendance this morning. The uninvited guest. And when the rector asks if there is any objection, I'll make my own."

"Why are you going on with this? Do you know how much you'll be hurting your own *son*?"

"Revenge, I suppose. Jealousy, perhaps, as you suggested earlier. When I cursed Francis all those years ago, I had no idea how much harm it would do. To him, to his sons, his grandsons—and you. He suffered, I can tell you."

The words hurt. "I've come to the conclusion you're nothing more than an actress hired to play a role," she retorted scornfully. "Was it Alasdair MacPherson that put you up to this? You're worth every penny he paid you."

"An *actress*! Well, I've been called many things, but never that. Alasdair and Thomas will soon be attesting to who I am. Although Thomas's daughter will be publicly branded a bastard when he does. I set that at your door, for not heeding me earlier. Why do you insist on this public denunciation? Why not simply call Richard to you and explain that it was a Hatton trick, you don't love him after all, and don't expect to marry him? He'll believe you then. Since you care so much for his feelings, it's surely the kindest way."

"Even kinder is for you to go away. Before your family turns on you."

"When I stand up in that church today, it will be noted that I came forward at great personal sacrifice to set the record straight. And I will be believed. People are always quite moved by sacrifice. I'll then be brave and ask Thomas for a divorce, and he'll be delighted to agree. My life will go on just as it did before. Incest is a crime, you know. And morally wrong as well. While there's more than enough proof that I'm Victoria Leighton, there's none at all to prove who you are."

"We'll cable Canada today—"

"By all means! By the time an answer gets here, the damage will be done. Richard will be gone. You won't easily persuade him to come back. If you'd walked away from him when I told you the truth, he would never have needed to know I was alive! But you're just as stubborn as Francis was, and you've made your own bed. Will that pompous solicitor of yours demand that you vacate this house? It would break Francis's heart."

"I think you're bluffing."

"I've never been more serious in my life. I didn't care for Richard when he was eight—I have no reason to care about him now." There was cold certainty in her voice, and whether she would be speaking the truth at the church, speak she assuredly would.

And Richard would have to stand there, in full public view, as his mother returned from the dead. He would have to listen to this malicious woman destroy his love for her, his love for Francesca, even the fragile happiness he was beginning to build out of the ruins of what his grandfather had made of him.

Or else be told in private that Francesca was calling off the wedding. Deserting him without explanation as Victoria had done when he was a child. Leaving him with silence, bitterness, and confusion.

To watch while the man she cared so deeply for suffered at her hands would be the worst punishment Victoria could inflict on her. Which surely was why Victoria was trying to drive her in that direction.

What's more, there was no certainty that Victoria would ever be satisfied. When would she come back again with another outrageous demand—holding Richard hostage, forcing Francesca to her will?

I can't go on like this, she thought.

But *incest.*

No, it couldn't be true! If it were, Victoria would enjoy nothing more than waiting until the ceremony was over, before making her appearance.

Or when the first child of the marriage had been born. When the anguish would be beyond bearing.

It has to stop. Somewhere, it has to stop.

Francesca drew her hand out of the blankets that covered her limbs.

It held Simon's pistol.

"You wouldn't dare!" There was amusement, not fear, in the attractive face.

"It's what my grandfather should have done all those years ago. Rid himself of you."

Victoria stared at her, thoughtful. "Perhaps you *have* inherited a little of me," she said. "But will you care to live, for the rest of your life, with the knowledge that you've killed your husband's mother? And your own? So that you might marry your own brother?"

"I won't think twice about it," Francesa asserted untruthfully.

Victoria Leighton smiled, but it did not touch her eyes. "Well, I must say I'm proud of you! You can't know until the service has begun whether I'll object or not. That's your punishment for defying me. Not knowing should make you a very flustered bride. The wedding guests will wonder what's on your conscience. Still, it makes your choice all that more interesting. Shoot me, and you'll never know how this would have ended. And you still can't marry your brother. On the other hand, if I walk out of here, I'll have several hours in which to think about what I'm setting out to do, and whether this is the best time to come forward. Perhaps even I'll wait and see whether you have the audacity to go through with this ceremony. How shocking that would be!"

"I can't trust you. The simplest thing would be to lock you away until the service is over."

"Do that! It will make what I have to tell that much more believable! My God, how Richard is going to hate you!"

Francesca said, "Richard will never know."

"You're so like your grandfather, Francesca. Francis always put logic before emotion. That's why you haven't the courage to fire, my dear. You think too much. I'm as safe as houses!"

She turned to walk out of the room, confident, her taunt hanging in the air behind her.

The first shot splintered the edge of the door frame.

Victoria laughed. "You're not as good with a pistol as Francis was—"

The second shot spun her around and Francesca could see, clearly, the shock of disbelief in her blue eyes—so like her son's.

"By God—" she murmured. Against the dark blue cloth of her coat, the blood was black, almost invisible.

Appalled, Francesca couldn't move.

Victoria stood there, smiling, surprised, almost pleased.

"You haven't got the courage to finish it," she said.

Francesca didn't know if she could pull the trigger a third time or not.

Then, without a sound, Victoria sank to the floor, as graceful in death as she had been in life.

Francesca cried out in horror, the pistol slipping from her fingers.

Miss Trotter was at the door, her face grim.

Kneeling by the body, the old woman felt at the throat for a pulse. She looked up, shaking her head.

"What have I done!" Francesca whispered wildly. "I've only made matters worse—" Then her mind seemed to clear, as if she had found her way. "Richard mustn't see her! He can't be told she was ever here. Or it's all for nothing. Miss Trotter—will you help me? There's no one else. I'm so sorry I must ask you!"

"It's no matter, Miss Francesca. I'll just find Bill."

"She's—"

"I've seen dead bodies before, Miss. And laid them out. I must find Bill, Miss. Mrs. Lane will be here in another hour. And we can't manage, the two of us. There's too much to be done. Don't fret, it will be all right."

She was gone, lily of the valley floating in her wake.

Francesca stared down at the body of the woman who had called herself her mother. *I can't feel anything for you,* she thought. *Except relief that it's over.*

In another few minutes Bill arrived, still pulling his suspenders over his nightshirt, a horse blanket under his arm.

"Whatever happened, Miss?" he asked, staring in his turn at the dead woman.

"She was intent on hurting Richard. She's his mother."

"In such close quarters you were bound to hit her. Well, Mrs. Lane will be here soon. I'd best hurry!"

He unfolded the blanket and bent to roll Victoria Leighton

into it. "She won't be getting away this time," he said harshly. "It's her. The one dying on the Murder Stone."

"I must help you."

"No, Miss, you won't do anything of the sort! We'll keep her out of sight for now, and I'll take her away later."

Francesca tried to think. "She had a carriage—something—she didn't come on foot. Mrs. Lane heard a horse, when Mrs. Leighton was here the first time."

"All the better. I'll just move it around to the barn, and who'll see?"

Miss Trotter came in, carrying a cup. "Drink this, Miss Francesca."

It was dandelion wine. Francesca looked at it, then at the old woman, fright in her eyes.

"There's only the wine, and a little something to soothe," Miss Trotter said kindly. "You'll need your wits about you. I'd drink it all, if I were you."

The body was bundled out of the room, and Miss Trotter was back again with bucket and water, a brush in her hand. "It won't do for the blood to stain the wood. There wasn't all that much. Her fine wool coat soaked it up. And there's nothing to be done about the splintered frame of the door. We'll just say you had bad dreams and in the night fired Mr. Simon's pistol, thinking someone was breaking in."

"People have broken in before," Francesca said. "Do you suppose it was she?"

"I wouldn't put it past the likes of her. Snooping." She picked up the dead woman's handbag, where it had been pushed behind the door. "We must be rid of this as well." She passed it to Francesca.

"Of course," she went on, "I was of the opinion it was Rector, come to look for the ledgers. He was one of the orphans, you know. He asked Mr. Hatton once if he could see them and find out who he truly was."

"Mrs. Passmore thought they were here, too."

"And so they were. But Mr. Hatton burned them all. When Mr. Harry died," Miss Trotter said. "I smelled the smoke on the night air. Mrs. Lane thought they were only the letters the boys wrote. But I know different. He'd always said he might burn them."

"He told you more than he ever told me."

"No, Miss, he didn't. I just knew him better than most. I came that night and looked through the ashes. There was a bit of leather from one of the ledgers that hadn't burned through, and a few edges of paper." She smiled sadly. "No one minds me, Miss Francesca. I'm old and not important. You learn a good bit, being invisible."

But Francesca had the feeling that sometimes her grandfather had talked to this woman, because she did see and understand so much.

"If I were you, Miss Francesca, I'd ask Mrs. Lane to dress me in my own bedroom. There'll be no need for her to come in here, until the floor is properly dry. I'll make up the fire when I get shed of *this*." She indicated the handbag. "Don't you worry. Nobody will ever find her. And if Bill takes the horse and carriage away tonight, after you're gone, why so much the better."

"It's not right to hush this up—"

"She killed herself. It's the kind she was. She dared you, and you're Francis Hatton's granddaughter. You did what was best for your family."

Francesca opened the handbag and looked inside. Under a lawn handkerchief, she found a photograph of an aging man sitting by the hearth, looking into the fire. His face was harsh, lined with more than age. Alasdair MacPherson, the man she'd glimpsed on the landing that day near Guildford. But how had it come to be in Victoria's possession? It had surely been taken in the last months. Perhaps to remind his grandson to hurry with his search.

Dear God! was her first thought. *Were they in this together? To prevent the marriage?*

By the time Mrs. Lane had arrived, Francesca was in her own bedroom, her bath finished, and her wedding clothes laid out. Mrs. Lane fussed over her hair, smoothed the pale rose gown Francesca had chosen for her wedding, and helped to snap the catch on the string of pearls that had belonged to her grandmother, Sarah Hatton.

Slipping her feet into her shoes, Francesca surveyed herself in her mirror, but seemed to see, behind her, the tall, slender figure of Victoria Leighton.

I can't marry him, not with your blood on my hands— But I couldn't let you hurt him—I couldn't let him see what you truly were! I can't marry anyone, not now. Not ever. But he'll be safe—

Victoria Leighton would win, even in death.

But Miss Trotter, her shawls floating like living things, handed her another small glass of dandelion wine, and Francesca obediently drank it.

Mrs. Tallon and her husband came for Francesca at a quarter to eleven, their spirits high, their voices loud in the house. Francesca had hoped to find five minutes to slip away to the stables, but it was too late.

She used her crutches as she'd promised, and had stepped into the drive when Bill came to the side of the house, dressed in his best suit, a hand-me-down from Francis Hatton. He smiled at her, and touched the brim of his hat in salute.

She tried to return the smile and felt it freeze into a grimace on her lips.

The drive to the church seemed to take forever. Half a dozen village children ran beside the Tallon carriage, shouting and wishing her well.

She felt cold as she came around the bend and saw that the church door was open, waiting for her.

Somewhere near the altar was Richard Leighton, looking for his bride.

I cannot do this—

The rector was standing by the door, taking her hands to steady her as she got down from the carriage. He passed her crutches to someone, and then tucked her fingers under his arm.

They began to walk slowly toward the altar, faces of guests upturned, looking at her, smiling.

She could see Richard now, tall and erect, his face smiling as well.

And on the walls of the nave were the memorials to her cousins, shining white in the light of dozens of candles. They *were* her blood...

There were no flowers, but silk ribbons had been tied in rosettes and hung about the columns, over the backs of chairs.

She could feel her shoes touching the long brass of the Somerset knight, lying in wait to trip her feet.

But she passed over him safely, and was nearly to the altar when a voice rang out behind her.

CHAPTER 37

A man was standing there, his bicycle just outside the heavy door, and there was an envelope in his hand.

"Is there a Richard Leighton here? I've an urgent telegram for him."

Richard was still, as if turned to stone. Then he strode down the aisle, touched Francesca on the arm as he passed her, and put out his hand for the telegram, offering the messenger some coins.

He held the envelope for an instant, looking at it as if reluctant to open it.

Over the heads of the wedding guests, she could just see Bill's face, a mask of fear.

She's going to tell them—from her grave—

Her knees felt as if they were buckling, but Stevens, his hand firm on her elbow, whispered, "Steady! It won't be much longer—your crutches are just there."

Richard was opening the seal, and she watched his face as he read the message inside. There was a frown, nothing else.

Folding it to thrust the telegram into a pocket, he walked back down the aisle, kissed her lightly on the cheek, much to the delight of the assembled guests, and took his place again.

"*Do you, Francesca Elizabeth Mary Hatton—*"

Francesca remembered nothing of the ceremony. She made her vows without hearing them, felt the ring being pressed onto her finger.

And it was over. She was married.

Someone handed her her crutches at the church door, smiling up at her.

It was Miss Trotter, her face bright with tears.

There's still time, she told herself, *to walk away.*

But Richard's face, bent toward her, was smiling as well, his hand warm in hers, a serenity in his eyes she had never seen before.

They were nearly to the Rectory, where the wedding break-fast was waiting, when he reached into his pocket and drew out the telegram.

"Not—now," she protested, not wanting to know.

"No. You must read it. It was held up by military traffic."

Your grandfather died this morning, 13 Dec., peacefully in his sleep. He maintained to the end that 2 nights ago Victoria had come to sit with him and talk with him. It gave him great comfort to believe it was true.

It was signed *Thomas Leighton.*

Yesterday.

They walked on. She said, "He was at peace at the end. I'm glad." Had MacPherson given his daughter the photograph that night? Or had she taken it?

"Yes. The mind's amazing, isn't it?" Richard was saying. "More than anything he'd wanted to see my mother again before he died. He brought her back in the only way he could."

Mrs. Horner was at the Rectory, waiting for them; Mrs. Lane, just behind her, had tears in her eyes, and Bill stood to one side, his glance fixed on Francesca's face.

It was an hour after the cutting of the cake before she

could find an opportunity to speak quietly with the old coachman.

"Richard's grandfather has died," she told him.

"Yes, Miss, thank you, Miss." He paused. "While you're on your wedding journey, we'll be digging out the Murder Stone and shipping it away, as your grandfather wanted. The sooner the better, in my view. There're too many memories—you won't want to look at it now."

"Yes. I'm grateful, Bill."

"And if you have no objection, Miss, before that I'd like to take a little time and visit my family in Bude. They're hard men, fishing men, and the boats go out in any weather."

Victoria Leighton would be put to rest in the sea.

"Beyond the Pillars of Hercules..."

Miss Trotter came up, shyly wishing Francesca happiness.

And then she said, "The dead don't walk, Miss. But that one will reach out of the grave and hurt you if she can. If you let her. You must make up your mind she'll do no more harm."

For the rest of the afternoon and into the evening, Francesca remembered the old woman's canny warning. She would carry it in her heart to the end of her life.

CHAPTER 38

There was once a white stone at the bottom of the garden. I remember it well. My cousins called it the Murder Stone. That was Simon's doing...he had a taste for war and bloody games.

When they dug it out to carry it away, there was a skeleton deep in the earth beneath it. Old bones, I was told. A Celtic woman from a time before the Romans, they said. I was on my wedding journey and never saw her. I have always wondered who put her there so long ago, and why. Was she murdered—or had she died young, a suicide? Was she sacrificed for someone else's happiness?

My cousins' tutor would have been pleased. He'd always avowed that the Murder Stone was older than Avebury and Stonehenge.

No one could tell me how she died. But there were gold amulets with the body, and a ring on her finger. It caused quite a flurry, and someone from a museum in London came to look at the jewelry.

It didn't matter. I knew now why the stone had always seemed to possess a life of its own. And I knew why my grandfather had wanted to be rid of it in the end.

It had seen too much blood.

Our new rector gave the woman Christian burial in the churchyard, saying that it was fitting and he hoped she'd found peace at last.

I put flowers on her grave from time to time. It comforts me.

I will go to my own grave soon. I'm an old woman now, and I talk to my dead when I sit in the late afternoon sun and drowse. They comfort me as well. I had a happy marriage. It lasted far longer than either of us had expected. And we watched our children grow up at River's End. They had been adopted from Falworthy; five boys and a girl.

The curse on my house was lifted, you see.

I have not set eyes on the sea again, not since the day I left Mr. Chatham's cottage that last time. The water was gray under a curtain of rain, and dreary. I have no wish to see it clear as crystal, the sun shining well into the depths, exposing the bones of wrecked ships and drowned sailors.

"You're so very like your grandfather...."

It was the only mistake she made.

THE END

A word to railway enthusiasts. I haven't overlooked the line that ran from Stoke Canon to Morebath, both a lovely excursion and a commercial success for so many years. The tracks were taken up in 1964, and this journey has become a distant memory for everyone but people who care about old trains, as I do. And so the right of way has returned to an earlier solitude and, when I was last there on a late winter afternoon, I saw another story to be told. The haunting whistle once heard echoing through the hills, like a spotted calf's cry, has become folk memory.

ABOUT THE AUTHOR

Charles Todd is the author of *A Fearsome Doubt, Watchers of Time, Legacy of the Dead, A Test of Wills, Wings of Fire,* and *Search the Dark.* He lives on the East Coast, where he is at work on the next novel in the Inspector Ian Rutledge series, *A Cold Treachery.*

If you enjoyed Charles Todds's
THE MURDER STONE,
you won't want to miss any of his rich and
suspenseful mysteries. Look for them at your
favorite bookseller's.

And read on for a tantalizing preview of the
newest Inspector Rutledge mystery,
A COLD TREACHERY,
coming in February 2005 in hardcover
from Bantam Books.

A COLD
TREACHERY

An Inspector Rutledge Mystery

by CHARLES TODD

CHARLES TODD

BESTSELLING AUTHOR OF THE MURDER STONE

A COLD
TREACHERY

a novel of suspense

A COLD TREACHERY

by CHARLES TODD

On Sale February 2005

CHAPTER 1

The North of England
December, 1919

He ran through the snow, face into the swirling wind, feet pounding deep trenches into the accumulating drifts. Rocks, their shapes no longer familiar under the soft white blanket, sent him sprawling, and he dragged himself up again, white now where the snow clung, and almost invisible in the darkness. He had no idea what direction he had taken, enveloped by unreasoning panic and hardly able to breathe for the pain inside him. All he could hear was the voice in his head, shouting at him—

"You will hang for this, see if you don't. It's my revenge, and you'll think about that when the rope goes round your neck and the black hood comes down and there's no one to save you—"

The sound of the shot was so loud it had shocked him, and

he couldn't remember whether he had slammed the door behind him or left it standing wide.

He could still smell the blood—so much of it!—choking in the back of his throat like feathers thrown on a fire. He could feel the terror, a snake that coiled and writhed in his stomach, making him ill, and the drumming wild in his head.

They would try to catch him. And then they'd hang him. There was nothing he could do to prevent it. Unless he died in the snow, and was buried by it until the spring. He'd seen the frozen body of a dead lamb once, stiff and hard, half rotted and sad. The ravens had been at it. He hated ravens.

Half the countryside knew he'd been a troublemaker since the autumn. Restless—unhappy—growing out of himself and his clothes. They'd look at what lay in that bloody room, and they'd hate him.

He was crying now, tears scalding on cold skin, and the voice was so loud he knew it was following him, and he ran harder, his breath gusting in front of his face, arms pumping, pushing his way through the snow until his muscles burned.

"You'll hang for this—see if you don't——!"

He would rather die in the snow of cold and exhaustion than with a rope around his neck. He'd rather run until his heart burst than drop through the hangman's door and feel his throat close off. Even with the ravens eating him, the snow was cleaner....

"You'll hang for this—see if you don't——!

That's my revenge... my revenge... my revenge...."

CHAPTER 2

Paul Elcott stood in the kitchen beside Sergeant Miller, his face pale, his hand shaking as he unconsciously brushed the back of it across his mouth for the third time.

"They're dead, aren't they? I haven't touched them—I couldn't—Look, can we step outside, man, I'm going to be sick, else!"

Miller, who had come from a butcher's family, said stolidly, "Yes, all right. The doctor's on his way, but there's nothing he can do for them." Except pronounce them dead, he added to himself. Poor souls. What the devil had happened here? "We might as well wait in the barn, then, until he's finished."

Elcott stumbled out the door. He made his way to the barn, where he was violently sick in one of the empty horse stalls. Afterward he felt no better. He could still see the kitchen floor—still smell the sickening odor of blood—

And the eyes—half closed—staring at nothing the living could see.

Had Gerald looked at Hell? He'd said the trenches were worse—

He sat down on a bale of hay, and dropped his head in his hands, trying to regulate his breathing and hold on to his senses. He should have sent the sergeant back alone. He'd been mad to think he could face that slaughter again.

After a while, Sergeant Miller came across to the barn, and the doctor was with him, carrying a lantern. Elcott lifted his head to nod at Dr. Jarvis. He cleared his throat and said, "They didn't suffer, did they? I mean—no one lingered—"

"No. I don't believe they did," the doctor answered quietly, coming to stand by him and lifting the lantern a little to shine across Elcott's face. He prayed it was true. He couldn't be sure until the autopsies. Without moving the bodies, he'd been able to find only a single gunshot wound in each, to the chest, with resulting internal trauma. Sufficient to kill. A surge of sympathy swept Jarvis and he reached out to press Elcott's shoulder. The bloody dead were this man's family. His brother, his brother's wife, their children. An unspeakable shock...

The doctor himself had been badly shaken by the scene and found it difficult to imagine how he would answer his wife when she asked him why the police had come to fetch him in the middle of his dinner. Nothing in his practice had prepared him for such a harrowing experience. It was, he thought, something one might see in war, not in a small, peaceful farm house. At length he said gently to Elcott, "Let me take you home, Paul, and give you something to help you sleep."

"I don't want to sleep. I'll have *nightmares.*" Without warning Elcott began to cry, his face crumpled and his chest heaving. His nerve gone.

The doctor gripped the shattered man's shoulder, and looked to Sergeant Miller over his head. "I wish I knew what's keeping Inspector Greeley—his wife told me he'd gone out to see if the Potters needed help getting out. I hope to God he hasn't stumbled on anything like this!"

"We'll know soon enough," the sergeant replied.

They listened to the sobbing man beside them, feeling helpless in the face of his grief.

"I ought to take him home," Jarvis said. "He's no use to you in this state. You can wait for Greeley. When you're ready for me, I'll be with Elcott."

Miller nodded. "That's best, then." He glanced at Elcott, then jerked his head, moving to the door. Jarvis followed him. The two men stood there in the late afternoon light, gray clouds so heavy that it was difficult to tell if dusk was coming, or more snow. It had been a freak two-day storm, fast moving with a heavy fall, and the skies still hadn't cleared. The roads were nearly impassable, the farm lanes worse. It had taken Miller a good hour to reach the house, even following in the ruts left by Elcott's carriage.

"There's one still missing." Miller pitched his voice so that Elcott couldn't hear him. "I daresay Elcott's not noticed. I've walked through the rest of the house. He's not there."

"Josh? By God, I hadn't—Is he in the outbuildings, do you think?" Jarvis shivered and glanced over his shoulder at the unlit interior of the small barn, with its stalls, plows, barrows, tack, and other gear stacked neatly, the hay in the loft, filling half the space. Two horses and a black cow watched him, ears twitching above empty mangers. "Gerald Elcott was always a tidy man. It shouldn't take long to search."

Miller counted on his gloved fingers. "Elcott penned his sheep, against the storm. I could see them up there to the east of Fox Scar. Stabled his horses, and brought in the cow. At a guess then, he was alive this time Sunday, when the snow was coming down hard and he knew we were in for it. But the cow's not been milked since, nor the stalls mucked out, nor feed put down."

"That confirms what I saw inside. I'd say they've been dead since late Sunday night." Jarvis frowned and stamped his feet against the cold, torn. "I should stay until you've found Josh. In the event there's anything I can do..."

"No, take Elcott back. If the rest are dead, the boy is as well. I'll find him."

The doctor nodded. He was moving toward Elcott again, when Miller cautioned, "Best to say nothing about this." He gestured to the house. "In the village. Until we know a little more. We don't want a panic on our hands."

"No. God, no." Jarvis handed the lantern to Miller and settled his hat firmly on his head against the wind. Raising his voice, he said, "Now then, Paul, let's take you home, and I'll find something to help you get past this."

"Someone has to look after the animals," Elcott protested. "And I want to help search. For whoever it was did this. *I want to be there when you find this bastard.*"

"That's to your credit," Miller answered him. "But for now, I'd go with the doctor if I was you. I'll see to the beasts, and there'll be someone to care for them tomorrow. Leave everything to us. As soon as we know anything, I'll see you're told."

Elcott walked to the barn door and stepped outside, unable to turn away from the silent house just across the yard. "I wish I knew *why*," he said, his face ragged with grief. "I just wish I knew why. What had they ever done to deserve—?"

"That'll come out," Miller told him calmly, soothingly. "In good time."

Elcott followed Jarvis to the horse-drawn carriage that had brought the doctor out to the isolated farm. The only tracks in the snow were theirs, a hodge-podge of footprints around the kitchen door of the house, and the wheel markings of the two vehicles, cart and carriage. Beyond these, the ground was smoothly white, with only the brushing of the wind and the prints of winter birds scratching for whatever they could find.

As if only just realizing that the cart was his, Elcott stopped and said, "Dr. Jarvis—I can't—"

"Leave it for Sergeant Miller, if you will. He'll bring it back to town later. I expect he'll need it tonight."

"Oh—yes." Dazed, Elcott climbed into the carriage and

settled himself meekly on the seat, stuffing his cold hands under his arms.

By the time Inspector Greeley had completed his examination of the Elcott farmhouse, he was absolutely certain of one thing. He needed help.

Five dead and one missing, believed dead.

It was beyond comprehension—beyond the experience of any man to understand.

In Urskdale with its outlying farms and vast stretches of barren mountainous landscape, his resources were stretched thin as it was. The first priority was making certain that all the other dale families were accounted for, that this carnage hadn't been repeated—*God forefend!*—in another isolated house. And there was the missing child to find. All the farm buildings, sheep pens, shepherds' huts and tumbled ruins had to be searched. The slopes of the fells, the crevices, the small dips and swales, the banks of the little becks. It would take more men than he could muster. But he'd have to make do with what he had, summon the dale's scattered inhabitants and work them to the point of exhaustion. And time was short, painfully short, if that child had the most tenuous hope of surviving.

Overwhelmed by the sheer enormity of what lay ahead, Greeley did what his people had done for generations here in the north: He buttoned his emotions tightly inside and grimly set about what had to be done.

It was well after midnight when he got back to the small police station that stood six houses from the church on the main street of Urksdale. The Inspector laboriously wrote out a message and found an experienced man to carry it to the Chief Constable. "Make the fastest time you can," he was told. "It's urgent."

On his drive back to the police station, Greeley had already compiled a mental list of the outlying farms, roughly grouping them by proximity. And then, to keep his mind busy and away from that dreadful, bloody kitchen, he had considered what the searchers would need—lanterns, packets of food, thermoses of tea, rope. But that was easier, each man would know from experience what to bring. Locating lost walkers in the summer had taught them all how to plan.

Jarvis had said two days—that the Elcotts had been dead two days.

This madman had already had more than sufficient time to track the boy over the snow, and then vanish. Or spread his net to other victims...

What in Hell's name would the search parties discover, as they knocked on doors?

Greeley capped his pen and set it in the dish. A general warning now would come far too late to help anyone else. But the search had to go on. A search for the boy, for the killer— for other victims.

As he rose to leave, turning down the lamp on his desk, an appalling thought struck him.

What if the murderer was an Urskdale man? Where had he spent these last forty-eight hours? Safely at home by his hearth? If he hadn't found the boy after all, would he make certain that he was included among the searchers?

What if he, Greeley, was about to set the fox amongst the hounds, unwittingly sending the killer out with an innocent man, to search for himself?

He felt as if he'd not slept for a week—the tension in his body and the nightmare in his mind seemed to envelop him.

In the darkness the Inspector rubbed his gritty eyes with his fists. When he walked out the door to face the somber men collecting outside the station, would one of them look away, unable to meet his glance? Would he read suspicion in the turn of a head or the restless stamp of feet?

He knew each individual in his patch too well to believe one of them was a vicious killer. Or—until now he'd thought he did. More to the point, he needed every man he could lay hands to, he couldn't afford to speculate. Still, he would send them out in threes, not twos. Just in case.

As he finally strode down the passage, he could hear the first arrivals talking among themselves, coming in, some of them, as soon as the news reached them. A few at a time, on foot, on horseback, their numbers slowly swelling.

The blast of icy air hit him in the face as he went through the door, a shock to warmed skin. Nothing, he thought, to match his shock at the Elcott farm.

In all his years as a policeman, he had never seen anything like that scene in that farmhouse kitchen. Try as he would, he couldn't imagine the kind of malevolence that could do such a thing. Try as he would, he couldn't shut it out of his mind. He and his men had lifted the five stiff bodies onto blankets and carried each out to the waiting cart. He could still feel the small bodies of the children, resting so lightly in his arms. Blind anger swept him so that he felt sick with it, helpless and, for the first time in his life, vengeful.

As the searchers turned toward him, prepared to receive their orders, he winced, his eyes evading theirs, staring over their heads as he began to speak. *How could any man kill like that, and not wear the guilt of it, like an ugly brand?*

Greeley realized he wasn't prepared to read guilt in any face. Not yet. Not until his mind found a way around the horror. Then he would look. . . .

He was moving on nothing but fear now, his legs pounding through the snow that was sometimes as deep as his knees. His heart seemed too large for his chest, but his brain was wild and tormented, refusing to let his body rest. He paused from time to time, listening, his face turned to the wind like an animal, certain he could hear steps behind him, a voice calling to him. But there was no one alive to come after him.

It never occurred to him that it would be easier simply to stop, to lie down in one of the drifts and let himself fall asleep forever. What followed him was so terrible that his dread of it catching up with him ate him alive. Like the ravens, it would pick and dig at him, even in death. Fleeing was his only salvation. Far beyond reach. As far and as fast as he could manage.

He had no idea where he was—in which direction he'd run or how well he'd kept to that line, once out of sight of the lighted windows of the kitchen. He had no idea how long he had been running. Everything was measured by his feet, how far they were taking him, how fast they could go. Away from the menace behind him.

But the voice was always in his ears, in spite of the wind. Always pushing him on when his lungs begged him to stop for breath, always at his heels like a living thing intent on savaging him.

"You will hang for this, see if you don't. That's my revenge, and you'll think about that when the rope goes around your neck and the black hood comes down—"

As a goad the voice was crueler than any whip.

He was terrified of it.

Sometime later he fell, the air whipped out of his body and his chin buried in the snow. For an instant he lay there, listening. Was it his heart beating so hard that it choked him—or was it the crunch of footsteps coming down the swale after him? Frantic, he clawed his way to his feet again. He turned to stare into the darkness behind him. But the sky and the land seemed inseparable, a blank gray-white swirl that offered neither hope nor sanctuary.

There was no one behind him. There *couldn't* be. And yet he could almost feel the warmth of a body coming toward him. He could see shapes dissolving and solidifying in the wild eddy of flakes caught by the bitter wind. Like a ghost.

A ghost . . .

He began to cry again as he ran on, wishing it was over, wishing that he was dead, like the others.

But he couldn't be dead like the others. He would be hanged when they found him, and the last thing he would ever feel was the jerk of the thick rope around his neck. . . .